Never Too Old to Save the World

Edited by
Alana Joli Abbott and Addie J. King

NEVER TOO OLD TO SAVE THE WORLD
All stories within are copyright © 2023 their respective authors. All rights reserved.

"Jackalope Wives" copyright 2014 by Ursula Vernon. First published in Apex Magazine, January 7, 2014.

Published by Outland Entertainment LLC
3119 Gillham Road
Kansas City, MO 64109

Founder/Creative Director: Jeremy D. Mohler
Editor-in-Chief: Alana Joli Abbott

ISBN (paper): 978-1-954255-47-0
ISBN (eBook): 978-1-954255-48-7
Worldwide Rights
Created in the United States of America

Editors: Alana Joli Abbott & Addie J. King
Galley Proofer: Tara Cloud Clark
Cover Illustration: Ann Marie Cochran
Cover Design: Jeremy D. Mohler
Interior Layout: Mikael Brodu

Printed and bound in the United States of America.

Visit **outlandentertainment.com** to see more, or follow us on our Facebook Page **facebook.com/outlandentertainment/**

— TABLE OF CONTENTS —

LEAN IN: THE LORD
— OF HELL IS COMING —
by Ericka Kahler

Vincent followed the man he was pretty sure was a demon into the office of the CEO of MA Culpepper, LLC. It unnerved him that they both wore similar suits, though the demon's tie was bright crimson silk while his was a boring polyester navy blue. Vincent adjusted his tie tighter against his Adam's apple. His fingers gripped the handle of the briefcase as he sat in the chair the demon gestured to.

Mary Ann Culpepper breezed in behind the demon. "Thank you, Dipshit," Mary Ann said. Vincent blinked in surprise, but realized she was talking to the demon, not him. He shifted his eyes to the creature. Instead of going on a demonic rampage, it simply nodded its head at Mary Ann and left the room. She sat down into an over-sized leather chair that vaguely resembled a throne, despite being an ordinary executive office chair.

"So, Mister..." she trailed off expectantly.

"Uh, Vincent Dunferline." He fumbled his briefcase onto the small table next to his chair. It tipped over and crashed to its side on the polished veneer. He patted it nervously before looking up at Mary Ann again. Her hand was stretched toward him, inviting him into a handshake. He took a very deep breath before reaching out and clasping it. Her hand felt warm and soft. Ordinary.

"I have a very busy day, Vincent. Can I call you Vincent?" Mary Ann asked.

This was it. This was the moment he'd been preparing for his entire adult life. He took a deep breath. "Mary Ann Culpepper, you've been chosen."

She tilted her head to the side. "Wait, you aren't the guy from the IRS?"

"Oh, I am," he said. "But I am also a member of an ancient order that is charged with saving the human race from the demon incursions. I took your case so I could make contact with you and tell you about your sacred duty."

Mary Ann sat up straight in her chair, then let out a huff of breath. "Well, finally."

Vincent blinked. "I'm sorry, what?"

"Hold on a sec," she pushed a button. "The IRS auditor is also a member of the Order. I'm going to need you to make some more room on my schedule for him."

"The Lord of Hell is coming," a deep, gritty voice said through the speaker.

"I know. Today of all days, right? Thank you, Dipshit." Mary Ann sat back. "So you finally figured it out. You picked a rather inconvenient day to show up, but I think I can make it work. Should make the IRS audit a bit easier, so that's a bonus. Come on, make your pitch."

"My pitch? I don't think you understand. I am a member of the Order of St. Anthony of the Tomb, and we've been searching for the Chosen One, the one prophecy tells us has the power to see the demons—"

"Wait, wait," Mary Ann leaned forward toward him. "I started this company three years ago, and I met Dipshit two years before that. Seems like your Order doesn't have a very efficient process for locating your Chosen One. But anyway, you were saying, about a prophecy?"

Vincent sat on the edge of his chair. "Once a generation a woman is born who is the inheritor of the legacy of St. Anthony. She has the power to identify and slay the demons hiding in our world. The Chosen One is the only one who can save us from the demon hordes coming out of Hell. Our Order is charged to find you and teach you how to use your gifts to protect humanity."

Mary Ann sighed in a sort of nostalgia. She glanced down at her watch. "Don't worry about your prophecy, I got it covered."

"Got it... covered?"

Mary Ann twisted her head to look over at the door. "It might be faster if we covered the Chosen One stuff and the supposed labor law violations at the same time. The Lord of Hell is coming, and my afternoon is pretty booked."

"So, um, you know about the demons?"

Mary Ann snorted. "Obviously. Most of my labor force is demons."

"WHAT?" Vincent took an unsteady breath and glanced around the office. He'd been right; the man escorting him in here had been a demon. He popped the locks holding his briefcase closed and pulled out his case file for the audit. Flipping it open, he scanned the corporate summary he'd prepared on MA Culpepper, LLC. The paper fluttered at the edges as he re-read the information. "You have over 150 employees."

"Independent contractors."

"What?"

"Legally, they aren't employees, they're independent contractors."

Vincent looked up from his folder. Mary Ann held out a hand and gestured at his folder. "The audit? We can do that part first if you like. It's the official position of my company that the demons are independent contractors, who are responsible for their own social security and Medicare taxes. I'll have Dipshit bring in the records." She hit a button on her desk phone. It buzzed. "Bring the 1099 forms and payroll ledgers," she said.

"Yes, ma'am."

Vincent glanced toward the door. He had to lower his folder back to the table to keep his hands from shaking. "You're saying there are almost 150 demons, just in this building alone?"

"Yeah. You and your Order didn't notice?"

Vincent closed his eyes a moment, mentally shifting from the page of numbers in his hand to the last time he'd updated the Order's number. "We...uh. Well. We can't see them, and the demon infestation fluctuates periodically. We just thought there had been a decline in demon-related—wait, *you're* tracking the numbers of demons on Earth?"

He caught Mary Ann's eyeroll before she answered. "Of course I keep track. They get pretty violent if left to their own devices. I think of them like toddlers. Set a few rules, make sure they know you're enforcing them, and provide plenty of rewarding activities to fill their time so they don't destroy everything they touch."

Vincent gasped, and he felt his mouth drop open in a moment of shock. As soon as he realized he was sitting there gaping at her like a stunned fish, he snapped his mouth closed again. He'd wanted to seem cool and competent, but Mary Ann must have seen his reaction, because her earnest expression turned into a smirk.

"Oh, you assumed the only way to handle demons was to bind them and kill them? You're obviously not mothers. Tempting as it is, we're forced to find other solutions. Ultimately, that works out better for humanity."

"With the demons?"

"With the toddlers. But turns out, works like a charm on demons, too."

The door opened, and the man who had originally escorted Vincent through the office entered with a large stack of file folders. Mary Ann pointed at the table in front of Vincent, and Dipshit—heaven help him, now *he* was thinking of the demon by that name—set them down next to his briefcase. He then stepped back to stand next to Mary Ann.

Vincent stared at the two of them. He was so good at arguing, at poking holes in defenses, in bringing people around to his point of view—and all of that had abandoned him. He knew he should be feeling something, but his mind couldn't process the unexpected turn this conversation had taken. "I prepared for this. I thought of every argument to convince you demons are real. I practiced for weeks. And when I finally get the words out, you— You already know." He stuttered to a stop.

Mary Ann went on as if she didn't notice the seismic shift of his reality. "Of course I know. I can see them. It's part of the Chosen One gig. It was my first clue, actually. I noticed my first demon, Dipshit here, at the park when I took my kids to get out some of the excess energy they always seem to have. At first, he manifested as distorted space, where the air seemed to have molecules big enough for me to see, swirling around each other like water in a flowing river."

"The Order calls it the Roil," Vincent found himself saying on autopilot. He'd rehearsed this, too, not knowing how much she would be open to learning in their first meeting. He shook his head to clear the fog. "When they manifest. We call it the Roil."

Mary Ann snorted. "That's dumb. I'm not calling it that. So anyway, there I am watching this thing appear right next to my children, who are screaming like demons in the little plastic tube slide. I had no idea what it was or where it came from, so I did what any good mother would do and went to collect my kids. But by the time I got there, there's this creepy guy standing near, and his face looks all wrong. Deformed and grotesque."

Beside her, Dipshit growled. Vincent tensed, waiting to see what Dipshit would do. But then Mary Ann put up a hand, her face contrite.

"No, wait, I'm sorry. I am sorry. I'm not supposed to use language like that to describe how I perceive demons. It's hurtful."

"You're being politically correct with demons," Vincent blurted out before he could stop himself.

"It's not politically correct," Dipshit's low voice put in. "It's part of the corporate communication agreement."

Vincent shifted uncomfortably in his chair. "I'm not sure I heard that correctly—corporate communication agreement? You're the Chosen One. You can't have demons working for you."

Mary Ann's eyebrows drew together in confusion. "Is that a legal opinion? Because I'm not sure how your religious beliefs pertain to my employment practices." Beside her, Dipshit snickered. She patted his sleeve, and his face settled into neutrality. "But I got off-track. I was telling you how Dipshit and I first met. So there he is, and I can tell he isn't just some creepy guy. There was this whole dangerous aura around him, as well as the face, what's the word...?" She tapped on Dipshit's arm.

"The alternative aesthetic."

"Yes. His face, with its alternative aesthetic. Then he took a step toward my kids. I was afraid if I tried to just walk away he'd hurt us, so I got up in his face and yelled, 'Back off, Dipshit!'"

Vincent jumped back in his seat. Surely, this would be the thing to set the demon off on a killing spree. Instead, Dipshit laughed. "What did I say to you, again?"

Mary Ann smiled. "You said, 'Dipshit. That's so rude. I like it. You may call me Dipshit.'"

Dipshit grinned. "And she did. She repeated it many times during her tirade about what she was going to do to me if I touched her children. It was wonderful. When they hire in, she names every new demon that comes to work here. Just like she did me."

Mary Ann leaned toward Vincent. "I give them rude names. Anything that would make a twelve year old giggle. I think it appeases their anti-social instincts to have a name that shouldn't be said in a professional setting. The latest worker satisfaction surveys indicate the naming ceremony is one of their favorite things about working here."

Vincent reached out to touch the edge of his briefcase. Inside, he saw the artifacts he'd brought, to show her, to prove her noble destiny. Next to it was the very ordinary looking stack of manila file folders Dipshit had brought in, full of 1099 forms, they claimed. His briefcase held the cherished treasures of the Order, yet they didn't have any place here, among a building full of demons with a corporate communication agreement and welcoming ceremonies. How could he pull them out now? "We— I— The Order must have made a mistake. You can't be the Chosen One. The Chosen One slays demons, she doesn't employ them."

Mary Ann vented a huge sigh of frustration. "They're legally listed as independent contractors." She pursed her lips and tilted her head, then continued in a calmer tone. "Demons can't get social security numbers. Yet. We've got a demon about to graduate law school who has some exciting ideas around requesting asylum status, but that's not worked out yet."

Vincent started shaking his head in tiny motions back and forth, as if by repeating it enough times he could deny the reality of demon immigration she'd so calmly proposed. "Demons can't be reasoned with," he said. "They are agents of chaos and evil on this earth."

Dipshit growled again, this time staring down at Vincent. His hand started clenching into a fist. Vincent inched his hand toward the briefcase on the table, wondering if he could grab the holy cross before the demon could grab him. Mary Ann crossed her legs and leaned back, letting her foot bob up and down. He thought she looked like she was waiting for something.

"That's a very insulting stereotype," Dipshit said after a moment. Mary Ann clapped her hands together lightly. "Well done."

"The corporate communication agreement does not allow me to rip his head off," Dipshit mumbled.

Mary Ann handed him a coffee mug. Dipshit crushed it in a one-handed grip. Vincent jerked as pieces of ceramic crashed to the floor, breaking on the hard surface. Dipshit stomped on the pieces until there was nothing left. Mary Ann waved Dipshit to the door. He took a few more moments to glare at Vincent, but finally left.

Mary Ann closed her eyes and took a deep breath. "You hurt his feelings."

"How did he do that? There's nothing left of it. Not even dust." Vincent leaned over, searching for any remnants of the cup on the floor. Nothing.

"Surely your folder there lists what this company does."

Vincent pulled himself away from the blank, empty spot on the floor and turned to the folder lying out on the table. "Umm... construction."

"Well, yes. But we're best known for demolitions work. I can undercut the competition by twenty percent because I don't have any waste disposal costs."

Vincent found himself intrigued, despite himself. "What do they do with it?"

Mary Ann's face tightened. "I don't know, exactly. Dipshit tried to explain it once, but he kept talking about unmaking, as if that was something anyone could do. He was a little surprised I didn't know how. I brought in some scientists once to study the unmaking process, but truthfully, what they told me didn't make any better sense than Dipshit's explanation. They all got very excited and started spewing physics things like 'conservation of matter' at me. The best I understand it, the demons are breaking down the molecular structure and turning it into atoms, or something. The demons assure me it's not dangerous. The scientists aren't so sure, because they can't figure out how the demons do it without things exploding. But I'm thinking of branching out into hazardous waste disposal as soon as those scientists can assure me there won't be any negative side effects from the unmaking."

Vincent, again despite himself, let the possibilities fill his head. The way Mary Ann was talking, demons could solve humanity's problems, not just go on a genocidal killing spree until they were stopped. It ran counter to everything the Order had taught him. Not in the details, that was the strangest part. She didn't deny the demons were demons, and she claimed they had all the powers the Order had carefully deduced they had from centuries of written reports. She just—used their abilities toward her own ends. What was wrong with that?

"That is blasphemy," he muttered, more to himself than her. But she must not have realized that, because her face suddenly grew more intense as she leaned in to respond.

"It's the corporate dream," Mary Ann said. "Amoral, soulless employees who thrive doing the work the company needs them to do? Demons enjoy both mind-numbing, tediously repetitive tasks and violent destruction. It would have been blasphemy not to take the big, fat business opportunity Dipshit and his kind presented." She paused. "Look, I was in the middle of a messy divorce with two kids and a crappy, dead end job. And then I started to see these demons everywhere I went. And they were acting out all the rage I felt inside, but I didn't have the luxury of destroying things to make me feel better. I had to build a life for my kids. So I used the resources I had available. I put the demons to work. I like to think they, and I, can make the world a better place."

Vincent looked at her, but his mind was too busy to see the woman in front of him anymore. She didn't seem to have any idea of the danger she had put herself and all of humanity in. He tried to think of some way to tell her, something that she might understand. "But demons can't be trusted."

Mary Ann smiled and held one of her hands out, palm up. "Turns out they take to therapy really well." She flipped her hand over and started gesturing as she continued. "The tedium of corporate day-to-day tasks soothes them, and spots on the demolition crews allow them to actualize their violent tendencies in socially constructive ways. My crew of demons can tear apart a skyscraper down to the molecular level, so there is literally nothing but a bare patch of dirt left when they're done. Now that is the service our clients pay a shit ton of money for. And the demons love it."

One hundred fifty demons all working in concert, doing something they loved? Vincent's stomach churned. That number was far more than the Order had calculated, and they were being used to destroy entire buildings. But, if the algorithms he'd written to detect demonic violence patterns were correct, they weren't doing much else. After a moment, he asked, "If you have 150 demons working here, how many have you sent back to their home in Hell?"

"Sent home?" Mary Ann frowned. "I think, like three, but that was before the therapists came on staff and our HR department has really got the hang of rolling on the new arrivals. I think word's gotten out, and they are leaving Hell to come here."

Vincent grabbed the knot of his tie with a shaking hand. Some of what she said made sense. How wonderful would it be if the demons were no longer a threat? Becoming productive members of society? Solving ecological problems the human race had created for itself? Could demons actually be made—good? For a moment Mary Ann's vision bloomed in his head. He knew the numbers, and how to balance the books. What she was talking about tilted them, turned them upside down, and shook the foundations of theology. The universe, even. Mary Ann Culpepper, saving the world through demons.

Or destroying it. She said it herself. The demons were coming here, and she encouraged them to destroy things. Did she really have the power to contain that destruction? He remembered the priest who had inducted him into the Order. His favorite line was "The Devil won't come as a beast; he'll come in a business suit." Vincent was pretty sure the old man quoted it more often when he was around because he worked for the IRS. Perhaps Vincent had let himself believe the works of the Devil would be easier to spot, despite his mentor's rather pointed warning.

He'd been silent too long. Mary Ann was frowning and tapping her foot on the carpet. He tried to backtrack to the conversation again. Beast in a business suit. "So are you paying them overtime in accordance with the employment laws?" It just burst out of him.

The smile came back to her face. "You're sneaky. If I admit to paying them per hour, then you can argue they aren't independent contractors."

"Actually, no," Vincent admitted. "Independent contractors can, in fact, get paid by the hour. Like a plumber or an electrician. The usual test is if you are providing their tools or workspaces, or if you dictate the hours they work to complete their contract. As an independent contractor, they have the right to set their own schedule. Technically. It can be a fine line sometimes." He snapped his mouth closed. It shouldn't be fun to talk shop with the Chosen One. IRS shop, not demon slaying shop. But he had the picture of Dipshit in his head, and suddenly the idea of slaying that demon didn't sound so appealing, either. He'd been so courteous, until Vincent himself had ruined it.

Mary Ann chuckled. "It sure seems like there should be a different set of rules for demons. Totally off the record, I will admit it's been challenging negotiating the right balance of motherhood, CEO, and demon rehabilitation. The paperwork is a nightmare. But I assure you, it's all in order. I pay some very good accountants for that. We have proper 1099 forms for all of them, and shell companies to disguise the fact that a demon doesn't have a social security number."

Vincent let the words run over him, staring blankly at her. All he could think to say was, "Aren't you scared?"

She leaned back in her chair, clasping her hands together in her lap and looking down at them. "I was, at first. They were intimidating, and I was alone, and I could barely keep the house from falling apart as Dipshit terrorized the neighborhood. But I realized something. Men save the world by destroying their enemies. Women save the world by making them not enemies anymore. I've given the demons a purpose and a common goal, and in turn they have made me a better person. Not to mention wealthier and more powerful than I ever imagined."

The phone beeped. "Ma'am, the Lord of hell has arrived," a deep voice said.

"Oh," Mary Ann said. "He's early."

"No, ma'am."

"Thank you, Dipshit."

"Yes, ma'am."

Almost as soon as she'd finished speaking, Dipshit opened the office door. Mary Ann looked up at the demon as he gently closed the door behind him. "Are you ready, Dipshit?" she said.

"I left the Lord of Hell waiting in the lobby until you completed your business with—" Dipshit cut himself off and gestured toward Vincent, still with shock in his chair.

"Thank you. Please escort Mr. Dunferline to HR so he can examine our vendor contracts." She brought her gaze back to Vincent. "I trust you'll find everything is in order."

Vincent took a steadying breath. "I—I suppose I will. Good Luck, Ms. Culpepper. If you ever need anything from the Order..."

"I doubt it," she said, her face softening into a smile. "But thank you, anyway. If my way doesn't work, maybe you can teach me karate or something."

Dipshit snickered, but quickly brought his face back under control. "This way, sir."

Mary Ann buzzed her intercom and asked another demon to escort the Lord of Hell to her office. Vincent stood and gathered his briefcase, full of papers and artifacts he never needed to use. He fumbled his legal pad when he realized the page was completely blank. He hadn't taken any notes at all. Feeling Dipshit's eyes on him, Vincent gripped it between his fingers and let the hand fall to his side. He'd take notes once he got out of the room that would shortly host the Lord of Hell. He followed Dipshit toward a door on the opposite end of the room from where he'd originally entered. As he went out, he felt a malevolent presence, almost a physical touch on the back of his body. He looked back.

The Lord of Hell stepped in. Vincent could feel it was him, even though the body standing there simulated a middle-aged white man with salt-and-pepper hair. A perfect seeming of a high-powered CEO or equally respected businessman. Dipshit tugged his arm, drawing him away from the scene. Vincent flinched and dropped his briefcase. As he bent to pick it up, he heard Mary Ann Culpepper address the Devil.

"Thank you for meeting with me. Are you interested in a franchise opportunity?"

BIG MOMMA
— SAVES THE WORLD —
by Maurice Broaddus

Dialing back knobs like she prepared to land a starship, Lavitra Campbell fussed at the oven. Her floral-patterned dress fluttered as she took a step back, admiring the tray of macaroni and cheese as it perched—almost regally—on the top shelf. With a fork, she turned her fried chicken in the cast iron pan on the stove. She already knew it would be fire because she was the one making it.

"Oh, is it almost ready?" Her daughter-in-law, Karen Campbell, slunk into the kitchen. With her blond hair swept away from her face, she'd slung a sweater over her shoulders like it was too fashionable to actually put on. She stretched her hand out, poised to open the oven door. "Let me see."

"Chile, I swear if you touch that oven door, you'll draw back a stump," Lavitra growled.

"I just wanted to see the masterwork in progress."

"It's a 'masterwork' because I don't have folks opening and closing my door disrupting the process."

"Leave Momma to her mission." Quentin swept in, his long overcoat made by a designer Lavitra had no interest in pronouncing, on which her son probably spent more money than common sense allowed. All for people at his company who he didn't like and who didn't see him. "In here, she gives the orders, and if you stray from her directions, you might catch the switch."

"We're long past the age of switches. I keep my last one above the mantle there to remind me to not pass down abuse as my legacy." She glanced over at it. Mounted like a trophy, the switch had been chopped from an old pin oak tree, which had long been felled, and no more grew in the area. It was the finest switch that had ever been cut and had caught many a spry behind in its day.

"I'm sorry, Momma. I didn't mean no disrespect," Quentin said.

"Hush, baby, I know. Those were different days, and we raised how we were raised. But as we live, we learn and we grow. I'm good with that. Now." Lavitra kissed him on his forehead. "Supper's almost ready."

The dining table had been set for four, though it could seat six before adding any extending leaves. Lavitra took the head of the table, where her husband, Mr. Campbell, used to sit before he passed. Quentin sat to her right with Karen on the other side of him. A young girl scampered into the room and climbed into the chair on Lavitra's left.

"Who are you? I don't let just anyone sit next to me. You gotta be mighty special to take that spot," Lavitra said.

"It's me, Big Momma. Chira!" The little girl squealed, threatening to collapse into a fit of giggles. Her hair had been braided nicely into pigtails off to each side. Karen did a passable job but was still learning what to do with Black hair. The girl's large eyes danced with delight, as if everything she saw brought her joy.

"Where'd you come from?" Lavitra surveyed the array of bowls and covered dishes, assessing any last second needs.

"Playing."

"You sure you wouldn't rather be called something like 'granny'?" Karen asked.

"Ain't no grannies up in here. I..." Lavitra tilted her glass, first suspicious, then in careful consideration. "Oh Lord."

"What's the matter, Momma?" Quentin asked.

"Didn't I tell you not to drink from this cup?" Lavitra waggled the cup in front of Chira.

"Yes, ma'am." Chira lowered her eyes, careful to avoid Lavitra's steady gaze.

"Ain't nothing but a swallow left in here. Who drank it?"

"Not me," Chira said sheepishly.

"I see. 'Miss Not Me' done broke into my house again. This time drank all my special juice." A playful tone returned to Lavitra's voice.

Chira chanced a thin smile. "Sorry, Big Momma."

"I done told you, my juice—like much of our food—comes from an old family recipe. This one used fruits I grow in the backyard."

"But it's so good!"

"I *know* it's good. I made it and it was mine." Lavitra's smile spread, and she scooted out of her chair to walk back into the kitchen. She returned with a full decanter. "Luckily, I made a whole pitcher."

The Campbell family had a special connection with each other. It didn't matter how long they were apart or where they found themselves in life, when the family came together, it was as if no time had passed. The special bond of their family was built on their Sunday dinners, which they had every week from when Quentin was a baby. Lavitra, Mr. Campbell, and Quentin, though they often invited others—friends, folks from church, sometimes neighbors—and welcomed them to their table. Of course, holidays were bigger—Thanksgiving, Christmas—involving more folks, more food, more laughter. When Mr. Campbell passed, Lavitra continued the dinners, because that's how the ritual of family traditions worked. They survived the individual yet also carried their memory down generations.

Someone pounded at the front door like they'd lost their minds. Or were police. Quentin and Lavitra glanced at each other. Not expecting company, she shrugged and shuffled to the door. Quentin rose, ready to back her up. Bracing the door handle, her face collapsed when she recognized the figure on the other side. She swung open the door despite her better judgment. "What you want, Harold?"

"Uncle Harold!" Chira yelled.

"Hey, baby girl." His voice a rheumy gurgle, Harold stepped into the foyer and scanned the living room, searching out the sources of the voices and the situation as if everyone and everything was suspect. Thick spectacles hung along his nose, too big for his face, magnifying his ever-bloodshot eyes. His grey fedora matched his shoes, and his off-white, seersucker suit hung off his too skinny frame like an ill-fitting shoe. Though he was her brother, the rest of the family tended to dodge him, because, always claiming to be broke, he constantly hit folks up for money. "I just wanted to see if y'all was going to make it to the cookout next week."

"It's the 100-year anniversary of our family moving to these parts. Always the same weekend, at the same time, every year, the way it's always been done. You already know we're gone show out. I'm even breaking out all the big guns: Grandma Jackie's peach cobbler recipe. Didn't no one dare try that except her, but she passed me her recipe." Lavitra beamed with pride and nodded toward Karen.

Uncle Harold's unhurried, stooped shuffle did not quite completely mask a severe limp. His left knee looked like it had been shattered at some point a long time ago and he never went to the doctor to have it properly set. It was painful to watch, so few people stared at his walk for very long. He tucked his hands into his pockets but continued to crane his neck about the room like an addict making a mental inventory list. "That's the other reason I swung by. I wanted to see if you had any other of Grandma Jackie's recipes."

"What for?"

"What you mean 'what for?'" He sucked his teeth.

"Harold, you couldn't find your way to a kitchen with a GPS." Not liking the vibe he put off, Lavitra blocked him as he started to wander toward the dining table. "You ain't gone do nothing but drink at the cookout noways. You and your boys will be huddled around a car trunk sipping a little something like some geriatric mod squad."

"We a council of O.G.s," Uncle Harold protested.

"Not unless that stands for Old Goofies. Get on outchea with your foolishness. If you were meant to have Grandma Jackie's recipes, you'd have been entrusted with them."

Over his protests, she ushered him out the door. Closing it behind him, she waited until he stumbled off down the sidewalk before she returned to her seat. "Must be a full moon or something tonight."

Quentin sat down only after she did. "People are really feeling the family reunion this year. They must be excited."

"I made something, too. I wanted to test one of my own family recipes for the cookout." Karen drew the cover from her dish revealing a potato salad. It had *raisins*.

"Damn, Karen!" Lavitra almost jumped back as if to avoid being bit. "You know, your invite to the cookout is always on a contingency basis."

"Momma," Quentin said.

"She never liked me." Karen crossed her arms and plopped back against her seat.

Lavitra stirred the salad. "I'm getting bubble guts just looking at it."

"Momma!"

"Well, baby, you tried. I guess." Taking her hand, the light of mischief curled Lavitra's lips, taking a bit of the sting from her words. She had to admit she was beginning to warm up to Karen. That special connection of family had blossomed, and it would be sad to see it extinguished at this tenuous stage. "You at least know better than to come to a meal empty handed—and to bring something homemade, not store bought—so you on the right track. But whatever ancestral memory demands you to put fruit where it don't belong, you deny, deny, deny. And we'll be good. For real."

Karen cracked a tentative smirk and heaped a mound of her potato salad onto her plate, knowing she'd be doing the heavy lifting of eating it. She passed a warning glance at Quentin. If he knew what was good for him, he'd better pile some on his plate, too.

"Can I stay the night?" Chira asked.

"Ion know. You gone be trouble?" Lavitra asked.

"No."

"Swear?"

"I swear." Chira held her pinky out.

"Alright then." Lavitra hooked her finger to it and winked like they shared a joke no one else understood.

With her mask no longer keeping a tight seal, Lavitra's CPAP machine blew intermittent spurts of air into her face, just enough to wake and annoy her. She half-stirred with a snort. The rollers in her hair jostled as she turned over, preparing to flip her pillow—to give herself its cool side—when her brain registered the set of eyes staring at her from the shadows.

"Lord Jesus!" Her hand clasped her chest, fearing her heart might leap out.

"It's only me, Big Momma." Stepping closer, Chira held a lone finger to her lips.

"Baby, what is it? You need some water?" Lavitra whispered.

"No. There's someone downstairs."

Lavitra bolted upright, fully alert. Ears attuned like sonar locking in on a target, she wrapped her robe around her and held her hand out, gesturing for Chira to stay in the room. Lavitra crept down the stairs. The sound of someone rustling through papers emanated from the kitchen. She flipped on the lights. A man dressed in all black—his face wrapped in bandages like a ninja cosplaying as a mummy—stood over the kitchen table. Poring over a stack of old family recipes dumped out from the boxes sorted in the cabinet above the oven, he froze. The man chanced a glance at her before grabbing a fistful of recipes and sprinted toward the living room. Lavitra dashed through the dining room to head him off. A thin plastic cover stretched across the length of the couch. A carpet runner marked a trail through the living room. The man hopped on her couch preparing to vault for the door.

"You. Did. Not. Just. Jump. On. My. Couch." Searching for anything to use as a weapon, Lavitra's hand reached out. "You uncouth, no good, dirty...where's my switch?"

"Right here, Big Momma." Her face full of glee at someone else about to get in trouble, Chira held it out with both hands.

"Baby, what are you..." Lavitra snatched the switch at the sound of the man making his move. Despite its thinness, the branch had a heft to it, the weight of purpose and intent. Perfectly balanced in her hand, it whistled through the air until it caught the backside of the intruder. He let out a surprised yelp, tumbling over the back of the couch instead of clearing it. Lavitra pounced on him before he could move. He scrabbled about underneath her, unable to get traction in the pool of spilt recipes. He shielded his face and upper body as best he could as the switch lashed at him.

"What are you doing in my house?" Lavitra raised her arm, ready to bring the switch down again if she didn't like what she heard.

"You and your family possess something that is not rightfully yours." The man's accent was foreign, though not from a place she recognized. Perhaps Iowa.

"Unless you coming with a reparations check, that's the history of this whole country."

"We know who and what you are. I'm here to stop you and your mission."

"Uh huh. Since you being all mysterious, you bout to make me do something I don't do unless times are desperate: call the police."

"Call them. Reveal yourself as one of the long line of the Order of the Mint Rose."

The name struck Lavitra so hard she almost dropped the switch. Noting her stunned silence, the man wriggled free and scrambled out of the door. Chira rushed to the entranceway, but Lavitra shook her head.

"No, baby, get away from there."

The girl buried her face into Lavitra's robe. "Who was he, Big Momma?"

"I don't know."

"What did he want?"

"I...don't know." Lavitra hesitated, not wanting to lie to the girl.

"I'm scared. I want daddy."

"I don't blame you. Let's call him. I think there are some things it's time for him to know."

"The what?" Quentin paced back and forth in front of the couch, careful not to stray from the runner. He bristled, wanting to call the police but being blocked by his mother every time he brought it up. He was so full up with mad, he had trouble understanding anything she said.

"The Order of the Mint Rose." Sighing, Lavitra lowered her voice as if not wanting to startle him.

"Is that some sort of cult?"

"No. It's our family's...duty."

"I don't understand any of this." Karen hugged Chira, who stared at Lavitra like she was a stranger.

Quentin folded his arms across his chest and waited impatiently in front of the mantle. "Someone needs to start explaining things."

"Someone needs to watch their tone and take a seat." Lavitra hard-eyed Quentin until he sat down on the couch with the rest of his family. "Now there are stories that are told only in the hood. One such tale started decades ago when Duke Ellington visited the Sunset Terrace on Indiana Avenue. It was a Sunday night, back in the 1930s. The rumor goes that when he was on stage, he heard the sounds of fighting from somewhere in the dark among the audience. The crowd threw whiskey and beer bottles toward the stage, mussed up his suit something fierce. And he loudly proclaimed that he'd never return to the Sunset Terrace. Never. But that whole event was orchestrated by a secret brotherhood, a sacred order of griots. He'd come to pass along messages about one of the most massive and sweeping undertakings in the history of Black folks. He was an emissary with a message about the long-prophesied Mother Plane. Made like the universe, it was spheres within spheres, by our people who live in the future. They said that they will return one day if the appointed signal is made at the right time to collect our people. We outchea!"

"Outchea?"

"Boy, you heard me. Let me slow down for you, I guess. We out here. Act like you ain't heard me speak on it before. When I shine, you shine; we shine together. Let's get it. Outchea."

"Come on, momma. This is a lot to take in, and when you get to feeling it..."

"Allow me to more clearly enunciate," she said, over-pronouncing each word, "'cause there's one last thing. This secret appointment has been passed down through generations, transferred through recipes as part of our living culture as memory, through the matriarchs of certain families."

"The Order of the Mint Rose?" Karen asked.

"Yes. Ours is a sacred duty. Making the meals passed down to us in hopes that one day our dreams, our future, will come to us."

"So, Black folks have been in communication with future space Black folks who are waiting for the right time to come ally with us?"

"Yes."

Quentin rubbed his temples. "Momma, you've been under a lot of strain. If you aren't feeling well..."

"If any part of me didn't feel well, I'd put some Vick's VapoRub on it." Lavitra slumped at the kitchen table. She reviewed some of the recipes over, putting them back in the proper boxes. "These are the stories that help us understand our past."

"And the man who broke into your house?" Quentin asked.

"A reminder that we will be hunted wherever we go, whatever we do. Sent by one of those who hate themselves. Who are so embarrassed of who we are, our stories, our ways." Lavitra sorted through the remaining recipes. "This is the key our ancestors left us. A recipe for fighting back. The stories are firmly etched into your DNA, your cultural, ancestral memory. To try to run from them is to hide from who you are."

"Why didn't I know?"

"It's passed through matriarchs, one generation to the next." Her eyes drifted to Chira. "When they are ready."

Quentin took the yellowed slip of paper from her. "It looks like a recipe for oxtail stew. So what, this like Black Passover? We painting a raised Black fist over our door?"

"It's a map."

"Show me," Quentin said.

"Are you sure?" Lavitra peeked over the remaining recipes she fanned in her grip.

"I'd think you were crazy, but a mummy ninja breaking into the house adds a certain credibility to your story," Quentin said. "Besides, if you're part of this sacred order, then it's partially my burden, too."

"And you shouldn't have to carry this burden alone," Karen said. "That's what family is for."

"Then let me see if I can decode these instructions." Lavitra plopped onto the couch and read. "It will lead us to the final recipe."

The Norwood neighborhood of Indianapolis was a Freetown founded by the surviving soldiers of the U.S. Colored Troops, the 28th Regiment, after the Civil War. Two rivers and four railroads met there, and at its heart was a great, old-growth forest. An orchard practically ringed the town, with each yard seeming to hold a portion of it. Many of the troops and families of Norwood were buried in the New Crown Cemetery, the grounds of which Lavitra and Quentin currently skulked.

"I'm not even going to pretend to know how you translated your code." Quentin kept low, alert for cars, especially police patrolling.

"That would come in time, with the training that happens as you actually try to prepare the recipes. It's kind of like getting a feel for music: there are the notes written down and the ones that are felt. Just like you have to know what not to play and when to improvise."

"Art and science." Quentin cast his flashlight across the ground, scanning the headstones. "So what are we looking for?"

"The key is this line: 'Here lies a knight interred, whose funeral was presided over by a prophet.'"

"A knight? That could refer to a soldier, I guess."

"Exactly. Look around us: this section of New Crown was where many of the Colored Soldiers from the 28th Regiment were buried. Over there!" She gestured toward a grave marker.

Quentin turned the beam to the stone, hovering the light on the corner over the image of a rose. "I'm betting this must be the one."

"It's the sign of the Mint Rose. Many of the soldiers were ex-slaves who came up from or through Kentucky."

"On the Underground Railroad. Wait." Quentin grew silent, lost in his thoughts. "Mint Rose. I get it. A play on Araminta Ross, the birthname of Harriet Tubman. She must be the prophet."

"She always had her soldiers, protecting those robbed of their power, those who were oppressed. We continue that mission." Lavitra tipped the monument. Its base shifted, and within a divot left by the tombstone was a box. Quentin fished out the box, which matched the set from Lavitra's cabinet. He handed it to Lavitra, who turned its lid back, forth, and around in a particular order until it opened. She withdrew several pieces of paper.

"What do they say?" Quentin reached for a slip. "A macaroni and cheese recipe?"

"No, that'd be too obvious. But the dish does have to be something baked." Lavitra flipped through the others. "Hoe cakes. No, wait. This is it. Sweet potato nut bread."

"How can you tell?"

"It's the beauty of the recipe. Look how it calls for a pinch of some ingredients and a dash of others. That's the sign of magic."

"The notes unplayed?" Quentin nodded.

"Exactly. Only then is the key unlocked. Come on, we have ingredients to buy and not too long to make sure I can do this recipe right."

The steady din of loud voices greeted folks as soon as they entered Pride Park. It was a family reunion for anyone who called this place, or the Campbells, home. Peals of laughter followed kids racing between stands of adults. Among the competing grills, the heavy aroma of home cooking trailed like a low-lying cloud through the families. Succulent greens. Bins upon bins of fried chicken. Sweet New Orleans cornbread. Bowls of dirty rice. Ham. Baked beans slathered with dark and rich brown sugar and the fat of bacon strips trickling throughout.

Within minutes Lavitra started to recognize some of the faces, as if—despite the dimming of memory time created—just being around her people was enough to stir memories. Aunt Margaret guarded—with justified vigilance considering she was Harold's wife—against people coming through the line too many times and fixing take-home plates. Her spiteful eyes even scrutinized the portions of each person's tray, occasionally grunting her disapproval if she suspected that the allotment would go to waste. Aunt Viola and Aunt Ruth—fraternal twins, the youngest of five children, ladies whom she had called 'Aunt' for so long she wasn't sure how they were related to her—paraded behind the dessert table, displaying their wares. Aunt Viola displayed a batch of pies, from butterscotch (Mr. Campbell's favorite) to sour cherry to peach cobbler. Apparently, Aunt Ruth showed off her angel food cake, a pineapple upside down cake, and a pair of lemon meringue pies, claiming to make the best meringue this side of the Mason-Dixon line. Their passive-aggressive competition ended the same way each year: insults about their dry-ass meat dishes, inability to keep a husband, and how much of their hair was actually theirs. They'd repair their rift at Christmas, only to repeat the cycle next year.

Karen insisted on arriving at the announced time of the cookout and posted up near the Campbell section of the table. By the time Lavitra strode toward her, Quentin looked beyond bored. At her approach, Chira perked to life at her cue to run and join the other children. Karen beamed as soon as she spied Lavitra, who tried to hide her scowl of leeriness at the container her daughter-in-law had covered in front of her.

"Baby, I'm gone ask this as gentle as possible, but what did you bring to represent our family?" Lavitra set down her still-warm sweet potato nut bread.

Karen whipped the cloth cover away to reveal a tray of macaroni and cheese.

"Is that...American cheese slices on top? And penne pasta? There better not be any nonsense like peas in there. You can't just stroll into a cookout with macaroni and cheese. That's a privilege to be earned. This is a sacred responsibility, the signature dish of a family."

"I also brought aluminum foil." Karen held up two rolls. "I don't know what happens, but there never seems to be enough."

"You manage to make me feel like there's hope for you sometimes."

"Some of the cousins just invited me to play Spades," Karen said.

"Please tell me you said 'no,'" Lavitra said.

"I tried to tell her," Quentin whispered.

"Why would I do that?" Karen asked.

"Because you ain't ready," Lavitra said.

"I learned. It's just like Euchre."

"Chile." Somehow the word now had three syllables. "Aw, hell no. You're about to get your invite revoked."

Karen backed up, bumping into Uncle Harold.

"Watch the shoes." He strutted about dressed like the player who was a bit too old for the club, with his brown polyester suit and flyway collars.

"Oh, excuse me." Not wanting to piss him off, Karen threw him a conciliatory smile.

"Folks always showin' too many teeth, especially when they ain't got nothin' to smile about." Uncle Harold perused the food offerings along the table. Yellowed eyes, his blood vessels like red tentacles about his pupils, carefully gave the table the once over, pausing at the sweet potato nut bread. "New recipe?"

"Uncle Harold, walk to my car with me." Wrapping his arms around him, Quentin was old enough for the rite of passage from the kiddie table to the grown folks table to the gathering at the car trunk, with its passing of the brown liquor.

"Who's this stranger?" Uncle Harold's deep baritone voice croaked, a slow, low rumble that melted with warmth whenever he was around Quentin. Or the thought of brown liquor. More like an older brother he wanted to hang out with but couldn't. "I almost didn't see you there. You tryin' to hide from me, boy?"

"You get anything to eat?" Quentin asked.

"No, not yet," Uncle Harold said. "It's not time yet."

"Better hurry up. You know how folks are with free food."

"Hell, I fixed me a 'to go' plate as soon as I got here." Uncle Harold patted a small tray that sat discreetly next to him. An odd menagerie of sides and desserts peeked out through the slits, like he'd tried to grab a sample of every dish made.

The DJ let enough of the opening notes of "Cupid Shuffle" play out to signal folks to make their way to the dance area.

"It's about that time," Lavitra said.

"I got this." Karen placed her hand on her mother-in-law's shoulders. "It there's one thing I *can* do, it's line dance. The instructions are in the lyrics!"

The dance floor swelled as folks made their way to it. Within a few beats, Karen was a whirl of elbows and kicks as she spun and shimmied "to the left, to the left, to the left, to the left." Lavitra refused to be distracted. She studied the tree line. In the shadows, she knew the figure who sought the family recipes lurked. A strange fear, close to panic, threatened to choke her. Lavitra cut through the dancers to make her way to the DJ. Unable to breathe as the bodies pressed in, her relatives no longer seemed familiar. No longer real, images distorted by a darkened funhouse mirror.

With cloying sweat, her clothes felt uncomfortably tight; the sounds of the gathering coalesced into a thick murmur of clustered voices. The microphone squealed as Lavitra snatched it. "Alright everyone, let's say grace." The crowd dispersed, heading to their respective tables to await the ritual passing of food. "Lord God, Heavenly Father, bless us and these Thy gifts which we receive from Thy bountiful goodness, through Jesus Christ, our Lord. The eyes of all look to you, O Lord, and you give them their food at the proper time. Amen."

Chira skipped over and jumped into Lavitra's lap once she was seated. Uncle Harold took a circuitous route from the dance floor, one that took him to the edge of the park, his eyes anxiously flitting about like he was searching for someone. Or waiting for a signal. When folks told her who they were, it was always easier if she believed them the first time. But her heart broke all over again with the dawning realization. Uncle Harold glanced about and immediately reached for the sweet potato nut bread.

"Going for dessert first?" Lavitra asked.

"You know how I do," he grumbled.

"This is what I was trying to tell you: all skinfolk ain't kin folk" Lavitra said to no one in particular. "You looking to sell out the family, Harold? What did they promise you? Money? House? Car? A good-paying job?"

"I..." His fork hovering over a piece of the nut bread, he glanced around the silent table. "It's not like that."

"What you once despised, was ashamed of, is now part of the essential beauty that is us." The words tumbled out of her like an incantation.

"Do you have any idea what we are supposed to be guarding?" he countered. "They opened my eyes to it. It's too much, Lavitra. Why should it always be on our shoulders—your shoulders—to fix what's been broken. When can we finally relax and just be free? Haven't we earned that yet?"

Lavitra walked around to him and just set her heavy hand on his shoulder and began to sing. *"One glad morning, when this life is over, I'll fly away..."*

Aunt Margaret, Aunt Viola, and Aunt Ruth screamed like a panicked choir as the bandaged figure stumbled out of the shadows and rushed to the dessert table. Big Momma charged at him and slammed her full weight into him.

"I got something for you. Let me finish what I started." Her hand grasped at air, so she tugged at her belt.

"You going to make me cut my own switch this time?" the figure growled.

Headbutting him, she backed away a step to give herself some room. Her first punch landed in his gut. The second caught him in the side of his neck. The bandaged figure dropped to the ground. Lavitra bobbed on her feet. The man spun, sweeping her legs out from under her. She flew into the air, landing flush on her back with a heavy thud. The man paused, as the rest of the family closed the circle about him. He lumbered toward the nut bread.

"Y'all are wrong about me!" Uncle Harold yelled. "I'm a part of this family, too. I'll prove it. They'll choose me as their rightful vessel!"

The bandaged figure reached for Karen's macaroni and cheese and took a large bite. Within moments of his swallow, he clutched at his throat. His face contorted. Spirits swirled out of the macaroni and cheese like errant embers. They spun about, elongating flames trailing as they moved.

The angry spirits leapt to him. He swatted at them, even as they seemed to ignite at the touch of them. The figure screamed as the spirits consumed him. Uncle Harold sprang up. Checking the pile of ashes—fearing they'd come for him next—he eyed the swirling judgment of his ancestors, and the family parted to allow him to run out of the park, his to-go plates in tow.

"Damn, Karen!" Lavitra, said watching him depart. "I know you ain't out here trying to bring about the apocalypse with your macaroni and cheese recipe."

With everyone's attention focused on the smoldering bandaged figure—conversation already turning to whether they should dip now rather than try to explain this scene to the police—or the fleeing Uncle Harold, no one noticed Chira. She ambled up to the table, took a slice of the nut bread, and bit into it.

"Child, no!" Lavitra yelled.

Within a few heartbeats, Chira's muscles seized. She threw her head back and began to tremble as if caught in a sudden surge of power.

"Chira!" Karen rushed toward her. Just as she reached her daughter, a beam of white light shot out of her mouth, eyes, and nose into the heavens. The skies darkened as if thunderstorm clouds had suddenly moved in. Spent, Chira toppled off the bench, but Lavitra caught her.

Quentin shoved everyone out of his way to reach her. He dropped to his knees to check her airways and pulse. "She's okay. Her breathing's normal."

"And she's already coming around," Lavitra said.

"I'd still like to get her to a hospital."

"You may want to skip the beams of light shooting out her face as part of her medical history," she said.

"Momma..." he started.

The clouds thickened, becoming roiling inky waves. A terrible roar erupted all about, a thrum that reverberated through her chest. The winds picked up. The family began to make their way to the park shelter. The clouds took on a sinister aspect, until a piercing while light outlined them. Lavitra held her ground. Visoring her eyes with her hand, she whispered.

"'Behold, the four wheels by the cherubims, one wheel by one cherub and another wheel by another cherub; and the appearance of the wheels

was as the color of a beryl stone. And as for their appearance, all four had one likeness, as if a wheel had been in the midst of a wheel.'"

"What does that mean?" Quentin asked.

Lavitra took his hand. "We outchea."

— A LEGACY OF GHOSTS —
by Sarah Hans

I haven't seen my mom in the flesh for over a decade, but the exact moment she dies, she appears to me. She materializes like condensation on a bathroom mirror, as if she's been waiting for this moment, hovering on the other side, anticipating the instant when the hospital would remove the tube from her lungs.

Of course, her ghost doesn't look like a sixty-four-year-old woman in a wheelchair, skinny and ravaged by lung cancer, so for a second the pieces don't connect. I squint at a brunette in her thirties, wearing neon green leggings, an oversized sweater, and white Keds, like something out of a Van Halen music video. I can't see it, but I know with a sixth sense her teased ponytail is held in place with a scrunchy, probably a pink one.

My brain is just starting to recognize the mom of my childhood when she shouts, "HA! You *can* still see ghosts!"

I flinch. "You've been waiting a long time to say that."

"You bet your ass I have." She takes a drag on an ephemeral cigarette; my nose burns with the smoke of ghostly tobacco. "How do you get them to leave you alone?" She glances around, surprised,

I guess, to find herself alone on the corporeal plane in my house. Her home would have been crowded with the dead, all clamoring for her attention, an endless parade of the desperate and damned. I shiver, remembering cold hands plucking at my childhood pajamas. "They don't mess with me, and I don't mess with them." She narrows her eyes.

My phone rings. I usually let it go to voicemail, but I really, really need an excuse to stop talking to my mom, so I grab it and turn away from her ghost. She materializes in front of me again almost instantly and my lungs clench tight in my chest. "Hello?"

"Miss Huddle? My name is Candace. I'm a nurse at Mercy Hospital. Are you sitting down?"

"My mom is dead. Yes, thank you, I know. Anything else?"

"How—how do you..."

"You know what my mom did for a living?"

The nurse hesitates. "She was a psychic, right?"

"Yep. I inherited her gift. She's here with me now." My eyes flick to my mom, long legs pacing around my tiny kitchen, cigarette dangling precariously between two fingers. "She wants you to know she really appreciates all the care everyone at your hospital gave her. Thank you for calling."

Mom glares at me as I lower the phone. "Why'd you say that?"

I press my lips together to hold back a sharp reply: *Because caring for you was no picnic, and I'm glad I didn't have to do it.* Slipping into my teenage habits instead, I say only, "It was a nice thing to do for someone who lost a patient today."

Mom's nose wrinkles. "You were always so fucking nice. I see that hasn't changed."

And you were always so fucking nasty; that hasn't changed, either. "Thanks, Mom. I try." I offer her a sarcastic smile and go into the living room. I kneel at the altar against one wall and start pulling items from the drawers: a silver athame, a bowl made of bone, a silk cloth embroidered with runes, a candle made from human tallow.

"You don't do the work anymore, so why do you still have all that?" Mom asks. "Thinking about taking up the family business again now your competition is out of the way?"

"Something like that." I don't look at her. I drape the cloth over the altar, lay out the knife, go to the kitchen to fill the bowl with water. I light the candle and slit the tip of my pinky finger, letting my blood drop into the bowl. Then, I begin to chant the words, the words that will send my mother's ghost out of the corporeal plane, banishing her to the ethereal forever.

I've prepared for this spell for years. What I didn't prepare for was my mother.

Peals of hard-edged laughter fill the house. I cover my ears but her voice grinds into my head anyway. The reek of cigarette smoke fills my throat until I gag. The lights flicker and go out; the candle flame wavers and flares like a blast from a blowtorch, sending me reeling back from the altar.

Something cold rakes my back, something cold and sharp, like claws, like the fingernails of a dead woman.

"You haven't used your gift for a lifetime," my mother thunders, a lamp flying across the room to shatter against the wall. "You never let me finish teaching you everything you needed to know, and the most important lesson was that a medium only becomes more powerful in death."

The floor bucks violently, the house trembling as though caught in a sudden earthquake. It sounds like a freight train bearing down on the house, like an airplane about to crash-land on the roof, like a herd of elephants stampeding across the yard. I want to do what I did as a child, curling into a little ball with my hands over my ears.

I remind myself: I'm not a child anymore. I'm forty-two years old, a grown woman! I force myself to my feet and snatch my purse from the hook by the door as I rush out of my own home. I run down the sidewalk and throw myself into my car, starting the engine and backing out of the driveway.

I pause in the street to look back at my house. Even with the car windows up and the motor running, I hear crashing sounds, the blare of a TV or radio—maybe both—turned to maximum volume. The lights in the windows flicker and flash. The front door opens and slams shut. Rage claws its way up my throat and exits my mouth in a long, low wail. She's destroying my home, my carefully constructed safe space, purely out of spite. Again, I fight the urge to shut down, swallowing my sobs.

It's time to go to Plan B.

Danielle greets me with open arms when I arrive on her doorstep. Her dark hair is streaked with gray, and her eyes are surrounded by crow's feet, but otherwise she looks much as she always has. She smells of sage and sandalwood as we embrace, and memories assault me, memories of my teenage years, spent hiding out at Danielle's new age shop when home became particularly unbearable. I can almost feel her well-worn tarot cards under my fingers, taste the peppermint tea she always made to soothe my nerves, hear the tinkle of bells on the front door as customers entered and exited the shop.

Of course, the shop is long gone—now Danielle sells the same mystical items online, from the comfort of her own home. She invites me in, past a dining room stacked with boxes and bags of inventory, and I say hello to the big black tomcat, Merlin, her familiar and pet. I'm amazed Merlin is still alive—he must be more than twenty years old—but I don't say so, not in front of him.

The murmur of muffled voices reaches me, and I glance at Danielle.

"Coven is on the back patio," Danielle says, and my eyes again well with tears, but this time they're tears of gratitude.

Twelve women are gathered under the tin roof of Danielle's patio, their faces dimly lit by citronella candles. A few I remember from my time in the shop, regular customers, but the rest are new. Most smile at me, but a few frown and look away.

Danielle steps onto the patio and places her arm around my shoulders. "This is Morgan, everyone." She turns to me and whispers, "Not everyone agreed with the vote, but they'll still help."

Someone drawls, "The tyranny of the majority."

Others sigh or chortle, and the woman nearest me rolls her eyes. She stands, and she's well over six feet tall. Her voice is surprisingly deep and sonorous. "Welcome, Morgan. We're happy to help you, if we can. I'm Jessica."

I shake Jessica's long-fingered hand. She has a firm grip and looks me directly in the eyes, and I appreciate both. I take comfort from her confidence. There's something familiar about her, but I can't quite place where I know the planes of her face and the bright amber of her eyes.

Jessica smirks. "We had classes together in high school. I was called Evan, then."

I nod, remembering a quiet, shy young man I never really got to know. A far cry from the woman standing before me, whose charisma seems to take up the whole patio, a radiant Amazon. "You look better as a blonde."

Jessica laughs, a loud bark too goofy to be fake. Her smile broadens and her posture relaxes. Her eyes go from amber to gold as her expression softens.

Danielle clears her throat, bringing me back to the patio, with its cloud of citronella and cigarette smoke and the assembled witches watching me intently.

I turn to the coven. "Right. I really appreciate all your help. We don't have any time to waste. Mom's weakened by her earlier outburst at my house but she'll regain her strength quickly. Best to banish her while she's not at full strength."

Jessica nods and grins. "I've never banished a ghost before. It's exciting."

The rest of the group seems less enthusiastic. One woman stubs out her cigarette and shakes her head.

"I know this is asking a lot for someone most of you barely know. I can't thank you enough," I say.

"Just remember that the next time we call you with a favor," another woman says.

I nod, agreeing to this price. I would agree to a lot more, to rid myself of my mother's ghost permanently, but they don't need to know that. Merlin watches me from the window, blinking his big, round eyes, two glowing green lanterns in the dusky light.

As one, the group rises and goes into the yard. They've already placed their brooms in a circle, and I step into it. Danielle pours salt around the circle, an added precaution. The wind stirs the trees ringing Danielle's backyard, pushing the swing on her ancient swing set so it issues a rusty squeak, tugging at my hair like the icy fingers of the dead.

Someone lights a candle, and the flame is passed around the circle. With each woman holding a candle, it looks like I'm surrounded by glowing, disembodied heads. The night beyond each woman seems endlessly dark and cold, the stars and moon overhead blotted out by clouds. When everyone has quieted, Jessica raises her candle and calls to Hecate for her help. Jessica's voice is powerful and dramatic, and I can understand why they chose her for this part of the ritual. The neighbors are miles away and they can probably hear her appeal; surely the gods themselves can't ignore us.

Danielle begins the chant of the same words I used in my banishing ritual, a jumble of Gaelic and Latin, a few Germanic words thrown in for good measure. Like all magical language, it has power because we lend it meaning. The words themselves could be the ingredients from the back of a cereal box, but thirteen women reciting them as a mantra while focusing their will can make them into a powerful spell.

I just hope thirteen women will be enough.

The other women pick up the chant and it rises in volume and speed, the words crawling across my skin and making my hair stand on end. Danielle was true to her word: even the reluctant members of her coven chant with purpose and intensity. The air crackles with magical energy.

I stand in the circle for what feels like eternity, the wind whipping my hair into a tangled mess. The candle flames waver and flicker and a few have to be relit. The coven's voices rise and fall, the chant becoming a pulse that batters the inside of my skull. The minutes slouch into hours. Where is my mother's ghost? Did she drive herself into such a frenzy at my house that she effectively banished herself? My instincts say no. I have to wait. Patience has never been a virtue of mine, and I fight the urge to check my watch for the time. The women in the circle sway with boredom. My legs ache. I'm ready to give up and start brainstorming a Plan C.

And then the barometric pressure drops so fast I feel it in my head, my belly, like I'm in an elevator that made an abrupt stop. I lean forward, suddenly nauseous with dread, a feeling I haven't missed since I mastered my ability to channel spirits twenty years ago. Behind the women in the circle, faces appear in the darkness, gray and drawn, eyes bright with hunger like silver coins. The faces of the dead.

Surprise and fear ripple around the circle as the women notice the visitors. Danielle continues chanting, raising her voice insistently until the other women rejoin the mantra, but their voices are tentative now, and even Danielle's hands tremble holding their candle. Her eyes meet mine, communicating a silent plea: *Hurry.*

"You can't rush the dead, honey." Mom materializes inside the circle, leaning over to speak in Danielle's face. She glows with unearthly, ephemeral light. She looks, now, how she looked on her television show: a forty-something woman in a blue skirt-suit, her bottle-blond hair expertly styled into a French twist.

"This is how you want to be remembered?" I ask, filling my voice with contempt, hoping to draw her attention away from Danielle.

When she turns to me, her face is so coated with pancake makeup it looks blurred, soft-focus, wrinkles smoothed over and age spots concealed. Beautiful...but also plastic, fake, like a genuine smile would crack her face in half. She chuckles, sauntering over to me on heels that never sink in the grass. "Why wouldn't I want to look like this? I was one of *People*'s most beautiful people in this outfit."

"Thanks to a team of stylists and speech writers and marketing experts. You look like President Barbie."

The cigarette appears again between her fingers, and she takes a long drag, ghostly smoke expelling from her nostrils as she talks. With her eyes glowing and smoke wreathing her head, she reminds me of a dragon. "You never approved of what I did with the gift. I can't help it if you rejected your legacy, but why does that have to apply to me?" She flicks the cigarette away and it cartwheels through the air, a slim, glowing white stick with a burning red tip. The coven watches as it lands on one woman's chest. I think her name is Lorraine? I remember her from Danielle's shop. Back then she was the type who never deviated from the pagan uniform of broomstick skirts, loose blouses, and velvet kimonos, and she hasn't changed in that respect in twenty years.

There's an instant of silence and hesitation where we hold our collective breath.

Lorraine screams and brushes the apparition from her shirt. It evaporates in the air but leaves behind a scorch mark in her blouse and a small, round burn on the revealed flesh of her sternum. Danielle shouts at them to stay and hold the circle, but two other women hustle Lorraine, still shrieking, out of the yard and into the house, and then we're down from thirteen to ten—eleven, if you count me. I'm going to have to count for double, I guess.

Mom laughs, the sound like rusty chains dragging on rough asphalt. "If that's all it takes to scare off your pathetic wannabe-witches, Danielle, this is gonna be easier than I thought."

"Hold the circle!" Danielle barks. She takes up the chant again. The remaining women close in, filling in the gaps, bringing the circle tighter. Their chanting is louder now, more urgent, the words tripping over one another. I close my eyes and let the magic wash over me, an ocean of electricity where I can float.

Mom's power is a hot slap ripping me from the cool tide. When I open my eyes, the other women have been knocked to the ground. Shouting in panic, they scramble to their feet and run for the house. All except Danielle and Jessica.

Now we're down from thirteen to three.

I step out of the circle and grab a broom. The three of us close in around Mom, chanting. Danielle has always been powerful, and Jessica's formidable magic crackles from her aura like a raging bonfire, and then there's me.

Mom laughs again, even as the circle shrinks around her, barely wider than her ghostly hips. Her eyes are the burning red cherries of her cigarettes. Behind her, the hungry dead surround us, pressing in, wearing expressions of pain and longing. They whisper in my ears, a susurrus of misery, and over it all, my mother's voice: "You'll never beat me. You came from me; you're a fraction of me and my power. You should really give up before someone else gets hurt, Morgan."

Under the reek of cigarette smoke, the air smells like ozone, like a summer storm, like lightning about to strike. My gut clenches tight, threatening to make me expel everything I've eaten today.

"Stop holding back," Jessica interrupts the chant to shout at me. Her eyes glow like twin suns. Danielle squeezes my hand, nodding agreement, never breaking the chant. Her hair is bright white flame, and her voice is impossibly loud, the chanting of multitudes issuing from one mouth.

I shake my head, trying to communicate that this is it. This is all I have. Mom is right; I've never been as powerful as she is, and I never will be. I gave up magic a long time ago, and with it I gave up the ability to free myself of my mother's ghost. Despair sinks inside me like a lead weight.

"She'll never be able to match me," Mom bellows. The wind tears at us, a cold blast laden with the stench of brimstone and nicotine. The dead howl around us, a ravenous maelstrom, ragged fingers tearing at our hair, our clothes, our skin. The creaking swing issues a rusty scream as it tears away from the swing set and disappears over the roof of the house. Tree branches crack and tumble to the ground all around us.

"You betrayed me, Danielle, right up until the end." Mom rears back, the size of a skyscraper, a mountain, a massive churning tsunami. I scream Danielle's name, but it's too late. Mom's ghost crashes over Danielle, and the last thing I see is Danielle looking at me, opening her mouth as if to say one last desperate word, and then we're all engulfed in darkness.

I come up from the darkness, and I'm surrounded by bodies, too many of them, none giving me air. The faces are wan, their fingers touching me are cold, and their voices pleading with me are soft and despairing. Their eyes shine like pearl buttons. Am I in the afterlife? Have I crossed over?

I push the apparitions away, both physically and psychically, so I can get my bearings. I'm not sure what happened to my shoes, but there is grass tickling the soles of my bare feet. When I stand, the ground is solid beneath me. The breeze ruffles my hair. I breathe a sigh of relief; not dead.

As the spirits step back, Danielle's collapsed form is revealed. My stomach drops and I run to her. My fingers pressing at her neck can't find a pulse. Her skin is already going cold.

A hand on my shoulder makes me look up. Jessica looms above me. "We have to finish this."

Mom's ghost is gone, probably too weak to stay corporeal. The other ghosts swirl around us, moaning and weeping and gnashing their teeth. It's hard to think with all the uproar.

"I can't do it," I whisper.

"What?" Jessica grabs my arm and hauls me to my feet. "Danielle just died for this."

"I don't think I'm strong enough, even with your help." I can't look Jessica in the eyes. Tears sting my cheeks.

"Then call Danielle from the other side."

I shake my head and step back from her. "You don't know what you're asking."

"Why not? Danielle would give anything for you."

I sigh. I've never told anyone this, except Danielle. "Being a medium isn't what you think. I quit because the ghosts were being called from the other side to talk to their loved ones and then they couldn't get back. They become the hungry dead." I nod to the twisted, desperate, gray faces that surround us, their moans rising briefly with the recognition. "Mom was using the ghosts for financial gain, then leaving them to wander the corporeal plane for eternity."

"So, if we called Danielle from the other side…"

"She'd be doomed to the same fate. I can't do that to her." A sob chokes me. "Danielle was like a mother to me when mine didn't want me anymore."

"And that's why your mom is haunting you. Because you didn't want to scam families out of money to torture their dead loved ones."

"When I rejected my gift, she took it personally. We haven't talked for more than twenty years. She's waited a long time to be able to punish me."

Jessica nods. "A tale as old as time."

That startles a laugh from me. "Sure."

Jessica finds two candles on the ground and fishes in the pocket of her denim skirt for matches. "No, really. I'm a therapist in my day job. Most of my clients are people who couldn't live up to a parents' expectations—or didn't want to." Jessica hands me a candle, lights a match, lets the wick catch, and then uses the match to light her own candle. The air fills with the scent of sulfur and wax burning. "You know Danielle talked about you a lot."

I meet her eyes in the soft, golden candlelight. She's so pretty, my stomach does a flip. "She did?"

"You were like a daughter to her. She was so proud of you for making a life for yourself, getting past your mother's abuse."

I sniffle. "It wasn't abuse. She just disapproved of me."

One of Jessica's eyebrows arches. "You don't think this—" She waves her hand to encompass the dark backyard, the sighing ghosts lingering in the shadows, Danielle's body cold on the ground. "—is abusive?"

"I guess I never really thought about it that way before. I think she got angrier as she got older, too. She wasn't like this when I was young."

"Stop making excuses for her and listen—I don't think we have much time before she comes back, and we need to be ready."

I shake my head. "Thank you, Jessica, really, but I can't risk your life, too." I start toward the house, where a few fearful witches watch us from the dark kitchen window. "I should go home."

Jessica catches my arm in a firm grip. "This is your home. Danielle's house and her coven will always be your home."

"I can't ask anyone else to die for me." I pull my arm from her grasp and turn away from her.

"Danielle believed in you, Morgan, and she believed you aren't a psychic medium at all."

The wind is picking up again, and the hungry dead are growing louder, more raucous. "I can hear the dead right now, Jessica. Even when they're on the ethereal plane, I can hear them. All the time. They never shut up."

"But you were able to live a life anyway. How? How did you control your power?"

"I made them leave me alone!" The wind tugs at my hair. The ghosts issue a collective, panicked wail, and my ears pop, as if I'm on an airplane descending from cruising altitude. "She's back." Now it's my turn to grab Jessica's arm and pull her toward the house. "You should get inside."

Jessica fights me, and she's taller, stronger, has more leverage. She has to shout to be heard over the screaming ghosts, the tearing wind. "How did you control your power?"

"I bluffed, okay? I told them not to come near me or I'd send them all to Hell!"

Mom's ghost pops into existence beside me, blowing a cloud of cigarette smoke into my face. "Sadly for you, Hell doesn't scare me."

Jessica shouts, "Morgan, don't you get it? They *listened* to you."

Mom's eyes slide to Jessica. She raises her hand and flicks her wrist, like she's swatting an annoying fly, and Jessica hits the ground, so hard the air is knocked from her lungs, and she lays there, flailing and gasping for breath.

"You ready to go home now?" Mom's gaze returns to me.

"Why do you want to spend your afterlife haunting me?" I ask, watching Jessica out of the corner of my eye.

Mom laughs, a throaty, malicious sound, and takes another drag on the cigarette. "You need my help, Morgan. Your life would be so much better if you would just accept your gift and use it."

I'm left speechless for a second, and then I manage to stutter, "I don't need you. I got by just fine without you for twenty years."

"Oh please. You live in a one-bedroom apartment and you work in a call center. No husband, no children. No legacy. You always needed me to guide you and tell you what to do. My only mistake was letting you move away from me and thinking maybe you could make it on your own, without your family."

The dead scream now, so loudly I can barely hear Mom's words over their shrieking. "Danielle was my family, and you killed her."

She flashes me that bright television smile that charmed millions of viewers all over the world for nearly a decade. "No, *you* killed her. All you had to do was cooperate. But you had to fight me—you always had to fight me. I'm your mother. I know what's best for you."

On the ground, Jessica sits up at last, sucking in deep breaths. Relief washes over me, and I realize just how afraid I was that she might die, too. She meets my eyes, trying to communicate something to me. An instant later she's invisible, the dead crowding in around me to shout in my ears, blocking her from view.

Mom keeps talking. "The first thing we'll do when we get back to your place is call the network. If you lose a few pounds there are no flaws makeup can't cover."

My hands go to my ears, trying to block out Mom's voice, trying to block out the chattering, wailing ghosts, but of course it doesn't work. Panic rises in me. What was Jessica trying to tell me? I'm not a medium. The dead listen to me. Those two things couldn't coexist. So, which was it? Why did it matter? I wish everyone would just shut up so I can think for a second.

"GET BACK, GET BACK, GET AWAY FROM ME." The words erupt from my mouth, deeper and louder than I've probably ever spoken. The other ghosts whirl away from me, their voices quieting, and even Mom takes one step back, a hand fluttering to her chest dramatically.

Jessica stands, dead leaves crunching under her shoes, and I can hear her footsteps, it's so quiet. My own frantic breathing is loud in my own ears. From the house, I can hear the concerned murmuring of the witches watching us through the window.

My eyes go to Danielle's limp form. What had she figured out that I didn't know?

"The ghosts listen to me," I say to Jessica.

She nods, once, and a smile curves her lips.

Revelation crashes over me. I turn to my mother. "The ghosts listen to me. The ghosts *never* listened to you."

"Of course they did," Mom says. "I summoned thousands—"

"Sure, you summoned them, but you could never send them back."

She snorts, affecting a casual pose. "And you think you can?"

I study her face. There's a flicker of fear there, a crack in her confidence. "I do, yeah. I think I can. I can send them all back across the veil, and I can send you there, too. Because I'm more powerful than you are, and I always have been." My heart is thumping hard now, but it's not with panic. I'm excited. "That's why you were always trying to control me, and put me down, and make me feel small. Your gift was everything to you, and you couldn't stand the thought of being surpassed by your own daughter."

She sniffs. "Don't be ridiculous."

I glance around me at the ghosts. They're still and silent, but their expressions aren't fearful or angry or even hungry anymore. Their gleaming eyes are brimming with hope.

They want me to send them back. They're waiting for it, and they've been waiting for a long time.

I take a deep breath, and I recite the banishing spell. I don't need to chant it as a mantra, or even say it more than once. The words are merely a focus for my will, and my will alone is enough to rip a hole between worlds, a jagged tear with its own gravity that threatens to suck me into it. I dig my heels into the earth as it starts to pull the ghosts into the brightness beyond. I flail, grabbing for something solid to hang onto.

Jessica's strong hands close around my waist.

We watch as the ghosts disappear into the light like water swirling down the bath drain. Mom is the last to go, her hands reaching for me, clawing, desperate. She doesn't want to go, and it's because she's afraid. She's afraid to confront the souls of those she wronged on the other side—and she's afraid to leave me, afraid of what I'll become, or what I won't become, perhaps. She's terrified to leave her legacy in my hands, the hands of someone she's never understood, never accepted, and never really liked.

"It's okay, Mom. I'll be okay," I tell her. She screams something unintelligible as the vortex sucks her into it, and then she's gone.

I need a focus to close the portal, and my exhausted mind can't think of anything but the birthday song. After the first few words, Jessica joins in, her voice lending strength to mine. The tear in reality mends itself closed and Danielle's backyard is her backyard once again. Toads croak in the pond nearby, and crickets chirp in the grass at our feet. The last notes of the song fade away and the breeze ruffles my hair softly, without insistence.

I can breathe—really breathe—for maybe the first time in my entire life.

Jessica's RV always smells like sandalwood and sage—like home—no matter where we find ourselves. A photograph of Danielle graces the wall beside the kitchen, which is also the living room and the dining room, and sometimes also the game room or the nooky room when we're feeling amorous. Jessica is making beans on toast with just a sprinkle of cheese, my favorite breakfast, and I'm tracing a route to the next town on the map, when Merlin gives that peculiar chirp he only does when company's arriving.

He hops down from the seat beside me and retreats into the bedroom just as the knock sounds at the door.

The woman standing outside looks like she's had a hard life. Her skin is deeply lined in the way of heavy smokers, and for an instant my nose fills with the reek of my mother's cigarettes. "Can I help you?"

"I heard you're some kind of a psychic." She gets right to the point in the way of the desperate.

"Sorry," I say with a shrug. "You were misinformed. I'm not a psychic. I can't read your tarot or help you talk to your loved ones who crossed over."

"But Cheryl Stokes across the lake said you got her brother's ghost to stop haunting her. For free."

I smile. "I did. That's kind of what we do."

The woman blinks at me. "Look, I think something's haunting me, too. Are you a psychic or not?"

I nod, gesturing for her to come into the RV, eyeing the restless ghost that lingers behind her. "I can help with the haunting. But I'm not a psychic or a medium."

"Then what are you?"

From the kitchen, Jessica says, "She's a necromancer. Do you want butter or jam with your toast?"

— THE M.A.M.I. INCIDENT —
by Guadalupe García McCall

When news breaks out that one of our Macrocosmic Artificial Maternal Intelligence, a M.A.M.I. living on the Northern shore of The Isle, has drowned her twin Sons in one of our many communal pools, the news folios go crazy. With Isabel quietly eating her oatmeal beside me, I scan through every folio within a twenty-grid radius. The story, being repeated in graphic detail, is live on every folio-feed. Even after I turn away, the plethora of chatty monitors on our First Wall, footage of the M.A.M.I. wringing her drenched apron and crying out repeatedly, "Mis hijos, mis hijos," continues to play out in my mind. Remembering the sight of the encased bodies being transported by the coroner out of Buenas Brizas del Mar torments me every time I close my eyes.

How could one of our M.A.M.I.s do such a thing? Especially now, right before our centennial birthday, when our Commemorative Cyber Celebration is around the corner? Ten days, and we'll have come full circle. Every President, every Magistrate, every Leader in the province will be there with their wives, and, of course, their ever-present special companions, our M.A.M.I.s and their offspring.

"Mom!" Isabel drops her spoon. "Do we have to watch this? I'm trying to eat."

"Then eat in the kitchen. This is important," I say, pulling my Network Control Pad, the NCP I carry everywhere, out of my bag and logging into the neuro-netsystem's CC, the Cerebral Cortex that binds us all together—the Señora Madres, our M.A.M.I.s, and our beloved children.

"Seriously?" Isabel pushes the bowl away and rests her chin on her elbows at the counter. "You're such an egomaniac."

Ignoring her, I click buttons, swipe through the neuro-net, and scan comcasts, but it's useless. There are no alerts. No advisories. No warnings.

But why is the M.A.M.I. in question only 8% tethered to the CC? How is she still functioning when she is almost completely dislodged from the neuro-netsystem? That certainly explains the dishevelment. Though nothing can explain the crying. Who would disconnect her without my permission? The only other person who has the coding sequence is...

Horrified, I look up at the monitors.

"There is no need to panic. We have retrieved our M.A.M.I. and are transporting her to the lab," Julian Neruda, my husband and Program Administrator in charge of Domestic Services at our main facility, *ANHELO* Headquarters, tells the correspondent on the news folio. "Everything is under control."

"Señor Neruda, what can our Señora Madres at home do to ensure the safety of their children? Are there signs, odd behaviors, red flags, things we should look for in our M.A.M.I.s that would warrant a shut down? And can we do that ourselves—shut them down I mean—or do we have to call Domestic Services for that?"

"A-a-absolutely not," my husband insists, stammering the way he always does when he's not sure of what he's saying. "Our

Reproductive Interlaces do not kill their own children. It's just not in their DNA encryption. I assure you, this is an isolated incident. Nothing like this has ever happened before, and it is unlikely to ever happen again. I urge everyone at home not to panic. Please. Don't touch your M.A.M.I.'s neuro-netting."

"But it did happen, Mr. Neruda!" The correspondent's eyebrows knit together. "So how can we be sure it won't happen to us? I have a M.A.M.I. sitting at home right now. She's alone with our Daughter and, frankly, I just want to rush back there and pull the plug on her, " the correspondent points out.

"Señora Treviño, I assure you, there is no reason to *pull the plug* as you say," Julian continues, his stammer under control as he speaks calmly to the correspondent. "Certainly, be cautious, vigilant even, but if you have any concerns, call Domestic Services. We'll be happy to tap into your M.A.M.I.'s neuro-net and look into any and all of your concerns. The important thing is not to panic."

"So, you're saying this is a fluke, another glitch in the system?" the correspondent presses further.

Another? No. No. That other thing was an isolated incident. Besides, that was decades and decades ago. Why can't reporters leave well enough alone?

Julian shakes his head. "Our M.A.M.I.s are genetically flawless, engineered to love, nurture, and protect their—*your* children. They are predisposed to feel every emotion that you are experiencing right now. Every Señora Madre should expect a certain amount of hypersensitivity coming from their M.A.M.I.s at this challenging time. But trust me, the sooner we get into this M.A.M.I.'s neuro-netting and find out what went wrong, the sooner we can prevent it from ever happening again. Thank you very much for your time. I have to go now. There's much work to be done."

When my Isabel and I turn off the monitors, we can't help it. We swivel sideways in our chairs, turn our heads, and peer out, past the glass partition in the dining room and into the garden, where our M.A.M.I. stands frozen, holding the rake straight up in the air with both hands, her eyes shut.

"What's she doing?" Isabel whispers, almost afraid to break the silence cast on the house when we shut down the monitors. "Is she...crying?"

As if to prove she could sense our Daughter's every need, suffer her every worry, our M.A.M.I. opens her silvery eyes and looks straight at us. The act is so sudden, so unexpected, that I jump in my chair and knock over my beverage, breaking the glass container and spilling orange juice all over our Daughter's lap.

"Mom! Be careful!" Isabel shrieks as I swipe at her Bluesilk with my cloth napkin. I do my best to mop off the juice before it spills over the edge of the counter.

"Are you okay?" Our M.A.M.I. is suddenly at our side, pushing Isabel's hair out of her face, looking into her brown eyes, and pulling her hand away from the glass shards she is trying to pile together. "Don't. I'll get that. You didn't cut yourself, did you?"

"No," Isabel says, her voice weak.

"I'm so sorry," I say as I help pile the glass shards in M.A.M.I's open palm. "I just...it just, happened. I didn't mean to."

"Of course not, my Señora Madre isssss..." M.A.M.I.'s head twitches. Her neck twists to the left and pops back several times before she regains her composure. "Perfect!" M.A.M.I. screams out the word, triumphantly finishing her thought.

She has a strange smile on her face; her soft, pale lips catch the light and glisten where the lower crease has been meticulously highlighted with a thin, honeycomb glob of gleaming glitter. Every M.A.M.I. is designed to look fresh and pretty, like she's just stepped out of her dressing room to start a busy day.

"Are you all right, M.A.M.I.?" Isabel frowns.

"Yes, yes," our M.A.M.I. says, and she kisses Isabel's forehead and steers her toward her room. "Go. Get ready for your Thursday course sequence. Your Señora Madre can't be late for work on your account. Unless you want me to take her, Señora Madre."

"No," I say, sighing at the sight of Isabel's ruined Bluesilk. Strange how M.A.M.I. hasn't offered to clean it at once. She is always so quick to care for our Daughter. "I'll take her. I just have to change first."

"It's Thursday. I don't have first course design today," Isabel reminds us, looking from Interlace to me and back to our Interlace again. She can see me forgetting that, but not our M.A.M.I.

M.A.M.I.s never forget.

Our M.A.M.I., especially, is always on top of things. She has to be. She is the most sophisticated, most entrusted Interlace in the collective. Of course, like her predecessors, our M.A.M.I. exists for the sole purpose of meeting our maternal needs. She more than bore us a perfect Daughter, she is perfection herself.

"It's Thursday. I don't have first course design today," M.A.M.I repeats Isabel's comment, word for word, and Isabel frowns at me.

"M.A.M.I.?"

I put my hand on M.A.M.I.s arm. The thin coils of her neuro-system undulate beneath her shell, biogenetic skin as dark and lambent as my own. Even at my age, more than a century old, it is hard to tell which one of us was designed by mother nature. We could be thirty-something identical twins, thanks to *ANHELO's* groundbreaking work in aesthetic enhancements. "What's going on? Do you need an adjustment? We can go to the regenerating station. Switch you on for a few minutes. I've got time."

"No need!" M.A.M.I. says, selecting and quickly displaying an unexpected smile, the one that shows only a small amount of upper teeth. Ironic-4. I recognize my handiwork. Though I would have preferred to see Gracious-08 or even Dismissive-1, but Ironic, in any of its subtle iterations, fills me with trepidation.

"Something's definitely bothering her," Isabel whispers when M.A.M.I goes to dump the shards of glass into the garbage lift in the garage. Has she heard the newsfeed all the way from the garden? I wonder. Is she as horrified as we are? Was she crying outside or just adjusting her ocular implants? These are important questions. I need answers. When our M.A.M.I. turns back to us, I look at her face for signs of distress, but there are none. There is, however, moisture residue clinging to the tips of the lashes over her left eye, a hint of a tear, perhaps, but I can't be sure.

"Oh, you're right, of course," M.A.M.I. says, putting a hand to her chest and shaking her head as if she is trying to reboot her system, casting off a temporary fault in the recesses of her peripheral neuro-netting.

"M.A.M.I.? Are you all right?" Isabel asks as we watch her close her eyes again and freeze in complete silence.

"Si Cariño, I am all right. I just need to hold you," M.A.M.I. finally whispers, opening her sleek, silvery eyes and reaching for our Daughter, holding her tight against her breast.

Isabel stands, bearing the weight of our M.A.M.I. as the Interlace leans into her and kisses her head and cries into her dark hair, as if just holding her tight is all she needed to console herself. But it's wrong. M.A.M.I.s don't need consoling.

I made sure of that.

At first, I don't know what to do or say. There is so much love in our M.A.M.I.'s voice. Her silver eyes, with their dark obsidian irises, hold a sad, desperate pain that moves me, and I let her cling to our Daughter, allow her to hold her tighter than programmed.

I have only seen our Interlace like this twice before, the day Isabel cut her leg on a nail from a wooden fence she was trying to climb and the time Isabel twisted her ankle at track practice.

However, something about the drownings this morning, makes me want to jump into action.

I have to fix it. Before...

"M.A.M.I.!" I scold as I pry this biogenetic version of myself off of our Daughter and point for her to step back and sit down at the end of the counter. "Que te pasa? Why are you acting like this? You must stop immediately."

"*You must stop immediately!*" M.A.M.I. repeats my words.

"Now," I command. "You're scaring Isabel!"

"It's not sanctioned. Breaking Imperatives 2 and 3," M.A.M.I. whispers.

"Exactly. Now sit down and let me take a peek at your lacework," I demand, hooking my fingernail against the hard metal on the underside of her left earlobe. The tiny button flips up and comes off. It bounces off her shoulder, and I catch it in mid-air before it rolls off the counter.

"I just don't understand," M.A.M.I. says, hugging herself so tightly, I can see the fibrous coils wrestling under her skin, trying to adjust to the pressure. "I don't know how anyone could ever do what that Interlace did to her Sons... It just breaks my heart. I could never, ever hurt my muchachita!"

"So you *were* listening?" I ask, pulling back a little to look into M.A.M.I.'s glistening eyes. She is not supposed to cry. Ever!

I made sure of that.

"How can I not? It's happening over and over again," M.A.M.I. whispers.

"What's happening over and over again?" I ask, but instead of answering, M.A.M.I. does something I am not expecting. Something I did not program into her or any other M.A.M.I. I've designed over the course of my life's spiritual work.

She blinks and the wall of monitors behind us comes on, filling the room with the hazy noise of a hundred news folios, still chatting about the M.A.M.I. incident. Before me, our M.A.M.I.

presses her hands against her ears and wails, "Over and over again!"

This is not supposed to be happening.

I pull out a chair and gently guide our M.A.M.I. onto it. "Sit down, M.A.M.I. I can't explain it, but I think you're in shock, like the rest of us. We're all in shock," I say, and I pour a glass of water and hand it to our M.A.M.I. "Here. Take a sip and breathe in, then breathe out. Do it again and again. It will calm your nerves."

It takes M.A.M.I. a few minutes, but she finally does calm down. Then she apologizes, gets up, and immediately goes to work, cleaning up the rest of the broken glass while our Daughter goes to her bedroom to change.

The phone rings. I walk down the hall and take it in our bedroom.

"Hey. Is everything okay?" It's Julian, but he's whispering, so I know he's as unsettled as I am.

"Yes, I think," I say.

"Think?" he asks. "What is it? Should we shut her down?"

"No, no," I insist, speaking calmly, because our M.A.M.I is in the kitchen, but her auditory sensors are amplified, and she can pick up on my every emotion by the tone of my voice. "Where are you?"

"On my way to a meeting," he says. "With the Commonwealth. Your Proselytes will want to look at the M.A.M.I.'s analog and meet to discuss next steps."

"I expected that," I say. "Let me know when it's scheduled. I'll come in to set it all up. What a mess!"

"Yes, but, for now, if something happens," Julian whispers again. "If she even sneezes wrong, you do it. You switch her off. Without prejudice or procrastination. Understand?"

"Sneezing? Really?" I ask. "Isn't that a bit...overzealous."

"No, not when it involves our Daughter."

I nod and whisper. "Fair enough. I've got my NCP, so I'll be able to check her neuro-stats."

I walk back into the kitchen. Isabel comes rushing back, dressed in a violet running suit. Svelte and sleek, she is a younger, prettier version of us.

That is the whole point of having a genetically engineered M.A.M.I., a perfect Interlace of our Señora Madres. Interlaces are designed to carry our babies, birth and breastfeed them, raise them, toil over them, worry about them. Our M.A.M.I.s take care of absolutely everything to do with our fertility, as we can no longer do that for ourselves. Through them, our benevolence, our genetic blessings, can live on. Because of our M.A.M.I.s, childbearing won't take its toll on our Proselytes. Oh, we will age, even as biological enhancements, virtual exercise, and botanical baths sanctify all of us, but at a much, much slower pace than we used to before the Cleansing.

"I love you." Julian's words are still ringing in my ears as I watch our M.A.M.I. standing with the oven door wide open, frozen again.

"M.A.M.I.!" I call out. "Is everything all right in there?"

"Si, Señora," M.A.M.I. trembles a bit, then she shakes herself into alertness the way a dog would shake off the excess water after an unwelcomed bath. "My neuro-netsystem is strong."

I overlook the strange response, pushing it aside for a moment as Isabel and I watch M.A.M.I. close the oven door, program the temperature, and start washing the vegetables she brought in from the garden.

"How about we take the morning off and go out for a spa day?" I ask Isabel, because I can't help it, I want to get out of the house, away from M.A.M.I. for a while. "I could use a good scrinching. Wouldn't you like to get rejuvenated? It's never too early to start slowing the aging process. We could have your face reframed. Here. Let me scan you."

Rolling her eyes, Isabel pushes her hair off her face and sighs heavily. I take her chin in my hand and move her head sideways to get a good reading with my NCP. "What do you think, M.A.M.I.? A face reframing in order for our Daughter?"

M.A.M.I.'s hands freeze at the sink. She looks up, blinks, and then answers, "The left side of Isabel's face is perfectly proportioned to the right side. Her eyes are balanced over her nose at the best angle and her hairline is exactly the same distance along her temples from her eyebrows. She is perfect, just as she is. I would not recommend a reframing. She is—our Daughter—but, as always, the Señora Madre has the last word."

"Thank you!" Isabel leaves me standing alone in the living room. She walks into the kitchen and hugs our M.A.M.I. "I'd rather spend the day doing tomorrow's course designs than getting my face pinched and tucked by robotic insects, like you and your weird disciples!"

Instead of chastising Isabel for being disrespectful, M.A.M.I. freezes. Her hands stop mid-scrape, her body stiffens, and she stands completely still in Isabel's arms, like an immovable trunk within the circle of our Daughter's embrace.

Isabel drops her arms, steps back, and looks over at me, brows furrowed and eyes glistening. Then she scuttles around the table. Taking my hand, she pulls me across the hall, to my office. She locks the door and hugs me, wrapping her thin arm tightly around my neck. "We have to get out of here." Her voice is a mere whisper in my ear, her breath a shuddering exhalation. "She wants to kill me."

"What!?" I ask.

"She's been thinking about it all morning. Ever since she saw that M.A.M.I. on the news folio." Isabel's voice cracks. "It's vibrating in every nerve cell in her body. I felt it, just now, when I hugged her."

"Okay," I say. "I left my NCP on the counter. I'll pick it up on the way to the garage. You grab the key fob."

We leave the office and walk back into the kitchen.

"What were you two doing in there?" M.A.M.I. asks. She is standing at the end of the counter, observing us. The obsidian irises of her eyes hyper-dilate, signaling the worst. Something has triggered her Combat Mode.

Outside, a soft, sonorous sound is building momentum, getting closer and closer. Sirens wail, one after another, as a horde of ambulances and police cars whiz by. The sight of them is alarming. The world begins to encroach on us. Deafening shrills. Honking horns. Crashing cars. Screaming. The screens light up on every monitor on all three walls, flipping through a carousel of foils, up and down, up and down, up and down.

Before us, our M.A.M.I. picks up a meat tenderizer, a small mallet, and tests it, back and forth in her hands. Left to right. Left to right. Left to right.

"Well?" our Interlace asks.

"Just working out our agenda," I say, trying to act calm, but secretly wondering how long it will take for this confrontation to be over. I am sure I don't have the option to run out and flag down one of those police cars. At this point, I am not even sure I can get us out of here. "Things are getting out of control out there. I need to go to the lab."

"Isabel should stay here," M.A.M.I. says, inching closer. "I will protect her."

"Thank you, but I'll feel better if she's with me right now," I say.

I tap Isabel's back and look over at my key fob on the hook by the garage door, trying to make sure she knows what I need her to do. But our M.A.M.I. doesn't give us a chance. She jumps, lunging at me and howling like an enraged orangutan.

I twist sideways and push her away, using the force of her own momentum to send her crashing to the floor. She falls forward, dragging the collection of aluminum pans on the sideboard with her. While M.A.M.I. scrambles, I reach over the kitchen counter and pull the thin cutlet knife out of the block pedestal. It makes a sharp, metallic sound as it slips out of its groove.

M.A.M.I. snaps her head up. Targeting me with her obsidian eyes, she jumps up and grabs me. She tries to squeeze the breath out of me, but I use the knife to slash her arm. She looks down at her wound. Taking advantage of the moment, I thrust the blade into her neck and twist it violently counterclockwise through the lacework of neuro-netting where I know it will do the most damage. Somewhere behind me, Isabel screams, and I put my hand out.

"Don't!" I shout. "Stay back!"

Instead of talking, M.A.M.I. sputters. Silver wires embedded in her muscles spark and sizzle, starting to catch fire. The scent of burning flesh makes me gag, and I step away, careful not to trip on the pots and pans. M.A.M.I. stands up. She looks at the exposed coils snaking around within the wound on her arm, broken dark biogenetic tissue that was meant to protect her neurological cords from damage. Then she collapses again, biofluid pooling around her.

I grab the key fob and we fly out the door. I don't know how we do it, but Isabel and I get through the chaos of cars and pedestrians, of smoke and sirens, of running and screaming and crying humans, mothers, fathers, M.A.M.I.s, and their Sons and Daughters in less than fifteen minutes.

When we get to the facility, located on the highest peak on The Isle, the building is quiet, a complete contrast to what is happening in the extensive nervous system of the mapped boroughs in the valley. We go inside and I call out for my husband as we rush through the hive of hallways and interconnected offices. Where is everybody? The place is desolate. Abandoned.

"Julian? Honey?" I yell. "Are you here?"

We go to the Cerebral Cortex, the largest, safest office in this building, where every M.A.M.I. is monitored, programmed, and assessed. Where they are either absolved or refurbished. I turn on the central neuro-netsystem and start walking around, checking vitals, looking for patterns, but there are no patterns. Every Interlace in the world is completely out of control in her own irrational way.

"What is it?" Isabel asks. "What's happening to our M.A.M.I.? Can you fix her?"

"I don't know," I admit, trying desperately to locate our M.A.M.I. on the grid. But it's useless. She's in Combat Mode, so she would have shut off her tracker.

"What do you mean you don't know?" Isabel cries out.

"I mean I don't know where she is. I don't know what she's doing," I tell Isabel. "She's gone rogue on us."

We hear a loud crash, like a car smashing against a wall. A lock clicks, the door opens, and our M.A.M.I. rushes into the Cerebral Cortex. She looks grotesque, sallow skinned, and drenched in dark biofluid. In seconds, she is upon me, thrusting me against the wall, slamming my arm against the glass pane of the emergency call box until my hand breaks through it.

I scream, a loud, bestial noise that I haven't heard coming out of my own lips since childhood, more than ninety years ago, when I fell through the skyline of our kitchen in the country house in rural Texas, landing on my mother, killing her instantly when a shard of glass severed her carotid artery and she bled out on our linoleum floor.

All that blood.

And no one there to help us.

Before I know what is happening, Julian is there. He grabs onto M.A.M.I.'s shoulder, pulls her off me, and slams her into the console. They struggle. Isabel rushes over and wraps her arms around me. I pull my wounded hand to my chest and inspect it.

All that blood.

"Let. Me. Go." M.A.M.I. snarls at Julian. Then she puts her hands over his ears and pulls sideways, snapping his neck instantaneously. It happens so fast, I don't know what she's done until she throws his limp body aside. Julian lands on his newly generated knees and topples over, like a felled redwood. When M.A.M.I. turns to us, I push Isabel behind me. We step back slowly. And when she least expects it, I push hard against a heavy equipment rack. M.A.M.I.s are built strong enough to defend themselves, especially in this new Combat Mode. Like all others, our M.A.M.I. was given this latest modification, but even she is not strong enough to keep the twenty-foot rack from falling on top of her.

Isabel screams.

I disentangle myself from our Daughter, *my Daughter,* and pick up the massive paperweight on my desk, a stout metal figurine of a mother embracing her child, an anniversary gift from Julian. Raising it high up in the air, I hit our M.A.M.I. on the back of the head over and over again, until she is completely still. Then, because I can't examine her to make sure she is deactivated without risking further injury, I run to the wall of lockers around the corner and press on the lip of the shelf mounted beside them.

The weapons room, a secret armory Julian installed for our protection, opens with a soft sigh that sounds like a sustaining breath to me. I reach inside and grapple for the loaded weapon Julian hung there. My fingertips touch the heavy metal and I pull it off the wall.

On hands and knees, our M.A.M.I. crawls toward me. Her hair is burnt to a dark, matted stump on the left side of her head, but she is not giving up. So, I do the only thing I can do. I shoot. Her head doesn't come completely off, but it flips backward and swings back and forth before it settles over her left shoulder blade. I walk around and take a look at it. She is practically decapitated, only her eyes, silver once again, are still flickering, and she's blinking, confused.

She tries to talk, and I lean over and listen.

"Isabel," she whispers. Then she drops to the ground with a loud thump. No more flickering. No more sparks. Just biofluids and smoke.

Sensing something moving ever so slightly behind me, I turn around quickly, so quickly I don't see the cutlet knife before it is already buried to the hilt into my left side, just below my ribcage.

"Isabel?" Her name is more than a question, it's a recrimination. "Hija mia? Why...would you...do this?"

"Don't call me that." Isabel twists the knife counterclockwise, and I almost pass out from the pain.

When she steps back, I put my hands on the knife handle and test it. The slight pull sends another wave of excruciating pain to the whole of my abdomen. It radiates into my back and up to my chest, and I can't breathe.

Isabel picks up M.A.M.I.'s prone body and pushes it up to a sitting position onto my desk chair. "I'm not your Daughter. This Interlace was more of a mother to me than you ever were. How do you think I felt, being raised, cared for, and loved by a fucking robot?"

"What are you talking about?" I ask. "You're *our* biological Daughter. She's me, incarnate, flesh of my flesh. Sangre de mi Sangre. I couldn't have you without her. Our bodies can't do that anymore. It would mean certain death to even try."

"You don't get it, do you?" Isabel's eyes glint with unshed tears. "This isn't what nature intended! This whole thing is an abomination, a house of horrors, and you...you're the director who wants to play the god from the machine. Here to save man from extinction."

"I did what I had to do to protect the world. The human race would die off if we didn't have M.A.M.I.s," I tell her.

"Then death it is!" Isabel walks over to the master control panel and starts pushing buttons on the screens, sending sirens blaring throughout the facility.

I try to walk, to move toward the flickering monitors. She doesn't know what she's doing. "Isabel, please," I whisper, as I lean against the wall.

"It's over Mother," Isabel says, flipping levers, clicking buttons, and entering data, until a series of red lights turn on, and I understand what she came here to do.

"Extinction-Level Event Sequence initiated," the neuro-net's computer-generated voice announces. "Seventy-five seconds to the destruction of all Macrocosmic Artificial Maternal Intelligence."

"Isabel! What are you doing? Where did you get the code, the information, to call on this catastrophe?" I whimper, trying to walk toward her, but failing because the cutlet knife impedes it.

"From M.A.M.I. She had no other choice than to get it for me. It took her months to figure it out, of course, but she couldn't stop researching. It's the ultimate imperative," Isabel says, and from the floor, behind me, I hear a small sound.

"Protect and provide support for anything and everything that inspires our Daughter." Our M.A.M.I.'s last words slip out of her as a hissing final note that exhausts her before she goes dark.

"Fifty-five seconds," the neuro-netsystem calls out.

When I see that she is not going to stop this, that she is going to destroy the M.A.M.I.s and everything we value, everything we need to survive as a species, I put my hand on the hilt of the knife handle, form a fist around it, and pull it out in one quick motion. The pain is vulgar, vile, and I scream and wobble a little as I try to endure it.

Isabel leaves the console and tries to take the knife away from me. We wrestle, fall to the ground, struggle, grunt, until it happens. The knife hits its mark—the jugular. Isabel spurts out blood, spasms, and then stills in my arms.

"Twenty seconds." The neuro-netsystem continues her countdown.

I let go of our Daughter and crawl up, over the console. Except for the last efforts at breathing, Isabel is completely quiet. I enter a sequence of numbers and letters. Our birthdays. Our anniversary. The dog's name. The coordinates on the map for the Basilica de San Juan, and suddenly, the red lights turn off. The countdown freezes with eight seconds to spare.

Heartbroken, I place Isabel inside the rebirthing pod. Every fiber of my being, my flesh, my sangre, the molecules of my very tears, quiver as I watch the gray, galvanized tentacles pop out of the bio-casement and embrace our Daughter, swaddling her like the fetus that she is, the underdeveloped human I so desperately wanted to call my descendent.

I should have known better. She was born with free will, but she refused to use it to our advantage. This was solely her fault. Her doing. Like every other known and unknown M.A.M.I. incident we've had since the inception of our woven dream, the realization of *ANHELO* and all the technological advancements our new order has brought this dying planet, this was not our M.A.M.I's fault.

It's never the M.A.M.I.'s fault.

Never.

— ADYA AND THE MESSENGERS —
by Jaymie Wagner

Adya was planting potatoes when the first messenger came to her.

He was a portly man dressed in green, his robes accented with gold necklaces and jeweled rings.

When she looked up at the sound of his approach, she immediately felt sorry for the horse that pulled his cart, a little grey mare that was sweated through thanks to the humid weather.

"Dear woman!"

She went back to planting.

"I say," the messenger continued in a voice that sounded like it came from the bottom of wine casks, "dear woman, I must speak to you!"

Adya finished placing another cutting into the earth and covered it before she looked up to meet his eyes.

"Water your horse."

The messenger blinked at her. "I beg your pardon?"

Adya drove her spade into the earth and pointed to the trough. "Water. Your. Horse."

"Oh, ah...very well..."

The messenger dismounted and unhooked his cart, and Adya waited for him to lead the horse to the trough before she finally left the potato field, dumping some salt into the water for the poor beast.

The messenger puffed himself up, straightening his hat and extending a hand dramatically. "I have come here from Posna to seek—"

Adya put up a hand to stop him. "Posna is *four days' ride*. Did you truly let this poor beast go without water that whole time?"

"No?" The messenger seemed completely baffled by the question. "I'm sure the stable hands took good care of him this morning."

Adya considered making the point that it was now the middle of the afternoon, but she decided it would be better to let the man speak and hopefully send him on his way once his horse had been properly fed and watered.

She gestured for him to go on but laid out a little extra hay and straw beside the trough.

"As I was saying," the messenger said as he struck a pose that was probably inspiring to the courtiers and servitors back in the capital, "I have come here from Posna to see you—Adya, the *Chosen One!*"

Adya blinked.

"I see you are awestruck." The messenger stepped back and offered a gesture to his cart. "Please, come with me, and I shall explain on the way."

"I am not awestruck," Adya countered as she dug her heels into the ground. "I am *offended*."

The messenger's face went through a series of expressions, his mouth moving silently as if he had never heard the word.

"Offended!?"

Adya nodded, gesturing to her potato field. "I have never heard such a ridiculous thing, especially in planting season! Did someone put you up to this? Are the farms in Sivrin so scared of competing against an old woman's crop at the market?"

"My Lady Adya—"

Adya snorted. "I am a farmer's widow. There are no ladies here."

The messenger shook his head. "You must understand, this is your destiny!"

"My destiny was to marry my Petyr and have a good life raising our children and working the land after he returned from the war." Adya couldn't stop her bitter laugh. "My destiny ended on the point of an Adrenni spear."

"I am sorry for your loss," the messenger said with what seemed like real contrition. "But you are wrong. The prophecies are clear. The dark child now rules the Adrenni empire, and it is you who will vanquish him."

"I'm a potato farmer," she stated, in case the man had missed the obvious. "I am no warrior, and I am no chosen one."

"Then you will not come?"

She shook her head firmly. "I will not."

"Very well," the messenger said regretfully before there was a sound like tearing cloth, and the guise he had been wearing melted away.

Where the portly man had been, there now stood a great green spirit made of leaves and fronds, his jewels replaced with vibrant blossoms, the golden adornments turned to fronds and vines.

"You are wise not to trust a stranger speaking of Prophecy," the spirit said in a voice like wind through trees. "But know this, Adya: your destiny is at hand. Another shall come to speak to you soon."

Adya bowed to the spirit with far more respect than she'd given his earlier guise. "Tell them to come after planting season, then."

The spirit chuckled, and when Adya looked over to the trough, the horse had turned into a grey cloud of mist that wrapped around its master like a shawl.

"*I shall inform them,*" the spirit rumbled, then tilted its head as the mist made a soft hissing sound. "*And I have been asked to thank you for the water and hay.*"

She smiled at them and nodded. "Of course."

There was a gust of wind and a scent of fresh leaves, and then they were gone.

At the end of planting season, Adya expected another messenger, but no one came to her farm or her village from Posna or anywhere else.

After a few weeks had passed, she decided it best to simply keep doing what needed to be done, and that the spirits would do as they pleased.

The rains came, and Adya put fresh earth around the potato plants as they grew. She made trips to the village for things she needed, and occasionally things she didn't.

Adya would visit her neighbors to trade food and gossip. She would make tinctures and poultices when someone grew ill, and brewed tea from mint and nettles when she started sneezing.

On a cool night after the rains ebbed, a visitor came to her land. She had skin the color of rich loam, and wore simple but sturdy traveling clothes, with a deep blue cloak that brought out the watery blue in her eyes.

"I have come far," the traveler said when Adya came out to meet her with a lantern. "May I ask for a bed, and some tea?"

"Come inside," Adya replied with a nod. "I have soup on my hearth."

"You are most gracious." The traveler gave Adya a courteous bow.

The woman was like nothing she had seen before, and Adya was quite certain she must be another messenger. She wondered why they played at being human, but she knew that spirits often did such things. Adya served the traveler a bowl of warm soup and a mug of good tea and offered to let the woman dry her cloak by the fire.

"I thank you for your hospitality, Lady Adya."

"I don't recall giving you my name," she replied mildly.

"I was told this was your land when I passed through the village."

Adya snorted. "Then they should have also told you I was no lady. I am an old widow who works her farm and trades for her needs, not some noble wasting away in a tower."

The woman's eyes twinkled. "An old widow who is loved by her neighbors and appreciated by her village."

Before Adya could respond, an urgent knock came from her door.

"Grandmother! Grandmother!"

"I wasn't aware you had grandchildren," the traveler murmured.

Adya snorted as she stood and went to the door. "What is it?"

A boy from the village stood panting at her door, his eyes wide. It took a moment, but Adya recalled his name was Kartha just before he had enough breath back to speak.

"My mother—she said it's time! Said to get you as quick as I could!"

Adya nodded and patted the boy's shoulder gently. "And so you did." She looked over her shoulder to the traveler who was absolutely not a spirit and raised an eyebrow. "Do you know much of midwifery?"

The traveler shrugged.

Adya grunted as she picked up a basket she kept near the door and checked that she had put fresh linens and a sturdy stool in it.

"Come anyway," she said with a little smile as the woman stood and then nodded to Kartha. "Lead on."

When they reached the house, there was only mild chaos.

The father, Nael, was the village smith. He was keeping himself occupied with heating water and trying not to fret over his wife,

Taya, who was trying to walk about the front room despite her obvious discomfort.

"Oh, thank the spirits," Taya gasped with relief as Adya set the basket down, then looked over at the traveler. "But who is this?"

"A guest," Adya said before the spirit could reply. "I thought she might be able to help."

Taya nodded, and the three of them went back into the bedroom. The spirit helped Taya remove her smallclothes and the dress she had worn over her chemise, and Adya arranged the birthing stool at the foot of the bed, then took a pillow from the bed to use as a cushion.

"Come. Sit. How long have you been feeling the birth pains?"

Taya carefully lowered herself onto the stool, sweat beading at her forehead. "Just after sunset. I sent Kartha when they began to speed up."

"Good," Adya said with a reassuring smile, and reached out to gently feel Taya's full belly. "The baby seems eager!"

"He *kicks*," Taya groaned before she let out a grunt of pain.

The spirit settled on the floor at Taya's other side and offered a hand for her to squeeze. "A good sign," she said. "Full of life."

Adya nodded agreement before starting to gently rub soothing oils into Taya's thighs. "These will help."

The labor was short—it took only a few more hours after their arrival for the baby to come. A girl with a healthy set of lungs, who made her displeasure about leaving the womb known until the spirit swaddled her and placed her on Taya's breast.

"She will be trouble," Taya murmured, but her eyes shone with joy. "Already proving her father wrong."

Adya chuckled and stayed at Taya's side until the afterbirth had come, wrapping it in the old linen she'd brought for the purpose.

"When the rains stop, where will you bury this?"

"In the garden," Taya answered with a weary smile.

"Good. May the spirits bless you, and the baby."

"Thank you, Adya. May they bless you, too."

Adya glanced at the messenger thoughtfully, and before long she had repacked her basket and taken the spirit back to her home.

"How many children have taken their first breath in your hands?"

Adya shrugged as she made a fresh pot of tea. "How many potatoes have I taken from the ground in my harvests? I have been a midwife almost as long as I have been a farmer."

The spirit hummed, then took a dainty bite of a roll. "Is that why you denied the first messenger? You had no wish to take life?"

"I had no wish to leave my field while there was work to be done," Adya said firmly. "Nor do I see a reason to leave my home when my farm still needs tending, and babies need birthing."

"There are others who could work in your fields," the spirit pointed out. "There must be others who share your skills."

"There must be others who could be your 'Chosen One,'" Adya countered as she brought the tea and filled their mugs. "What makes an old woman so important?"

The spirit took a sip and smiled. "The heavens called for you, and the prophets spoke your name."

Adya rolled her eyes. "They should have said it years ago. When I was young and silly, and not set in my ways."

"Perhaps," the spirit said mildly. "Perhaps not."

Adya drained her cup and ate the rest of her roll before she spoke again. "It has been a long evening, spirit. You have my hospitality for the night. Let us sleep, and in the morning, you can be on your way."

The spirit set her mug aside and stood gracefully. "So it has. But I will not be the last to seek you out, Adya."

"Of course," she sighed as she showed the spirit where she could sleep. "Of course."

When Adya woke and dressed in the morning, she found the messenger watching clouds forming in the skies.

"It will be a good crop," the spirit said confidently. "The rain will provide, and the earth will nourish."

"I hope so," Adya agreed. "But I will still work to bring the fields through the rains, and until the harvest."

"Then I suppose that is your answer."

Adya huffed in amusement. "I suppose it must be."

"Very well, Lady Adya."

The traveler pulled at her robes, and the woman who had shared tea with her was gone. In her place was a spirit of water that flowed between a woman's shape, a fall of rain, and a rush of flooding.

"Another will come, Chosen One. They will seek out the bringer of life."

Adya nodded and bowed to the spirit, for what answer could she have to that?

The spirit seemed to smile before vanishing, and a few minutes later Adya could hear a rumble in the distance as the rains began.

The weather grew hot, and Adya worked her field, making sure each plant had what it needed to thrive. She gathered and dried herbs from her garden and made gifts of pressed flowers and jars of herbs when a few of the village girls were wed.

As the season began to turn, she hired a few hands to help her harvest the plants, cellar the tubers she would keep for the winter, and haul the rest to the market. She laid in salted meats and preserved foods for the winter and pretended to "accidentally" add a few extra pennies to the wages when she sent her hired hands home.

When the village and its surrounding farms gathered to celebrate a good year's harvest, she joined them in dances and songs to thank the earth for its bounty. When the local priest led them in prayers, Adya bowed her head, asking the land and the spirits for another year of plenty.

She had a feeling that someone was listening to her prayers, and deep inside Adya knew that no matter what the next year held, she would not be in her village to see it.

The next morning, as if on cue, there was a person wrapped in a monk's robes at her door. "May I speak to you, Lady Adya?"

They had a soft and reedy voice, with pale eyes and skin that had been tanned by the sun. It was difficult to tell much of their shape beneath their robes, but the hand that held their walking stick had a lean strength to it.

Adya sighed as she gestured for the monk to come in. "So, we're back to 'Lady Adya,' are we?"

The monk smiled as they sat down on a stool. "It is always best to be polite."

Adya sighed. "I have told the others that I am no lady, and I am no chosen one. I'm a farmer, a midwife, and a widow."

The monk raised an eyebrow. "Why should a chosen one not be any of those things?"

"Your friend said I am supposed to 'vanquish' the new emperor," Adya countered. "I am no warrior."

"Prophecies are often mysterious and vague." The monk shrugged. "Perhaps my friend assumes too much."

Adya hummed as she considered that. "Perhaps."

The monk chuckled as they stood back up. "Of course, I may be assuming too little."

"You're not really encouraging me to follow you," Adya observed, but she still began to pack for the journey.

"It is always best to be honest," the monk said. "You are ready, then?"

Now it was her turn to shrug. "As ready as I can be."

Once Adya finished packing, she put two baskets in her cart and hitched it to her horse. The monk walked beside them as she visited the neighboring farm and told them she had to travel to see one of Petyr's relatives, and they agreed to mind her house and fields until she returned.

She offered the monk a seat when she began to turn the cart toward the road to Posna, but they declined with a little shake of their head.

"I thank you, but I prefer to walk—and besides, you are going the wrong way."

"The first messenger claimed we needed to go to Posna."

"That was some time ago," they said gently. "Now we must make our way to Adrenna."

Adya let out a shocked gasp. "Adrenna?! How will we cross the border? How will we cross the *mountains?*"

The monk laughed and reached up to give her hand a comforting pat. "With the help of our friends!"

It should have taken many days to reach the border of the Andrenni empire. Even with a cart to ride and a horse to pull it, the journey was not easy. But somehow her old bones did not tire, and her horse made better time than it should have.

"I know you're cheating," she told the monk when they stopped to eat and rest. "We should barely be to Tejna, not on the banks of the Yna."

"You know much of the way to Adrenna," the monk observed as they put chunks of potato into the stew pot over their fire.

Adya also knew that she had only packed enough potatoes, salted meat, and preserves for a four-day journey, expecting to buy more in Tejna. Somehow those supplies showed no sign of running out.

Blasted spirits.

"Petyr sent me letters," she admitted as she watched the flames lick at the sides of the pot. "At least for a while. Told me about where he'd visited. I thought once I might travel to see them, after. I'm afraid I became rather set in my ways over the years."

The monk chuckled. "But now, here you are!"

Adya frowned at the dirt. "I suppose I am, but I never imagined anything like this. I didn't want to be alone and old. I thought..."

"You thought you would be a mother," the Spirit of the Rains said as she approached the fire, once again in her traveler's guise. "You thought you might travel here with your husband and your children, and perhaps even your grandchildren, one day."

Tears that Adya thought she had left behind many years ago pricked at her eyes. "Yes. Perhaps."

"But are you not a grandmother?" The Spirit of the Land asked as he settled his portly bulk atop a tree stump that had not been there a moment ago, the gold rings on his fingers dancing in the firelight. "Have you not brought dozens of children into this world?"

"You use my words against me now," Adya murmured in a low, thick voice.

"We tell the truth as you shared it with us," the monk pointed out in a gentle murmur, and Adya felt the Spirit of the Rains touch her shoulder with the gentle comfort of cool summer rain after a hot day in the field.

Adya bowed her head and let the tears fall at last, and the spirits talked of gentler things for the rest of the evening.

In two more days (that should have been ten), they could see the border crossing stretching across the banks of the Verika. In Petyr's letters, he had described forts on both banks of the river with walls of stone and dried mud, reinforced with timbers. He had been awed by the stone bridges the forts guarded, built in happier times, broad enough to allow five men to walk shoulder to shoulder as they crossed.

Now the fort on what had been the Adrenni side of the river was reduced to a collection of low walls. A much larger fort had been constructed on what had been the Posnaian side of the bridge— with an Imperial flag flying from the battlements.

Adya frowned as she looked out at the great bridges. They were just as stunning as Petyr's letters had made them out to be, but how would they be able to cross them?

When she said as much out loud, the Spirit of the Land chuckled. "My dear Adya, please leave that to me."

When they broke camp the next morning, the Spirit of the Rain had changed her dress from simple robes to fine silks. She carried herself with a regal bearing as she climbed into the cart, her hair down and brushed into glossy, flowing waves. The sacks of food and waterskins had been moved to the front of the bed, and a plush looking cushion had appeared for her to sit on.

The monk sat with her, perched atop a wooden crate. Their robes had been washed clean of the dust and dirt of the road, and their mala and bowl looked freshly polished.

Adya looked at them as she climbed up to her seat and clucked her tongue. "So you would appear to them as a wealthy trader and her servants?" She looked down at her simple clothes and felt terribly out of place.

"Indeed," the Spirit of the Land said with a pompous bow. "But you have nothing to fear, Adya. See? I shall aid you."

Vines and flowers rose from the earth, seemingly of their own accord, until their blossoms, fronds, and leaves draped over Adya. As each touched the rough spun fabric, they rippled and softened, until the fabric took on their rich colors, turning fine and supple.

"Tomorrow," the spirit said as he took his place, "all shall be as it was. But for today, it will suffice."

When they reached the road, it was easy enough to join a handful of carts and wagons traveling toward the fortress as they made their way to the river crossing. The guards at the fortress gate searched each wagon and traveler. Some travelers passed through, some were sent away, and a handful of the more belligerent were dragged into the fortress, yelling insults or pleading their innocence.

The chill that ran through Adya's bones had nothing to do with the late autumn winds.

The monk put a reassuring hand on her shoulder. Adya looked back, shared a moment of eye contact with them, and nodded. She still didn't believe in the "Chosen One," but she would trust these strange friends.

She slowed and stopped the cart when the Adrenni guards came forward, dressed in their brown and red uniforms. One of the Adrenni soldiers approached, a stout looking man with a bored look on his face that turned calculating as he took in their robes and finery.

"State your business."

The Spirit of the Land bowed so deeply in his seat that his head nearly touched the floor of the cart.

"We are traveling back from Posna, good sir. My Lady has been seeking trade among them and working to enrich our glorious empire!"

The soldier grunted as he walked around the cart with obviously exaggerated care, and the Spirit of the Rains made a point of ignoring him with equally exaggerated indifference.

"We've had problems with contraband lately, and I don't recall you traveling through this crossing before."

"Indeed, you have not," the spirit agreed in his most obsequious voice. "We made our crossing farther south, near Revu, but My Lady caught word of a most impressive crop of potatoes growing in Sivrin. She directed us to take her there to see for herself before we returned."

The soldier completed his circuit as the spirit gestured vaguely to the west, giving them another calculating look. "I see no potatoes in this cart."

The Spirit of the Rain sighed, finally breaking her silence. "Of course, you do not! I bought twenty hundredweight to sell back in Revu. A river barge will carry them there."

"So you say," the soldier said skeptically.

The Spirit of the Land took over from her just as smoothly as he'd made up the first half of the story. "So we can prove, my good Sir." He turned to one of the sacks that held their improbable supply of potatoes and drew one out before offering it to the Soldier.

"A sample of the wares," he said as he held out the potato, and Adya missed the gold coins tucked between the tuber and his palm until the soldier slid them from the spirit's hand to his own.

"Hm." The soldier seemed to give the potato the same sort of inspection he'd given the cart, then took a healthy bite, chewing on the raw flesh while he tucked the coins into his belt pouch. "Not bad, for a Posani potato." Stepping back from the cart, he gestured toward the gate with the hand still holding his snack. "Be on your way."

"My thanks, sir, and a pleasant day to you!"

"They can pass," he ordered the other soldiers, waving for them to clear the road. "Open the river gate!"

A few minutes later, they were crossing the great bridge, the *clop-clop-clop* of hooves echoing against the stone before it was swallowed by the sound of the river passing beneath them.

Adya gave the Spirit of the Land a carefully restrained look. "You said that tomorrow, all shall be as it was?"

The spirit nodded, a satisfied smile on his face. "Indeed, and our friend shall learn a very important lesson about greed."

As he broke into a boisterous laugh, Adya found herself grinning as they finished crossing the Verika, another step closer on their journey to Adrenna.

The strangest thing about being in the Adrenni Empire to Adya was that it wasn't that strange. When she had read Petyr's last few letters, they made the Andrenni sound like fabulous creatures, more beast than man. He'd passed on stories he'd heard of how they were unnaturally tall and strong and drank the blood of the fallen. She'd taken it all with a grain of salt, but some part of her hadn't expected them to seem so *normal*.

They weren't even that tall, really. Petyr had only been half a head taller than Adya when he'd left their farm, and most Andrenni appeared only a head or two taller than that.

As they passed by villages much like her own, Adya saw fields being harrowed and tended to prepare for the colder months, just as her hired hands would likely be doing now, and when they occasionally stopped in a tavern or inn, she found the people they spoke with to generally be pleasant.

The biggest difference, she decided, was the army.

She knew all too well how the King's Council in Posna would call for conscription, but it was a temporary measure in times of war. There was a Standing Guard in the capital, but nothing like what she saw as they traveled closer to Adrenna. Every town had a garrison that patrolled the streets, and the sound of hobnailed boots was ever present.

"Don't they tire of having the soldiers around?"

The monk shrugged as they walked beside the cart, watching a patrol march past.

"Does a fish tire of the water?"

Adya sighed. Another riddle.

"I suppose you expect me to say it does not," she answered. "Because it is all the fish has ever known. But the fish does not swim with a sword to its neck."

"Is the sword to their necks? Or is it placed before them as a defense?" The monk's smile was still teasing, but their eyes had become more serious. "You see them as a threat, but your village must have had those who turned away bandits, or who punished thieves."

"None who marched about constantly in uniforms and armor. They were people of the village—not held apart."

The monk hummed and wordlessly pointed out where a soldier had stopped in front of a bakery, chatting idly with a woman who had given him a roll and a mug of something steaming.

Adya frowned and gave a soft huff of annoyance. It wasn't the same, really—even if she went to bed thinking of the conversation, unable to justify her feelings.

It should have been a month's journey from the border to Adrenna, but just over a week had passed when they took a winding road over and through the Certain Mountains. As they descended through the Farenn Valley, they could see the great white walls of the Imperial capital in the distance.

Petyr had never written of the city, but Adya knew a little from travelers' stories and tavern tales. A great circle of white stones around the city protected it from harm, broken only by the River Adren where it passed through the heart of the old city. There were songs about the bravery and foolishness of warriors who had tried to use the river to aid them in conquering Adrenna, and how the river itself had crushed their boats and smashed them against the walls and channels rather than let the city come to harm.

She tried not to think too much on that as they approached one of the great gates set into the stone. Ranks upon ranks of soldiers marched along and atop the walls, and Adya could see them stopping to search carts and inspect travelers.

"I don't think your coin trick will work here," Adya murmured as she maneuvered the cart into the end of the line.

The Spirit of the Land gave an uncertain hum before finally shaking his head. "No. No, dear Adya, I fear it will not."

The wind rustled, and Adya shivered despite the fur-lined cloak she'd bought in Revu.

"I can aid you here," the Spirit of the Rain said in a soft rumble, "but it will mean I can go no further."

Adya felt a pang of sadness at the thought of parting with the messenger who had quickly become a friend. "Do you believe it is the right thing to do?"

The Spirit of the Rain nodded slowly, her movements filled with the weight of storm clouds. "I know this is what I was meant to do for you, Adya."

Adya reached out to take her hand and felt the rightness of it. "Then please aid us, Spirit. I hope someday I will see you again."

The Spirit of the Rain smiled at her and bowed her head, then seemed to fade from view as the skies darkened with clouds, and the winds grew stronger. The scarf that had covered the spirit's head whipped away in a gust, and as it disappeared into the skies, the rest vanished, leaving nothing but a slight indentation in the bag the spirit had been sitting on.

As cries of concern rose from the carts, wagons, and travelers waiting to be allowed into the capital city, the first drops of rain began to fall.

When the storm began, Adya did not think it was a coincidence that she could hear her name in the rumbling thunder.

"In!" One of the soldiers ran through the rain, his boots sinking into the fresh mud with every step. "In, IN! The Gate is open—just drive, you fools! Get inside the walls before the storm washes you down the river!"

As the travelers in front of them sped toward the gate, Adya took up the reins and urged their mare to pull the cart as quickly as it could.

After so many months of messengers and strange travels, they had reached Adrenna.

Adya felt a pang of sadness for the departure of their friend as she listened to the clop of hooves and the sound of wheels against the cobbled roads, every sound amplified as they passed through the great walls.

The storm had calmed to an early winter's drizzle as they reached the end of the tunnel, and Adya could not help her gasp of shock as they emerged into the city proper.

"There are *so many*," she breathed in surprise as she tried not to gawk like a fool. People of seemingly all ages and all colors, dressed in outfits that ranged from the practical to the ridiculous, moved about the streets, some stopping at market stalls to haggle for goods or to nab a snack. The soldiers were here too, and in force, but they seemed just another part of the throngs that gave the city life. She had to give the monk their due—they did not seem so overbearing here.

"I know of an inn where we can rest," the Spirit of the Land said as he gestured vaguely to the right. "Once you have had a chance to prepare, we will take you to the palace."

The reminder of her "destiny" sobered Adya.

"I suppose that is where we will find the 'dark child' you spoke of."

The spirit nodded.

"I have no weapons. No training. How will I 'vanquish' someone if I cannot fight?"

The monk looked up from where they were walking beside the cart.

"When the time comes, you will know. That is what destiny means."

Adya snorted. "Weren't you the one who said we assumed too much?"

The monk's laugh sounded like wind running through chimes. "Indeed!"

It was not terribly reassuring.

The inn was pleasant enough. Certainly, it was better appointed than many they had seen on their way through the empire, and Adya admitted she had been in dire need of the warm, sweet-scented bath the innkeeper's wife drew for her.

They ate well that night, but the Spirits insisted Adya give herself another day or two to rest from their journey before they investigated the palace. She spent that time speaking to other travelers, learning about the lands they had come from. She spoke to those who had lived in the great city all their lives, and those who were as humbled by its massive buildings and throngs of people as she had been. Adya traded more of her improbably fresh potatoes and a soup recipe to the innkeeper's wife for another luxurious bath and listened carefully to the gossip of others in the inn.

The Emperor had caused quite an uproar by marrying a foreign girl, it seemed. There were whispers of intrigues in the Imperial Court, and no one had seen the Emperor or his bride for several months. Troops had moved around lately, but it seemed like they were gathering around the city, not preparing for a war march. Generally, the people seemed positive, but there was an undercurrent of tension, a tightness around the eyes and mouth Adya noticed despite their smiles. No one breathed about the possibility of a civil war, but Adya could tell they all feared one.

When she returned to their rented room after dinner, the two spirits were waiting.

"Do you know what has happened to the Emperor, or his new bride?"

The Spirit of the Land shook his head. "We know that the dark child has taken the throne. The stars themselves spoke of it, but I fear they offered little else."

Adya sighed. "Other than my name."

"Indeed," the spirit rumbled.

The monk had been resting on the floor in some sort of meditation, but their eyes opened at that remark.

"Perhaps it is time we found out."

When they snuck out of the inn that night, the air was so chilly, Adya could see her breath escaping in little puffs of steam as they crept across streets and alleyways, the sound of their footsteps oddly quiet and muffled. The monk kept their eyes closed even as they led the way through the streets, and Adya understood the spirit was doing something to keep them from being heard.

After what seemed like hours of wandering through alleys and passages with no apparent rhyme or reason, they emerged from the shadows to stare up at the towering Palace Imperial, arched entryways rising to broad balconies and terraces before forming towers and spires. Adya gave herself a moment to appreciate its beauty, then let herself be practical again.

"What level would the Emperor and Empress live on?"

The monk chuckled. "The very top, of course!"

"I don't suppose either of you can fly..."

"There are other ways to reach them," the monk suggested, looking back to the Spirit of the Land.

The spirit sighed and produced a silk square to mop his brow. "So, there are." He turned to face Adya and bowed deeply to her.

"My dear Lady Adya. I can help you reach the top, but it will mean I can go no further."

Just as with the Spirit of the Rain, Adya felt a pang of sadness. "You began all this with me, Spirit."

He nodded, a sad smile on his lips. "I had hoped to see you through the end, but it seems I have another part to play in your destiny."

"Pompous old fool," she murmured with a smile, and gave the spirit a hug. "Go, then. Please, help us, and don't forget to water your horse the next time we meet."

The spirit rumbled with laughter as he stepped back from the hug and gave them both a final bow. "I daresay I shall never forget that again!"

With that, the Spirit of the Land exchanged a solemn nod with the monk and left them to walk toward the palace. He paced along the wall until he found a patch of ground where the cobblestones had been loosened, and weeds had begun to grow.

The spirit became a towering form of plants and leaves, and Adya heard the cracking of stones and splitting of earth as great roots sank into the ground. Planting himself firmly, the lush green of the spirit's body turned to new colors as his arms stretched into branching, climbing vines that swiftly ran to the top of the palace walls.

They watched the spirit's body turn to sturdy bark, branches spaced to allow for good foot and handholds. The vines thickened and twisted in on themselves until they became as stout as strong rope, knotting together every so often to allow them to complete the climb.

When it was done, the great tree that now clung to the walls seemed to have been there for hundreds of years, the vines worked into the very stones of the palace—but there was no sign of the Spirit of the Land. It was a magnificent tree, but merely a tree.

Adya blinked back tears as she reached out to touch the rough bark.

"Do not worry," the monk said as they put a comforting hand on her arm. "Our friend is still out there—and I think you shall see him again."

"Another prophecy?"

The monk shook their head before they boosted themselves up to climb. "No. Just understanding the ways of good friends."

Heartened by that, Adya found a good foothold in the bark and hoisted herself up as well. The climb was long, and harder work than she'd done since the last planting season. Still, as she let herself down from the vines and onto the palace floor where the monk waited, Adya's legs did not wobble, and her hands did not shake.

Blasted Spirits, she thought.

"I don't suppose you know where the Emperor's chambers would be?"

The monk winked and gestured for her to follow as they went inside.

A turn, a corridor, another turn, and an opulent hallway later, they stood before a set of doors carved and polished from some strange dark wood, with inlaid metals and jewels that picked out the Imperial Seal.

"Are there no guards here?"

The monk winked again, then pushed the heavy doors inward with a muffled creak.

The carpet of the Emperor's suite was a rich plush red as deep as the loam in Adya's fields, with chairs and lounges that could have paid for her entire village many times over. Again, Adya expected there to be guards or courtiers, but none were there. Padding across the room to the next doorway, there was a great bed with carved spears at each corner, holding up a canopy of gauzy fabric, pillows piled high as mountains, and no one in it.

Adya had been about to say something to the monk when she heard a quiet cough, and the sounds of movement from the room beyond. She pushed past the monk and stepped through, her eyes going wide at what she found.

"A baby...?"

The child couldn't have been more than six months old. They had been wrapped in robes of gold-embroidered red silk, their skin a shade just slightly lighter than Adya's own, and a head covered in dark hair. They reached through the bars of the crib as she came closer, making a soft "ackle" sound as Adya knelt down to offer a finger for them to grab, watching the delight in the baby's eyes.

"Where are your parents, little one?"

"Dead," the monk said sadly, looking mournfully down at the child. "His father died to an assassin's knife after one of the Imperial consuls realized the Emperor had already sired an heir with his Posani bride."

Adya's brows rose with surprise. "And his mother?"

The monk shook their head. "The prophecy spoke true—the first life the dark child claimed was the one who bore them into the world."

Adya gave the monk a sharp look. "There are many reasons that one can die in childbirth. None of them are the child's fault."

The monk laughed softly, and when the so-called dark child giggled back, they made silly faces until the baby began to doze again.

"Perhaps it was not his fault, but their deaths have placed him on the throne. Those still loyal to his father's house are trying to guard his claim, but they rightly fear a war might be needed to keep him there."

The baby stirred again, and Adya leaned over to pick him up without a second thought. Walking and gently rocking him in her arms, she kept the boy close to her breast, humming softly as she considered what the monk had said.

"Who is caring for him now?"

The monk shrugged. "A nursemaid sleeps in the next room."

"He has no other family?"

"The Old Emperor and his wife passed a few years into their son's reign. There are a few cousins—many of whom might challenge for the throne."

Adya smiled as the boy settled against her, then looked at where the monk was leaning far too innocently on their staff. "What of his mother's family?"

"They have no idea," the Monk said with a hint of mischief in their eyes. "The Emperor met her by chance during his last tour of the border. A commoner, to their minds, and unimportant."

"You knew all of this."

The monk smiled innocently. "When one wanders, they hear all sorts of interesting things."

"You led us all this way, letting me believe I would have to kill a child."

"I led you all this way knowing you would not."

As Adya cradled the sleeping baby, she finally heard the sounds of alarm and running feet that she'd expected when they first reached the palace. The sound of heavy boots grew nearer as she gently placed the baby emperor into his crib, and Adya summoned up all her stubbornness and strength as she turned to meet the guards who had come to protect their little lord.

"Don't you *dare* wake my Grandson," she said in a harsh whisper before anyone else could speak, and with the same force of will she'd used to stand her ground against the Land, the Rain, and the Wind, Adya pointed to the outer chambers. "Go out there and *be quiet*. I will join you in a moment."

When they had retreated beyond the bedchambers, Adya looked over to the monk.

"I don't suppose you might send for my things."

The monk bowed deeply. "I regret that I cannot—but your neighbors and friends will tend to them all until you can return."

Adya returned to the crib and reached down to gently brush her new grandson's hair. "I have no idea how to raise an emperor."

"Raise him as a farmer, then," the monk said with a knowing smile. "As long as you raise him to be a good man, I think the results will be much the same."

The weight of responsibility on her shoulders was heavy, but as Adya watched her grandson dream, it did not seem so bad.

"I suppose this is where you leave me now, too."

The monk nodded. "For now. But do not worry, Adya. We will watch over your new family."

Adya bowed her head in thanks as a breeze passed through the open window, and when she looked up, the monk was gone, leaving nothing but a few wisps of gray mist and the sound of the passing wind.

"Blasted Spirits," she murmured fondly, and turned to go meet her Destiny.

SOCCER MOM
— SAVES THE WORLD —
by Addie J. King

I moved my brother Andrew's holy water garden sprayer and my cousin Gregory's "demon" banishing kit aside to make sure I had everything I needed for the day. Of course, we couldn't go anywhere without their tools, no matter how much space they required. Sigh.

Folding chairs for all of the adults? Check.

Rolling wagon? Check.

An extra blanket for the kids to relax on between games? Check.

Cooler of drinks and snacks? Check. I even remembered the orange slices, in separate baggies to prevent the kids from fighting.

Handheld fan? Umbrella in case of rain? Check and check.

Camera and cell phone backup batteries? Sunscreen, first aid kit, sunglasses, visor? Check to all.

It was another soccer weekend, at a tournament an hour from home. I was used to my SUV being jam packed with thirteen-year-old girls. My daughter played soccer nearly year-round. She and several of her friends played on an elite club team in the spring, and we spent darn near every weekend traveling all over the place for her to play in various events. This was the closest we had been to home for the last six months. I was really looking forward to being able to sleep in my own bed instead of the varying qualities of hotels and motels we'd experienced as we traveled for her to play. Being this close to home meant that I guilt-tripped my brother and my cousin (who was close enough to be like another brother), committed bachelors both, into coming to watch their niece play. But neither of them would leave the "demon" banishing equipment behind, and it took up so much room in the back of the car!

Andrew leaned up against the side of my SUV, laughing softly to himself. "What in the world are you taking so much stuff for? Aren't you coming home again tonight?" He snickered at me, struggling with the cooler and Gregory's case of supplies, and hesitated just a bit before coming over to help me cram it all down to close the door.

"Of course we're coming home tonight. There aren't any suit-cases, are there?" I huffed back at him.

"Why are you taking so much stuff to watch soccer?" Gregory asked, carrying a small, soft-sided briefcase with him.

"Okay, first of all—" I crossed my arms over my chest to show how frustrated I was with them, and leaned back against the closed door, using my hip to push it the rest of the way closed. "She has three games today, and if they do well, two tomorrow. We've played at this field before, many times, and there aren't a whole lot of good healthy places to get lunch while we're there. The kids will be hungrier than you expect. If you don't take healthy snacks, the kids end up with food truck and concession food, and that's not good if it's hot and the kids are running all over the place."

Andrew nodded. "Completely understood the cooler. And you've told me that there are no bleachers, so I understand the chairs. But it's like you're packed for bear, and you won't be gone twelve hours."

"Shows how much you know. These teenage girls will want somewhere to sit, and food. They will want towels to keep the sweat out of their eyes and fresh socks to change into between games. Plus a dry shirt between games. Trust me when I say that this is packing light for a tournament weekend. I packed essentials for the two of you as well, since I figured you guys wouldn't know what to expect." If I got any more frustrated with the two of them, I knew there would be steam whistling out of my ears like Grandma's old tea kettle. I closed my eyes briefly to keep from losing my temper.

Gregory was laughing at Andrew, who had clearly been trying to get a rise out of me. I was not going to put up with their antics.

"I have no idea why the two of you are insisting on bringing work supplies. Do you honestly expect to be attacked by rogue 'demons' at a tournament field with a bunch of teenaged girls?" Yes, I used air quotes. There was a small part of me that figured that a demon, if they actually did exist, would actually want to shy away from these girls, rough and tumble as they were. Ali and her friends were going to be forces of nature when they were grown. They pretty much took over every space they inhabited now.

Ali, my long-legged daughter, came bouncing out of the house, her hair already braided in double French braids and pinned up to her head tightly, ready to play. She took one look at us and rolled her eyes. That was pretty normal for her too. I ignored it.

"Mom, are you three going to snipe at each other all day? I mean, you and Dad were sniping at each other pretty good last night, and I kinda want to know if I'm gonna have to listen to it all day today too."

"Probably," Gregory said easily, tugging on the collar of his shirt. As much as I'd tried to get him to wear something a little less formal, he had insisted on a short-sleeved clerical shirt and collar with slacks. I mean, I understood that he felt he had to wear it, but that much black in the hot sun would be uncomfortable. I'd tried to tell him. He hadn't listened.

Andrew, on the other hand, was wearing a work polo, when I really had wished he wouldn't. Andrew was fifty, but he'd already retired from the police department several years earlier due to some injuries from a shooting. He's fine these days, but he now ran a company called Demon Busters. He said that they were supernatural exterminators, but I never would have thought he was into bugs, and I couldn't believe that they were actually making money at it. I was sure that Ali would protest when Andrew showed up in his work shirt, but she hadn't said a word, just looked at it meaningfully and ignored him again. "Why do you guys have to take work stuff with us?" I asked.

"Being prepared. Just like you are," Andrew said.

I blew out the breath I'd been holding, probably a little bit louder than I normally would have, then told everyone to get in the car. It was already six in the morning, and we should have left fifteen minutes earlier. I'd deal with Ali's comment about her dad later. At the moment, I couldn't deal with that drama too.

That was the longest drive I'd ever done in my life, despite being less than an hour away. Andrew and Gregory were talking some sort of nonsense about a theory that one of Andrew's employees was cooking up. It all sounded like they were nuts. I'd heard stories about the two of them battling a demon when they were younger and thought it was some kind of weird prank. No way was this crap real. But they were Ali's favorite people in our family, so I grinned and gritted my teeth the entire drive. That demon stuff was crazy talk right out of a fantasy novel.

I was very glad for the large travel mug of coffee I'd made sure to bring. And the healthy snacks. I had already seen the food trucks setting up as we pulled into the parking lot; Belgian waffle, snow cone, chili dog, and walking taco trucks were already getting things cooking for the first wave of hungry kids and parents after the first round of games. They'd make a fortune this weekend. And I'd save my money to take Ali out to celebrate her wins at her favorite Mexican restaurant at the end of the weekend. It was our thing. And if her dad got off work early enough, maybe he'd be able to join us for a celebratory dinner.

The girls were off and running, going through warm up drills for their first game. I made the two blockheads—er, Gregory and Andrew—help me to load up the wagon to pull all of the supplies to the side of the field. The walk was long enough that the wagon was necessary, as I'd expected. It took longer than it should have to get the chairs set up, umbrellas at the ready (there was a chance of rain, but also there was a chance of it being warm, sunny and humid—the umbrellas could attach to the chairs for shade if need be). I put on the sunglasses and visor and started applying sunscreen while the two of them looked at me in disgust. "Skin cancer is a thing, guys. And you will bake out here without even realizing it." They shook off my offer of sunscreen and bug spray (there was a creek nearby, and plenty of mosquitos would come out if it got more humid), and they were joking around about some sort of dude who researched demons in the sixteenth century. Okay, they were nuts, but I loved them anyway. I ignored them and got my camera ready for action shots.

Ali waved over from the middle of the field. The guys enthusiastically waved and clapped and cheered for her, and she beamed from ear to ear. This was why I was putting up with their kookiness. Her smile made my heart skip a beat from sheer joy. I just felt bad that she'd heard her dad and me arguing the night before. She didn't need to worry about whether I was going back into the workforce or not. I'd been a stay-at-home mom for years, and while the soccer travel took up my weekends, it was also a mounting expense. Her dad wasn't wrong that a part time job would help with the expenses, and I didn't want to tell her no when her heart was all in for soccer. I just had to find the right job that gave me weekends off and had me only working during the school day. I hadn't found it yet.

I pulled a granola bar out of my purse and put my chilled water bottle from the cooler in the mesh drink holder in my chair, waiting for the game to start.

The whistle blew and launched the girls into action for one of the first games of the morning. Ali scored the first goal. By halftime, her team was up three to nothing; Ali herself scored two of the three goals. The teams huddled together at opposite ends of the field, talking strategy, while the parents stood up, stretched, talked among themselves, and reapplied sunscreen.

Andrew leaned over to me. "She's really good," he said, reaching into the cooler for the bag of grapes I'd cleaned the night before.

"Thanks," I said. I wanted to snark at him that he would have known that if he'd come to any of her games in the last five years, but I didn't want to ruin the day for her, and it was such a nice morning.

Was.

The sky darkened, and the clouds turned stormy with a thunderclap noise that had me grabbing at my ears. Flames burst on the field, and from the fire grew a large cloud of smoke. I elbowed Andrew. "What's that?" I asked.

"A demon," he said.

No damn way. I thought for sure he was kidding. I rubbed my eyes and turned to ask him something, only to see him and Gregory racing for the car. "KEYS!" Gregory yelled.

I tossed him the keys, happy to be accurate in the toss, but he missed the catch and my keys bounced off his chest. He tripped over himself, grabbed them off the grass, and stumbled back to his feet to toss them to Andrew, who had gotten to the car first.

And then I realized...I could have unlocked it from where I'd been sitting in my chair with the key fob. Good Lord, I sure hoped they were better at the demon exterminating than they were in the execution here.

Demons were real.

They weren't actually killing bugs with a goofy name.

And that meant the stories about them running into demons when we were kids...weren't made up.

Wait a minute. Where was my kid?

I didn't want to call her name. I didn't want attention drawn to her. But where was she? I started inching toward the goal post where the team was huddled. I needed to see that she was okay, but I didn't want whatever-that-thing-was (okay, yes, a demon) to look at me either. I made my way slowly off to the side as I saw a snake-like head rise above the smoke.

And then I saw it. The demon was wearing a uniform shirt from Ali's team. It was the new girl, Betsie Lauder, the one that had joined the team just a week earlier, who had to get special permission to join the club midseason. How did I know that? Because her number was right there, right on the back of the shirt, just before the shirt split as the demon's wings tore through the fabric. We only had one number 23 on the team, and it was Betsie. So, either something had happened to Betsie, or she had a secret that was literally out of the bag now.

I saw Ali's head pop up from the huddle, taking in what was happening on the field. "Mommy," I heard her whimper, and I took off at a run. Only dimly did it register that Andrew and Gregory had caught up to me and were headed in the same direction, toward Ali and her teammates.

The demon shrieked and spat sulfur-smelling fumes into the air. "Brimstone," Gregory huffed, clearly out of breath.

I must have been losing my mind, but I didn't even skip a beat. "If this is your thing, what do we do? How do we get these girls out of here?" I demanded.

"We don't," Andrew said. "If we try to evacuate, there are too many people. There's already a panic. It will become a stampede, and everyone gets hurt. We've got to stop this right here."

I looked around. Nearly half of the parents were staring in shock. The other half were looking around for their kids and their keys, and running to their cars. "I think you already have a stampede in progress," I said, deadpan. Even the kids playing on the other fields had stopped, whistles blown, and the folks watching them were also taking cover. All except for the dude at the snow cone truck, who had headphones on and was dancing to whatever music was in his ears, oblivious to everything around him under the whir of the snow cone machines. Given that he was the closest truck to where we were, it was almost funny, but I kept my eye on him, trying to figure out how to get his attention without leaving my girl in an unsafe position.

Andrew got ahead of me and laid down a strip of holy water from his garden sprayer between the girls and the demon, who just seemed to be angry and shrieking as loud as she could.

The coach? Well, I think the coach had gone bye-bye. By that, I mean that she was in complete shock, her mouth hanging open, and not responding. I grabbed Ali by the arm and pulled her and her friends behind me and behind Andrew's holy water line, Gregory helping to herd them. I grabbed the coach as well. Thank goodness her feet and legs seemed to be responding, and she cooperated in being moved with the girls. I heard a wail and realized it was the coach, but I couldn't turn and look. I was too busy watching the flailing demon throwing a temper tantrum at midfield.

"What happened?" Andrew asked. "Was there something that started this?"

Ali pushed her face over my shoulder and next to my ear and said, "Coach got after Betsie because she was coming too close, too often, to being offside. She was lucky they weren't calling it. Betsie got upset that the coach was singling her out and yelled back. I don't think Betsie understands the offsides rule. When some of us tried to explain, she got mad, and her face got red, and then we saw steam...and then we saw...*that.*" She nodded in the direction of the demon. "Is that really Betsie?"

Gregory nodded, opening up his case. I had no idea what all he had in there, but there was a wooden cross as well as several small vials. He already had his stole around his neck and a wooden rosary in his left hand. "She's been possessed. We're gonna have to banish the demon, and that's not gonna be pleasant for her."

I looked toward the demon before asking, "Is she going to be okay afterward?"

Andrew didn't look hopeful. "I hope so," he said before he headed right toward the demon version of Betsie, trying to talk her into calming down, the garden sprayer bouncing against his leg with its nearly full weight as he walked unevenly across the field.

I nudged Gregory, who was mid-prayer. "Is he really going to go after a demon with nothing but holy water?"

He nodded, his lips moving silently as I saw the beads of the rosary slipping through his fingers. I could see the words on his lips, and couldn't help but echo them in my head, good Catholic girl that I was. *Hail Mary, full of grace...*

"Is there anything else we can use?" I asked, thinking hard and coming up with nothing.

He finished his current prayer and looked me in the eye. "Part of the benefit of me being along is that anything liquid can be blessed. You'd be surprised at what we've used."

"Like what?"

He grinned. "Well, we've used water. I've blessed chocolate Yoo-hoo drinks before. Even a garden hose."

I looked up, right at the snow cone truck. "What if it isn't liquid right now?"

He followed my eyes and nodded.

We got the girls to move over to the snow cone truck. The attendant had finally pulled the earbuds out of his ears and started screaming, as ear piercing and shrill as a three-year-old girl. Ali's best friend, Rachel, slapped him across the face to get him to stop—for which we were all grateful. Gregory launched himself into the truck and started blessing the ice, the syrup, and everything else he could get his hands on that was, or could become, liquid. Ali and I started to dish up cone after cone of packed ice, loading up the girls' arms with the sticky concoctions. By the time we were done, each girl, Gregory, and I had at least four snow cones in our arms.

"Girls, none of you have to do this," I told them. "If you're scared, that's fine. I won't make anyone do this. But the goal is to get in as close as we can and start pelting Betsie from all sides with this stuff so that Andrew can soak her down with his sprayer." They all nodded. "Okay, so Betsie is the goal. Throwing, not kicking. Constant marking. No misses." Again, uniform nodding.

I was so proud of the girls I could've cried, but I still was worried. If something happened to one of them, what would I tell their parents? And then I saw a line of parents behind them. Rachel's mother was leading the crowd. "We won't be as fast as the girls, but if they're willing to do this, we can do what we've always done: support them as much as we can," she said firmly. "We'll throw from a distance, and some of us will hang back to handle refills."

I fist bumped her. I couldn't help it. And the girls were off. Ducking and diving, dodging and weaving around each other, just like they did on the soccer field.

Demon Betsie roared her anger even louder. I ran in, trying to stay out of the way of those incredible girls, who were landing their Holy Snow Cones around Demon Betsie's knees and ankles. I yelled, "Aim higher! Over the bar, not under it! We don't know if her shin guards are still protecting her legs!"

Ali nodded at me and pointed higher. The girls immediately started throwing toward the demon's waist and torso. She roared even louder. I guess the shin guards were still working to protect her legs, but she didn't have any protective gear on her torso and upper legs.

Andrew came running over, panting and out of breath. "That's one stubborn demon."

"Those are some pretty stubborn girls," I replied, rearing back to throw another snow cone at the demon's chest. It landed with a sizzling thump, and Demon Betsie tried to swipe it off, only succeeding in spreading the cone, which acted like acid, leaving burning welts as it melted through her shirt and into the demon flesh beneath. My advice to aim higher seemed to be helping, as the lower aimed cones hadn't done much against what was left of Betsie's socks and shin guards on the lower legs of the demon.

"Reload!" I yelled, pointing at the snow cone truck. A couple of the girls peeled off and circled around to the snow cone truck, their parents giving them as many as they could run with. As they returned to the front lines, the others began cycling through, doing the same thing. I could hear the girls talking to each other, working together to coat the demon around the waist with sliding snow cones burning down the demon's torso, leaving a line of charred demon flesh under the glaze of the multicolored syrup and melting ice. I looked down and realized that Andrew's garden sprayer was empty.

"You're out?" I panted.

He nodded. "I soaked the grass underneath the demon so that she couldn't light it on fire."

The grass?!?!?! "Why didn't you soak the demon herself?" I asked.

He looked annoyed. "Because I've done this a time or two thousand. It's not just about the demon. It's also about the collateral damage. If that grass went up, I don't know how far or fast the fire would spread. It's a bit dry."

I realized he was right. But would the snow cones be enough?

I knew the answer.

Ali's friend Megan came up, and her mom, Kim, knew the answer. "The Gatorade jugs. On the team benches." Kim pointed to the team benches, abandoned amid a sea of duffel bags, sandals, towels, and water bottles. Each team had two ten-gallon coolers filled with Gatorade, as well as squeeze water bottles for during the game. The coaches generally made sure the coolers were filled to the brim at the beginning of the day, and they'd be empty by night, the last of the watery sports drink gone and last melting ice cube evaporated after a tournament weekend. They were heavy. And at only half of the first game done, they would still be mostly full.

We took off running, other parents continuing to reload the girls with snow cones. We dodged around the girls, who had definitely noticed we had a plan of some kind. I ran to the first cooler, the one closest to us, and screwed off the top lid. "Still pretty full," I yelled. "Gregory, start here! We'll check the others!" Kim ran with Andrew to the other end of the bench and started opening the other cooler to check.

Gregory started praying over the liquid the minute he caught up, lips moving as fast as he could go, moving one hand over the liquid as he crossed himself with the other. I had no idea how long such a blessing needed to be, but it apparently didn't take long, because he followed me quickly. "How are we gonna lift these?" he asked before dropping back into prayer on the second jug, which was about three quarters full.

Good question. I couldn't lift one by myself. If they were full to the brim, those coolers would weigh over a hundred pounds each, and they were awkward to lift. Gregory kept going, and we got all four coolers opened for him to pray over while Andrew and I ran back to the first one. Without speaking, each of us grabbed a handle and started moving as fast as we could toward the demon.

The girls saw what we were doing and followed suit, some of them stopping their snow cone assault to run after and grab more of the coolers and follow us into the fray. As we got closer, Andrew told them to try to get more angles, to circle around the demon, who hadn't tried to go anywhere as the holy water wetted grass burned her feet. She stomped a few strides in any direction and came right back when it wasn't better. It reminded me a lot of Ali, who was my fierce girl, but tested boundaries in a very cautious way, giving up too easily when she got pushed back by Momma Bear. It must be common to the age, I thought, and wondered how long that tentative nature would last before we had full-blown teenaged rebellion.

Andrew barked orders to the girls, who listened intently as he directed them around the demon, yelling a countdown. When he hit zero, we all dumped the entire contents of the coolers (two blue, one orange, and one red) on the demon, who screamed even louder, and melted down to a normal-sized teen girl, whimpering in a wet multicolored heap on the grass.

"Ali, go grab your extra t-shirt. Her uniform shirt got shredded," I whispered. "Or a towel or something to help cover her."

My daughter had been staring at her friend. She started, and then ran over to the mound of duffel bags, pulling out a sports towel and a clean shirt. She seemed older than she had this morning, as if she'd lived five years in the two hours since we'd left the house—mature and battle tested, one might say.

Andrew and Gregory told the girls to stay back, but my Ali wouldn't let them stop her. "She's probably scared and confused.

You are strangers to her. Let me go with you and cover her up. She won't be thrilled at her shirt being ripped, or about anyone seeing her vulnerable."

I had to give them credit; they listened. I was in awe of my daughter and her composure.

They went in with the towel and helped Betsie sit up, wiping off the worst of the sticky liquids she was covered in before helping her into the shirt, over the shredded uniform and sports bra barely covering her.

I ran in to where my daughter was comforting Betsie, who was still whimpering softly. "Are you okay, sweetie?"

My daughter, my heart, replied, "She's fine, but she's not at fault here. Her older sister has been dabbling in demon summoning."

I didn't know that was an activity for schoolgirls these days.

Luckily Ali didn't look at my expression. "Mom, we need to get her sister to talk to someone. She's pretty depressed and tried suicide by demon."

Um. I didn't know *that* was an activity for schoolgirls these days. Gulp.

"We will get her help," I promised. "Are her parents here?" I didn't remember ever meeting them.

"Her mom is a politician; her dad is a surgeon. They almost never come to games, and the housekeeper brings her to practice. She's really lonely, and so is her sister." Ali gave Betsie's hand a squeeze and glanced over her shoulder at me. "Can I invite her to my birthday party next month?"

My heart broke for my beautiful girl, in a million pieces of love. My child had watched her friend fall apart completely in anger at a coach, turn into a demon, get vanquished by her friends, and still wanted to welcome her and be friends with her. I couldn't be prouder of her than I was at that exact moment, while still worried that it wasn't a good idea. I turned to Andrew. "Is the demon gone?"

"Yes. It's gone." He looked about as sure as I've ever seen him, and it helped unclench the moment of worry at the base of my heart, sneaking around the pride. "She really was possessed, and it doesn't look like she's the one at fault. She didn't invite it. Which is part of why it was so easy to get the demon to leave."

EASY?

Andrew, that jerk, looked me directly in the eye. "Your daughter is a natural for the family business. You know that, right?"

My heart landed somewhere near my feet. I wanted her to go to college, to have a career, and to find her own community. But I also recognized what he was saying. She wanted to protect and help others, something both Andrew, as a retired police officer and now, I guess, demon exterminator, and Gregory as a priest, knew a little bit about. Would I stop her?

"I know." I couldn't stop her from being herself, no more than my mom could have stopped me. "But I'm in. You've been asking about me getting involved. I'm in."

Andrew breathed a sigh of relief. "We really do need someone good about being prepared and organized to keep us on the straight and narrow. Otherwise, it's mass chaos out there. And we need someone who will keep their head in a crisis. Ask Leslie, our newest employee; it's not easy to be the new girl, the recent non-believer. She'll tell you it's a weird transition. But you as our dispatcher and receptionist should help relieve our issues with volume. Something's coming. We will need a ton of help. Are you in?"

My husband worked a ton of hours, so Ali and I were close. But my girl was growing up. She wouldn't need me as much, as she'd just proven. It was time to get back out of the house and do what made me feel useful: helping people. Ali walked up and hugged me tight. "You'd be awesome at it, Mom." I guess I had her seal of approval.

"So long as I'm out for the day before school lets out, and there's no weekends involved? And you guys make a bigger effort to come watch more of her soccer games? I'm in." I hugged my girl, fighting back proud tears.

My child was going to change the world. And I was going to be along for the ride, doing my part. My husband would be relieved to have the extra help with soccer expenses, and I couldn't be happier. I was going to order a margarita tonight at the Mexican restaurant, calories and salt be damned. I felt like celebrating.

I was ready for it. Bring it on.

— MY ROOTS RUN DEEP —
by John F. Allen

CW: This story features racist individuals who use bigoted slurs. John F. Allen is a Black author, and his writing mirrors his own personal experiences.

Mia Harrison took a sip of lemon Moscato and wiggled her toes with excitement. It was Friday evening, and she wasn't grading a stack of exam papers from angsty high school students looking forward to their pending graduations.

Retirement suited her and she was excited to embark on *finding her groove*. It had been five years since Eriq died and left her a widow. And with their daughter away at college, she had just recently gotten a taste of being an *empty nester*. She found it quite refreshing.

Mia sat in her king size bed, wearing rainbow striped toe-socks, a flannel bathrobe and doo rag covering her silver, twisted locks. Old school R&B from the 60s, 70s, and 80s played softly in the background as she squinted at her laptop screen. It was the only source of light in the room, except the half dozen scented candles burning.

Mia sat down her wineglass and lifted the laptop off her knees. Her arthritis had begun to flare up lately. Bio-Freeze helped, but she'd been so busy working on the grand opening of the Myra Jackson Community Center, named after her great-great-grandmother, she barely had a moment of still time.

The specialized ringtone on her smartphone went off, letting her know her daughter was calling.

Her eyes squinted behind progressive lenses housed in her large, Michael Kors designer frames, as she grabbed her smartphone off the nightstand.

"Hello?"

The cheerful voice of her child responded, "Hey Mommy!"

"Hey Honeybear! How's my favorite Martin University senior doing?" Mia asked.

Leesa Harrison giggled at her mother. "I'm fine. I was calling to remind you that I'm coming home this weekend."

Mia smiled. "Yes, sweetheart I remember. I'm just excited that you've penciled in your mother for one of your spring-break weekends."

"Mommy," Leesa sighed. "You know I'm coming home for the community center grand opening on Monday."

Mia chuckled. "I know Honeybear, I'm just teasing you. Should I expect you to bring Roderick when you come?"

"Of course," Leesa said, her smile bright enough to hear through the phone. "And when you meet his father, please be nice."

"Harrumph. Child, when haven't I been nice? It's not my fault that you decided to date the son of the center's newly revealed benefactor."

"You know I had no idea Mr. Petersen was a contributor to the center, anymore that you did," Leesa chided, sounding as though she was trying to hold back a laugh. "Besides, wouldn't meeting the man be of any interest to you at all?"

Mia held the phone for a brief pause. "I suppose. It's just that this is a family legacy project. The idea that the city denied our bid for making the site a historical landmark, and suddenly, at the last minute, a mystery man invests in the center? It's too much of a coincidence for me."

"I would think that Mayor McGinnis's endorsement and his public track record would ease your mind," Leesa said.

Mia sighed, "I suppose, but I felt much more comfortable when *all* of our contributors were a part of the community and *not* wealthy, white real estate developers."

This time, Leesa was the one to hesitate. "You didn't get any *vibes* on him, did you?" she asked cautiously.

Mia rolled her eyes and harrumphed, "Girl, no! How many times do I need to tell you I don't have ESP?"

She reflected on her daughter's adherence to superstition regarding their family lineage. Mia remembered how it had always seemed as though her grandmother had eyes in the back of her head. She had made the mistake of sharing with Leesa the stories her grandmother told her as a child. About the women in their family having *The Gift*. Mia never put any extra thought into it. To her, they were merely stories told to children and not to be taken seriously. Whenever she might have displayed any extra intuition, she attributed it to being observant. If life had taught her anything, it was to be a realist. She had too many tangible things on her agenda than to put stock in some old *hoodoo* wives' tales handed down from the past.

Leesa sucked her teeth. "Whatever Mommy, I'll take that as a 'no,' and if that's the case, we have to take help wherever we can get it. It's a *brave new world* mother."

"Yeah, that it is," Mia said with a sigh.

"Well, I'll let you get some rest. Monday is a big day, and you have a lot of preparations to make for the ceremony. I love you!" Leesa said.

Mia smiled. "Goodnight, baby. I love you too."

She placed her phone on the nightstand and drank the last of her wine before turning off the light. Besides, rest wasn't for the weary.

Kentucky 1975

Great-Granny sat in her wooden rocking chair as Mia and her younger siblings, Matthew and Carla, sat on the floor surrounding her. Mia stared in rapt attention at her great-grandmother as she spun tales from the life and times of their famous ancestor, Myra Jackson.

A large, oval shaped picture frame hung on the wall in their great-grandmother's living room. It housed the black and white portrait of their infamous ancestor. She was quite striking even as an older woman for the time, as their great-grandmother often recalled from her memories of her mother.

The stories chronicled Jackson's life as a Union scout and spy, who led many other negroes to freedom through the Indiana track of the Underground Railroad during the Civil War.

As Great-Granny spoke, she deftly fondled the silver and wooden talisman hanging from her neck. She fidgeted and twirled the trinket between her spindly fingers, as though by nervous habit. She never failed to utter the words passed down the generations from Myra: "My roots run deep."

Mia remembered the story behind the talisman, told to her when her sister and brother were far too young to remember. Of how it had been brought to America during the Middle Passage, taken from an ancestor by a slave ship captain named Peters.

Over one hundred years later, it found its way back to the bloodline of its true owner...to Myra Jackson.

Mia felt a burning throughout her body, from her head to her toes. As the inferno raged within her, she shot upright in her bed. A waterfall of sweat rolled down her face, neck, chest, and back.

It didn't feel like a hot flash, and she was three years postmenopausal. This was at least ten times more intense. Whatever had come over her was unlike anything she'd ever experienced before. After a few seconds she calmed enough to glance at her nightstand. Glowing red numerals read three thirty-three. Mia made her way to the bathroom and splashed as much cold water on her face as she could.

What the hell is going on with me?

The image of her ancestor's face, remembered from the portrait, flashed in her mind. Myra Jackson's eyes again bored a hole into her soul. Before she knew it, Mia was standing in her attic, staring at an old, large, wooden chest. She remembered that it had been her grandmother's and was passed to her mother, who passed it on to her before she died almost ten years ago.

Why was she here?

A powerful urge burned inside of her. The fire from when she awoke flared up even more intensely than before. Mia crumpled to her knees as invisible flames engulfed her. She stifled a scream as she wept.

A soft voice whispered in her ear, *"It's your destiny child. The sacred fetish beckons you. Accept your birthright."*

She had to open the chest.

Her trembling hands lifted the lid, and her eyes saw a glint of metal in the dim light. Mia reached into the chest and pulled out a silver and wooden talisman, partially hidden beneath a menagerie of old photographs, post cards, papers, and ceramic figures.

It was her great-grandmother's necklace. Myra Jackson's necklace.

The talisman tingled in her hands and emitted a light glow.

As a child, she and her siblings weren't allowed to touch it. Her mother refused to buy into her grandmother's stories and had packed it away without a second thought...but now, Mia believed.

She eased the talisman around her neck and the burning she felt immediately disappeared. Suddenly, she felt dizzy and lethargic. Mia made her way back to her bedroom and fell across her bed as her vision faded to black.

It was nearly twelve hours later when Mia stirred from her slumber. As she groggily rose into a seated position on her bed, she reached for her cell phone and looked at the time and date on its display.

What the hell? she thought.

It was almost 3 p.m. Saturday afternoon. She must have been more tired than she thought, and she'd had one hell of a dream. Mia supposed her body needed the rest and forced her to take it, even though her mind may have had other plans. She felt almost twenty years younger, with an increase in clarity. The air smelled clearer, the sounds of cars driving by outside louder, and her energy was noticeably increased.

Leesa must've spoken that superstitious, mumbo-jumbo into her mind last night for her to dream about her great-grandmother's talisman. As Mia turned, a glint of silver caught her peripheral vision, and she looked down to see the talisman around her neck. Her eyes widened and her breath caught in her throat.

Apparently, it wasn't a dream after all.

Mia got showered and dressed before heading to run some errands around town. As she closed her front door and made her way to the car, she noticed her next-door neighbor, Mrs. Dillard, checking her mailbox.

"Good afternoon Mrs. Dillard," Mia said with a smile and a wave.

The older woman looked up and smiled. "Hello, dear. Getting a late start today?"

Mia grinned. "Well, it's Saturday."

"Harrumph, just like some lazy ass colored woman to sleep in all day and make a joke about it."

Mia stopped in her tracks. "Excuse me, what did you say?"

Mrs. Dillard's smile remained unchanged. "Why nothing, dear. I didn't say a word."

Mia fought the frown she knew had formed on her face.

"Stupid ass black bitch."

Mia opened her mouth to speak but stopped when she realized that her neighbor's mouth had remained closed when Mia heard the words. She scrambled to get into her car and sit down.

What the hell is going on? Mia thought.

A sparkle of light from the talisman caught her eye, and she looked back at Mrs. Dillard, who had already made her way into her house. She never would've guessed that her neighbor's racism was so blatant, at least in her mind.

How did she hear Mrs. Dillard's thoughts?

Whatever was going on, she wasn't going to figure it out without some insight, and she knew just the person to call.

Benny's Bistro on Mass Ave had a mild mid-afternoon crowd for a Saturday. This was likely because of the Earth, Wind & Fire concert starting in a few hours at the Gainbridge Fieldhouse.

Mia sat at in a corner booth near the front window, sipping a white mocha latte and nibbling on a slice of cherry-lemon pound-cake. She was usually a bit more conservative with her sugar intake but today, *diabetes be damned.*

She and Benny had been good friends from high school, and it was her late husband Eriq who developed the commercial property where his bistro was located almost thirty years ago, shortly after college graduation. Eriq and Benny became fast friends, so much so that Benny took Eriq's death almost as hard as Mia had.

"Hey, Mia," a baritone voice cried out from the back of the bistro. Benny Perez flashed a wide grin as he approached. His pecan-hued skin, which seemed to almost glow, along with his black wavy hair, bespoke of his Puerto Rican heritage.

"Hey, Benny," Mia said, returning his grin.

Benny sat across from her. "So, what brings you to my *fine establishment* today? Are you heading down to the concert later?"

"Naw, I'm actually meeting Devlin," Mia said.

Benny smirked. "You mean that nerdy dude that followed you around campus like a *puppy dog* in college?"

Mia chuckled. "Seriously Benny? He wasn't all that bad. Besides, we were always just friends."

"So, what's the occasion now?"

Mia took a sip of her latte.

"He's helping me with a project Benny, that's it."

Benny leaned back and harrumphed. "Does he know it's *only* a project?"

Mia cut her eyes at Benny and shook her head. She was used to the playful banter from him, but there was some underlying truth to his words. She knew that Devlin had a crush on her in college. He had even asked her to go out on a date once, but she was already seeing Eriq at the time.

"Benny…he's helping me with the Myra Jackson Community Center. It isn't a date, and he knows it. Besides," she said, pausing to look down at her latte, "I'm not really ready for that sort of thing yet."

Benny nodded. "I'm sorry. I was only kidding you know?"

Mia reached across the table and grasped Benny's hand tightly. "I know."

Benny pursed his lips. "I better get going now. I'll tell Alma that I saw you today. She'd be here, but she's off to be with Marcia, shopping for a prom dress."

Mia smiled. "Please give your wife my best."

Benny nodded with a solemn expression as he stood from the booth and walked toward the back of the bistro. Pangs of pain stabbed her gut. She sighed in exasperation and guilt. Mia knew that Benny didn't mean any disrespect. She was sure his teasing was just that. Eriq's absence left a void in both of their lives, for different reasons.

The front door opened, and the attached bell chimed.

Devlin walked through the door wearing a tweed sportscoat, a wool scarf, a maroon polo, blue jeans, and brown loafers. A herringbone newsboy cap sat atop his head, which he removed as he entered, exposing his shiny, mahogany, bald head. He looked every inch the professor he was—department head of African Studies at Martin University and an expert in African antiques.

"Devlin, over here!" Mia called as she waved to him.

He made his way to the booth where Mia sat, removing his coat and hat before he sat across from her.

"Hey there lady," Devlin said with a smile.

Mia smiled back. For the first time since she'd known him, she noticed how his boyish charm forced a feeling of happiness from her.

"Thanks for meeting me on such short notice," Mia said.

Devlin smirked. "No problem. It's a chance to get out of the house and to have lunch with my best friend. What's going on?"

Mia sighed. She lifted the talisman from around her neck and showed it to him. He leaned forward to examine it more closely.

"May I?" he asked.

"Oh sure," Mia replied.

Devlin held it in the palm of his hand and measured its weight. He carefully assessed the craftmanship and materials of the talisman. When finished, he laid it on the table between them. "It's exquisite! I can tell you that it's African in origin and very old. But I'd need more time to determine exactly how old and from where in Africa," Devlin said.

Mia knew she'd come to the right person for answers. "It belonged to my great-great-great-grandmother, Myra Jackson. But that's not the most interesting thing about it."

She took a deep breath and explained to him about her dreams, lost time, and her encounter with her neighbor. Devlin sat patiently with a focused expression on his face.

Silence seemed to stretch on after she finished speaking.

"I know you think I'm crazy," Mia said, with a nervous laugh.

Devlin shook his head. "Not at all. I happen to have a very healthy respect for African mysticism, and I've read stories about a talisman that allowed its owner to see the auras of evil people and hear their thoughts."

He took out his phone. "May I take some pictures of it for research?"

Mia nodded. "Sure."

When Devlin finished, he gently slid the talisman back across the table to Mia.

"Thanks," she said, as she placed the talisman back around her neck. "Are you coming to the grand opening of the center?"

Devlin flashed a sheepish grin. "I will now that I'm invited."

"As if you didn't know you were," Mia teased.

Devlin chuckled. "Then it's a date."

Mia woke up both excited and reserved about the grand opening. She was eager for the center to serve the community and give hope to a city gripped in terror from record gun violence and drug related deaths.

The morning newscast had reported another five shootings overnight, two of which were fatalities, both fifteen years old. That segment was followed by a brief announcement about the center's grand opening, swallowed up and wedged between a story on the increasing rates of COVID-related deaths in the state. None of that had eased her nerves.

She was also a bit apprehensive at meeting Walter Petersen.

According to Leesa, he was an extremely charming and handsome man. Mia had encountered plenty of men with those attributes who were also devious, manipulative, and untrustworthy. Despite never having met the man and knowing his glowing reputation within the real estate community, something nagged at her she couldn't explain. She was almost certain this gut feeling had nothing to do with the talisman and the uncanny abilities it gave her, yet it was undeniable all the same.

Mia knew she didn't have time to dwell on her suspicious thoughts. She quickly jumped in the shower before getting dressed and heading downtown.

Mia walked into the center as the eyes of her guests—community leaders, clergy, and journalists—met her with interest. She wore a canary yellow business suit with royal blue accents and matching pumps. Her silver and black braids were neatly pinned at the top of her head and covered with a large brimmed yellow hat with a blue band. She also wore the talisman, which surprised her by seeming to go well with her ensemble.

"Mother, over here," she heard Leesa's voice shout.

She saw her daughter standing with her boyfriend Roderick, Mayor McGinnis, and a tall, distinguished looking man who Mia knew to be in his early sixties, even though he didn't look a day over fifty. He wore a navy-blue Armani with a pale gray dress shirt, a navy and pink paisley tie, and matching pocket square. His dark hair contained streaks of silver at the temples, which contrasted nicely with his tanned skin.

"Mr. Petersen, I'd like to introduce you to my mother and chairwoman of the Myra Jackson Community Center, Mrs. Mia Harrison," Leesa said.

Mia held out her hand to Petersen, who took it into his and kissed the back. His sapphire eyes bore into her soul as the hair on the back of her neck stood at attention. For a fleeting moment, his eyes glowed with a fiery light and his aura took the form of a hideous figure.

She gasped as she pulled her hand from his and attempted to maintain her composure. Luckily, the adaptive lenses of her eyeglasses hadn't yet readjusted from the sunlight, and they helped to hide her expression.

"Hello," Mia stammered.

Everyone seemed to ignore any unnatural behavior she had exhibited and smiled at her.

"I must say, you're a stunning figure Mrs. Harrison," Petersen said, with a sly stare.

Mia could feel the gooseflesh rise on her arms as a light sheen of perspiration formed on her forehead.

"Thank you, Mr. Petersen," she managed.

"We were just discussing the wonderful architecture of the building when you arrived, Mia," the mayor said. "Mr. Petersen was also telling us how he'd like to say a few words today, if you're okay with that."

Mia swallowed before she spoke. "I suppose that would be fine, considering Mr. Petersen is a major contributor to the center."

After several community leaders and clergy made their speeches, a brief intermission was called, and Mia made her way outside of the auditorium to get a cup of punch from the concession table.

The number of attendees was near capacity for the center, and there was a plethora of black and brown families in the crowd. Her heart lifted at the sight of them as smiles beamed on their faces. Just maybe, all the years of planning and hard work would pay off, and Indianapolis could take a breath of relief and experience even a moment of peace, in the midst of turmoil. First COVID, which resulted in thousands of deaths and widespread job losses, then increased gun violence across the city, most of the victims being black youths... How much more could the community take?

She continued to scan the outer corridor as she noticed a path being cut through the throngs of people. A tall man made his way through the crowd toward her. Mia recognized the face immediately.

"Mia," Devlin called.

"Devlin!" Mia greeted him warmly. "I didn't think you were going to make it. Is everything all right?"

Devlin gave her a wan smile. "No, but it will be. Petersen cannot be trusted."

Mia nodded. "I already know. But what did you find out?"

Thirty minutes later, Petersen took to the stage with a wide grin and roaring applause. When he stood at the podium, he waved at the crowd for quiet. After several moments, the din died, and he began to speak.

"Thank you all. I'm honored to be here and to be a part of this momentous occasion. The grand opening of the Myra Jackson Community Center is the most important event that Indianapolis has seen in recent years."

Mia watched as Petersen's aura shifted and morphed into the demonic image she'd seen earlier. His spoken words began to fade and were replaced by his thoughts.

"These black bastards are so gullible. They don't know that over the course of twenty years, I've secretly bought the inner-city properties they once called home. Once the market was right, I sold the land to developers for several times what I bought them for. And this bitch thinks my investment was charitable, when it was simply money laundered from the Patriots First Organization. In a few years, once these monkeys are complacent, our bank will foreclose on this property and repossess it."

Mia steeled her resolve as he glanced over at her. The bile rose from the pit of her stomach and left a bitter taste in her mouth. Instead of a grimace, she smiled and held her emotions in check.

"The only reason we went along with secretly funding this project was to keep them from proceeding with making this site a historical landmark and keeping us from ever getting possession. Dumping a few hundred thousand into the mayor's lap kept him with the program and eager to run interference when we needed him to."

Mia nodded at his thoughts, while everyone presumed it was at his words. She was simply biding her time.

"And without further ado, I present the chairwoman of the Myra Jackson Community Center, Mrs. Mia Harrison!" Petersen said, with a wide grin.

Mia strutted past Petersen and took her place behind the podium. She scanned the sea of black and brown faces, men and women, young and old, who cheered her with applause and raucous excitement.

"Thank you," Mia said.

She took a deep breath before she spoke again.

"I'm not the person you should be applauding. None of us would be here if it weren't for the heroic actions of my great-great-great-grandmother, Myra Jackson. She led many slaves along the Underground Railroad to freedom, here in our fair city. Her courageous and selfless acts are a beacon of hope, to a community fighting for its life. But while I would like to bask in your applause for her, alas, *my roots run deep*."

Mia looked around the crowd and felt the energy emanating from their souls. She could see the auras of the crowd glowing as intently as their rapt attention to her voice.

Mia cast a sidelong glance at Petersen. "Which is why the truth must prevail and justice be served."

Puzzled expression and murmurs spread throughout the assembly as she continued. "There is an enemy among us, and his name is Walter Petersen."

The din of the crowd rose as Mia steeled her gaze at Petersen. He narrowed his eyes, and his monstrous aura raged around him in a shroud of evil.

"You see, Mr. Petersen isn't who we thought he was. He used his influence to secretly buy real estate in our inner-city neighborhoods for pennies on the dollar and sold the land to rich developers. He forced many of you out of your homes, homes that your parents and grandparents built or struggled to purchase from hostile individuals who fought to keep them away."

Loud gasps and profane language emerged from the assembly. The scorned glares squarely focused on Petersen. He started to move toward Mia, but Devlin stood in his path.

"Don't even think about it," Devlin growled.

Mia pressed on. "See, Petersen sold the land to members of a White Nationalist organization called Patriots First, of which his family, formerly known as the Peters, are founding members. And they wanted it all, including the ground this building was built on. But they knew that because of its notoriety as a hub along the Underground Railroad with ties to my ancestor, it would draw unwanted attention to their true motivations."

As she looked upon the crowd, five men and two women wearing suits, along with a dozen uniformed police officers, entered the auditorium and slowly moved toward the stage.

"When our bid to have this ground declared a historical landmark was denied, thanks to a payoff to Mayor McGinnis, our backs were against the ropes. Yet, Petersen and his cohorts knew that they couldn't sweep in and simply take the land, because local, grassroots community organizations would've thrashed them in the court of public opinion. So, they sent in Petersen to secretly fund the building of the center, with laundered money from Patriots First, only to stage a series of unfortunate accidents. Then our insurance companies, which they secretly own, would deny our claims, and their bank, who secured our loan, would foreclose on the property so they could eventually claim it for themselves."

The assembly became even more raucous and started to surge forward, but the uniformed officers kept them back. Petersen fumed, his tanned skin turning fiery red, and his aura expanding into a demonic maelstrom only Mia could see.

"Lies! This woman is lying! She has absolutely no proof of anything she's said," Petersen spat.

"But oh, that's where you're wrong Petersen. My friend Devlin called in a favor to his cousin, FBI Special Agent Jayson Martin." Mia smirked, reflecting on the conversation with her friend in the courtyard. "Agent Martin's team has been investigating Patriots First. He and his team stumbled upon a connection to your family's past. They also confirmed that Patriots First owns the insurance company and the bank associated with the center. This is a direct conflict of interest, a violation of real estate laws, and fraud."

Petersen glared at Mia, "You nigger bitch, I'll kill you!" he yelled as he rushed toward the podium.

Devlin lunged between them, pushed Petersen back, and punched him in the face. Blood spurted from his nose, which he immediately grabbed.

"That black mother fucker hit me!"

Devlin shook out his right hand in pain as Agent Martin and two of his team came onto the stage and surrounded Petersen.

"Mr. Petersen, you're under arrest for conspiracy to commit fraud and bribing a public official," Martin said.

"Fuck you monkeys! My lawyers will have me out in time for the evening news," Petersen said.

The mayor attempted to ease his way off the stage, but two more of Martin's team stopped him. He stammered excuses and pledged that he would have their jobs, but they ignored him as they read him his rights.

Devlin walked over to Mia, who was wrapped in Leesa's arms, trying to keep from shaking. "Are you okay?"

Mia turned to Devlin. Her back straightened, composure regained and resolve steadfast. She felt her eyes narrow as a smirk slid across her face. "Yes, thanks to you. Can I repay you with a proper date?"

Devlin's expression was of mild shock with a nervous grin. "Sure, I'd like that."

The three of them stood and watched as Petersen and the mayor were escorted off the premises. Roderick stood at the edge of the stage and stared after his father, looking lost. He turned to Leesa helplessly. "I don't know what to say."

Leesa chuckled. "There really isn't anything for you to say. You aren't your father, are you?"

Roderick hung his head. "No." Then he turned back, facing the door the agents had escorted Petersen through. "But he is my father."

Leesa nodded. "Then I suppose you need to go attend to him."

He looked up as though to speak, but Leesa had turned her back to him. Roderick's footstep echoed as he walked out of the assembly and her life.

Agent Martin walked up to Mia and Devlin with a satisfied smirk. "With the evidence we had already and what you gave us, Devlin, those two are facing a long court battle and jail time," Martin said.

He fist-bumped his cousin, nodded at Mia, and followed his team out of the auditorium. The crowd looked to the stage; their eyes begged for answers.

Leesa and Devlin stood to the side and looked to Mia, who nodded and moved to stand behind the podium. She took a deep breath and smiled as she addressed her community.

Three years later...

Mia stood on the balcony of her tri-level home overlooking the Geist Reservoir. She had been there since the predawn light first peeked above the horizon. Birds sang their sweet songs of spring. The scent of the cool breeze off the water tingled her nose and gave her body a quiver.

She sipped her Sumatran blend coffee with three Splenda packets and a splash of cream. The heat from the oversized smiley-face mug generated a pleasant sense of warmth against the chill. Her monogramed terrycloth robe helped, but there was something special about hot coffee in the morning.

Mia smiled at the feelings of comfort and security her wedding gift from her husband brought her. Those thoughts were reenforced by the feel of her husband's arms wrapped around her.

"Good morning gorgeous," Devlin said before he began to place soft kisses on her neck.

"Hmmm," Mia purred. "It's spring break. Shouldn't you be sleeping in?"

Devlin pulled her into him tighter. "I noticed an empty bed and decided to investigate."

"You've found me. Now what?" Mia asked.

Devlin rubbed his hands across her hips. "I'm never letting you go."

Mia smiled. "That sounds great, but I need to go downtown to the center today. We've got a tour stop scheduled with Oprah and Tyler Perry tomorrow, and I've got to make sure everything is in order."

"Ahh...the work of the CEO of the Myra Jackson Community Center is never done."

Mia chuckled. "No, it isn't."

Devlin pulled back Mia's robe to expose her neck; her family talisman gleamed in the light of the morning sun. He gently kissed her as she moaned in ecstasy.

"Mmm...maybe I'll let Leesa know I'll be running a little late," Mia said, as she and Devlin made their way back inside.

Neither of them noticed silken wings beating against the sky and across the water: a beautiful, black butterfly, embodying the message of freedom and faith as sure as the stars.

— IT'S MY NATURE —
A "Monster Hunter Mom" Adventure
by JD Blackrose

Captain Morgan—yes, his real name—called me in when the fourth person vanished while walking in a city-run multi-acre nature preserve.

"Morgan, are you seriously telling me that four people have already died? Why did you wait so long to come see me?"

Morgan wore a black shirt, pants, tie, and a black baseball hat with the police emblem. Each of his shoulders sported two gold bars. "*Suspected* dead," he corrected, "but we aren't sure. We didn't think they were related at first. Two teenagers, one older adult, and a twenty-year-old. They didn't know each other."

I couldn't believe it took the department so long to ask for my help.

"What happened to the kids?"

"After talking with the teens' parents, we surmised that they may have run off. The adults didn't approve of their relationship. Stupid, if you ask me. A kind of *West Side Story* vibe."

I couldn't imagine turning my children away, ever. Morgan and I stood outside on my porch watching my kids play on the lawn. I didn't worry too much about my children's safety within my yard. My wards shocked anyone who came too close to my house with ill intent. Morgan never had any problem because he was a good guy. The witch who'd performed the ritual to create the wards was a giant pain in my patoot though. Lila brimmed with powerful magic, but she also overflowed with powerful attitude.

The police captain gave my youngest, Daniel, the thumbs up when my little guy caught a soft underhand pitch from my daughter, Demi. David, the oldest, coached his younger brother. My husband and I had stopped at three children. It was enough. I had the stretch marks and crow's feet to prove it.

David and Demi were normal kids. They went to school, played with friends, fought with one another. Typical.

Daniel, however, worried me. The kid tended to be in places and do things beyond three-year-old abilities. The vampire blood running through my veins might have passed down to him.

The cupid thing hadn't helped, either.

But that was a different story.

Anyway, it was good to watch him do something normal, like try to catch a softball.

Morgan crossed his arms and rocked back on his heels. "The teens were the first. Then the eighty-six-year-old man, one Mr. Bodhi Singh, took a stroll with his dog. He walked that path every day, but his neighbor thought maybe he'd gotten lost, 'given his age.'"

"With his *dog*? On a path he walked all the time?" I crossed my arms. "Unlikely. The dog would have found its way home all by itself."

Morgan patted his duty belt. "That was my thinking. Also, despite the neighbor's fiddle-faddle, his kids said their dad was sharp as a tack. It's possible he's visiting a friend. He sometimes does that, according to the family, but they can't reach him on his cell phone, or the friend either."

"In other words, the teens could have run off, and the dad might be out of town with a bum cell phone battery and no charger."

Morgan pinched the bridge of his nose. "That's correct."

"But your instincts say otherwise?" He nodded. I picked at a cuticle, thinking. "What about the young woman?"

Morgan removed a small pad of paper from his front shirt pocket. He cleared his throat while he flipped to a page. "The twenty-year-old woman disappeared in the same preserve a week after the teens, two days after the older gentleman. Out jogging, like normal, and poof! Disappeared." He closed the notepad.

I considered the situation, worrying my lower lip. "No deaths that you can prove, but four people have disappeared in the same nature preserve in a single week."

"That about sums it up."

I stared out into the yard. Observing my oldest son helping my youngest hold the baseball mitt made my heart happy. I leaned over the railing and yelled to David. "You're a good teacher, kiddo!" Turning to Morgan, I asked, "Do you have any leads? Anything at all?"

He handed me a plastic bag containing funky green leaves. The darn things stretched out long and thin with tiny curved, sharp edges.

"This looks like a briar mated with a weeping willow."

He snorted. "That's as good any description. Don't touch it. That's when it gets weird."

I held the bag up to the light. "In what way?"

"Touch your finger to the edge of the leaf and it cuts you."

"Okay," I said, still examining the plant. "It's prickly."

"Then it drinks the blood and hums."

I dropped the bag on a patio chair. "Are you kidding me?"

"Nope." Morgan tipped his hat and moseyed down the steps. "That's why I'm talking to you about it, Jess, and not a botanist."

He nodded to me. "Let me know when you've got something to report."

I pinched the bridge of my nose and closed my eyes. I needed to consult a demon.

Murmus, the Night Demon, dropped his black cloak and stomped a hairy foot. "I haven't run over an old person in a while and I'm getting kind of antsy."

"We've discussed this."

"I know, Jess," the Night Demon whined. "But it's my nature."

"Nature, smature," I snapped. "Don't even think it. That's what that is for." I pointed to a copper bracelet encircling his sixth leg. "Remember, I already got a pulse from that once. I get a second pulse and you're banished."

"You said I could live on campus. The community college is the only one that offers night classes."

"Sure, if you want to get a degree in architecture, go ahead," I said agreeably, "but don't kill anyone while doing it."

In the centuries past, Murmus wore armor and rode a gryphon, the crown on his head identifying him as an Earl who ruled legions. In our modern day, he'd ticked off his boss, and now he hid on Earth as a college student. I allowed him to stay in my city because he helped me from time to time when I needed to find a monster on the run.

Shoulders slumped, the demon shoved his crown deep into a drawer. The small dorm room contained a bureau, a tiny closet, and a twin bed. Murmus had a single. I'd arranged that, quietly, since living with a demon could have deleterious effects on a roommate's health.

Turning back to face me, the demon recovered his joie de vivre and shot me a sly wink, his green, slitted eyes sparkling in the light of his desk lamp. "Jess Friedman, monster hunter and mom of three, rescues demon on the lam. Some would say you're going soft."

I crossed my arms and gave him the beady eyeball. "I tolerate you. I didn't rescue you. You lay low and I won't be forced to rat you out. I keep you around for your divination abilities, Murmus. You're useful. The second you stop being useful or become too dangerous for the local populace, you're going back."

The demon rolled his shoulders and sniffed. "I barely touched the guy. One wheel into his hip, that's all. And he's *eighty*. Almost time for him to go anyway. Running people over is so much fun. You should try it."

"He's a respected biochemistry professor, you lout, and he almost fell and broke that hip," I said with a wag of my finger. "I should take your motorcycle away."

"But how would I get to you when you need me?" He held out a protesting hand. "Fine. It's not my fault humans smell so intoxicating, but I'll behave."

I zipped my jacket. Evening weather in Northeastern Ohio had gotten chilly. "You're off the sauce, M. Focus on your studies. No partying."

The demon hung his head. He looked like a normal, dejected human. I had to remind myself he wasn't, so I said, "Back to business. What did you say the plant monster is called again?"

I'd given Murmus the weirdly shaped leaves and he'd crushed them into tiny bits and dropped the pieces into a silver bowl. A little mumbo jumbo later and he'd been able to tell me about the plant.

He waved in the general direction of the bowl. "It's a Jidra. Highly violent, very strong, and carnivorous. It's a human/plant combo and related to the Mandrake."

"Sounds pleasant. It's stationary, right? Can't move?"

"Planted in the ground and not mobile, but don't underestimate it. To kill it, you must slice through its roots. Adults are big."

"How big?"

Murmus shrugged. "If it's started eating people, I'd say at least seven feet."

"That's not too bad."

"You and I have different ideas of 'bad,' then." Murmus fished in his ear with an outstretched pinky. "It survived on small rodents and deer thus far. It's turning to humans and their dogs because it's gotten bigger."

"Now I feel sorry for it. It can't help that it's growing up and needs to fuel itself. Sharks gotta eat. Hawks gotta hunt. Jidra are the same, right?"

Murmus fixed me with a hard look. "Don't be tricked. They're smart, nasty buggers." He pointed at my chest. "Be careful. Remember that you're my meal ticket. It's not just you at risk here."

"Feeling the love, as always." I turned to go. "Remember the rules. Stay sober or get sent over."

Murmus huffed an exasperated breath. "Fiiiiine."

I packed a bag and carried a shovel. The park had been closed to visitors, so there was no one to give me a second look. While the police didn't know exactly where each victim had disappeared, the older man's family mapped out his regular constitutional. That was as good a place as any to start as any.

The shovel weighed heavily on my shoulder, but I trudged along, taking my time, searching for the prickly, blood-sucking leaves. I figured that if any of the victims had struggled, they might have torn off a branch. The man's route extended two miles, so it wasn't a lot of real estate to search, but enough that I needed a clue.

I got one.

Sometimes clues are subtle, but other times, they hit you in the face like a deer head in the middle of a dirt path.

The deer's head had been torn off, not cut, sinew and skin hanging from it like spaghetti off a spoon. Not much bothers me, but I almost vomited at the sight of it—but not the smell. The lack of decomposition odor told me that this was a recent kill.

Instantly on alert, I dropped the bag, opened it so I could reach my tools easily, and peered around for the Jidra.

"Okay, you obnoxious plant, I know you're out there. You can't hide. Show yourself."

A slithering sound came from behind me, and I whirled around. A creeping vine with those sharp-edged, long slim leaves wiggled toward me.

"I don't want to hurt you," I said, backing up. "I understand you have to eat. Predators do that. But the authorities take umbrage when you consume humans. And their pets."

The vine continued toward me, and I hopped to the side.

I reached for my bag, withdrew a fixed-blade tactical knife, removed the sheath, and faced the oncoming vine, knife in my right hand and shovel in my left.

And I completely missed the vine that shot out of the woods behind me and snagged my ankle.

"Damn it!" I yelled, bending at the waist to hack off the vine. I did so, but the one approaching from the front got my right wrist. I slammed the shovel point on it and broke that off, too.

The noon sunshine vanished as a sudden darkness descended on the path. Birds stopped singing. Even the wind died down. I looked up to see a massive green head with wild eyes staring down at me.

"You're bigger than I expected," I said to the Jidra.

"You're smaller than I expected," it growled back. "You're the human's champion? An older woman? What happened to the teenage heroes of yore I've heard about?"

"They grew up, you pompous prick, and watch who you're calling old."

"I'm going to eat you anyway," it said. "I'm a growing boy and I need my protein."

"Not today, stick boy."

The Jidra soared up to its full height. It stood closer to seventeen feet tall, not seven. Damn that demon and his incorrect information. The knife-like leaves hung from the Jidra like a shaggy suit. Underneath the leaves were arms, a torso, and a thick trunk of craggy bark. It released an unspeakable odor as it rose, like a stagnant swamp. Yards upon yards of normal vegetation rose with it. It had burrowed underneath the ground, and as it stood tall, it shredded the root systems of the regular trees and bushes. Dirt rained down on me, getting into my eyes and mouth. I spit it out and blinked rapidly to clear my vision.

It opened its black maw and revealed razor-sharp teeth the same shape as its leaves. Like a villain in old black and white movie, it gnashed its teeth at me and let out a scream. It's rancid breath nearly blew me over, but the volume of that screech is what shocked me. I'd expected a low snarl but got a high-pitched shriek, more akin to a bald eagle, instead.

It lifted its mighty arms and brought them down full force. My knife and shovel were useless against something this size. I stopped, dropped, and rolled to my right, onto the edge of the path, then army-crawled forward as fast as possible, getting out of the range of its initial strike. Its gargantuan fists crashed down only inches from my feet.

I hopped up and ran, but it swept a long arm and scooped me up, wrapping its wooden fingers around my waist. I hung there like Ann Darrow in the original *King Kong* movie. I hacked at the leaves and bark with the knife, but it didn't faze the Jidra.

Visions of my children and my husband flashed through my head. I'd beaten a vampire, a zombie gorilla, and an elf that ate children, but the plant monster was going to get me. I'd let my family down and tarnished my mother's monster-hunting legacy.

All of this flashed through my brain as the Jidra lifted me toward his mouth. It let out a belly laugh and opened wide to chomp off my head.

In desperation, I stuck the shovel between me and its tongue and pushed as hard as my dubious position would let me. It wasn't much, but I cut the roof of its mouth, and a green fluid poured out. The creature released me, and I fell.

I dumped the knife and shovel and snagged a ball of vegetation on the way down to slow my fall. Pulled by my weight, a strip of bark and leaves peeled from the Jidra's body, and I slipped down its side into the thorny, broken underbrush. I bled from numerous cuts and had lost my weapons, but I still had my head, so I considered it a win.

The Jidra fumbled in the scrub for me. I squeezed through foliage, tripping and rolling as I went. I left behind a blood trail any predator could follow.

The monster's heavy fists crunched the ground next to me with the force of an earthquake. The ground crumpled and I fell, again.

I'd escaped its grasp once, but I wouldn't do it a second time. I said a small prayer and squeezed my eyes shut.

And waited for the end to come.

But it didn't. A bark pierced the air, an insistent yap-yap.

I hauled myself to my feet and, limping out of the green tangles of bush, tree, and vine, I staggered back to the path. Up above me, the Jidra stood stock still.

An elderly man approached with a Pomeranian on a leash. He pointed a finger at the Jidra. "You promised!" The man had white hair and a stooped frame. He wore brown suit pants, a white button-down, and a Mr. Rogers's navy-blue sweater.

The Jidra shrugged. "Sorry old man. It's my nature."

The Pomeranian kept barking.

"Enough, Atlas," said the man to the dog.

Blood continued flowing from my wounds, so with careful movements, I inched to my bag and removed a medical kit. I began cleaning and taping the worst of the cuts.

"I'm so sorry he got out of control," the man said.

I hazarded a guess. "Mr. Bodhi Singh?"

He bowed. "At your service."

"Mr. Singh, you planted the Jidra?"

He sighed and nodded. "I brought him home from India. I had to smuggle him in, you know. He was barely a seedling. Adorable."

"You understand that Jidra are humanoid meat-eating plants? And by meat, I mean they eat people."

Mr. Singh shrugged. "A lot of monsters do that."

"Which is why we call them monsters."

"You eat plants," Mr. Singh argued.

It was hard to come back from that, but I countered with, "Yes, but they aren't sentient." I hesitated. "At least as far as I know."

Mr. Singh bent to pet Atlas. "The Jidra are related to the Mandrake."

"That's what my research said, too." I bandaged the last of my injuries.

"People don't appreciate them."

"I understand that the Jidra are rare, but what do you want to do about your pet here? It can't stay. We thought it had killed you and Atlas, but obviously not." I rubbed my face. "It tried to kill me, and it got two teenagers and a jogger."

"Him, not it." Mr. Singh let Atlas have a long lead and the dog ambled over to me. The canine sniffed my feet, and I gave him some good skritches under the chin. The Jidra grumbled above me, shifting with impatience. "And I was just out of town and forgot to charge my phone."

"But he did kill the teenagers and woman, right?"

"Yes," Mr. Singh said, on a sigh. "He did."

His dog licked my fingers.

"Atlas, be polite," Mr. Singh admonished.

"Oh, he's being polite—"

Mr. Singh used his dog as an excuse to crouch near me. "You have to get to his roots," he whispered. "I'll distract him while you go for it." His voice hitched. "He's got a single, thick root right at his trunk's center. You'll have to cut through that."

He didn't give me a chance to respond but stood up and started talking to his pet. "Remember when I brought you home, Jidra?"

The plant swept an arm down into the foliage and caught a pigeon. It shoved it into its mouth and chewed. It spit out feathers as it said, "Oh, I love this story. This is the story of the day we met. My gotcha day."

"That's right. I planted you in a small pot."

"Your uncle gave me to you. I was so happy to have a home."

Moving efficiently, I put my bag on my back and snuck off back into the woods.

"Wait. Where's she going?" the Jidra asked.

"She's leaving. Don't worry about her. Let's tell the story," Mr. Singh said. Despite his age, he sank gracefully on the ground and petted Atlas.

"You put me in a bag. I didn't like it because it was dark, and I couldn't see the sun."

"Right, but I told you you'd see the sun soon."

"That I had to be patient." The Jidra bent and rocked back and forth with the memory.

I crept closer to the Jidra's trunk and placed the bag on an old stump. I removed my hatchet, a magic one that I'd purloined from a local museum. It liked me, and if I dropped it, it came back on its own.

Mr. Singh kept talking to the monster plant, like a parent telling a child his favorite bedtime story. I swallowed hard and focused on what had to be done.

"I kept you in that lovely hanging planter with the sunflower on it? Do you recall?"

"Yes!" said the Jidra. "I loved it, but I got too big for it quickly because you fed me mice."

"You remember everything. I'm so proud." Mr. Singh's soothing voice continued the tale. "Remember the day you caught your first squirrel?"

Speaking of squirrels must have reminded the Jidra how good they tasted because it knocked one off a telephone wire directly into its mouth. "But people are so much better. These squirrels are hardly a snack anymore. People are yummy."

"What about deer? Do you recall when you completed your first deer hunt?"

The Jidra's voice lit up, happy at the recollection. "It was the first time I wasn't hungry in so long. But they don't come here anymore. They're afraid of me."

I tip-toed right next to the trunk, and with my heart in my mouth, swung the hatchet directly into the body of the tree. The hatchet sang with triumph as it cut through the bark and directly into its heartwood.

The Jidra shrieked that high-pitched scream and swung its enormous arm down along its side. I twirled out of its way and struck again. The hatchet flew true and the Jidra's trunk cracked. The Jidra listed to its side.

"Father!" it cried. "Why?"

Mr. Singh stood in the center of the path and looked up at the plant. "I'm sorry, my son." He sobbed. "I'm so sorry."

Wanting to end this quickly, I put my all into it and chopped through the main root.

The Jidra whimpered as he crumpled, reaching out for Mr. Singh, who caught his hand, ignoring the leaves' sting. Mr. Singh's red blood joined the Jidra's green blood, mixing with their tears as the Jidra died.

That night I held my children close and crooned their favorite lullabies and read them their favorite stories.

Daniel hugged me extra tight and pointed to my forehead and then my mouth.

"Yes, you perceptive little boy." I kissed his cheek. "Children, let me tell you a new story. It starts with a plant who grew bigger than this house. A man loved it very much. He could see the plant's beauty even when others could not."

"What happened to it, Mama?" asked Desi.

I told them the ending I wished had happened.

"When it got too big to stay where it was, the man carefully dug it up and replanted it in a forest with other trees of its kind."

"And it lived happily ever after, Mom?" asked David.

What could I do? I lied.

"Yes, David. It lived happily ever after."

Jess Friedman is a Jewish, suburban, monster hunter mom working for the Holy Roman Catholic Church. Read about her adventures in The Devil's Been Busy, published by Falstaff Books.

— TRUTHTELLER —
by Linda Robertson

Author's note: *I have borrowed from history to create realism in this story. Some details have been purposely maintained while others have been purposely skewed and/or altered. Please, dear reader, accept the story as a work of fiction and without an expectation of historical facts.*

1891 April 30 Saturday

Nearing the only intersection in town, Lydia Mae Thompson glanced westward. The sun hung on the horizon like an egg yolk peeking around the pan lid. It hadn't rained in a week. Scant few drops had fallen this whole month. Every wispy breeze filled the air with dust.

She turned east toward the church.

It was colder than usual, too. Even so, sweat beaded on her brow and itched under her pinned-up hair. The lady-fever started at the backs of her knees, traveled up her spine and over her scalp. This sensation groped her often and for no obvious reason. Sometimes, though, when tense, it bushwhacked her.

Like now.

She would have worn a thinner dress if she had any that fit. The fevers steadily thickened her. At forty-four, half of her brown curls had gone silver. She blamed the fevers for that, too. If pressed, she could name many other reasons for the prematurity, but she didn't dare give such words voice.

A thinner dress wouldn't have helped anyway. The fevers burned just as hot when she wore only her nightgown.

Besides, if Patience, the preacher's wife, caught her wearing unseasonable clothes, she'd do more than sneer from the upper window. Patience regarded Lydia's saloon as an enemy, so the old crone would've disparaged Lydia to the preacher. Then tomorrow's sermon would be peppered with a rant about the Whore of Babylon. Again.

The pair always took Sunday dinner at some churchgoer's home, then came to stand in the saloon doorway on their way back to the parsonage. They never entered, but the preacher harangued them with threats of hellfire and brimstone, recapped the sermon, then spoke a berating prayer for their wicked souls.

All the while, Patience would glare, like she did now from the top window.

Chin level, Lydia walked past the church and strolled along the cemetery fence. Those regular tithers who bequeathed a sum to the church laid within the picket boundary, enjoying the privilege of eternal rest in blessed ground. All others received burial outside the fence.

The sun had gone when Lydia reached the graves at the far corner—the area reserved for pariah. She halted before the markers with a lump wedged in her throat. She surveyed the distance as if her heart would rather be there than here.

A hundred yards north, the twisting and fast-flowing Neosho River rounded a sharp bend, and a shallow pool formed. The lack of rain had the river down. The pool was mostly dry, but the current looked healthy.

When the lump dissipated and her words sat ready on her tongue, she read the chiseled names and dates.

Nettie Ann Thompson	Kit David Thompson
December 9, 1824	March 3, 1811
September 27, 1861	April 30, 1861

"Been thirty years, father." Tears burned, hot as the fever. She let them fall but resented the tightness in her throat. The words were important. She had a truth to tell, and the saying needed to be unmistakable.

Grief swelled. Her silence lingered.

Her fingers slipped into the folds of her skirt. A smooth, smoky crystal weighted her pocket. The thick crystal filled her palm like a good knife handle. Each of the six sides had a smooth face. One end tapered to a point. The other had many short, ragged peaks. Touching it brought reassurance, but it didn't diffuse sorrow.

Darkness settled before clarity returned to her voice.

"I am sorry, papa. I didn't mean to—"

Movement by the river caught her eye. A woman stumbled along the pool. Waterlogged skirts clung to her legs. She fell and didn't rise.

Lydia hurried to her. A slight thing, no more than sixteen, she didn't rouse when prompted or when Lydia performed a quick search for wounds. She was, however, pale, cold as ice, and breathing shallow.

How long had she been in the river?

The church was dark. The preacher and Patience arose with the sun and crawled into their beds when it sank. Lydia searched along the backs of the nearest buildings. None of them were lit, either. Except for the undertaker.

She smoothed back the girl's dark, wet hair, watching her chest rise for a few shallow breaths. They were getting deeper. "I don't think we'll need *him*."

Instead of returning to the street, Lydia cut diagonally across the land and straight to the small pasture on the back of her saloon, half dragging and half carrying the limp dishrag of a girl. When they neared the barn, Hooch, her buckskin stallion, nickered a warning from inside. It was almost a growl.

"It's me," she said.

Hooch repeated the sound, this time a higher, curious note.

Inside, Lydia maneuvered the girl into her private room. She laid the girl on the floor, removed the girl's boots and wet dress, then hefted her onto the bed.

She lit the lamp and checked the girl over again. She found no pox, snakebites, or wounds, but the girl's hands and feet had no warmth at all. Lydia wrapped the bed linens around the girl, added two quilts, and stoked the fire in the hearth before heading into the saloon via the kitchen doors.

Beyond, it sounded like Henry, the young bartender, had the crowd well in hand. She smiled to herself. He'd come looking for work last winter. She trusted him. Plus, the townsfolk liked him more than they liked her.

She kindled the stove and set water on to warm. When ready, she filled some canning jars, screwed the lids tight. As she transferred them into a bucket, Henry came in.

"I thought I heard you in here." He noted the jars. "Are you sick, ma'am?"

Letting him think she was ill would give her time to tend the girl. Lying to him would have a consequence, but even *that* might be a good thing. She transferred the bucket to one arm and pushed her free hand into her pocket. Gripping the crystal, she said, "I am feeling unwell."

The stone vibrated as it absorbed her lie and diffused it into the ground. Lightning flashed beyond the windows. A loud crack split the night. The bar fell silent, but the horses tethered out front gave shrill and startled neighs. Thunder rumbled like an approaching stampede.

"Can you tend the bar alone tonight, Henry?"

"I'll manage. Should I send for the doc?"

"No."

His eyes moved about her face. "Your marks are darker than usual."

The words of his unexpected statement echoed in her ears like tinkling bells resounding with truth.

Lydia nodded reassuringly and returned to her rooms. Already the wind howled and whistled through cracks in the window. The much-needed rain was coming.

She placed the jars between the covers near the girl's hands and feet. She massaged each cold limb in turn. After a few rounds of this, the girl's color improved and she breathed deeper, easier.

Assured the girl would recover, Lydia stepped to the vanity with Henry's words in mind. Studying herself in the dusty mirror, she stroked her cheeks.

Lightning flashed and boomed like the bolt had landed right outside the window, but she didn't flinch. She'd felt it coming.

Lines like feathers or willow fronds trailed from her temples across her cheekbones and down to her lips. Other lines curled around her ears. Thicker lines trailed down her throat.

They *were* darker than usual.

Shortly before midnight, Bill Rudabaugh returned home with two friends. As the trio unsaddled their horses in the barn, Bill considered how to tell his father the news. As a child, the two words he'd heard most were, "Go away." At least the words implied he'd been seen.

He remembered when, a decade ago, his mother served cake after dinner.

His father scowled. "This is no holiday. Why would you waste the sugar?"

"A better question is why would I waste my life in this nowhere town with an oblivious, indifferent sot like you?" She left the room, weeping.

"It's my birthday," Bill said.

His father faced him then and squinted like he didn't recognize him. "How old?"

"Twelve, sir."

"You seem small for twelve."

Not long after, his friend Virgil burned his arm on the potbelly stove. Bill saw Virgil's pa dote on him. Bill reasoned that if he got hurt, his father would do the same. He'd screwed up his nerve and branded his own arm, convinced his father would tend him after the "accident."

His father never even checked on him. Bill had felt more invisible than ever.

But he wouldn't be invisible after tonight.

For as long as he could remember, his eccentric father had been obsessed with the land around the town of Parsons. He spent his days on horseback, his evenings creating maps. Bill never understood how this held his father's attention day after day, year after year.

Recently, though, he developed a theory: the Union Pacific Railway was coming west. If it ran through Parsons, then people and businesses would follow. They'd all need property. The demand would cause land values to soar.

This notion stemmed from chaotic days in January, when his father sought to purchase a hundred acres south of town. "Levi's selling cheap. Now's the time."

"It's cheap because it's worthless!" his mother fumed. A week later, she'd moved to Topeka, taking what she called "her family fortune" with her.

She'd asked Bill to accompany her, citing the likelihood of finding a wife there.

Though tempted, he'd declined. He reasoned that in her absence his father would engage with him. He hadn't.

As Bill led his friends toward the house, he recalled being in the barn early one morning last week. His father came and saddled a horse. Bill noticed lanterns in the saddlebags and asked where he was going.

"To explore Levi's mine south of town."

Three years back, the city founder, Levi Parson, invested in mining the caves on his property. When two shafts collapsed, he'd boarded up the opening and sent the miners away. Levi said any gold down there could stay there. They were lucky no one perished.

"It's not safe there, father," Bill said.
"You sound like a woman." His father mounted the horse.
"How'd you get Levi's permission?"
"Pliny's ointment."

Bill understood that meant his father paid Levi. He'd watched his father ride away then, saddened to think the man was so desperate to own the land that he'd willingly risk mining in a dangerous shaft.

Today, a unique opportunity had presented itself. It came with a terrible deed—killing a few innocent people. But it could fix everything.

Concerned for his father's safety and eager to allay his desperation, Bill had seized the opportunity.

He glanced at his friends, carrying the small, heavy chest.

Even split three ways, Bill's share of the contents would ensure his father could buy all the land he wanted. There'd be enough to keep applying "ointment" and ensure the Union Pacific station came to Parsons instead of Independence or Coffeyville.

After this, he'll not only see me, he'll have to love me.

Unsurprisingly, Oberon Rudabaugh sat at his desk, pen in hand, scratching on a paper. Pages littered the desktop and the floor. Dirty dishes stacked precariously on the side table.

"You're home late." Oberon didn't look up.

Feeling smug, Bill said, "I know," and rested his hip on the desk edge. He wanted his father to see this grin on his face.

Oberon's eyes flicked to Bill's hip, but not up. "You're also wet."

"I am. Ask me why."

Instead, Oberon said, "Off," and kept writing. "That storm catch you?"

Bill didn't stand. "No, sir." He realized his father was writing, not drawing a map.

"I smell whisky. You were at Boudro's."

"We had reason to celebrate."

"Will you be too hung over to collect something from the livery inn tomorrow morning?"

"No. I'll gladly fetch your package." Bill tried another tactic. "You know that French thing you quote at me a lot? There is no opportunity which comes again?"

"Il n'est chance qui ne retourne."

"Yeah that."

Oberon finished the sentence, stabbed a period at the end, and ceremoniously set down his pen. Sitting up straight, he scowled as he finally looked at Bill. "Off!"

Still grinning, Bill leaned across the desk. "I discovered an opportunity and took it."

Leaning back, Oberon folded his hands across his middle. The sapphire ring on his index finger caught the lamplight. "What opportunity, exactly?"

"Virgil! Leroy! Bring it in." Bill watched his father's face as the chest came into view. Oberon's expression filled with distaste as he glanced from the chest to the desk to Bill.

Standing, Bill hurriedly shuffled pages together to make room as his friends hefted the chest onto the desk. Attempting to straighten the pages he held, Bill realized they were all the same. Familiar letters grouped in ways that only hinted at words he knew.

It was French. Maybe Latin.

He scanned the fallen pages. More copies.

As planned, Virgil and Leroy stepped back to wait. Bill had wanted to be the one to open the chest, but his glee faded. "Father, what is all this?" He shook the papers in his hand.

"Manifestation, William. One must convince the mind that what one wants to make real already exists. There are better ways, but for now, what is available to me is this."

Looking closer at the topmost page, Bill saw *terra* repeated many times. *Land.*

The mention of manifestation and the use of Latin meant this nonsense had roots in his father's correspondences with London spiritualists and mediums, with Marie Laveau in New Orleans, and with Paschal Randolph, that Rosicrucian fellow in San Francisco.

He squinted at his father, questioning if he knew this man at all.

"Are you going to show me what's inside the chest, William? Or are you waiting to see if it leaks on my desk?"

Bill jerked the chest open. Gold coins gleamed in the lamplight. "We heard a bank man was on a stagecoach coming through.

Heard he wasn't on holiday. Heard he was carrying gold to establish a bank and start the incorporation of Cedar Vale."

His father looked him right in the eye. Bill's chest swelled.

"A stagecoach from where?"

Bill choked. "This is thousands of dollars in new coins. You can melt it down and say you mined it south of town. You can buy the land, father! Where the wagon rolled in from doesn't matter."

"It matters more than you can imagine. Was it from Kansas City, Fort Scott, or Fayetteville?"

If this doesn't please him, there's nothing that can. "Fort Scott."

Oberon stood. "You two. Get out."

At those words, Bill's stomach knotted.

"But our shares—" Leroy said.

"You'll get it," Bill said, teeth grinding.

When they had gone, Oberon turned his back. "What became of the passengers?"

"They're dead."

Oberon's hands clenched, knuckles popping. "If you've ruined the Fate I put in motion, boy, there'll be Hell to pay."

1891 April 31 Sunday

The cock's crow woke Lydia. She'd slept in the chair. The storm roused her several times, but blessed sleep always returned. Now, heat simmered at the backs of her knees and rose to her scalp again.

Once a lady-fever set in, there'd be no return to slumber.

She sat up, hissing as neck muscles struggled to loosen and move. She'd taken her hair down last night, so she pushed thick curls aside and rubbed the achy spot. Doing so, she checked the bed. The woman had hauled a quilt corner around her head like a hood, and she peered out from the fabric cocoon, brown eyes steady but wary.

"Did you sleep well?" When the girl did not answer, Lydia stood, stretched out the stiffness, and hobbled toward the chamber pot. Afterward, she fetched an older dress from her closet. She'd never squeeze into this one again, but it would fit the girl. She draped it over the chair.

"I'm going to make breakfast. I'll be back soon."

She prepared eggs and bacon and cut slices of bread. When she returned, the girl had dressed, drawn back the lone curtain, and was making up the bed. The canning jars sat on the vanity.

Lydia slid the tray onto the small round table. "Come. Eat with me."

The girl came eagerly, but as she neared her steps abruptly slowed. Unsurprised by the girl's stare, Lydia said, "Lightning struck me as a child. The lines never faded. What's your name?"

"Esther Jennet Hughes." She sat across from Lydia, expression sober. "I am quite grateful for your help." Her words had the lilt and accents of British folk. That didn't matter. The joyful chime of truth resounding in Lydia's ears, however, did.

"You're welcome, Miss Hughes. Your eggs are getting cold."

"Please call me Jenn." She lifted the fork. "And you?"

"Lydia Thompson. These rooms attach to my saloon." When their plates were empty, she asked more. "Why are you so far from home?"

Jenn's cheeks flushed. A pained expression knit her brows. "I am far from home, aren't I?" Her nose and eyes reddened. "I came to marry. My father and brothers died in March last year. They were miners at Morfa Colliery in Port Talbot. A gas explosion killed them and nearly a hundred others. My mother didn't last the winter. I was alone and afraid. I wanted to matter to someone. I signed with an agency and corresponded with a few gentlemen.

William's letters made me feel important. He sent funds for both travel and a proper wedding dress."

"Where were you headed?"

"Parsons."

Lydia smiled. "This is Oswego. Parsons is ten miles northwest. If you're up to it, I'll have you there by sundown."

The statement brought no relief to Jenn's features. Her rigid posture crumbled, and she slumped against the chair. Her jaw trembled. Tears slid down her cheeks.

"I mustn't go. Not now."

"I don't understand."

Jenn hesitated. "Thieves shot the stagecoach driver from a distance."

"What?" Lydia grasped Jenn's hand. "Is that how you ended up in the river?"

Jenn nodded. "The team ran wild and left the road. Men with covered faces raced their horses alongside. My seat was in the back row. The man reached out for the break lever or the grip on the driver's box. A cattle brand scarred his forearm. XII in a circle. I knew the driver was gone. I knew the team would tire eventually," she sniffled, "but I kept foolishly believing we would get away."

"What happened?"

"The team charged into the river. The stagecoach slowed so fast it threw me against the seats ahead of me. I fell to the carriage floor. I heard shouts and splashes. Bullets pecked holes all around. The man seated in front of me fell to the floor. Under the seats, we locked eyes; then he was dead. Everything was so loud. The horses screamed. The people in the coach screamed. Guns cracked like thunder. The coach jerked and bounced. Water rushed under the doors. The woman I'd sat beside opened her door. A bullet splintered the door in a spray of red, then she fell, tearing the door away."

Jenn covered her face with her hands.

Lydia fetched a handkerchief from a drawer and gave it to her. Jenn dried her eyes. "When I heard the thieves say 'get the chest' I realized how quiet it had become. Everyone was dead. They climbed onto the coach. Their weight made it sink more. Water rose and the current pulled at me. I took a deep breath and maneuvered myself out. I stayed face down, praying they thought me already dead and didn't shoot me."

"That was very clever," Lydia whispered.

"Clever," Jenn repeated, unimpressed. "The current swept me into rapids. The river threw me like a doll. I fought to keep my head up for what seemed like hours before I escaped the current and crawled ashore."

Lydia knew every word of this sad tale was true. She clasped Jenn's hand again. "Why must you not go on to Parsons, though?"

Jenn wiped away fresh tears. "The man at the agency gave me a package to deliver to my father-in-law. He said if I opened it or lost it, I'd be better off dead." She swallowed. "It was small and in my purse. That warning ensured I kept it close. I had it with me for a while, but I lost it in the river." Jenn's features pinched up and she sobbed. "My future depended on delivering that package. Without it, I cannot go to Parsons. I'll never meet my sweet William."

Detecting not one syllable of a lie, but suspicious of the delivery arrangement, Lydia felt intrigued. "I will help you." The words slipped out before she even considered them, as if old regrets and years of diligent consideration hadn't taught her a damn thing.

Another lady-fever swept up her back.

Bill sat astride his horse by the river with a rope attached to the saddle horn. He'd tied the other end around Virgil, who'd waded into the river swollen with storm water. The stagecoach had completely disappeared under the surface.

Leroy paced the water's edge.

Bill still couldn't believe what his father had told him.

"I purchased a rare power stone from Miss Claire de la Voyante, a Spanish mystic and London sensation. I've been studying the research on these stones. For some, they provide astounding abilities."

"Sounds like a fairy tale."

Oberon moved as if to shoo a fly, but his strike knocked Bill across the room.

When Bill could sit up, his father wiggled the fingers of the hand bearing the big ring. "Do not doubt my research, boy. I need the darkened stone."

Bill rubbed his jaw. No wonder the gold meant nothing. His father had found something more powerful than wealth. He stood.

"Miss de la Voyante refused to risk the safety of such a valuable item in the post, but she required a ridiculous sum to cover the cost of delivering it. So, using your name, I corresponded with an agency for mail-order brides and arranged for a Miss Jenn Hughes to deliver the stone, albeit unknowingly." He smiled. "Steerage passage for one poor girl is little more than the post."

"Why would the mystic part with it?"

Oberon wiggled the ring again and raised his brows.

Bill's toes curled in his wet socks. Focused on all the gold represented, he'd given little thought to the lives he'd ended. Hearing a young woman had traveled across the ocean believing she'd be marrying him, however, and knowing that one of his bullets probably took her life, a cold shame overcame him. He gripped the desk edge to steady himself. "The livery. I was to collect her."

"Indeed. My letters ensured she'd cast smitten eyes upon you. It would have been enough for you to accept the arrangement. This is just as well... so long as you find the stone."

The invitation to move to Topeka had tempted Bill. There were few women here. Maybe a woman's love would've made up for what his father denied him.

Considering his parents' relationship, though, maybe love was a myth.

Virgil surfaced and pulled himself back to shore using the rope. "They're all still there, except that one that floated off while we got the chest." He tossed three purses to Leroy.

"It'd be wrapped in paper. Sealed with wax," Bill said.

Leroy transferred a few coins to his pocket, but ultimately dropped each purse back to the embankment. "Nothin'."

"Get the suitcases," Bill said.

Virgil huffed but waded back into the river.

While Jenn rested, Lydia donned her boots and set about her chores, first of which would be tending to her horse. When her door shut, Henry called from the saloon. "I fed Hooch already."

Surprised, Lydia passed through the kitchen and found Henry wiping spots off clean glasses at the bar. "Thank you."

"I put him out to pasture after," Henry said. "If you'd like, I could feed him every morning."

"Did you give him two scoops of grain?"

Henry nodded.

In her ears, Lydia heard a whisper snarl, "One scoop."

She stomped closer, hands on her hips. "After all these months, you dare to lie to me, and you lie about *that*?"

Henry blinked. "Hooch don't need more. It's spring. He'll graze all day. If you cut back until winter, I reckon you'll save enough to buy that catalog dress you admired."

Heart-warmed that he'd accept a chore to con her into saving money for a new, better-fitting dress, she couldn't stay angry. Besides, he spoke truly now. "Do you really think a few oat scoops will equal that tea gown?"

"It might." Henry squinted. "I've seen you call dozens of fellas on their lies. How do you always know when someone ain't truthful?"

"Don't all women know?"

Lydia returned to her rooms and found Jenn dusting items on the dresser top. "You don't have to do that."

"I do. You've been so kind, Ms. Thompson—"

"Please. Call me Lydia." She lifted her dirty clothes basket.

Jenn twisted and untwisted the rag. "The American frontier sounded like a dream. Like a romantic fool, I wanted to find love. I've come so far, but I'm scared to even meet William now..." She sank onto the chair.

Lydia added Jenn's dress to the top of the basket. "And?"

"I want to go home."

Lydia set the basket down.

The girl rushed closer. "Let me cook at your saloon. Please. I'll work hard. Help me save enough to buy passage home."

Lydia heard truth in every word. "Are you a good cook, then?"

"I am. My mother was a baker. I can make many kinds of bread."

"Can you make biscuits?"

"The fluffiest biscuits!"

Lydia wanted to agree straightaway but paying another employee would cost more than she could hope to save reducing Hooch's oats.

If I find her purse, the item inside is surely valuable. Then Jenn would have the choice of going to Parson and meeting William or using it to buy passage home.

But to find the item, Lydia would have to use the power she'd sworn to never use again.

"Will you let me think on it?"

"Of course." Jenn returned to dusting.

When Lydia returned from washing the clothes and hanging them on the line, Jenn asked, "Are these your parents?" She held open the little wooden book from the dresser top.

Realizing she hadn't delivered her message yesterday evening, Lydia sat the empty basket down. Jenn brought her the daguerreotype.

Lydia had forgotten how heavy the little case was, but she remembered well the swatch of velvet on the left and the portrait behind ornate edging on the right.

"This was their wedding day." She handed it back.

"They look as happy as any two people could be." Jenn swooned as she studied it again.

Everyone deserves happiness.

"I will allow you to cook. You can stay in the smallest of the sleeping rooms upstairs."

Jenn beamed.

Lydia dug a pair of pants from the dresser's bottom drawer. She slipped her skirt off and the pants on. "Stay here. I have an errand. When I return, I'll introduce you to my bartender."

Astride Hooch, Lydia rode to the spot where Jenn collapsed. She dismounted and crouched at the river's edge. "Mama, papa, I'm sorry."

She touched the ground and whispered, "I know where the package Jenn carried rests." This was not true, but as she repeated it a light as bright as lightning filled her eyes. She was *making* it true.

A velvet bag, sky blue, edged with fringe and embroidered with little white birds, lay under the water. A heavy white silk cord secured the top shut. The image moved away until she saw, above the water, a stand of trees at the water's edge.

In a blink, the image disappeared. Lydia stood. Warmth dribbled over her lip. She dabbed a handkerchief at her nose and wiped away the blood. The fever burned up from her knees and had sweat beading on her brow before she'd mounted Hooch. They raced north along the river.

Miles away, she spotted the trees. After dismounting, she tied a rope to one of the trees, then waded in. The current pulled her, but her grip on the rope kept her steady. She had to go under to get it, but she knew exactly where to reach to grab hold of that white silken cord.

The purse looked exactly like she knew it would.

What she did not expect was the stone in her pocket thrumming like a heartbeat, or the object in the purse answering with a thrumming of its own.

Long ago, her father had bought a colt and named him Hooch, saying it suited a saloon owner's horse. Lydia walked the colt on a lead rope after lunch every day. Two weeks later, during their walk a sudden storm darkened the sky. Lightning spooked the colt. He reared and jerked the rope from Lydia's hands. The colt ran off. She followed and got lost in the storm.

Being struck hadn't felt like anything.

She awoke later in a cave. A frontiersman sat beside her, chanting. His eyes were closed. He was dirty and he smelled of sweat, but she didn't feel afraid.

The storm continued to rage outside. She scooted closer to the small fire for warmth and realized a cloth wrapped her hand. She could feel a long, smooth stone in her hand. The cloth kept her from letting go.

When finally his chant ended, the frontiersman opened his eyes. He moved to the far side of the little fire. "Do you know the Thunderbird Heloha?"

She shook her head.

"The people of this land taught me, and now I will teach you. Heloha lays eggs that roll around in the clouds. To catch them, her mate, Melatha, flies so fast he creates lightning. The great horned serpent created words with his forked tongue, but men corrupted this gift by telling lies. Now Melatha touched you. He gave you the power of truth. He made you Nanishtahullo."

"I don't understand."

"You can hear the difference between lies and truth." He told her a series of lies and truths until she understood her ears now knew the difference.

"Why's my hand wrapped up?"

"So you don't lose the stone." He leaned closer. "You can ask questions all you like. If you speak, you must tell the truth, for if you lie, there will be consequences. If you must lie...hold the stone. It will take the power of your lie and disperse it. The consequences will not be avoided, but they will strike elsewhere.

"What if I lie without the stone?"

"Hear this, child, and never forget: What is, is. What is not, is not. But what you say...might become."

The next morning, she awoke alone in the cave. Her hand was unbandaged and, if not for the stone in her pocket, she might have thought she'd dreamed the conversation with the frontiersman. Outside, rocks laid in the form of an arrow. She walked that direction.

She hadn't gone far when she spotted carrion birds ahead. Filled with dread, she ran, shouting to scare away the birds. She found Hooch, cold and dead and heavily picked by the birds. Her knees weakened and she cried. Papa had trusted her. Now the colt was dead.

"This can't be. Hooch can't be dead..."

Lightning struck in every direction at the same time. She cowered and covered her ears...until something nipped at her hair.

She hadn't believed the frontiersman, but when she saw Hooch standing before her, she couldn't deny it. She grabbed his lead rope and said, "Let's go home."

She thought nothing of it, until she noted all the dead vultures in their path.

The memory filled her as she stood at the river's edge, her shirt and trousers clinging. Every fiber in her being said throw the purse back in the river. But the pulsing stones said, *Don't.*

Hooch watched her calmly, expectantly. She'd never been afraid of him.

But fear did come, years later, when her mother was dying.

Her papa stepped outside to shed his tears, as he had often done that week. This time, Lydia wrapped both of her hands tightly around her mother's hand. "You're going to live. You aren't sick after all." She said the words over and over, willing them to be true.

Lightning flashed and thunder roared in the distance.

A little later, when she looked for her papa to tell him mama felt better, she found him lying in the field. Dead.

The frontiersman had been right. There were consequences.

Her mother recovered physically, but not mentally. "I don't belong here," she often said. A few months later, Lydia found her hanging in the barn.

The preacher refused to bury her mother next to her father, close to the church.

Lydia had her father exhumed and put her parents together in the far corner. Most townsfolk thought her wicked for doing this. Some even whispered accusations that her scars were evidence of evil. One Sunday evening, from the saloon doors, Patience suggested Lydia's scars brought death to those around her.

Henry had pointed out that both he and Hooch were doing just fine.

But would that be true if there were two stones?

As the water ran from her clothes, Lydia wished her fear would drain away, too. She didn't want to possess this second stone, didn't want to know what it might do, and she didn't want anyone else to have it either.

The warning the agent had given Jenn made sense now. This was a powerful stone. But why would an agent in England have it? Why would they be sending it to Jenn's father-in-law in Parsons?

She pulled the package from the purse and flung the purse back in the river. For now, she'd hide the package. Jenn could work for her and start saving. In the meantime, Lydia could decide what to do.

Hooch nickered as she approached. She stroked his neck to soothe him. He was over thirty. Most horses would've died of old age, but he was as strong and fast as ever. "Can you guess who's getting two scoops of oats every day?" she whispered. Hooch bobbed his head as if he understood. "Good. Let's go home."

Bill and Virgil and Leroy rode along the river, hoping to find the body of the woman who'd floated away. They'd found a wedding dress in one of the suitcases, but the stone hadn't been inside. That meant it was in the woman's purse. "What if she's already in Lake Hudson?"

"Even the storm current isn't that fast," Virgil said.

"What if she sinks?"

"It's more likely she'll get hung up on the branch of a fallen tree or something. Just keep an eye out for blue plaid." Bill wondered if she'd been pretty.

Lydia's new cook made an excellent pan of biscuits. So good in fact, that Lydia got lost in enjoying one with a drizzle of honey and didn't see the trio of men wander in and take a table.

When she did notice them, she hurried to their table. "Hello gentlemen. Have you come for dinner or drinks?"

"Both." The man gestured at her. "What's on your face?"

"Lightning struck me when I was little. Left these marks. You've obviously never been here before. Where are you fellas from?"

"Parsons."

Her heart lurched in her chest and a lady-fever shot up, heating her up to her scalp. "I haven't been there in ages. Would you like the chicken dinner or pork?" She took their orders and strolled into the kitchen, where Henry assisted Jenn. "I need you fill this order, but hold it here until I come back to fetch it?" She paused. "I want you both to stay in this kitchen until I say otherwise."

"What's going on?" Henry asked.

"Will you trust me to explain later?"

He nodded.

By the time she'd served the men their drinks, the pair had filled the plates. Lydia delivered the food to the table. Anticipating their meal, the men had rolled up their sleeves. One had a circled XII brand on his forearm.

Lydia nearly spilled their plates.

A second lady-fever hit her. The last one had barely passed.

Others came in, and Lydia collected the other orders before returning to the kitchen. After giving them to Jenn, the girl passed them to Henry and pulled Lydia aside.

"You're sweating like mad. What's wrong?"

"The men at the first table are from Parsons. One has the brand you described on his arm."

Jenn gasped.

"Will you promise to stay in here?"

Jenn nodded.

Lydia wiped her sleeve over her sweaty brow and returned to the saloon floor. When the men finished, she approached with the bill in hand. "What did you think, gentlemen?"

"Mighty fine biscuits, ma'am."

"Good. Good." She laid the bill down and collected the empty plates. "Will you be telling everyone in Parsons about the fine food here in Oswego?"

"Indeed."

As Lydia turned to leave, he added, "Maybe you can help us with something else, too."

"Perhaps."

"We're looking for a young woman."

Lydia shook her head. "You don't think this is *that* kind of place, do you?"

"You misunderstand. We've been following the river," the man explained. "Just north of here, at the river's edge, we saw some tracks. Looked like someone came out of the river, but that storm made tracking a chore. Have you seen any strangers in town?"

"Have you checked the inn?"

"Of course we did," he snapped. He met her gaze with all the directness of a bull preparing to charge. "The tracks we found came this way."

Despite the fear churning in her stomach, Lydia forced a smile and tilted her head as if thinking. She shifted the dirty dishes to one arm and slipped her hand into her pocket. "I haven't seen any strangers."

Lightning flashed and thunder boomed in the streets. People at the other tables commented loudly, enthusiastic for more rain. When Lydia's attention returned to the men before her, she pulled her hand from her pocket.

The branded man took note of it.

"Is the young woman you're tracking a criminal or something? Should I warn my neighbors be wary?"

"No. No. Nothing like that," the branded man said. "As I understand it, bandits shot a stagecoach driver and the team went wild, ran off the road into the river. The young woman was to be my bride. She wasn't among the dead. She'd come all the way from Wales. I'm just...heartsick over what might have happened to her."

"Oh my." Lydia put her hand on her chest. She hadn't heard any lie in his words, though the voice in her ear corrected *heartsick* to *nervous*. "I certainly wouldn't want to see any young woman forsaken among murderous bandits. Would you like another round?"

"Yeah. And we'd like to know—"

"Hear me, ye sinners!"

Lydia jerked, startled at the shout. She hadn't noticed the preacher and Patience taking their Sunday evening positions blocking the saloon doorway. "Excuse me, gentlemen." She carried the dishes to the kitchen. As the preacher harangued her customers with his sermon recap, she leaned on the sink trying to work this out.

Jenn grasped her arm. "What it is?"

"The man with the brand," Lydia whispered, "is your intended husband, William."

"What?"

Henry came closer. "What's going on, Lydia?"

"Can you get Jenn out of here?"

"Why?"

She had to be careful of her wording, but a question was hard to form. "Isn't my concern enough reason?"

"It's unlike you."

Lydia faced Jenn. "I trust Henry. Can you explain the situation to him?"

Jenn nodded again, and Lydia returned to the saloon. The preacher's eyes were shut tight as he offered a prayer for the wicked souls in their community, but Patience glared at Lydia, who filled a shot glass and lifted it in toast before drinking it in a single gulp.

By the time she'd poured fresh glasses for the men at the first table, the preacher and Patience had left. Lydia set the glasses down and collected the empty ones. "I apologize for the preacher, gentlemen. That round is on the house."

The branded man seized her arm.

"Preacher interrupted me earlier." He stood and glowered down at her as he jerked her a step closer. The other patrons fell silent. The branded man's friends stood, too. They tapped their gun belts. It encouraged the patrons to scurry away. One man stayed near the branded man. The other took a position at the doors.

"There's a dress on the line out back." He looked her up and down and sneered. "It won't fit you. Where is she?"

Lydia couldn't answer truthfully. She struggled for a convincing question answer. "Why do you care what laundry hangs on my line?"

"Because the woman on the stagecoach wore blue plaid."

His grip was beginning to hurt. "Didn't you say you hadn't met her? How would you know what she wore?"

He leaned closer. "I was there," he whispered. Swiftly, he reached for her pocket.

Lydia tried to stop him. The glasses fell and shattered. Fragments skittered across the floor. He held the stone up between them. "Look what I found, boys." He pushed her.

She stumbled and fell on her backside. "You don't want that." Her lie had no guide for disbursement. She felt the sting of a vein pricked open. Warm blood leaked from her nostril.

"According to my father," he said to Lydia, "these stones can change the truth. That blood on your lip means you lied and tried to change my truth. How many lies can you survive?"

"What do you mean *stones*?"

"This one's bigger than my father said it would be. Where's the other one?"

Lydia said nothing. Had the stone protected him from her lie? Or had it been the truth?

He drew his gun and pointed it at her. "Where?"

"You're William, aren't you?"

"Check the kitchen," he told his friend at the table. As the man walked off, he asked Lydia, "Where'd you get this?"

"A frontiersman gave it to me after the lightning struck me." Lydia scooted to lean against the bar. "I don't think it's safe for you or your father to use the stones."

William shrugged. "Gonna find out. My father wants to draw maps and play at being a mystic...but I think...I'm gonna rule the railroad."

Pots and pans clanged in the kitchen. Lydia couldn't be certain if Henry and Jenn had left in time or if the bandit tore up her kitchen out of frustration.

"Do you truly think that's possible?" Lydia asked.

"Why not? Is that goal not big enough?" William held the stone before him. "Maybe I should want to rule the *world* instead. I mean, why not dream big? I have the ultimate power right here in my own hands!"

She drew a breath and whispered to herself, building her will into her words as she shouted, "You don't *have* hands!"

White light flashed before her eyes, like lightning in her brain. She heard the crack of a gun and William screamed. When her vision returned, William was on his knees whimpering. Shriveled nubs of flesh hung from his wrists. His gun and the stone lay on the floor between them.

Blood gushed from her nose. Everything hurt.

The friend who'd been watching the door rushed to William, then spun and aimed his gun at Lydia.

"You all want to leave now," she whispered.

Again, lightning flashed in her mind. She screamed before his bullet pierced her. When she could see, William's friends were carrying him out, eerily silent as her words became truth.

Lydia looked down, surprised to see two bullet holes in her dress. She hadn't felt William's shot find her. *Damn it.*

The kitchen door opened. "Lydia?" Jenn's voice.

"I'm here."

Jenn rushed around the bar and dropped to her knees beside Lydia. "I'll return your favor and take care of you," Jenn said.

"Nothing to take care of come morning." Lydia squeezed Jenn's hand. "You're home. You're standing on a familiar street in Talbot Port...."

A light shone around Jenn, bright like the dawn. The smell of a salty seashore filled the air, then Jenn disappeared.

Lydia was barely aware of Henry coming in and carrying her to her bed. "Will you bring me the stone from the saloon? And the other from behind the oil can in the barn?"

She focused on breathing slowly until he returned and placed them in her hands. He reached toward the bullet wound. "Don't bother."

"Lydia—"

"Will you bury me in the far corner with these stones? One in each hand?"

He nodded. "I will. I'll take care of Hooch, too. And give him two scoops of oats every day."

She heard bells tinkle. "The saloon is yours."

— UTOPIA —
by Vaseem Khan

- 1 -

My name is Robert Sheldon and, once upon a time, I was a prophet. Of sorts.

Don't get me wrong. God didn't speak to me; I never took His word to the masses. I simply made certain predictions about the future. I worked for an investment firm—one of the older ones on Wall Street—and my job was to anticipate movements in the prices of precious metals.

I was good at my work. I made a great deal of money—for myself, my colleagues, and for our clients. I was feted, and for my sins, they called me Magus.

But, for all my ability to read the entrails, to gaze into a crystal ball and chart the course of the future, I never saw *them* coming.

And I never saw *him*.

The man who would save us all.

- 2 -

On the day the Invaders arrived they promised us a utopia.

What we didn't realise then is that utopia meant something totally different on their world. Perhaps we should have. After all, the writer who coined the word did so from the Greek *ou-topos*, meaning: "no place on Earth."

To the Invaders, utopia was to be found in order. In efficiency. In the clean lines and moral geometries of social engineering.

They began by eliminating all borders: geographical, political, economic, social. We became, for the first time in human history, a single species, united by the edicts of our new masters.

All human activity was put under the microscope. The creative arts were banished. Frivolity was outlawed.

The thesis by which we were ordered to live was simple: if an activity did not aid the collective, did not materially progress the human species in some small way, then it was of no value.

How was *progress* defined? In ways we could not fathom.

And then the individual testing began.

Great centres were set up around the globe. Thousands of them. Every man, woman, and child was required to present themselves for "assessment."

What were they assessing?

Everything. Our physical, intellectual, and psychological makeup. The gestalt of our abilities. Our fitness to the grand plan, a plan only they could see.

What happened to those deemed wanting?

It's still difficult to talk about those days. A great wail arose around the world—but it was too late, too ineffectual. After all, in the face of their technological omnipotence, what could we do?

We were powerless and we knew it.

We were ants, bees, enslaved to the hive's masterplan, our identities as individuals erased like patterns drawn on water.

- 3 -

I first met Rohan Das a year after I'd been reassigned.

My wife and child never made it out of the great Re-Ordering. Nandita, to whom my parents had introduced me at a Calcutta garden party and who'd taken years to make up her mind; Rahul, fifteen years old, a soccer-player in a country where cricket was the prevailing religion, a child I'd had too late and whose absence I felt like a hole excavated from the very core of my being.

I'd considered following them into the darkness, but, in the end, courage failed me.

I couldn't die, and so my only choice was to live.

With no stock markets, no individual assets of any form, my talents had been deemed worthy of a role I could not have imagined for myself had I lived another ten lifetimes.

I was sent to the Thar Desert in what had once been known as India and tasked to work on the hardiness of grain yields.

I plotted data points on charts; I monitored outcomes against predictions. In some ways, I was doing the same job I'd excelled at for three decades.

Das was another member of our half-a-dozen-strong unit. A small, slim man in his early sixties, with a head of peppery grey hair and a trim moustache. There was an air of quiet assurance about him that I found by turns comforting and infuriating.

He seemed imperturbable in the face of our plight; an automaton.

We lived together in a communal dwelling on the edge of the Thar, seventy-thousand square miles of scrub, sand, and salt pans.

On the day that everything changed—again—he and I were out together, deep in the desert, checking on a field of hardy durum transplanted from the Arizona lowlands.

A comet streaked across the sky. We looked up and watched it. Instead of curving away or vanishing into nothingness, the object grew, rending the air with its passage, until it became obvious that it was an aircraft, one of the strange, propulsion-free vessels the Invaders used to move around in, an egg-shaped, silver capsule.

The rounded bullet stuttered, and then fell, vanishing into the glare on the horizon a few miles west of our position.

A thunderclap rolled toward us, and then the crackling silence of the desert returned.

I looked at Das. He was as still as a big cat tracking prey.

"Let's go," he said, eventually.

- 4 -

Ten minutes later, we brought our jeep to a halt beside a smoking crater torn into the landscape, a hot gash interrupting the horizon-to-horizon uniformity of the scrub.

At one end of the crater, the Invader's vessel was crumpled into a ball, a great tear in its side exposing its innards to the elements.

We climbed down into the furrow, picked our way to the craft, and peered inside.

Nestled inside a webbed bucket seat, some ten metres back from the hull fracture, was an Invader.

We'd seen them before, of course. On screens around the world, before they'd banished all independent media. We knew what they looked like, but even so, it was a shock. I'd never been so close to one. Few of us had.

All our interactions—in the testing centres, at transport hubs— had been carried out by AI-powered machines. Robots, if you will, but of an order far beyond anything we had yet created.

To see a live Invader, in the flesh, was, in some ways, a privilege.

I slipped a Stanley knife from my tool-belt.

Das leaned into the vessel.

"Be careful," I muttered. Sweat trickled down my back.

"He's still alive," said Das.

"How can you tell?"

He said nothing. Instead, he bent low and worked his way into the ship.

"Goddamnit." I hesitated, then followed him, pausing at the opening to finger the edges of the gash. The tear had been blown outward. An explosion.

Inside, I found Das looking intently down at the Invader. The alien's eyes were closed.

"He's injured."

"We should leave him here. His...*people* will come for him."

Das had a look on his face that I couldn't fathom. He'd never been a talkative man. I knew next to nothing about him. None of us did. He was pleasant enough, made conversation in the way most of us did, to prevent the silences from tearing down what remained of our resolve; but his past had always been out of bounds.

I knew he was a city man. Bombay. Maybe, Delhi. But how he'd made his living before he'd been assigned to our detail, none of us knew... Had he been married? Were there children out there, somewhere? Or worse? Like me, had he arrived here trailing ghosts?

"No," he said.

For a moment, I just stared at him. His narrow shoulders. The grey of his hair. The fine down curling from the outer rim of his ears. Sweat darkened his shirt between his shoulder blades.

"Rohan. We need to get out of here before the cavalry arrives."

"Help me."

I blinked. "I don't understand—"

Before I knew it, he'd reached into the seat and unbuckled the Invader. He slipped one of the alien's arms around his shoulder and heaved it to its feet.

The Invader's head lolled forward; but its eyes remained closed.

"What the hell are you doing?"

"Help me," he repeated.

"Have you lost your mind?"

"If you don't help me, it will take longer."

I swayed on my feet for a moment, and then, cursing, moved forward.

- 5 -

It took us ten minutes to haul the Invader out to our flatbed truck.

We laid him out in the back.

"This is insane," I muttered.

Das said nothing. He rolled a tarp over the prone form, then hopped off the back and headed for the cab.

Once we were both inside, I said, "Now what?"

He pushed his wire-framed spectacles to the top of his nose, then started the engine, and reached for the gear stick.

It took us an hour to return to base.

When we got there, Das told me to stay by the truck. He walked inside and came back minutes later with a stretcher and with Nina.

Nina was another of our crew. Nina Alvarez. Formerly of Guadalajara, Mexico. Once upon a time she'd worked in a canning factory.

She and Das climbed into the back. When Das pulled aside the tarp, Nina froze.

I thought she would yell, but instead, she shivered—even though the temperature was over a hundred in the shade.

"Help me," said Das.

She looked at me, then back at Das. And then she nodded.

We took the Invader to the infirmary.

Once it was safely inside and laid out on a bed, Das systematically searched it.

He dug out various instruments, turned them over in his hands, then replaced them.

"Rohan, what the hell are we doing?" My anxiety lent my voice an unnatural pitch.

"Haven't you ever wanted to talk to them?" he said. "To ask them...why?"

I stared at him. I supposed there was a possibility that he'd lost his mind, but what did that matter?

We'd all lost our minds at some point in the past three years.

- 6 -

The Invader awoke three hours later.

We'd done our best to examine its injuries, but we knew nothing about their physiology. We had no idea how badly wounded it might be. For all we knew, death might have been hovering in the shadows.

Perhaps some of us even prayed that that was the case.

By the time it had gained consciousness, we were all back. All six of us.

Das, Nina, me. David Innes, an Englishman from York, a man who'd once written cartoons for a local newspaper. Rachel Kepler, a former aviation engineer from South Africa. And Peng Shen, a Chinese botanist who'd taught at Princeton for a decade.

We stepped outside for a heated conference. It became obvious that we were fracturing into two camps: those who felt Das had made a grave error; and those who, like him, were grimly excited by the possibilities of having our very own captive Invader.

In the end, fascination trumped fear. We were all in the same boat. We'd all lost the lives we'd known; we'd all lost loved ones. And none of us really understood why.

Das wasn't the only one with questions.

In the end, we waited a week before the interrogations began in earnest.

I suppose we thought that, at any moment, the Invader's compatriots or robot minions would descend on our habitat. We were the only manmade structure for twenty miles in all directions, an insulated blister of life in the middle of the burning vastness of the Thar. Even a rudimentary search spiraling outward from the Invader's downed vessel would have led to our door.

But no one came.

We puzzled at that, in a state of sweating semi-terror.

Nina began the questioning.

It was shortly after four in the afternoon. We were together in the habitat—myself, Nina, and Das; the others were out in the desert, having resumed their duties, eager to return to a semblance of routine. Das was the only one who refused to pretend that we could simply act as normal, whatever *normal* now meant in the long shadow cast by the invasion.

He spent all his time with the Invader; he'd even taken to sleeping on a gurney in the corner of the room. During that first week, he tended to our guest as if rehabilitating a loved one. Yet he made no attempt to communicate with the creature. It was as if he sensed that the Invader wasn't ready.

His restraint infected the rest of us, so that we too held back, until it seemed that the pressure was building inside us to the point that it might be released in some cataclysmic explosion that would take us and the habitat with it.

Nina broke the silence.

She'd arrived with the Invader's afternoon meal—a bowl of porridge. Out of all the things we'd tried to feed it—*him*, Das said—this was the only one he'd taken to.

His tall, lean form was restrained in the infirmary bed; he could move his head and not much else.

He'd taken to opening his eyes and staring at us as we moved about the room.

Like us, he'd said not a word.

We'd all heard them speak before—on a billion screens around the world. Some of us—Rachel and David, in particular—were convinced he was the representative of the alien race that had acted as "spokesman" since the day of their arrival. It was impossible to be sure. Certainly, it was a fact that none of the Invaders had set foot on Earth, and we had never seen more than one on any screen at any one time. It seemed an odd sort of hubris to believe that *our* Invader was the same one that had set out—in a soft, male human voice, translating through a device whose workings we could not guess at—the tenets of the invasion.

In some ways, our mutual silence became a chess game—who would make the first move?

"I had a fiancé," said Nina, eventually. "We were going to be married that summer. Honeymoon in Paris. We'd been saving up for years. I've never been to Europe. His name was Roberto."

The Invader blinked, but said nothing.

Nina set the spoon into the bowl and held his gaze. There was something beseeching in her eyes. "Where is he now? Is he alive? Please, tell me. I beg you."

Silence.

"Puta madre!" The howl was torn from an inner part of her. She threw the bowl at him.

He didn't flinch, didn't turn his head away. Instead, he allowed the bowl to strike his jaw; it fell back onto the bed and then to the floor where it cracked into two almost identical pieces.

I stood there, stunned, then looked across at Das who was watching with an expression that reminded me of a hungry dog.

If we'd expected a reaction from the Invader, we were disappointed.

Nina stared at him, then turned on her heel and marched out the door.

- 7 -

After that, the floodgates opened.

It was as if the Invader's failure to react had given us the confidence to act with impunity. We began with threats. Like children exhilarated by a dangerous game, we became intoxicated by a temporary sense of our own invulnerability.

At first, we took it in turns to pitch our questions to the alien, each desperate to know what had happened to our loved ones, desperate to understand why our lives had been snatched from us. When the Invader's supreme indifference to our personal grief became clear, we began to threaten him. We withheld food, water; we threatened to stake him out in the desert beneath the broiling noonday sun. We promised to beat him, to make him suffer in the way he and his kind had made *us* suffer.

The longer he remained silent, the more daring we became.

In the end, it was inevitable that someone would take that extra step.

I had expected it might be Nina, but, after her initial, unsuccessful attempt to uncover the fate of her vanished fiancé, she had remained on the periphery of our collective angst.

I was there, once again, to serve as witness when Peng Shen walked into the infirmary with a spray bottle, one of those he used to spritz his greenhouse cultivars. Before any of us really understood what he was doing, he'd walked up to the Invader and squirted whatever was in the bottle onto his thigh.

For an instant, nothing happened. And then the Invader began to jerk inside his bonds; a long low rumble escaped from his throat, scaling up into a full-fledged bellow of pain. His lean body thrashed around on the bed, and his eyes rolled inside his head.

"What was in that bottle?"

Das had materialised at Shen's elbow. The Chinese botanist was rooted to the spot, looking on in horrified fascination at the anguish he had wrought.

Das took the atomiser from him, unscrewed the top, and lowered his nose to the rim. His mouth set into a grim line.

He turned to me. "Hook up a hose to the cold-water tap. We're going to flush the skin. We'll need some sterile gauze bandages too."

I glanced at the Invader. A horrible weal had risen on his leg. The skin seemed almost to bubble.

"Robert," said Das, his voice still even, but gently persistent.

"Yes," I stammered, and turned toward the sink.

That was the last time violence was used against the Invader.

It was as if Shen's act had returned us to our senses, just as we had hovered on the very edge of falling out of ourselves into something else. Justifiable barbarity.

There was no need for us to talk about it, and so we didn't. Our feelings communicated themselves instinctively. Whatever else we were, or had become, we would not betray the very thing that kept us tethered to the gossamer thread of our stolen humanity.

Our collective sense of morality.

For his part, Peng Shen never again set foot inside the infirmary.

He retired to his greenhouse and his cultivars; we saw him only in fleeting glimpses after that, passing like a ghost through the common areas on his way to and from the kitchen. He no longer ate with the rest of us; he retreated into his own spaces and we were happy to leave him there. He had done the very thing all of us had secretly dreamed of: inspiring terror in the Invader. But in so doing, he had transgressed, moved beyond the white picket fence enclosing our shared mythos and into a place from which he could never return.

- 8 -

A second week passed.

The Invader healed. His silence, however, remained intact, an impenetrable forcefield that gradually pushed the rest of us back toward the refuge of our daily routines. Only Das remained by his side. Waiting. Watching.

One evening, I was sitting with him in the infirmary, neither of us saying much. He was reading, a book about mountaineering. I had no idea if Das had an interest in climbing mountains, but he'd had the dog-eared copy in his hands for several days.

I'd taken to bringing along my laptop. I was crunching my way through datasheets when I felt Das stir beside me.

I watched as he set down his book and walked toward the Invader.

The creature's eyes had opened while I'd been glued to my screen. He watched Das approach with that inscrutable gaze.

For a moment Das just stood there, looking back at him, as if staring at one of those mysterious Easter Island statues.

"What is your purpose?" he finally said. "I don't mean the reason that you came to Earth. Or the reason you've remade our world, our society, our lives. I mean *your* purpose. You."

Darkness falls like a stone out in the desert; in the past fifteen minutes the world outside had gone from dusk to glittering dark. The desert nights are freezing at this time of year, and the stars lent a pallid hue to the dunes visible through the infirmary's windows.

Silence howled around the room.

Finally, Das turned away.

"Isn't the purpose of every sentient being the pursuit of meaning? Of validation?"

Das froze. I saw his nostrils flare, and then he turned back to the Invader.

"And have you found it? Out among the stars? Here on Earth?"

I felt the desert tremble beneath us, down through the layers of moulded plastic, timber, and steel, down where, if you put your ear to the sand, the heartbeat of the world could be heard on the stillest nights.

"No."

"What about your compatriots? Your species? Are you *all* searching for meaning? For validation? By imposing your ideology on other civilisations?"

"I have no compatriots. I am alone."

"What do you mean? What about the others aboard your ships?"

"There are no others. Only machines. I am the only one left."

And in that incongruous human voice, he explained everything.

He was the sole remaining representative of a vanished race.

What had happened to them?

He did not know. He could not remember.

All he had was *snatches* of memory, from a time when he'd lived as part of a great community, an individual in a complex society as far beyond humankind as we were from petri dishes of bacteria. One moment he was among them; the next he was alone.

Since then, he'd been alive for a length of span unfathomable to the human mind, the inheritor of a great technology, the culmination of his race's aeons-long effort.

Over time, he'd harnessed the capabilities of his inheritance, tinkering, improving, creating for himself a race of machine helpers. These automatons, of a sophistication that humans had not come near replicating, beguiled him for the longest time. But, ultimately, despondency set in.

Purpose. He realised that what was missing was *purpose*.

And so he had set off to journey to the stars.

And as he did so, as he came upon world after world, as he studied the creatures that he found there, the first faint glimmerings of a grand design became visible to him.

Here was chaos. Here was mindless disorder, each species blindly ploughing forward hampered by inefficiencies that, from his omniscient viewpoint, seemed to him a simple matter to correct.

And so it became his great mission, enabled by his robot army, a mission he had pursued doggedly through the outer reaches of the galaxy. He had lost count of the races he had *perfected*, the worlds he had redesigned, the societies he had set upon a blazing new path.

"And did it work?" said Das. "Did you find meaning in such a purpose? Did you overcome your loneliness?"

The Invader blinked. "No."

"Your ship. The explosion that brought you down—it came from the inside of your craft."

The Invader said nothing. But I understood, in that dazzling instant, what Das had seen that I had not.

The explosion had been self-inflicted.

Das's gaze was tenderness itself. "Let me tell you about being *us*. We believe ourselves to be complex beings, but in truth we are simple creatures. Our lifespans are infinitesimal; we are physically weak and mentally immature. We fight, we kill, we stumble along blindly in our ignorance, inventing false mythologies to shield us from the terrors of *not knowing*. But for all that, we have something that you have lost. We have *empathy*." He stopped. "We have the ability, when we are willing, to feel the anguish of others. So let me ask you this: what is it that *you* really want?"

I listened to the ticking of my heartbeat. In the silence, it sounded like the beat of a giant drum.

"I want to die."

Das reached out and took his hand. "There's a better way. It's never too late to unlearn what you think you know."

The Invader became still. And then, after the longest moment, he said, simply: "Help me."

— JACKALOPE WIVES —
by Ursula Vernon

T he moon came up and the sun went down. The moonbeams went shattering down to the ground and the jackalope wives took off their skins and danced.

They danced like young deer pawing the ground, they danced like devils let out of hell for the evening. They swung their hips and pranced and drank their fill of cactus-fruit wine.

They were shy creatures, the jackalope wives, though there was nothing shy about the way they danced. You could go your whole life and see no more of them than the flash of a tail vanishing around the backside of a boulder. If you were lucky, you might catch a whole line of them outlined against the sky, on the top of a bluff, the shadow of horns rising off their brows.

And on the half-moon, when new and full were balanced across the saguaro's thorns, they'd come down to the desert and dance.

The young men used to get together and whisper, saying they were gonna catch them a jackalope wife. They'd lay belly down at the edge of the bluff and look down on the fire and the dancing shapes—and they'd go away aching, for all the good it did them.

For the jackalope wives were shy of humans. Their lovers were jackrabbits and antelope bucks, not human men. You couldn't even get too close or they'd take fright and run away. One minute you'd see them kicking their heels up and hear them laugh, then the music would freeze and they'd all look at you with their eyes wide and their ears upswept.

The next second, they'd snatch up their skins and there'd be nothing left but a dozen skinny she-rabbits running off in all directions, and a campfire left that wouldn't burn out 'til morning.

It was uncanny, sure, but they never did anybody any harm. Grandma Harken, who lived down past the well, said that the jackalopes were the daughters of the rain and driving them off would bring on the drought. People said they didn't believe a word of it, but when you live in a desert, you don't take chances.

When the wild music came through town, a couple of notes skittering on the sand, then people knew the jackalope wives were out. They kept the dogs tied up and their brash sons occupied. The town got into the habit of having a dance that night, to keep the boys firmly fixed on human girls and to drown out the notes of the wild music.

Now, it happened there was a young man in town who had a touch of magic on him. It had come down to him on his mother's side, as happens now and again, and it was worse than useless.

A little magic is worse than none, for it draws the wrong sort of attention. It gave this young man feverish eyes and made him sullen. His grandmother used to tell him that it was a miracle he hadn't been drowned as a child, and for her he'd laugh, but not for anyone else.

He was tall and slim and had dark hair and young women found him fascinating.

This sort of thing happens often enough, even with boys as mortal as dirt. There's always one who learned how to brood early and often, and always girls who think they can heal him. Eventually the girls learn better. Either the hurts are petty little things and they get tired of whining or the hurt's so deep and wide that they drown in it. The smart ones heave themselves back to shore and the slower ones wake up married with a husband who lies around and suffers in their direction. It's part of a dance as old as the jackalopes themselves.

But in this town at this time, the girls hadn't learned and the boy hadn't yet worn out his interest. At the dances, he leaned on the wall with his hands in his pockets and his eyes glittering. Other young men eyed him with dislike. He would slip away early, before the dance was ended, and never marked the eyes that followed him and wished that he would stay.

He himself had one thought and one thought only—to catch a jackalope wife.

They were beautiful creatures, with their long brown legs and their bodies splashed orange by the firelight. They had faces like no mortal woman and they moved like quicksilver and they played music that got down into your bones and thrummed like a sickness.

And there was one—he'd seen her. She danced farther out from the others and her horns were short and sharp as sickles. She was the last one to put on her rabbit skin when the sun came up. Long after the music had stopped, she danced to the rhythm of her own long feet on the sand.

(And now you will ask me about the musicians that played for the jackalope wives. Well, if you can find a place where they've been dancing, you might see something like sidewinder tracks in the dust, and more than that I cannot tell you. The desert chews its secrets right down to the bone.)

So the young man with the touch of magic watched the jacka-lope wife dancing and you know as well as I do what young men dream about. We will be charitable. She danced a little apart from her fellows, as he walked a little apart from his.

Perhaps he thought she might understand him. Perhaps he found her as interesting as the girls found him.

Perhaps we shouldn't always get what we think we want.

And the jackalope wife danced, out past the circle of the music and the firelight, in the light of the fierce desert stars.

Grandma Harken had settled in for the evening with a shawl on her shoulders and a cat on her lap when somebody started hammering on the door.

"Grandma! Grandma! Come quick—open the door—oh god, Grandma, you have to help me—"

She knew that voice just fine. It was her own grandson, her daughter Eva's boy. Pretty and useless and charming when he set out to be.

She dumped the cat off her lap and stomped to the door. What trouble had the young fool gotten himself into?

"Sweet Saint Anthony," she muttered, "let him not have gotten some fool girl in a family way. That's just what we need."

She flung the door open and there was Eva's son and there was a girl and for a moment her worst fears were realized.

Then she saw what was huddled in the circle of her grandson's arms, and her worst fears were stomped flat and replaced by far greater ones.

"Oh Mary," she said. "Oh, Jesus, Mary, and Joseph. Oh blessed Saint Anthony, you've caught a jackalope wife."

Her first impulse was to slam the door and lock the sight away.

Her grandson caught the edge of the door and hauled it open. His knuckles were raw and blistered. "Let me in," he said. He'd been crying and there was dust on his face, stuck to the tracks of tears. "Let me in, let me in, oh god, Grandma, you have to help me, it's all gone wrong—"

Grandma took two steps back, while he half–dragged the jackalope into the house. He dropped her down in front of the hearth and grabbed for his grandmother's hands. "Grandma—"

She ignored him and dropped to her knees. The thing across her hearth was hardly human. "What have you done?" she said. "What did you do to her?"

"Nothing!" he said, recoiling.

"Don't look at that and tell me 'Nothing!' What in the name of our lord did you do to that girl?"

He stared down at his blistered hands. "Her skin," he mumbled. "The rabbit skin. You know."

"I do indeed," she said grimly. "Oh yes, I do. What did you do, you damned young fool? Caught up her skin and hid it from her to keep her changing?"

The jackalope wife stirred on the hearth and made a sound between a whimper and a sob.

"She was waiting for me!" he said. "She knew I was there! I'd been—we'd—I watched her, and she knew I was out there, and she let me get up close—I thought we could talk—"

Grandma Harken clenched one hand into a fist and rested her forehead on it.

"I grabbed the skin—I mean—it was right there—she was watching—I thought she *wanted* me to have it—"

She turned and looked at him. He sank down in her chair, all his grace gone.

"You have to burn it," mumbled her grandson. He slid down a little further in her chair. "You're supposed to burn it. Everybody knows. To keep them changing."

"Yes," said Grandma Harken, curling her lip. "Yes, that's the way of it, right enough." She took the jackalope wife's shoulders and turned her toward the lamp light.

She was a horror. Her hands were human enough, but she had a jackrabbit's feet and a jackrabbit's eyes. They were set too wide apart in a human face, with a cleft lip and long rabbit ears. Her horns were short, sharp spikes on her brow.

The jackalope wife let out another sob and tried to curl back into a ball. There were burnt patches on her arms and legs, a long red weal down her face. The fur across her breasts and belly was singed. She stank of urine and burning hair.

"What did you do?"

"I threw it in the fire," he said. "You're supposed to. But she screamed—she wasn't supposed to scream—nobody said they screamed—and I thought she was dying, and I didn't want to *hurt* her—I pulled it back out—"

He looked up at her with his feverish eyes, that useless, beautiful boy, and said "I didn't *want* to hurt her. I thought I was supposed to—I gave her the skin back, she put it on, but then she fell down—it wasn't supposed to work like that!"

Grandma Harken sat back. She exhaled very slowly. She was calm. She was going to be calm, because otherwise she was going to pick up the fire poker and club her own flesh and blood over the head with it.

And even that might not knock some sense into him. Oh, Eva, Eva, my dear, what a useless son you've raised. Who would have thought he had so much ambition in him, to catch a jackalope wife?

"You goddamn stupid fool," she said. Every word slammed like a shutter in the wind. "Oh, you goddamn stupid fool. If you're going to catch a jackalope wife, you burn the hide down to ashes and never mind how she screams."

"But it sounded like it was hurting her!" he shot back. "You weren't there! She screamed like a dying rabbit!"

"Of course it hurts her!" yelled Grandma. "You think you can have your skin and your freedom burned away in front of you and not scream? Sweet mother Mary, boy, think about what you're doing! Be cruel or be kind, but don't be both, because now you've made a mess you can't clean up in a hurry."

She stood up, breathing hard, and looked down at the wreck on her hearth. She could see it now, as clear as if she'd been standing there. The fool boy had been so shocked he'd yanked the burning skin back out. And the jackalope wife had one thought only and pulled on the burning hide—

Oh yes, she could see it clear.

Half gone, at least, if she was any judge. There couldn't have been more than few scraps of fur left unburnt. He'd waited through at least one scream—or no, that was unkind.

More likely he'd dithered and looked for a stick and didn't want to grab for it with his bare hands. Though by the look of his hands, he'd done just that in the end.

And the others were long gone by then and couldn't stop her. There ought to have been one, at least, smart enough to know that you didn't put on a half-burnt rabbit skin.

"Why does she look like that?" whispered her grandson, huddled into his chair.

"Because she's trapped betwixt and between. You did that, with your goddamn pity. You should have let it burn. Or better yet, left her alone and never gone out in the desert at all."

"She was beautiful," he said. As if it were a reason.

As if it mattered.

As if it had ever mattered.

"Get out," said Grandma wearily. "Tell your mother to make up a poultice for your hands. You did right at the end, bringing her here, even if you made a mess of the rest, from first to last."

He scrambled to his feet and ran for the door.

On the threshold, he paused, and looked back. "You—you can fix her, right?"

Grandma let out a high bark, like a bitch-fox, barely a laugh at all. "No. No one can fix this, you stupid boy. This is broken past mending. All I can do is pick up the pieces."

He ran. The door slammed shut, and left her alone with the wreckage of the jackalope wife.

She treated the burns and they healed. But there was nothing to be done for the shape of the jackalope's face, or the too-wide eyes, or the horns shaped like a sickle moon.

At first, Grandma worried that the townspeople would see her, and lord knew what would happen then. But the jackalope wife was the color of dust and she still had a wild animal's stillness. When somebody called, she lay flat in the garden, down among the beans, and nobody saw her at all.

The only person she didn't hide from was Eva, Grandma's daughter. There was no chance that she mistook them for each other—Eva was round and plump and comfortable, the way Grandma's second husband, Eva's father, had been round and plump and comfortable.

Maybe we smell alike, thought Grandma. *It would make sense, I suppose.*

Eva's son didn't come around at all.

"He thinks you're mad at him," said Eva mildly.

"He thinks correctly," said Grandma.

She and Eva sat on the porch together, shelling beans, while the jackalope wife limped around the garden. The hairless places weren't so obvious now, and the faint stripes across her legs might have been dust. If you didn't look directly at her, she might almost have been human.

"She's gotten good with the crutch," said Eva. "I suppose she can't walk?"

"Not well," said Grandma. "Her feet weren't made to stand up like that. She can do it, but it's a terrible strain."

"And talk?"

"No," said Grandma shortly. The jackalope wife had tried, once, and the noises she'd made were so terrible that it had reduced them both to weeping. She hadn't tried again. "She understands well enough, I suppose."

The jackalope wife sat down, slowly, in the shadow of the scarlet runner beans. A hummingbird zipped inches from her head, dabbing its bill into the flowers, and the jackalope's face turned, unsmiling, to follow it.

"He's not a bad boy, you know," said Eva, not looking at her mother. "He didn't mean to do her harm."

Grandma let out an explosive snort. "Jesus, Mary, and Joseph! It doesn't matter what he *meant* to do. He should have left well enough alone, and if he couldn't do that, he should have finished what he started." She scowled down at the beans. They were striped red and white and the pods came apart easily in her gnarled hands. "Better all the way human than this. Better he'd bashed her head in with a rock than *this*."

"Better for her, or better for you?" asked Eva, who was only a fool about her son and knew her mother well.

Grandma snorted again. The hummingbird buzzed away. The jackalope wife lay still in the shadows, with only her thin ribs going up and down.

"You could have finished it, too," said Eva softly. "I've seen you kill chickens. She'd probably lay her head on the chopping block if you asked."

"She probably would," said Grandma. She looked away from Eva's weak, wise eyes. "But I'm a damn fool as well."

Her daughter smiled. "Maybe it runs in families."

Grandma Harken got up before dawn the next morning and went rummaging around the house.

"Well," she said. She pulled a dead mouse out of a mousetrap and took a half–dozen cigarettes down from behind the clock. She filled three water bottles and strapped them around her waist. "Well. I suppose we've done as much as humans can do, and now it's up to somebody else."

She went out into the garden and found the jackalope wife asleep under the stairs. "Come on," she said. "Wake up."

The air was cool and gray. The jackalope wife looked at her with doe-dark eyes and didn't move, and if she were a human, Grandma Harken would have itched to slap her.

Pay attention! Get mad! Do something!

But she wasn't human and rabbits freeze when they're scared past running. So Grandma gritted her teeth and reached down a hand and pulled the jackalope wife up into the pre-dawn dark.

They moved slow, the two of them. Grandma was old and carrying water for two, and the girl was on a crutch. The sun came up and the cicadas burnt the air with their wings.

A coyote watched them from up on the hillside. The jackalope wife looked up at him, recoiled, and Grandma laid a hand on her arm.

"Don't worry," she said. "I ain't got the patience for coyotes. They'd maybe fix you up but we'd both be stuck in a tale past telling, and I'm too old for that. Come on."

They went a little further on, past a wash and a watering hole. There were palo verde trees spreading thin green shade over the water. A javelina looked up at them from the edge and stamped her hooved feet. Her children scraped their tusks together and grunted.

Grandma slid and slithered down the slope to the far side of the water and refilled the water bottles. "Not them either," she said to the jackalope wife. "They'll talk the legs off a wooden sheep. We'd both be dead of old age before they'd figured out what time to start."

The javelina dropped their heads and ignored them as they left the wash behind.

The sun was overhead and the sky turned turquoise, a color so hard you could bash your knuckles on it. A raven croaked overhead and another one snickered somewhere off to the east.

The jackalope wife paused, leaning on her crutch, and looked up at the wings with longing.

"Oh no," said Grandma. "I've got no patience for riddle games, and in the end they always eat someone's eyes. Relax, child. We're nearly there."

The last stretch was cruelly hard, up the side of a bluff. The sand was soft underfoot and miserably hard for a girl walking with a crutch. Grandma had to half-carry the jackalope wife at the end. She weighed no more than a child, but children are heavy and it took them both a long time.

At the top was a high fractured stone that cast a finger of shadow like the wedge of a sundial. Sand and sky and shadow and stone. Grandma Harken nodded, content.

"It'll do," she said. "It'll do." She laid the jackalope wife down in the shadow and laid her tools out on the stone. Cigarettes and dead mouse and a scrap of burnt fur from the jackalope's breast. "It'll do."

Then she sat down in the shadow herself and arranged her skirts.

She waited.

The sun went overhead and the level in the water bottle went down. The sun started to sink and the wind hissed and the jackalope wife was asleep or dead.

The ravens croaked a conversation to each other, from the branches of a palo verde tree, and whatever one said made the other one laugh.

"Well," said a voice behind Grandma's right ear, "lookee what we have here."

"Jesus, Mary, and Joseph!"

"Don't see them out here often," he said. "Not the right sort of place." He considered. "Your Saint Anthony, now…him I think I've seen. He understood about deserts."

Grandma's lips twisted. "Father of Rabbits," she said sourly. "Wasn't trying to call *you* up."

"Oh, I know." The Father of Rabbits grinned. "But you know I've always had a soft spot for you, Maggie Harken."

He sat down beside her on his heels. He looked like an old Mexican man, wearing a button-down shirt without any buttons. His hair was silver gray as a rabbit's fur. Grandma wasn't fooled for a minute.

"Get lonely down there in your town, Maggie?" he asked. "Did you come out here for a little wild company?"

Grandma Harken leaned over to the jackalope wife and smoothed one long ear back from her face. She looked up at them both with wide, uncomprehending eyes.

"Shit," said the Father of Rabbits. "Never seen that before." He lit a cigarette and blew the smoke into the air. "What did you do to her, Maggie?"

"I didn't do a damn thing, except not let her die when I should have."

"There's those would say that was more than enough." He exhaled another lungful of smoke.

"She put on a half-burnt skin. Don't suppose you can fix her up?"

It cost Grandma a lot of pride to say that, and the Father of Rabbits tipped his chin in acknowledgment.

"Ha! No. If it was loose I could fix it up, maybe, but I couldn't get it off her now with a knife." He took another drag on the cigarette. "Now I see why you wanted one of the Patterned People."

Grandma nodded stiffly.

The Father of Rabbits shook his head. "He might want a life, you know. Piddly little dead mouse might not be enough."

"Then he can have mine."

"Ah, Maggie, Maggie... You'd have made a fine rabbit, once. Too many stones in your belly now." He shook his head regretfully. "Besides, it's not *your* life he's owed."

"It's my life he'd be getting. My kin did it, it's up to me to put it right." It occurred to her that she should have left Eva a note, telling her to send the fool boy back East, away from the desert.

Well. Too late now. Either she'd raised a fool for a daughter or not, and likely she wouldn't be around to tell.

"Suppose we'll find out," said the Father of Rabbits, and nodded.

A man came around the edge of the standing stone. He moved quick then slow and his eyes didn't blink. He was naked and his skin was covered in painted diamonds.

Grandma Harken bowed to him, because the Patterned People can't hear speech.

He looked at her and the Father of Rabbits and the jackalope wife. He looked down at the stone in front of him.

The cigarettes he ignored. The mouse he scooped up in two fingers and dropped into his mouth.

Then he crouched there, for a long time. He was so still that it made Grandma's eyes water, and she had to look away.

"Suppose he does it," said the Father of Rabbits. "Suppose he sheds that skin right off her. Then what? You've got a human left over, not a jackalope wife."

Grandma stared down at her bony hands. "It's not so bad, being a human," she said. "You make do. And it's got to be better than *that*."

She jerked her chin in the direction of the jackalope wife.

"Still meddling, Maggie?" said the Father of Rabbits.

"And what do you call what you're doing?"

He grinned.

The Patterned Man stood up and nodded to the jackalope wife.

She looked at Grandma, who met her too-wide eyes. "He'll kill you," the old woman said. "Or cure you. Or maybe both. You don't have to do it. This is the bit where you get a choice. But when it's over, you'll be all the way something, even if it's just all the way dead."

The jackalope wife nodded.

She left the crutch lying on the stones and stood up. Rabbit legs weren't meant for it, but she walked three steps and the Patterned Man opened his arms and caught her.

He bit her on the forearm, where the thick veins run, and sank his teeth in up to the gums. Grandma cursed.

"Easy now," said the Father of Rabbits, putting a hand on her shoulder. "He's one of the Patterned People, and they only know the one way."

The jackalope wife's eyes rolled back in her head, and she sagged down onto the stone.

He set her down gently and picked up one of the cigarettes.

Grandma Harken stepped forward. She rolled both her sleeves up to the elbow and offered him her wrists.

The Patterned Man stared at her, unblinking. The ravens laughed to themselves at the bottom of the wash. Then he dipped his head and bowed to Grandma Harken and a rattlesnake as long as a man slithered away into the evening.

She let out a breath she didn't know she'd been holding. "He didn't ask for a life."

The Father of Rabbits grinned. "Ah, you know. Maybe he wasn't hungry. Maybe it was enough you made the offer."

"Maybe I'm too old and stringy," she said.

"Could be that, too."

The jackalope wife was breathing. Her pulse went fast then slow. Grandma sat down beside her and held her wrist between her own callused palms.

"How long you going to wait?" asked the Father of Rabbits.

"As long as it takes," she snapped back.

The sun went down while they were waiting. The coyotes sang up the moon. It was half-full, half-new, halfway between one thing and the other.

"She doesn't have to stay human, you know," said the Father of Rabbits. He picked up the cigarettes that the Patterned Man had left behind and offered one to Grandma.

"She doesn't have a jackalope skin anymore."

He grinned. She could just see his teeth flash white in the dark. "Give her yours."

"I burned it," said Grandma Harken, sitting up ramrod straight. "I found where he hid it after he died and I burned it myself. Because I had a new husband and a little bitty baby girl and all I could think about was leaving them both behind and go dance."

The Father of Rabbits exhaled slowly in the dark.

"It was easier that way," she said. "You get over what you *can't* have faster than you get over what you *could*. And we shouldn't always get what we think we want."

They sat in silence at the top of the bluff. Between Grandma's hands, the pulse beat steady and strong.

"I never did like your first husband much," said the Father of Rabbits.

"Well," she said. She lit her cigarette off his. "He taught me how to swear. And the second one was better."

The jackalope wife stirred and stretched. Something flaked off her in long strands, like burnt scraps of paper, like a snake's skin shedding away. The wind tugged at them and sent them spinning off the side of the bluff.

From down in the desert, they heard the first notes of a sudden wild music.

"It happens I might have a spare skin," said the Father of Rabbits. He reached into his pack and pulled out a long gray roll of rabbit skin. The jackalope wife's eyes went wide and her body shook with longing, but it was human longing and a human body shaking.

"Where'd you get that?" asked Grandma Harken, suspicious.

"Oh, well, you know." He waved a hand. "Pulled it out of a fire once—must have been forty years ago now. Took some doing to fix it up again, but some people owed me favors. Suppose she might as well have it... Unless you want it?"

He held it out to Grandma Harken.

She took it in her hands and stroked it. It was as soft as it had been fifty years ago. The small sickle horns were hard weights in her hands.

"You were a hell of a dancer," said the Father of Rabbits.

"Still am," said Grandma Harken, and she flung the jackalope skin over the shoulders of the human jackalope wife.

It went on like it had been made for her, like it was her own. There was a jagged scar down one foreleg where the rattlesnake had bit her. She leapt up and darted away, circled back once and bumped Grandma's hand with her nose—and then she was bounding down the path from the top of the bluff.

The Father of Rabbits let out a long sigh. "Still are," he agreed.

"It's different when you got a choice," said Grandma Harken.

They shared another cigarette under the standing stone.

Down in the desert, the music played and the jackalope wives danced. And one scarred jackalope went leaping into the circle of firelight and danced like a demon, while the moon laid down across the saguaro's thorns.

— GRANNY —
by R.J. Sullivan

A s was her habit, Granny sat on her rocker on the cluttered front porch of the one-story family home, watchful of her neighbors. Her ancient eyes peered through the antique opera glasses to center on the house down the street. "I don't like the looks of it, Gregory." When she spoke, she addressed the garden gnome statuette facing her from the brick ledge surrounding the porch. As was *its* habit, it sat, watchful of Granny.

She continued to peer through the glasses. A car pulled up, and a group of three teenagers proceeded up a cobblestone path to the house. One of the teens knocked on the door, and, as Granny spied from between her hedges, a package and a folded bill exchanged hands between the visitors and the home's occupant.

Granny set the glasses onto the table and grabbed up her wireless telephone receiver. She paused a moment to regard the petrified gnome. "Don't just look at me, Gregory. Tell me what you think."

Granny had grown up in this house, her father's home, making her part of the second generation to raise families here. Back then, it was still a lovely neighborhood. When she married, she had no qualms about moving in with her husband Benjamin (now more than ten years in his grave) and starting their family. The neighborhood had seen better days, but she could still raise their six children in relative safety.

She'd lived her whole life here. She knew one day she would die in this house, but not today, and hopefully not soon.

Granny listened past the lawn noises of insects, passing cars, and the spring breeze. "I agree, Gregory. It's drugs. They're dealers" As the last of the neighborhood's first-generation homeowners, she considered it her personal duty to watch over the neighbors. More often these days, new neighbors meant temporary residents renting the property. It meant that someone had chosen to move into a crime-ridden area for one of two reasons. Maybe they'd come upon hard times and needed a low rental haven to get back on their feet. In those circumstances, Granny would do what she could to help them. As for the others...

Granny put the cordless phone to her ear. Under the phone was a business card with a number she had since memorized. She dialed the number while slipping the card into a breast pocket of her wrinkled blouse. "Lt. McDowall, please." After a short pause, the familiar voice answered. "Brian? It's Granny. I have another tip for you."

Knowing Granny's tips were more reliable than a magic crystal ball, Lt. Brian McDowall, a plain clothes detective with nearly twenty years on the Indianapolis Police Department, called in his team. Minutes later, he watched from the sidewalk while the uniformed cops did their job. He witnessed a textbook display as the team blocked the exits, knocked on the door, and brought the dealers out in cuffs. First the man, then the woman, each one slouched and ashamed, eyes cast downward. Both perps were basically kids, probably in their early twenties. Moments later a third trooper emerged, holding the bagged evidence that bulged enough to guarantee jail time for both.

Another tip from Granny had paid off. Lt. McDowall had mixed feelings about the matter. On the one hand, they had indeed busted another neighborhood drug dealer. On the other hand, a couple of kids selling dime bags of dope was not the sort of bust he thought would make much difference in the grand scheme of things. He hoped the perps would get an attorney that advised them to turn on their dealer for a more lenient sentence. Moving further up the supply source was the only way this bust was worth the bother. As he stood there, neighbors, mostly elderlies all around, peeked out the windows. Some watched from their porches, blatantly standing in the door frame. Red and blue lights attracted witnesses, even when the SWAT team never engaged the siren.

Lt. McDowall waited until his team drove away, then waited a bit longer until the curious got bored and went inside, back to their normal lives. He walked the perimeter of the property one last time, double-checking the distinctive Police Line yellow tape across both doors. He didn't mind waiting outside in the cool Indiana autumn afternoon. Next month, it might be a different story.

Certain he was no longer observed, he crossed the street, walked between two houses, accessed the back alley, circled around to "Granny's" home, and knocked on the back door.

Some time ago, maybe five years back, Lt. McDowall had questioned her for the first time as the call-in lead about a suspicious woman walking the neighborhood. Back then, he'd taken her story with a healthy dose of skepticism. In his years on the force, this wouldn't be the first false report he'd taken down from a bad actor looking to cause trouble for their neighbors for no good reason, and it wasn't his last.

But his concerns about Granny's motives proved unfounded. Granny's suspicions that a street walker was trying to establish a new territory turned out to be correct. After the arrest, he'd handed Granny his card and said, "Call me any time if you see anything else." This normally innocuous invitation he offered to all his witnesses proved to be the beginning of a long, mutually beneficial relationship. Over time, he stopped thinking of her as one of his most reliable contacts and came to regard her with affection.

At some point, he'd taken a note about her real name, Jane or Joan or someone, but that no longer mattered. If the word "Granny" existed in a personified form, it would look exactly like this tall, thin, gray haired creaky old lady with the creaky old voice. Besides, she preferred the nickname. Had embraced it and insisted on it long ago.

Granny opened the door and let him in. "Hello, Brian. Thank you for responding so fast to my call." As soon as he stepped in, he was momentarily overcome by "old person smell," an unpleasant blend of rotted wood and old perfume. It never lasted long, but the odor frequently distracted him during the first couple of minutes of any visit.

He stepped through into the kitchen. Its green tiles and white-painted cabinets looked like a period set from a 1940s classic movie. He knew the neighborhood pre-dated that time. The feeling continued as he stepped through into the dining room. Dozens of family photos covered every inch of visible wall space. Photo after photo of her six children, all fully grown, and her dozen grandchildren.

The front room resembled nothing if not a thrift store furniture shop, with oddball toys and random knickknacks from five decades back; Happy Meal toys, folding chairs, and old appliances filled out most of the space, including a stand-up radio that still worked and an old TV that could no longer receive a signal.

He worked his way over to a couch along the far wall (his usual spot) and settled in, sinking low into the worn-out old cushions. "Granny, I wanted to thank you, again, for the tip. We found all the evidence to arrest them. Even if they get out in a few days, I doubt they'll return to this neighborhood."

"That's what I hoped for, Brian." Her voice sounded strong and confident for someone who appeared so vulnerable. "Still, it's too bad you can't just keep them locked away until they've learned their lesson. I always thought that was the point of prison."

Brian knew from previous conversations that trying to explain the distinction between petty crimes and dangerous criminals would be wasted breath. To Granny, the world was crisply divided into saints and sinners. It was a generation gap that Lt. McDowall had no chance of closing.

Granny's tips always lead to an arrest, but whether the bust was worth the effort was another matter. And now, he had another concern. "Listen, Granny. I came the back way because I didn't want anyone to see a police officer approach your house right after the bust. I don't think I was seen, but I can't guarantee that."

"I'm not concerned if anyone sees you come to my house," Granny assured him. "You're a good man, doing good work. Gregory and I just do what we can to help."

By now, Lt. McDowall had had plenty of practice keeping a poker face whenever Granny mentioned the old garden gnome statuette. "I think you should be. You can't be the only person around here sitting, watching, and noticing patterns. I think maybe we should cool it for a few weeks. I'm afraid you're putting a target on your back."

Granny's lips pulled into a thin-lipped smile that revealed crooked teeth. Her eyes, a cloudy blue, reflected only bemusement with no hint of concern. "Thank you, but I'm not worried, Brian. What I do is important. I am watched and protected. Nothing will happen to me."

Lt. McDowall continued to keep a straight face. This wasn't the first time in their many conversations that the old lady had referenced her faith. "With all due respect, Granny, when criminal elements sniff out a snitch, we don't get a lot of warning before they strike. I've attended too many funerals for people of faith, including the pastor of my local church, who were sure God would protect them. It would break my heart if the next funeral was yours."

"That won't happen, Brian. But if it does, it just means that the Lord has called me home." She returned his worried gaze with a solemn look. "I am not afraid to die."

Lt. McDowall sighed. "Maybe so, Granny. But for me, so I know you're protected, maybe take a couple weeks off. Stay inside, or if you go out, stop looking so hard for trouble. People are going to notice if they haven't noticed already."

Granny smirked. "But what if I spot something even if I'm not trying?"

"Just lay low a couple of weeks, Granny. A $50 hooker or a few dime bag sales won't make a big difference in the overall crime. But it might keep you alive and well to spot something more significant later."

After a long pause, Granny answered. "It makes me sad, Lieutenant. When Benjamin and I bought this home from my parents, forty years ago, it was nice. Safe. A nice neighborhood to raise kids. Now my kids are out on their own, and I'm a grandmother twelve times over. And on various days and times, I've had to watch over every one of them. I can't just let them play. I must sit. And watch. And be vigilant. Because this neighborhood isn't safe anymore."

"And I'm sorry, Granny, but it's probably never going to be safe again. But I do want to make it saf-er. And I need your cooperation to make that happen."

Granny hung her head. "You're telling me to lay low for a couple of weeks."

"Yes. I'm asking you to trust me."

Granny raised her gaze to meet his. "Very well, Lieutenant. I'll mind my own business."

Lt. McDowall smiled, rose from the couch, and headed toward the back door. "Great. That's all I ask. I'll show myself out."

As soon as the nice police detective shut the door, Granny approached the front window and peeked between the slats of the blinds. What Brian failed to grasp is that protecting the neighborhood from criminals *was* her business.

She waited a few minutes to allow the detective time to return to his car and drive away, then opened the front door and stepped onto her porch. Smiling, she took her usual seat and reached out to the ancient CB radio. The microphone had long ago snapped off, but the receiver worked fine. Many afternoons, she and Gregory would sit together and listen to the police channel on the off chance they might hear something interesting.

A couple of days later, they did.

Guido crouched in the back seat next to the kidnapped teenager as his pal Danny guided the car into the back alley of their neighborhood and pulled around behind the house. His job was simple: keep the bound, gagged, and blindfolded kid as quiet and as still as possible. She'd put up a good fight when they'd first abducted her, but after a couple of backhands, she'd stopped fighting and simply sat, cowering and quiet. Twin tears had escaped from her blindfold to streak across her bruised cheeks.

He couldn't remember her name, and did it really matter? She was the daughter of the state governor, well connected and well-off, so Guido and Danny would get well-paid to return her back unharmed. That's what really mattered.

Abducting her had gone off according to plan. As a sort of local celebrity, they knew her on sight and had tailed her for days. They knew she had a daily routine on the private school campus of walking alone between two specific buildings at the same time every day. They simply waited at the curb as she walked by, earbuds on and oblivious to her surroundings. They had her shoved halfway into the back seat before she started to struggle.

Now came the subduing, the waiting, the planning. Guido hated this part of it, but this was what needed to happen. So too bad for the girl, but if everything went off according to the plan, she wouldn't be permanently harmed.

If her parents refused to pay, or called the cops...well, he would really hate what would happen next, but he hated getting caught even worse. If she had to die, too bad for the girl, but he had the stomach to waste her if he had to.

Guido watched as the gap between the houses glided past the windows. He felt the car shift as Danny clicked the garage remote and backed the car into the gravel drive. Best he could tell, no one saw them. *Once we hide the car, assuming no one sees us, we should be home free.*

Then it's just a matter of time, and I'll get well-paid.

He liked that part. A lot.

Granny first heard about the kidnapping of the governor's daughter during the radio morning news report. The newscast had included the mother's press conference, pleading for her daughter's life. When the police band put out an Amber Alert along with a call to all units to be on the lookout for a gray Honda CR-V last spotted going east on I-70, she listened to the details intently. If wouldn't take long for the kidnappers to travel from north of Indianapolis to this neighborhood if this was in fact their destination. She didn't know the odds, suspected they weren't good, but some instinct told her she should pay special attention.

Granny spared a glance at her stone overseer before grabbing up her opera glasses. "They're coming here, Gregory. I just know it. I don't know how I know it, but I do. Isn't that strange?"

Gregory returned his eternal mischievous grin. "You know I'm right, don't you?" Granny put the glasses up to her eyes and scanned between the houses across the street. Several minutes of intense searching revealed nothing, but then she detected the distinct sound of an automobile traveling the back alley behind the houses.

Sure enough, she glimpsed a gray SUV passing behind the arrested drug dealers' house. She shifted to the next property in time to see it pass between those houses, then the house after that.

But it didn't continue. Instead, she heard the mechanized sound of an automatic garage door opening.

She set the opera glasses on the table and centered the dilapidated single story green home in her vision. "She's there, Gregory. I just know it."

Gregory returned a knowing grin of support.

Granny grabbed up her walking stick. "That poor young girl. Stay here, Gregory. Watch the house. I'm going to take a closer look."

Granny suspected that if Gregory could, he would have flashed a thumbs-up to her suggestion.

Guido peeked out through the front window and scanned the houses across the street. Behind him, Danny worked the disheveled teenager into a sitting position on the floor of an equally disheveled front room that held old, dusty carpet, a single couch and a side table, and land line phone. They wouldn't use the land line, of course. Guido didn't even know if it still functioned. Instead, they'd use the newly purchased prepaid (and hopefully untraceable) flip phone Danny had bought for the purpose of calling the politician's office to make their demands. In the meantime, Guido couldn't help but feel uneasy, like he'd missed something. Some sixth sense beyond his ability to explain sent him to the back of the house to look out the back door.

A tall, elderly stick of a lady approached in an awkward hobble. He recognized the ancient old bag as the same lady he frequently spotted sitting out on her front porch. Many times. More often than made him comfortable. It didn't take him long to think it through. Given the position of her house, the route Danny drove, and the view from her porch… *Is it possible she saw something?*

She had already glanced over more times than necessary, and once he opened the door and the hinge squeaked, her gaze fell directly on him.

Guido felt himself flush red with anger. He stood as tall and imposing as he could. He let his coat slip open to show the handle of a gun.

"Hey! Lady! Get lost! You're trespassing."

The old bat stopped short. Her eyes widened. "I thought I heard something."

"Yeah? Well, you heard me." He considered drawing his gun and wasting her on the spot, but they didn't need anyone calling the police on them right now. And his gun didn't have a silencer. "Go back and mind your own business if you know what's good for ya."

The old lady stopped, then made a noise, maybe a scoff or a wheeze. Guido wasn't sure. "I didn't mean any harm," she said. The old lady turned in a hobbling spin and walked the other way.

From behind him, a noise escaped from within the house, a feminine moan or a cry, followed by a sharp striking sound. The hairs on the back of Guido's neck stood out and a chill ran through him.

The old lady paused in her retreat. "Did you hear that?"

"I said, beat it! Get your wrinkly old ass out of here and never come back!" Guido glared as the old lady hopped away, moving faster but still too slow for his comfort. It took several seconds for her to leave his sight, and he knew he had to go inside immediately and discuss options with Danny.

For the first time, Guido feared he wouldn't get paid, that he might actually spend time in jail. Guido would do anything necessary to prevent that from happening.

Danny listened to Guido's report and muttered a curse. "That's no good. She could be calling the cops already. We need to take care of that. Are you sure you know which house she lives in?"

Guido nodded. "Yeah, the old lady sits on her porch looking around every day, just up the road." He glanced at the girl, slouched and unmoving in the corner. "Is it safe to leave her here?"

Danny looked down at his freshly bruised knuckles. "She'll be out for a while. We can make the call after we take care of this." Danny's dead charcoal eyes met Guido's. "It's lucky you saw her. You up to this?"

Guido nodded. "I need to get paid, Danny. I won't let anything— won't let anyone—prevent that. Especially not an old lady who couldn't mind her own business."

"Okay." Danny grabbed his large hunting knife and shoved it down the front of his pants. "This will be quieter. Let's do this. Follow my lead."

Danny and Guido stepped out into the brisk autumn afternoon, crossed the street, and walked quickly up the block.

Guido recognized the old metal chair on the front porch barely visible above the border of hedges. He indicated the old brick house with a tilt of his head. "That's the one."

Danny released a frustrated breath. "I bet she's already inside." He glanced around at the completely still houses surrounding them. "Okay, let's go."

Guido followed him up the small path that ran between two hedges and ended at the set of steps leading up to the porch.

Danny and Guido ascended, and moments later, they stood next to each other on the front porch, facing the shut front door.

Danny opened the screen door and rattled the doorknob. "Locked." He swore quietly.

Guido took in his surroundings. From the street, he'd only noticed the old chair, but now he saw the table with the opera glasses and the police radio, and the garden gnome statuette seemed to be glaring at him with a menacing snarl on its frozen face. He turned away and focused on the task at hand.

Danny rapped hard on the door. "Hey. Old lady. Open up in there. We just wanna talk to you." Danny turned back to Guido and drew out his knife. He moved one finger to his lips. "Come on, open up!"

Guido grunted. *If I were her, I wouldn't believe him, either.* He heard something shift behind him. Movement caught his attention, and a growling hiss cut through the air.

Some *thing*, large, imposing, gray and deadly, stood between and towered above them. "Noooo!" a voice gasped. "You will not hurt Granny!"

The hulking creature, standing nearly seven feet tall, held out one hand and fanned its fingers. Sharp, deadly talons flicked into place. "Gregory will stop you."

Guido drew a breath to scream, but the creature's arm swiped at him with inhuman speed. Before he could respond, the monster tore a huge gash across his chest. He could only look down, stunned, watching himself bleed out. He instinctively raised his gun at the monster, but even as he pulled the trigger, the creature's claws had grasped his hand, twisted, and aimed the nozzle toward his friend. Before he could register his actions, he'd already fired three slugs into his friend.

Guido witnessed a look of dumb surprise on Danny's face as Danny's body slid down the wall, the life fleeing his eyes. *I guess I won't be getting paid*, he thought.

Then he died.

"What happened?" Lt. McDowall sat with Granny in the dining room at the back of the house, the door shut between themselves, the front room, and the bloody carnage still visible out the front door on the porch. He'd ordered forensics to take their photos, tag the evidence, and get the horrible mess cleaned up as fast as humanly possible. Granny herself had discovered the unbelievable bloody carnage. He had been talking to her on the phone, listening to her incredible story of how she'd found the kidnappers of the governor's daughter. Then he heard the gunshots, and her scream.

Fearing the worst, Brian called his team to speed directly to her home. He could not possibly have predicted what he'd find. Two bodies ravaged on the porch and a frail old lady inside overcome with the shakes. Moments later, his team located the kidnapped girl in the house down the road, bruised and in shock but very much alive, exactly where Granny had led them.

Lt. McDowall shifted between his team and his friend as information continued to roll in. The perps were two of Indiana's Most Wanted. One had a knife found near its mangled body, the other a gun. Clearly, they'd intended to kill their meddling neighbor, and just as clearly, they'd instead broken out into some sort of incredibly violent fight between themselves and offed each other.

Was it possible that Granny was one of the luckiest old women on the face of the planet?

Still...the blood...the bodies...what sort of argument... What causes two partners in crime to turn on each other and absolutely destroy themselves in such a fit of ferocious violence?

Unless...Lt. McDowall stood in the front room, taking in the carnage, then he turned back to Granny, then back again.

No. Surely not.

He mentally kicked himself. *No way Granny is capable of this.* If she were younger, stronger, then sure. It would make perfect sense, and ultimately, she would have gotten off with self-defense. *But...no.*

Clearly one of these two, maybe both, had harbored some deeply buried, incredible anger issues. And it happened to come out as they stood on the porch trying to off a harmless old lady.

He settled into a chair next to Granny.

The old lady wept into a tissue, her hands trembling.

Lt. McDowall put his hand over hers. He spoke in his most calming tone. "How are you doing, Granny?"

Granny shuddered. "I'm just...so glad the girl is safe. As for those men...they were terrible people, and one way or another, they got what they deserved."

Lt. McDowall grunted. "I told you to keep a low profile. This right here? This is the opposite of that."

Granny looked away but he saw the hint of a smile on her face.

"You're not going to stop, are you? Despite this? Despite everything we discussed?"

"It's necessary, Brian. You could say it's my calling. Not only that, but I also have this feeling that...every neighborhood, every community...has someone like me. Someone placed to watch, to help, to protect. Because it's necessary." Granny shrugged. "In this neighborhood, that person is me."

Lt. McDowall sighed. "And no matter what I say, no matter how dangerous it gets, you're going to continue to do this." He felt himself resign to this fact even as he spoke it aloud.

Granny's withered old hand squeezed his. "It's what we have to do, Brian. Me and you." She looked in the direction of the front porch. "And Gregory."

As usual, Lt. McDowall maintained his poker face. "Right. You, and me, and Gregory."

— LAUNCH DAY MILKSHAKES —
by Jim C. Hines

What kind of puppy-hating, orphan-kicking son of a biscuit sends thirteen Wyvern-X fighters to shoot down a seventy-nine-year-old grandmother?"

Barbie Owens's question was rhetorical. She had a darn good idea who was responsible for the red blips on the flight monitor screen that dominated the far wall of her virtual diner. A curved line projected the dots' course as they left Earth's orbit, and a small timer estimated twenty-four minutes until they intercepted the *Malena*.

Her front door opened with a pleasant jingle. A tall, broad-shouldered man swept in wearing faded blue jeans and an immaculate white leather jacket over a black button-down shirt. He removed mirrored sunglasses and surveyed the diner. His lips tightened into a sneer.

Barbie's chest tightened, but her avatar simply tilted her head. She'd spent her life working with—and eventually, working *through*—men like Geoff Reeve, and she'd be damned if she'd let him see one speck of the tension and anxiety she was carrying today. "Speak of the devil, and he shall log in. This is a private server. You might own the company, but I pay for privacy in my little virtual office."

"Privacy. That's cute. Our security systems detected unusual traffic at this node. I'm just..." He waved his hands as he strode toward her. "...making sure there are no problems. I know how much is riding on today. How much you'll lose if everything doesn't go just right."

He was gloating like the mission had already failed. She forced a brighter smile. "Who says you can't find good old-fashioned customer service anymore?"

He took the stool next to her and turned, surveying the diner's interior: the cherry red and mint green décor, the aluminum trim edging the tables, the jukebox by the far wall. "Infinite customization options, and you slap together this nightmare of century-old, Hollywood-fueled nostalgia."

"I like the milkshakes." Barbie gestured to her glass. The sides dripped with condensation. The whipped cream on top was untouched, save for a red swirl where she'd plucked off the maraschino cherry. Virtual milkshakes were never as good as the real thing, but the neural interface stimulated her taste memories, conjuring up road trips with her parents and brother from half a century before.

He raised one perfectly sculpted eyebrow before pulling a brand-name pouch of artisanal granola from his jacket pocket.

She crushed the urge to scratch her brow, where her physical body wore the interface like a crude crown. All she had to do was remove that crown, and she'd be safe and sound in her Tennessee home. But she hadn't backed down from a fight since she was eleven. Besides, it wasn't her own safety she was worried about.

Geoff chewed a mouthful of granola and thrust his chin toward the flight screen. "Congratulations on today's launch. An auspicious start to a century-long journey."

"Thank you kindly."

"You lost me a significant wager with my father. Running your little charities are one thing, but if you'd told me an over-the-hill country R&B star could snatch the Alpha Centauri contract *and* produce the world's first fully integrated brainship—"

"I hate that term," she said casually. "Makes it sound like Mabel Barton's just a brain floating in a jar in the middle of the *Malena's* bridge."

"Isn't she, though?" Geoff gave a practiced chuckle. "Sure, her brain's connected to an extensive artificial nervous system, and the jar is a state-of-the-art nutrient bath with more radiation shielding than a nuclear test site, but it's the same basic concept."

Barbie checked the screen. Seventeen minutes to intercept.

"It's a shame how much backlash you've been getting from the public," said Geoff.

Backlash he'd fanned, using his algorithms to boost critical comments and conspiracy theories while stifling supportive voices on his servers.

"Common people have always feared technology and the future," he continued. "Witchcraft and sorcery, they call it. They don't see the potential. Take your integration process. Assuming you didn't fudge the test results, you might have discovered the key to virtual immortality."

"Which you'd love to sell to those who can afford the transplant and a suitable shell?"

"Naturally." He clucked his tongue. "Then there are the military implications. No more drones means no more transmission delay from remote neural links. Imagine a soldier's brain wired directly into a modern tank. A thinktank, if you will."

"Clever. I bet that scored well in the test groups."

He looked at the screen and shook his head in mock sadness. "And now, to see those ignorant, frightened terrorists ready to destroy everything you've invested in. They must have launched their fighters days ago to get them into position. I imagine their control signals are untraceable."

"How ever did you guess?" Barbie asked dryly.

"If you'd brought me on board from the outset, I would have advised you to improve the *Malena*'s defenses, and more importantly, to choose a candidate better prepared to protect herself."

"A better candidate?" she snapped, raising her voice for the first time. "Mabel Barton—"

"Mabel Barton was a crippled old cat lady with dementia!" he shouted, rage erupting so suddenly Barbie sloshed milkshake onto the counter. "You've turned the future of our species into a soft-hearted, short-sighted *publicity stunt*."

She pulled a handful of napkins from the black-and-chrome dispenser and tried to hide the trembling of her hands. "That's why you want to destroy the *Malena*?"

"Destroy it?" His smile returned. He poured more granola into his mouth and crunched loudly. "As soon as I learned of this tragic but predictable terrorist attack, I sent a fleet of my own prototype fighters to assist. Sadly, they won't arrive in time to save poor old Grandma Barton, but they should be able to salvage the *Malena*. I know you overextended yourself with this project, but not to worry. I've already drafted a proposal to rebuild your ship, as well as a list of *proper* candidates to take her up next time. The *Malena* deserves a hero to take her to Alpha Centauri, someone brave and smart and—"

"And on your payroll?" Barbie didn't give him time to answer. "Mabel Barton was the best match from more than half a million volunteers."

"I've seen her files. The woman was one heart attack away from being eaten by her own cats. She could barely wipe her own ass."

"That wasn't one of the qualifications. Spaceships don't have asses."

Geoff slammed a fist on the countertop. Color flickered and faded, leaving them in a pixelated grayscale rendering of the old diner. He was showing off his control of her server, trying to make her feel powerless. "Pretending she's some kind of hero is like pretending you belting out those inane lyrics and shaking your ample ass for the crowds made you an artist."

He'd startled her before, but not this time. Not with that weak old attack on her music career. He had all of the same indignant rage as the critics who'd savaged her as a teenage star, with none of the verbal skill.

Twelve minutes to intercept.

Barbie leaned in. "How much gardening experience do your candidates have?"

"Gardening?" He scowled.

"Getting to Alpha Centauri is the first step. Once Mabel arrives, she's supposed to prepare the planet for human habitation. That means growing plants. The ship's equipped with farming drones, but tools are nothing without talent. Have you seen Mabel's orchids? Or tasted her green beans? Not to mention the catnip patch. She spent fifty years of her life conjuring magic out of the dirt. We're lucky to have her skill and experience."

"Gardening is secondary to—"

"The loneliness, yes. The farther she goes, the longer it will take to communicate with Earth. Then there's the solitude she'll face after she lands. We're talking four lightyears from the nearest human being. Are your candidates prepared for that? Mabel's been widowed eighteen years. She's learned to survive and thrive on her own."

"Oh, please. She was a professional housewife. She lacks the technical skill to—"

"Eighteen years," Barbie repeated. "She maintained her house, kept her old pickup running, built an addition for a small green-house, and more, all with her own two hands. Back before her arthritis got too bad, she even cobbled together an automatic irrigation system out of old plumbing supplies."

"So she could handle a few basic household repairs. Her addled old brain won't have a clue what to do with a state-of-the-art fusion engine."

"You'd be surprised. Ever since we got her brain into the ship's cradle and let the nutrient bath clean up the plaque and get the mental juices flowing, she's been on a learning kick. She passed the ship's repair certification exams four months ago. Last I checked, she was averaging six books a day, everything from Shakespeare to Stephen Hawking."

"Grandma Barton sounds like quite a lady," Geoff admitted. "It's a shame she's not a fighter. If you'd gone with a soldier and given the *Malena* the tools to defend itself, you might have had a chance. Though thirteen terrorist fighters are a lot, even for a trained soldier."

"Bless your heart. That woman is more of a fighter than a rich boy like you will ever understand." She checked the screen. Relief poured through her. Her body begin to relax for the first time in months. "And it's twelve."

"What?"

"You—I mean, the terrorists—are down to twelve of those fancy, expensive Wyvern-X fighters. Whoops, looks like eleven, now."

He glared at the display. "Are those *drones* going after the fighters?"

"Fabrication and repair drones, that's right. The *Malena* has a full complement of forty-eight FRDs. Looks like she launched thirteen of them back when she spotted her pursuers."

The fighters had broken out of their attack formation to engage the drones. For the next minute, Geoff and Barbie watched the battle in silence, following the drones' chaotic movements.

"They're moving independently," he said. "With no signal delay. That's not possible. No one can direct that many different machines at once."

A drone accelerated suddenly, pouncing directly at a swerving fighter. Two manipulator arms clamped onto the underside. Cutting torches raked the fighter's belly.

"Right as usual, Geoff. I told you we'd taken steps to help with the loneliness. It was Mabel's idea. She didn't care one whit about money or fame. Her only request was that her cats come with her on the trip."

"You wasted hundreds of millions of dollars putting *cat brains* into those things?" He couldn't have sounded more offended if she'd mixed kitty litter into his fancy granola.

"Aren't they cute? They think those Wyvern-X fighters are big old cat toys." Two more fighters fell away. The rest veered off, leaving the drones to play with the ships that were too damaged to retreat. "Maybe your 'rescue mission' can claim those fighters as salvage. I hear they're awfully expensive. Whoever funded these terrorists is going to be out a pretty penny."

Barbie finished her milkshake and stood. "This has been pleasant, but I need to log out and prep for another press conference. I can see the feeds now: 'Grandma Barton and her cats fight off a terrorist ambush.' I may not be a proper artist, but after thirty-eight top ten hits, I know viral gold when I hear it."

He simply stared.

"I think Grandma Barton is going to inspire a lot of good in the world. You feel free to stick around and watch as long as you'd like, all right? And try a chocolate milkshake. My treat."

— THE SUNSPEAR —
A "Greymantle" Story
by Alexandra Pitchford

O f the thousand different things Annwyn Rhys had imagined she'd be doing with her life by the time she'd reached her fortieth winter, staring into the yawning skeletal maw of some great beast with a head the size of a house hadn't been one of them. It was long dead, thankfully—the rest of the skeleton was likely buried under half a ton of rubble, with the skull resting in the midst of an ancient fortification at least as old as it was. A jagged crack had split the foundations of the place, a slope of rocks and other debris leading down into the darkness beneath the long-dead creature's head.

"And you want *me* to take you in *there?*" she asked, shooting a look at the woman beside her.

"Yes. I do. The dreams were clear. 'In the dragon's maw, the spear of the dawn's star will make itself known'. This is the place that I saw." Lyra Forrest nodded resolutely as she spoke, the slight sing-song note to her words making Annwyn grind her teeth. She clutched at the silver pendant around her neck, her eyes fixed on the monstrous skull ahead of them in the ruin.

"And you know what this thing looks like?"

"You've seen a spear before, haven't you?" Lyra finally met Annwyn's gaze, the lilt in her voice narrowly failing to hide an edge of nervousness. "I imagine it just looks like that. A spear. Grab the spear and we go."

Annwyn sighed, forcing herself to look away from the skull and back the way they had come, trying not to spit out the irritated response she had to the young priestess's question. The ruin itself was surrounded by sheer walls of stone, ancient cliffs that formed a narrow pass through the mountains. A few twisted trees dotted the barren soil here and there, long dead and bleached an ashen white, with nothing but the narrow path they'd climbed leading up the cliff face to where the tumble-down keep rested. The fact that Lyra had been able to lead them there at all was a miracle, she couldn't deny that, but the place set off alarm bells in the back of Annwyn's mind.

"I doubt it's going to be that simple. Lyra, I have no idea what's going to be down there. I'm a bodyguard, not a treasure hunter."

"Then focus on guarding me. Aryss will guide me to the spear. I just need you to keep me safe on the way there." Lyra beamed at her before walking toward the skull's open mouth, tentatively setting a foot on the slope. "It will be simple, I'm sure. Just one foot in front of—"

She cut off with a startled scream as the rocks slipped under her feet, the priestess vanishing as she tumbled down a slope within the skull and into the darkness below. Annwyn cursed under her breath and made to follow, sliding down the incline after her.

Annwyn crouched low as she slid, a gloved hand dragging over the debris and gravel behind her to control the speed of her descent. Light filtered down from the cracked foundation above, but it barely pierced the gloom. Her eyes were unable to pierce the darkness beyond a small circle of illumination at the bottom of the slope. A scattering of rocks littered smooth stone nearby, the debris disturbed where Lyra had fallen, though she couldn't see the young priestess anywhere.

"Lyra!"

The faint clatter of stones behind her was all she heard for a moment until a pained groan reached her ears from somewhere in the dark. Annwyn kneeled, shrugging off her pack and pulling a light rod from one of the loops on the back, a twist of the handle causing light to flare along the length and casting the chamber in a faint eldritch blue. Lyra lay a few feet from the slope against one of the chamber's walls, the younger woman stirring awkwardly and trying to stand after her tumble. Annwyn made her way over, taking the priestess's hand and helping her to her feet.

"I'm fine, really," Lyra mumbled, wobbling slightly until Annwyn put an arm around her to hold her steady.

"Not quite what you expected, is it?"

"I'm not sure what I expected, but immediately falling on my face wasn't part of it."

Once she was certain Lyra wouldn't fall over, Annwyn stepped away, turning her attention back toward the chamber they'd found themselves in. It was made of worked stone and mortar of the same style as the ruins above—a basement level of the fortification, dug into the mountainside. Curved spikes of pale white jutted down from above them—the beast's ribs, Annwyn dimly realized, forced down through the crumbling masonry by time and the weight of the rubble burying it. An archway stood at the room's far side leading to another chamber, though it was difficult to say just how far and deep the entire thing went without venturing farther in.

"Just stay close," Annwyn commanded. "If your damned spear is in here, we'll find it, but I don't mean to stay here longer than that. Got it? Gods only know what's made its home in a place like this."

Lyra nodded uncertainly, reaching out and taking Annwyn's arm until the older woman pulled away, drawing one of the daggers from her belt to press the hilt into the priestess's hand. "Cling like that and I can't do anything. Take this, and stab anything that isn't me."

Lyra stared wide-eyed at the weapon for a few moments before tightening her grip around the hilt.

"I understand."

"Good." Annwyn relaxed slightly, stooping to collect her pack and lift her glow rod over her head as she drew her sword with the other hand. As she started to move forward a thought occurred to her, and she hazarded a glance back at the younger woman over her shoulder. "Your order aren't pacifists, are they?"

"No. The Temple of Aryss boasts numerous warriors of great skill and courage. I...never excelled when it came to things like that." Lyra looked sheepish, and with the death grip she had on her loaned dagger, Annwyn believed it.

"And they didn't send one of them with you?" The other woman looked away, and Annwyn felt a dull spike of pain throb between her eyes. "Did they send you at all?"

"Not exactly, but my dream was clear! I saw this place, and the spear *will* be here, you have my word. Besides, I'm still paying you, aren't I?" Lyra still couldn't meet Annwyn's gaze even as she protested, and the bodyguard stared at her for a long moment before turning back toward the archway ahead of them.

"We'll talk about this later. For now, I'm not going to shirk a job, and I'm not about to leave you alone in the bloody wilderness, so just...relax. All right?" She sighed, starting to move forward. "We've got a damned spear to find."

The archway opened into a corridor that led deeper into the structure, narrow passages and half collapsed doorways branching off to either side as the two women made their way forward. Annwyn briefly paused as they reached each branch in the corridor, glancing down as far as the glow from her light rod allowed before moving on, Lyra hovering just behind her. The air in the place was still, with a musty note that made Annwyn's nose itch; each step they took stirred up the fine dust that coated the stone underfoot.

"Do you think there's anything here?" Lyra asked. Even with her voice barely above a whisper, it carried in the silence of the place. The rooms they'd passed had been empty save for dust and rubble—not even the remains of those that had occupied the place to mark whatever had happened there.

"I thought you were *certain* this spear was down here," Annwyn replied. "You saw it in a dream. Knew this place was here without it being marked on a map, right?" She stopped as the corridor opened into a larger chamber, where a vaulted ceiling disappeared into darkness up above them. "If it's not down here, it's not down here, but you're paying me to do this. I'm not going to turn around and leave without knowing for sure. So...take a breath, all right? Stay calm. So far all we've found is dust and shadows."

Annwyn took another step forward, her boot catching on something by her ankle. She threw herself forward as a sharp twang resounded through the chamber, a flurry of crossbow bolts streaking out of the darkness and sailing through where she'd been standing a moment before, shattering on the opposite wall.

"Annwyn!"

Lyra rushed toward her, past the snapped tripwire that had been strung across the doorway and stooped to help the older woman back to her feet. Other than a dull ache in one of her knees, though, Annwyn didn't feel any injuries—a quick check of her clothing as she dusted herself off confirmed that none of the bolts had struck her. Turning, she held her light rod up and moved toward where the bolts had come from. The tripwire led to a makeshift mount set a few paces from the doorway, a trio of small crossbows set atop it to aim across the entrance. The dust had been disturbed around it, a few faint footprints leading toward it and away again.

"I'm fine. But this…this was set up recently." Annwyn looked from the makeshift trap, adjusting the grip on her sword as she began to edge deeper into the vaulted chamber. Though the footprints were faint, she could barely make them out, following the trail until it stopped at a pile of blankets and a plain traveler's pack beside the remains of a fire. The embers were doused; no warmth radiated from the ashes as she hovered her hand over them. "Someone's here…recent enough, but they haven't been back in some time…"

"It *has* been a while, I'll admit." Annwyn spun at the sound of the voice, stopping short as the tip of a rapier nicked the flesh just under her chin. The woman holding the weapon smiled, pale skin radiant in the blue light even as the black blade of her sword drank it in. She hadn't been there a moment before, though with her black hair and fitted black leathers, she may have simply blended in with the shadows around them. "Still, I'd thank you not to rummage through my things, my dear."

"I hadn't intended to, so if you wouldn't mind lowering your sword?" Annwyn said, her words careful and measured as she kept her gaze fixed on the other woman's eyes. The stranger tilted her head for a moment before smiling and spreading her hands, the sword vanishing from sight as if it had never been there.

"Sorry about that. You can never be too careful in a place like this, though…" The stranger looked toward Lyra, still standing near the sprung trap and clutching her dagger tightly. "If you've got *that* one with you, I can't imagine you're here to hurt me. Not unless I am reading your friend there entirely wrong." She winked at Annwyn, brushing past her to crouch down beside the fire pit. The stranger swept a gloved hand over it; Annwyn caught a flicker of light in the woman's eyes before the fire re-ignited. "You're welcome to share my fire, if you like, though depending on what you're after, I'm not sure you'll find all that much down here. This place was picked clean *ages* ago, from the looks of it."

"Oh. Thank you, ma'am," Lyra replied before Annwyn could speak, stepping toward them and finally lowering her blade. "If you've been searching this place, too, then maybe you can help us find what we came here for? Or...at least tell us where you've already looked so we know not to waste our time there."

In the firelight, Annwyn could make out more of the stranger's features. She was slight, her face delicately refined with a slight mischievous tilt in how she smiled up at the priestess. Her tapered ears were enough of a giveaway that she wasn't human, though Annwyn couldn't recall having seen an elf with crimson eyes. Though she looked young, not too dissimilar in age to the honey-haired Lyra, her true age could be anywhere from a decade or two older than Annwyn herself to several centuries.

"And what are you after, sweetling?" The elf asked, the flicker of the flame making the shadows dance around her.

"Lyra, don't," Annwyn said, a warning note in her tone that the priestess ignored.

"The Sunspear," Lyra replied, taking a seat by the fire. "It's a relic of the goddess Aryss. If we can find it here we can restore it to the temple in Greymantle where it belongs."

"Yes, and once we find it, we can leave you to whatever you're after. We have no desire to impose," Annwyn said with a sigh, switching off her light rod and moving to seat herself beside Lyra. She kept her attention fixed on the elven woman, instincts setting her on edge.

"Oh, it's no imposition, really. We may even be able to help each other if you're interested. Though I'm forgetting myself." The elf looked toward Annwyn across the fire, drawing a knee up close to her as she settled in. "You can call me Sparrow, if you like. I'm something of a treasure hunter. Which is why I'm mucking around in this dusty old crypt in the first place."

"Well, I don't exactly have a clever alias, but you can call me Annwyn. I'm a bodyguard, though my usual jobs tend to stick close to the city or main roads. The priestess is Lyra."

"Well, then. Annwyn and Lyra. You're welcome to rest for a bit—the girl looks like she's had quite the spill, and I'm sure you could use a moment to calm your nerves as well. As for finding this 'Sunspear,' there's only one vault in this place that I haven't managed to search yet. I can show you where it is, though getting inside might be a bit tricky." When Sparrow smiled, it didn't quite reach her eyes. "Still, if we put our heads together, perhaps we can manage it, and all come out richer for our troubles."

The rest of the ruin was a warren of tunnels and chambers that twisted around on each other. With Sparrow as their guide, the trio made quick progress. Annwyn's light rod provided enough illumination for them as they went, the black-clad elf keeping a few paces beyond the ring of light without straying too far ahead of them. Finally, they arrived at a pair of heavy stone doors at the end of a broad passage. Sparrow came to a stop to one side, turning back to face them and making a sweeping gesture toward the doors.

"And here we are. The final obstacle to what we seek, perhaps. Or...the barrier keeping us from one last disappointment." Sparrow straightened, smirking at them. "It really could go either way, though I daresay I'm hoping for the former."

"Yes...lucky us," Annwyn said, stepping forward to bring their light closer. The doors were easily twice as tall as she was, the surfaces covered by worn carvings. Most were difficult to make out, weathered by decades, if not centuries, of neglect, but those that remained depicted a figure in armor holding aloft a shining spear against a twisting serpentine beast that had its maw open— poised to swallow the flame and star of the goddess Aryss etched across both doors. "And you couldn't get inside?" Annwyn looked at Sparrow. "They look too heavy for one person to move, at least."

"It's not quite as simple as that, no. While the doors are stone, yes, there's something else about them. Magic of some kind is keeping them sealed. It's old, but still strong, and I have had a devil of a time trying to find a way around it." Sparrow spread her hands with a grin. "Yet, just as I was ready to admit defeat, I stumble across an Aryssian priestess and her bodyguard? That sounds like providence to me."

Annwyn frowned, looking back at the doors and tracing the symbol at their center with her eyes. This all felt *too* lucky. Too simple.

"Remind me what it is you're looking for, here?" Annwyn prompted their guide. "We've told you what we're after, so I'd rather like to know what it is *you* want." She offered the elf a smirk of her own. "No offense, Sparrow, but I'd prefer not to wait until we get through this door to suddenly find out we're all after the same artifact."

"Annwyn, please. I don't think Sparrow would bring us down here just to double-cross us," Lyra said. "She's only been helpful so far."

"Oh, I have been helpful, sweetling, but your bodyguard is right to worry." Sparrow laughed, drawing closer to Annwyn until they were barely an inch apart, crimson eyes meeting the human woman's steel gray. "Were I after the artifact you seek, it wouldn't be beyond me to lure you down here to get your help, only to take it and leave the pair of you to find your way out on your own. Or, if you made it difficult...well, I've never been shy about drawing steel, should I need to. Luckily for the two of you, my employer isn't interested in any artifacts..." Her smile was languid, a gloved hand rising to gently touch Annwyn's cheek. "And I do find you far too *fascinating* to just double-cross like that, my dear."

Annwyn was caught off-guard by the touch, freezing briefly as Sparrow leaned in closer—jerking herself away from the elf at the last moment. As she did, she pressed her hand against the door, a low rumble in the stone snapping her attention away from the elf even as Sparrow stepped back with that same satisfied grin.

"Well...maybe it was easy after all," she said, the sound of grinding stone filling the corridor as the doors began to swing inward. The vault beyond was so dark that Annwyn's meager light rod couldn't hope to pierce the gloom, its glow seeming to shrink the closer it drew to the opened entryway and whatever lay on the other side of it.

"You knew that would happen?" Annwyn snapped, reaching for her sword as she fixed her gaze back on Sparrow. "How?"

"I didn't *know* anything, but I had a hunch..." The elf shrugged. "I sat and spoke with your priestess after you nodded off by the fire. When she mentioned having seen this place, and your spear, in some kind of prophetic dream...well, it didn't take too long to come to the conclusion that *one* of you would be the key. And if you weren't? No harm done, and I would be right back where I started."

The rumbling stopped with an ominous crash. The air flowing from inside the vault bit Annwyn's skin and even made Lyra shiver a few paces back. The priestess stared into the darkness, clear concern knitting her brow as she wrapped her arms around herself against the cold.

"This isn't right. The spear was meant to be here, not...this. What *is* this?" Lyra took a half-step back, unable to keep fear from creeping into her voice. "And...why Annwyn? She's just some bodyguard I hired. I'm the one Aryss blessed with visions of this place."

"Oh, that's simple!" Sparrow said, winking at Lyra. "Annwyn was simply closer to the door. Besides...gods and fate are funny like that." She started to say more, but an unearthly roar emanated from somewhere in the darkened vault, cutting her off. Even the elf looked startled. The eyes of all three women turned toward the black beyond as a chorus of chittering and hissing rose up in the roar's wake. "Oh. That's...not good..."

The darkness writhed, and black lupine shapes erupted from within, lunging toward the women with jaws snapping. Annwyn stepped between them and Lyra, slashing into one with her sword and slamming her boot into another as it leapt up at her, sending it skittering across the floor. The creature was back on its feet a moment later, snarling and charging forward again while more of the beasts emerged from the opened doorway.

"What in the hells are these things?" Annwyn snapped, bringing her arm up in front of her as one of the creatures snapped at her face. Her useless light rod clattered to the ground. They were wolf-like, but the similarities were superficial at best. Eyes burned like coals in faces without true feature or detail, their flesh appearing to be woven from the very darkness itself. The beast's fangs sank into the sleeve of her coat and the leather vambrace beneath, biting into her flesh and sending unnatural cold radiating up her arm, even as it tried to bear her to the ground. She felt the strength in her arm falter as she lost feeling; she snarled back at the beast and leveraged her sword up to drive through its ribs. It let out an odd yelp and then unraveled—dissolving into wisps of black smoke as Annwyn let her numbed arm drop to her side. Behind her, Lyra screamed, and Annwyn spun to see a pair of the creatures backing the priestess toward one of the walls.

Annwyn forced her left arm up despite the lack of feeling, tucking it against her chest and stumbling into an awkward run toward the young woman. Lyra held her dagger out toward the beasts, one hand gripping the pendant around her neck. Halfway there, something slammed into Annwyn's back from behind and sent her sprawling, her sword clattering from her grip and sliding off into darkness out of reach. She felt claws digging into her back and screamed, rolling and lashing out with her uninjured arm to try and knock the beast away. The same chill that had stolen the strength from her arm began to spread from her back. Tendrils of cold gripped her heart, and she gasped for breath, struggling for a moment before sagging back against the stone. Ahead, Lyra found her voice again and stammered through a prayer; a brilliant silver flame shot from her hands and consumed one of the beasts, but the second charged for her at the same time. Annwyn wanted to cry out, but the sound died on her lips. She could only watch as the lupine monster closed the remaining distance, its maw unnaturally wide.

Yet, before its fangs found the priestess, the shadows flickered and moved on the wall behind her. A mass of inky black formed on the worked stone, and a leather-clad shape emerged halfway from it to wrap her arms around Lyra as eyes of crimson found Annwyn where she lay. The last thing the bodyguard saw was Sparrow's self-satisfied smile before the pair tipped backward and vanished into the shadows again, the wolf-creature slamming into the wall and thrashing in confusion as it fell back to the floor. Annwyn forced herself to move as she struggled for breath, her heartbeat slowing in her chest as she managed to knock the creature from her back and roll to one side. Still, even doing that much made her falter and gasp. The remaining pair of the wolf-like monsters found their feet and padded in a circle around her as the shadows beyond the door pulsed and squirmed—the baying cries of more creatures echoed from somewhere within the vault. Lyra was gone. Safe, perhaps, but for how long? How many of those things waited beyond the door that *she* had opened? She had to get up. She had to close that door, or Aryss only knew what else would come slithering free of that place.

The baying cries grew distant, then. The light still emanating from the rod she'd dropped flickered and dimmed. For a moment, she thought it was her senses failing, yet even the creatures perked up and let out odd, chittering noises before taking a step back from her. Gritting her teeth, Annwyn found the strength to force her limbs to move. What started as a spark of determination grew into a faint warmth that spread through her as she found her feet, the feeling returning to her body followed by a sudden rush of strength that quickly grew into a fire under her skin. Even the chamber around her seemed brighter, the wolf-beasts scurrying back toward the passages that led toward the surface as the silver radiance emanating from Annwyn grew. They never made it, a thin black blade darting from the shadows to pierce through one as the other erupted into flickering purple flame. In an instant, both were nothing but smoke, and Sparrow stepped back out into the chamber with a look of genuine awe.

"Well, then...you *are* full of surprises, Lady Rhys, aren't you?" she asked with a slight tilt of her head. A moment later, that smirk of hers was back. "Or should I call you 'Sunspear'? I must admit, I had figured one of you was special, but I hadn't *quite* realized that you would *be* the very thing your prophecy spoke of. Almost seems like a wasted trip, doesn't it?"

"Stow it," Annwyn snapped. "We need to get that door closed."

"Closed? Darling, even if we did, that seal is broken. The door won't hold them for very long." The elf glanced toward the slithering black beyond the doorway and lifted her sword, nodding toward where Annwyn's blade lay a few paces to the side. "No, there's something at the heart of that vault that's controlling these things. If we want this done, we need to kill it. Which is something I get the feeling you were destined to do in the first place." She cast a look at Annwyn, crimson gaze sweeping over the bodyguard for a moment. "Not what I might have expected of a 'chosen hero' but...mmm...beggars can't be choosers, I suppose."

Annwyn glowered at the elf but gave a nod of agreement as she picked up her weapon and stepped through the doorway. The darkness beyond shrank back as she approached, the silver radiance still emanating from her causing the edges of shadow to hiss and bubble, like pitch. With a final look at Sparrow, Annwyn rolled her shoulders and focused straight ahead. Whatever evil was in this place, it was there. She could feel it.

"Keep the little ones off me!" she shouted back as she threw herself into the vault. The darkness burned away as she ran, parting like a fog bank. She heard more of the small creatures nearby, but from the screeches that followed and then abruptly stopped, Sparrow's work kept them at bay. Ahead, something twisted and coiled, sending tendrils of darkness lashing at Annwyn that she cut through with her sword. The blade began to blaze with the same silver radiance as the rest of her, the light forming into a wreath of fire around the weapon even as a serpentine creature burst from the shadows ahead. Its head was reminiscent of the skull that sat amid the ruins above, though half the size, and it made as if to swallow Annwyn whole. With a cry, she focused every ounce of the strength that had filled her into her weapon, sweeping it up through the serpent in a flash of blinding light.

Annwyn woke on a pile of blankets near a small fire, staring up at a vaulted ceiling that she couldn't quite make out in the gloom. She sat up, the sudden motion sending a spike of pain through her body that caused her to sink back down with a groan. Every part of her ached, the wounds in her arm and back throbbing, but at least without the numbness that had plagued her earlier.

"Welcome back," Sparrow said. The elf sat nearby with her back resting against the wall. She held in her hand a jagged black crystal about the size of a palm, the firelight glinting off the facets as she slowly turned it over. "That was impressive, taking that thing out like that. It's been a *very* long time since I've seen a display of divine power on that scale."

"What did you do with Lyra?" Annwyn pushed herself up on an elbow as she spoke, slowly this time. Sparrow tucked the crystal into a pouch on her belt and turned her head, nodding to the other side of the fire where the priestess was curled up.

"She's asleep. And don't worry—I didn't tell her about your little display down there, 'Sunspear.' I'll leave that for you to decide. Being 'Chosen' by a God is something few people get to choose for themselves, and while it's not *quite* the same thing, I thought it best to give you the option of...accepting that burden for yourself. You could just as easily tell her there was nothing in the vault once you valiantly slew the beasts. That her prophecy was little more than a dream."

Sparrow stood, plucking up her pack from the ground beside her and turning away from the fire. Annwyn tried to sit up again, reaching out to grab the elf by the wrist, but fell back against the blankets again as another stab of pain wracked her.

"What the hells were you after?" she managed to growl, eyes boring into the elf's back. "How much of what you said was even bloody true?"

"None of it. All of it. Does it matter?" Sparrow lifted a hand in a half-hearted wave, stepping out of the ring of firelight. "Do think carefully, before you choose. I certainly hope we see each other again, 'Sunspear.'" A moment later she was gone, swallowed up by the shadows.

Annwyn groaned, staring back up at the ceiling as she tried to make sense of any of it. By the time Lyra stirred and began bombarding her with questions, the weary bodyguard had come to one conclusion. She *hated* prophecies.

— ONCE A QUEEN —
by Alana Joli Abbott

S usie looked at the suitcase in her niece's bedroom and calculated. Clothing with pockets—how she wished she'd had
some of *those* with her when she first went. First aid kit? A
necessity, at least through the first week or two. Bug spray? Check.
Not that she remembered there being many bugs, but she remembered the climate, and how could there *not* have been? Definitely
sunscreen. She remembered a glorious sunburn that first summer,
after all the snow had finally, finally melted. Maybe aloe, too,
just in case. Susie closed her eyes and tilted her face toward the
window, still feeling those first warming rays that chased away
the cold.

But then she glanced at the clock. Shoot. "Claire, love, we'll be
late!"

Claire, a cynical eleven, leaned against the doorframe. "Are you
sure I can't take my phone, Aunt Suz?"

Susie was still uncertain why Claire's parents had gotten her a
phone at her age. "You won't have reception," Susie reminded her,
though they'd had this conversation before. "And honestly, you'll
be far too busy to text."

Claire pulled a Camp Halfblood hoodie off her dresser and pulled it over her shoulders. It was in the high sixties, and Susie was sure the bright orange hoodie would be too warm. But then, weather often worked differently than she expected, and it was hard to know what it would be like when they arrived.

"Hiking boots?"

Claire gestured to her feet, hiking boot-clad.

"Compass?"

The girl heaved a deep sigh. "I have one on my *phone*," she reminded Susie. "And a GPS."

Susie shook her head. "I promise you, there's no signal."

They zipped the suitcase shut, and Claire grinned up at her aunt conspiratorially. "You're sure my parents think you're just taking me to camp?"

Susie tugged one of the girl's two long French braids. "Same camp I went to," Susie promised. "And it's not even a lie."

When Susie was eleven, her life changed. She and her two best friends at Camp Totoket had learned to sail, to tie knots, to sleep in a tent in the woods without worrying whether that particular noise just beyond their thin walls was coyotes or another girl finding the outhouse in the dark. Luisa and Janae and Susie had been inseparable from the moment their counselors put them on the same art project, and Janae found a way to turn their dried pasta into strips of gold.

"Like Rumplestiltskin," Susie had said.

But Janae had just shaken her head. "I don't need babies, first born or otherwise. Who wants all those diapers?"

And they bonded because diapers were, of course, gross. But they all loved the Babysitters Club Books (Luisa liked the mysteries the best, while Susie preferred the Super Specials), and granted that if someone were *paying* them to change diapers, they'd make do. They taped up their gold pasta picture in the dining hall, where it captured the rays of the sun every morning at breakfast, sparkling like jewelry or priceless art.

They were always together, and this became an important detail when the portal opened. They went through, because what else did three girls who craved magic do when faced with the improbable, the impossible, the utterly miraculous?

It was winter on the other side, and they were all wearing shorts, because it was a healthy eighty-seven degrees at Camp Totoket. At least they all had their bows—they'd been headed to the archery range—so when the winter wolves set upon them, they were able to defend themselves.

They'd stumbled back to camp, and the nurse had been perplexed how three girls could get frostbite on their limbs in the middle of summer.

They were determined to be better prepared the next time. There would be a next time, of course, because how could there *not* be? They packed extra gear in their backpacks, wore jeans even on the hottest days, and waited for the portal to return.

And waited.

And waited.

Until three days before the end of camp, when they'd nearly given up hope, it came for them again. They leapt through greedily, hungry for more magic, to be *important*. They could stop the endless winter, they were sure, and be the heroes they knew they were meant to be.

When Susie turned twenty-one, she sent letters to Luisa and Janae. They'd written over the years, of course, but there were only so many times they could rehash the same old stories, though they'd had years and years of them. Being twenty-one the second time was a letdown, though it meant more in Connecticut than it had in Halavar. There, it had been the coronation of the triune queens that had been the highlight of her life, when they'd all come of age at eighteen. Twenty-one had been a festival, of course, because the people of Halavar, the talking animals, the elves and the orcs and the dryads, all loved to celebrate the queens who had come to them as children and ended the impossible winter. But it had only been another year among many, and the queens had been sure their reigns would last forever.

But there'd been that dragon. And then the portal. And then they'd stepped through and been eleven again. It was a crushing blow, a worse defeat than if the winter wolves had returned, and they'd had to face the Alpha at the palace of ice a second time. Susie had been so angry to have to go through it all again, in a place that did not know she was a hero, she almost couldn't stand it.

Here's to turning twenty-two for the first time, Luisa wrote back.

Back in Halavar, Susie had waited and waited for Luisa and Janae to realize they were meant for each other. They'd all been best friends, true, but Susie knew from early on that she never wanted more than that, that kissing wasn't a thing she desired. But Janae and Luisa—there'd always been a tension there that was different from Susie's easy friendship with them both. There was a question, unspoken, and a longing that Susie could see on both of their faces.

They got married in the spring of the year Susie turned twenty-nine. She was a bridesmaid for both sides of the aisle. Susie bought them both tiaras at a Renaissance Festival that reminded her of the crowns the three of them had once worn.

She still visited them, often. They had new stories now—travels across the globe to places Janae photographed. Luisa did some sort of computer programming Susie didn't understand, and she could take her work with her wherever Janae went.

Susie worked in a bookstore. It was small, and it smelled like Constantine's library in the capital city. When she shelved, she thought of the elf, who at four foot five had looked her in the eye when she'd arrived, but who she'd towered over by age thirteen (the first time). He'd been a mentor to them, the one who'd given Janae the chalice that, when filled with pure water, would cure all ills. Whenever Susie needed to work out a problem, she would turn to Constantine, and his wise words would never persuade her, just give her the perspective she needed to come to a solution on her own.

The bookstore didn't pay much, and it kept her from traveling. But it felt more like where she was meant to be than anywhere else in her life. Even though it still didn't feel quite like home.

The first time she was eighteen, she slumped into Constantine's library after a particularly difficult meeting with the Regent of Calamont. She rested her head on the smooth, cold oak of a large library table. A mug of tea appeared next to her in a way that seemed magic until Constantine pulled out the chair next to her. His robes slid against the oak with a brush that sounded like wind in leaves, high up in the canopy of the Whipporwood.

"It went well, then?" he said cheerfully. She could hear the clink of his own teacup against its saucer.

Her head lolled to the side so she could look up at him. "Because there's no screaming?"

He lifted his cup. "You have once again held back the threat of war, Your Majesty. That's to be celebrated."

It took more effort than it should have just to push herself back from her resting place, but a queen did not let her face smoosh against a table. Even in front of friends. At least, not for very long.

"Sometimes," she said, picking up her cup, "I wonder why the portal chose us."

Constantine blinked, slowly, but she could see that she'd startled him. "What makes you ask that?"

"It's just *hard*," she admitted. "When we started, there were villains, and a quest, and magic, and..." She waved one hand helplessly, as though she could pluck the right words from the air. Tea sloshed from the cup in her other hand, but Constantine made a tiny gesture that evaporated the drops before they could sully his table. "Now it's this job of making friends with people who don't want to be." She set down the cup and stared at the old elf. "Do you think that's why it brought us when we were children? I remember, when I was *very* small, long before I ever came to Halavar, that making friends was the easiest thing in the world. Making friends with Luisa and Janae—it wasn't a given. It had gotten harder by then to instantly connect with people. And I think it gets harder every year."

Constantine placed his teacup and saucer gently next to hers, then took both of her hands. His fingers felt raspy, like paper and comfort. "Perhaps there *was* a reason the portal found you as children. Those who travel portals often are still youths. But I think it's notable that, out of all the eleven year olds, it chose you three."

The smile started with her face, but it washed over her, chasing down her back, releasing her shoulders, loosening muscles near her ears and toes she hadn't realized were tight. "I think you give us too much credit," she said, "but thank you, Constantine."

He grinned as he leaned back and took up his tea. "If you're truly curious, I could look into it further. The portals have always been a curiosity of mine."

"And heaven knows we don't need an invasion of eleven year olds!" she joked. Her fingers reached for the handle of her own cup. "I suppose it's not important, but I would be curious to know what you find out. If you have time."

"Ah, time is one thing I have always had plenty of," said the elf.

———⟨●⟩———

Claire was born when Susie was thirty. Susie's younger sister, Tessa, had never gone to Camp Totoket, despite Susie's urging. Tessa had always been more interested in clothing and boys and bands, which didn't stop her from earning a PhD in economics and gaining a far more lucrative job than Susie could hope to have.

Tessa's daughter, on the other hand, was not particularly interested in clothing. She liked bugs and pollinator gardens; she liked wild spaces and climbing trees. Susie loved Claire from the first moment the chubby infant tugged on her hair, and she even willingly changed diapers if it meant she could stay for bedtime stories.

In Claire, Susie found an audience, a willing ear for all her adventures, someone who would believe every glorious word of Halavar's history, of Susie's own adventures. They played pretend in the woods behind Tessa's house, battling the winter wolves and facing the Alpha. But now, Susie thought of questions she'd never asked. Why had the winter wolves invaded in the first place? The eternal winter was bad, of course, but had arrows been the only solution?

"I think if I were there again," Susie said one night when Claire was seven, tucking her in, "I might try to find out what Halavar could do to help the winter wolves instead. Maybe they're still out there, still in need of a home."

"How would you get back?" Claire asked.

Susie smiled and tapped Claire on the nose. "I don't think a portal would come for me anymore. I'm too old."

Claire gasped in mock offense on her aunt's behalf. "You're not old Aunt Susie. You're not even forty."

But forty was looming. Susie didn't mind; she'd rather be old for the first time than have to go through puberty again. "Maybe you'll be the one to go back," Susie said, not really meaning it.

But she kept thinking about it. And Claire started planning. And soon, Susie couldn't remember a time when she hadn't intended for Claire to be her heir, running through the portal and saving Susie's kingdom from whatever had gone wrong after she left.

She was sure, whatever it was, Halavar would still need saving. Because that was how magic worked, wasn't it?

Camp Totoket had not changed in the thirty years since that fateful summer. The buildings had gotten new coats of paint, and the trail blazes looked fresh, but there was a sameness there that Susie appreciated. This would work. She knew it would.

Claire checked in and got her tent assignment. They hauled her suitcase up the hill, but instead of taking the left path toward Butterfly Vale, Susie veered her niece right, a shortcut between the platform tents and the archery range.

"You know that I'd be cool just going to my tent, right?" Claire said suddenly. "We don't have to do this."

Susie looked at her, shocked. "What do you mean?"

Claire crossed her arms over her chest. "Aunt Suz, I know we've been pretending about this for forever, but…I'm a rising sixth grader. I know that portals don't just pop up in the woods to take girls on magical adv—"

Which of course was the cue for the portal.

Susie had to blink back tears. It was gorgeous, a swirl of color brighter than she'd remembered, and she was so relieved that she could see it, that she hadn't been excluded because she was too old and too tired and too deeply a part of *this* world. Her fingers reached toward it, trailing sparkles like gold-painted pasta.

"Woah," breathed Claire.

"I know," Susie said, fighting the lump in her throat. "Grab your bag. You'll be back in the same instant you left."

But Claire didn't step forward. She just stared and stared at her aunt. "Everything you told me was true?" she said, with a seriousness that Susie had never seen in the girl.

Susie nodded.

Claire took a step back. "Being eleven once is bad enough," the girl protested. "I don't know how you could bear it, having to grow up twice."

Susie rubbed an aching spot in her chest. "It was worth it," she promised. "Every moment of being there was worth anything that happened after."

Claire's lip quivered. "But you had to leave," she said.

Susie's fingers danced in the light of the portal. "If there'd been a different way, I'd have taken it." She smiled wanly. "If the portal's open, it's because the people of Halavar need help. They need a hero."

"How do you know it's me?" Claire asked. "When you went before, there were three of you. You told me you couldn't have done it alone."

Susie frowned. That was fair; she hadn't had to go alone. Really, she hadn't thought through what would happen after the portal opened, if it opened at all; she'd been placing so much hope in Claire's age, knowing that the portal would only come at the right time to the right person. Which meant she hadn't planned for Claire's very reasonable, very mature hesitation.

It was all Susie could do, even at forty-one, to keep from diving right through the portal the way she'd done as a child. Even though she knew it wasn't meant for her.

"I…" Susie looked at Claire and nodded. "You're right. I wouldn't have. But I wasn't prepared the way you are." Susie reached for the girl, but Claire took another step back.

"It was fun when it was pretend," Claire said. She eyed the portal. "Now—"

And then she gasped, because one long-booted leg was coming through, followed by a dark blue robe and a brown, bespectacled face Susie had once known as well as she'd known her own.

"Constantine!" she shouted, and she rushed to hug her friend, not pausing when the realizations crashed around her.

The portal had never worked for Halavarians. Only the girls from camp had been able to go through. But here was Constantine, embracing her, though she had to bend for him to do so.

"Your Majesty," the elf said, "I'm so glad we've finally found you!"

Susie pulled back. "Found *me*?" She glanced over her shoulder at Claire, who looked utterly dazzled at the appearance of Constantine. "But..." She turned back to her friend. "I don't understand."

"Time dilation, I'm afraid," Constantine said sadly. "There's always been some trouble with the distance between our world and yours, and the magic that joins them." He dropped his hands from her shoulders and looked at her, more thoughtfully this time. "It seems it took me a bit longer than I expected, but the solution couldn't have come at a better time for Halavar." He tilted his head in that wonderfully familiar wry way she'd adored. "I'm afraid things have become a bit of a mess since your departure. I tried to keep things steady, Your Majesty, truly, but the Nortalians pressed for trade agreements that weren't advantageous, and the Calamonts have been testing our southern border. That's not to mention the problems that dragon has caused us in the last twenty years..."

"Thirty," Susie breathed.

Constantine nodded. "I imagine the dragon had a hand in that as well. But as I said, I believe I've fixed the issue. We should be able to keep the portal stable from here, especially if you need to get the other Majesties to join you..."

The elf looked hopefully over Susie's shoulder, and Susie followed his gaze, knowing that neither face he sought would be there. Instead, she saw Claire, tapping rapidly at her phone. "Auntie Janae and Auntie Luisa are in Sao Paolo," she said, "but they'll probably check their texts by tonight. I'm telling them now."

"Claire!" Susie gasped. "I told you not to bring your phone!"

Claire shrugged inside her oversized orange hoodie. "You also told me there was no signal out here, and your information was clearly out of date. I'm getting plenty of signal." The phone buzzed. "Oh! And Auntie Janae says they can be back in two weeks—can we hold the throne until then?" Claire grinned. "Like they weren't even surprised. That's pretty awesome."

Constantine took both of Susie's hands. "I know it's a lot to ask, Your Majesty. So much time has passed, and I know you have your own responsibilities. I wouldn't ask you to give everything up and return to us if our need weren't so dire."

Now, the tears did flow, and Susie did nothing to brush them away. "I will always come to Halavar's aid when I am needed," she pledged. "I remember my oath, and I shall always uphold my duties to the throne, and to my people."

"We got this, Aunt Susie!" Claire crowed.

Susie grinned back. She'd heard the word "we" from her niece twice now. Claire pocketed her phone, stepping toward her aunt and the elf, no longer as hesitant about the portal. "You told me you couldn't have done it alone," the girl reminded her. "And you're not prepared the way I am."

"You're absolutely right," Susie told her. "Since apparently signal's fine, we can call the camp and explain you'll be with me for the next two weeks instead."

"I already texted Mom and Dad," Claire said, shifting the backpack on her shoulders. "Let's do this."

Susie straightened her spine, remembering what it was to walk like a queen. Then she nodded at Constantine.

"Well then, my friend," she said, "I think it's time you took me home."

— BY THE WORKS OF HER HANDS —
by LaShawn M. Wanak

"I tell you the truth, wherever the gospel is proclaimed in the whole world, what she has done will also be told in memory of her."
Luke 14:9

LaTeiqua thinks she is too old for this.

The portal is swirly and purple and sparkly, just like in all the stories. It's hovering right next to the dirty wash water tub, popping into existence just as LaTeiqua was slinging the last of her wet laundry into her dryer. It even has a faint, tinkling sound to it, an ethereal swirling whirlpool sound. When LaTeiqua steps closer, the hairs on her arm all rise at once. In the light breeze that emanates from it, LaTeiqua can smell pine, ice, and mud.

Nope, LaTeiqua thinks.

She's read the stories. Portals only appear to white folks, usually British, usually young kids who live in humongous mansions, rich and broody, bemoaning their lives when all they needed was a good kick in the pants to pull their heads out of their asses and pay attention to someone else every once in a while. They're the ones crazy enough to dive through those portals and go off on adventures, mostly becoming the savior of someone else's land, because *of course they do*. That's what white people do. Insert themselves into someone else's land and make themselves the heroes.

Portals aren't supposed to appear in front of people like *her*. She's got enough to deal with in this world to go gallivanting about in some other world.

But that's when Lionel, her teenage son, her only son, thunders into the laundry room, sees the portal, gasps, "Holy shit!" and then he *jumps right into it*. Her son. Her sweet, loveable, *dumbass* son, diving into the portal as if it's a floating horizontal pool and he's a diver intent on swimming to the very bottom.

Lionel hasn't had enough time to grow suspicious of the world. She kept him away from boozeheads, frat boys, drug lords, and weed junkies, but had not counted on a freaking fantasy portal to open up in her house.

I'm too old for this.

She slings the wet sweater she's holding extra hard into the dryer, slams the door shut, punches the buttons to get it started, then, grumbling, grabs the nearest thing she can use for a weapon—it's a plunger, and how this can be a weapon, who the hell knows—takes a deep breath, and steps forward.

The land beyond the portal is just like how the stories usually go. The sky is a perfect blue. The grass is a perfect soft. The air is a perfect balm. Everything is pastoral and pristine and LaTeiqua is sure that it is the first time her lungs have processed clean air.

LaTeiqua has been searching for her son now for three days.

The portal follows several feet behind her like a devoted puppy. That wasn't in any of the stories. Usually portals just stay put or appear and disappear based on plot convenience. LaTeiqua doesn't know what to make of it but decides to roll with it. She does, after all, have work on Monday, and plus it'll make it easier when she finally catches up with Lionel and hauls his stupid ass home.

Instead, she comes across an orc.

It's green. It's muscled. It has tusks. It wears a loincloth. It stinks to high heaven as it shakes a club that looks like a shinbone of some devoured beast and snarls, the tusks slurring its words, "Die now, puny human—"

LaTeiqua was mugged in an alley once. Back then, she had pepper spray. She also had a wallet, which she threw at the assailant and ran as he bent to pick it up. She doesn't know if enough capitalism has reached these lands for her to stop the orc with money. The only thing she has is a plunger.

So she holds it out. "You know, this will make a better weapon than what you got right now."

The orc stumbles to a halt from its headlong charge and cocks its head, staring at the plunger. "Uh...what?"

Good. Keep it talking. "What's your name?"

"Uh...Grok."

"Grok," he says. Of course its name is Grok. Such an obvious orc name. The stories are right on this one.

But LaTeiqua also gets it. Even now, people still get that look when they learn her name. That smirk, that mocking twitch on their lips. Those syllables that made landlords tell her over the phone, "those nice condos are all filled up," and then suggest apartments in broken down, unsafe neighborhoods. When she was younger, she kept getting advice to change her name on her resume, because no one is going to hire a woman with such a rachety name. Her lovely, beautiful, ghetto name.

"*Grok*," she says again, putting all her respect into it. She can see its effect on the orc—its brows rise. "Tell me something. What have I done to you to make you want to kill me?"

Apparently, the question has never been posed to it before. "You, uh, enemy. You not orc. All those not orc must die!"

"Says who?"

"Say leader of orcs."

"Uh huh. And are you happy with that?"

The orc squeezes its beady eyes shut several times. "Happy?" It wraps its mouth around the word as if chewing on gristle.

"Does it make you feel good? Do you want to do it for the rest of your life?"

It lowers the club completely. "It no matter how feel. It what do. I kill for orcs. It our purpose." It blinks several more times, startled by its own epiphany, and struggles to get back into character. "You have weapon. You kill too, yes?"

LaTeiqua looks at the orc. She then looks at the portal behind her.

Hell, I am too old for this.

"Wanna see what this is really used for?"

There is an orc standing in her laundry room.

Now there is an orc in her hallway.

And now, it's in her bathroom, watching her as she uses the plunger in the toilet bowl.

Grok is astonished at the water swirling around the porcelain bowl. She has to distract it from drinking out of the toilet by turning on the faucet in the sink. As the orc twists the knob on and off, LaTeiqua decides not to start thinking about her water bill and instead shows it toothpaste. She gets it to brush its teeth. They use the entire tube on its tusks. When they're done, they gleam like ivory, like opal. They're surprisingly smooth.

Grok chugs the mouthwash down, and LaTeiqua really, really hopes it doesn't mess up its bowels.

She leans against the bathroom door as Grok searches through her deodorant, her shea butter lotion, her hair oil, sniffing each container with great interest. She should really go back for Lionel. She's worried about him. If there are orcs willing to kill, her son could be in danger. She shouldn't be wasting her time, watching an orc (*there's an orc in her house!*) go through her personal things. She shouldn't even have brought Grok here. There's nothing enchanting about her world at all.

But Grok discovers the shower and gives a squeal of such delight, LaTeiqua is not prepared for it. She also isn't prepared for the orc to jump into the shower, drop its loincloth, and ask her for help with the shower gel that smell like roses. In Grok's words, "Grok now can smell like flowers!"

Also, Grok is definitely, *definitely* male. Which becomes more apparent when he starts doing this thing with his muscles and gives a toothy grin. "Want join with Grok?"

"Uh." LaTeiqua is now the one at loss with words. Is that even possible? She's human, he's an orc. He's brand new in her world, she shouldn't take advan—holy hell, he could make *that* move too?!

"Uh…my son! I have to find him. Besides…um…what about your… your…tusks?! Yes. Tusks."

Grok stops moving all his body parts. "Oh. Oh! Grok now see. No worry. Tusk can be use more than eat." He waggles his thick eyebrows and drops his voice low. "Want see how tusk work?"

And oh god, it's so cheesy but at the same time so sexy and it's been such a long time since anyone made LaTeiqua feel this way…

Her son can be on his own for a little while longer.

LaTeiqua is a social worker. She's been one for thirty years now. Her main job is to find resources for those who are homeless or considered low-income. She was hoping when Lionel graduated from high school to go off to college (a challenge they had been dealing with all through his senior year), she could finally retire. All she wants to do is watch soaps all day, putter around in her backyard, maybe even work on a garden, because she never had time to and she always wanted one.

The portal doesn't follow LaTeiqua in her own world. It stays put in her laundry room, which is good. This way, she doesn't have to explain to her co-workers or her clients what it is, or really give a good reason why she's been walking funny for several days now with a goofy smile on her face.

(She did have a brief freakout after she first had sex with Grok because *she had sex with Grok* and while it wasn't like he was one of her clients, there was still ethics and power dynamics to think about even if it involved an orc from a magical world—

But then Grok took her hand and assured her that it was okay, he liked her...and it happened all the time between orcs. And he knew she wasn't an orc but she was still pretty and would it be okay if Grok showed her how much he liked her? LaTeiqua had been so charmed that she let him do so in the bedroom...and the kitchen...and twice on the stairs, oh god, the *stairs*.)

In Grok's world, the portal proves to be very handy. It's the first thing creatures see when she approaches them.

LaTeiqua comes across a troll while she's following a rumor of her son travelling with a band of elves. The troll is probably less intelligent than Grok, more interested in trying to club first than talk. But LaTeiqua is better prepared this time.

She holds up Lionel's Nintendo Switch.

Some goblins trying to rob her get excited when she tells them about Bitcoin. A ghoul attempting to suck her soul out pauses when she tells it she knows a place where she can get much better meals.

The deeper she travels in the other world, the more she comes across creatures who try to fight her, rob her, harm her. She talks to them, ask their names, and learns why they do what they do. She gets invited to burrows and caves where creatures' younglings creep around her, their toes damp, tiny eyes blinking up at her in disbelief.

It's not so different from visits to low-income homes, really.

LaTeiqua isn't a fighter, but she is a social worker and this is right in her wheelhouse. She has no sword or special weapons training, but she has *connections*.

She also has a neighborhood who, until a few days ago, didn't know that trolls or goblins or magical creatures existed at all. The ghoul she sets up in an alley that is known to be a gang's hangout. The troll becomes an excellent security guard. The goblins are surprisingly savvy bankers, and their presence is finally enough of a draw for reluctant tenants to come to their informational meetings. Sprites take up residence under stairwells. Harpies are more effective in keeping watch over women traversing the streets alone than any can of mace.

LaTeiqua hangs out with them, drinks beer and other libations with them. Wonders why she's not afraid of them as she should be. But she is learning the stories that cast these creatures are always about good or evil, never really considering that monsters could just as much want normal lives as the regular creatures of the portal's world. They just were never given the opportunity.

Thus, it doesn't surprise LaTeiqua that after a while "normal" fae folk seek her out. The reasons are varied, but they all boil down to one thing: they wish to exchange their idyllic world of meadows, lakes, and crystal-clear blue skies for the hustle and justle and cluttered dingy sidewalks of her own world.

A dwarf brings a willow tree nymph, delicate green fingers intertwined with the dwarf's stubby ones. In LaTeiqua's world, their uniqueness draws attention, but not their love. And soon there are others: a pixie that can't sing. A brownie white as snow. A faun who learned LaTeiqua's world had the means to turn her truly female despite her male body. They all share the same story of being shunned in their own world; rejects, castaways, those who are always whispered about.

LaTeiqua welcomes them all. Gets them set up in the right communities.

Except for the unicorn. It has no reason because it doesn't speak human language. It just appears one day and follows LaTeiqua through the portal. She lets it stay in her backyard where the children in her neighborhood feed it carrots and sugar cubes.

She still searches for Lionel, though as of late, she's been too busy. From time to time, she hears of his heroic deeds and is astonished to hear his name in the same sentence. She hears of prophecies, of other fighters of otherworldly origin. She hears of a god who walks in the form of a lion (or tiger or elk—it changes every time). Her son is sometimes at the god's side— his skin glowing like the last moments before dusk falls.

One day, she comes across the ruins of a recent major battle. She smells the rotten bodies first, hears the hoarse calls of vultures circling in the sky. The portal behind her appears to hang back a bit, unwilling to trod with her on the blood-soaked ground.

The stories never really tell what happens after a battle.

She has never seen so many dead bodies. It's hard to tell which side is whose. She doesn't find her son's body. That's a good thing, she thinks, until she realizes there are cries that are not from the birds.

Among the looters and the scavengers is an orc wailing as it kneels on the ground. She can't tell who the orc is keening for. Could be the orc's lover. Could be the orc's parent or even child. She thinks of Grok, back in her world, who could easily be numbered here among the dead.

She has heard rumors from neighboring villages that this battle had raged for seven days and seven nights. At the end, a beloved lord sacrificed himself and the god of this world cried. They carried the lord back to his castle, the god weeping crystalline tears as if the lord had been the god's only son.

Where is this world's god now? Who shall weep tears over all these corpses?

I am too old for this, LaTeiqua thinks as she goes to the orc.

She gets her answer a few days later when she steps through the portal to see the god of this world.

Today, he is a minotaur the size of a warhorse, which is just about a head taller than Grok would be. His flanks are the color of smoldering charcoal and for his eyes he has twin gouts of flame. Smoke churns around him like a cloak, but instead of brimstone, the sweetness of flowers lace the air.

"Where are you taking my people?" he rumbles.

"Where have you taken my son?" she counters back.

"Your son is doing important work for me."

"I can say the same for your folks."

"Do not assume you can do the work of a god. I can crush you underfoot like a grape."

He reminds LaTeiqua of when a CEO once came to their organization looking for a project to fund. The way he swept around, every detail of her grubby office caught by piercing blue eyes, analyzing the broken office chair she sat in, the computer years out of date.

He never offered to fund their project.

I am too old for this, she thinks, looking at the minotaur and seeing the same disdain. "Do you even know the reason why they're leaving? Why they don't feel safe here? Do you know their names? Their families? Their joys and sorrows? Do you even know *them?*"

The fires in the minotaur's eyes darken. "I know every breath they take. I know—"

"But do you?" LaTeiqua bites off whatever she's going to say next and rubs between her eyes, which is starting to get a headache. "Look, if you're so concerned, why don't you just come into my world and see for yourself how they are. You may say you know them, but you have never actually spoken with them, have you?"

The minotaur regards her with a look she decides to call flat as opposed to flustered. "Very well."

In her neighborhood that is now overrun with creatures that are definitely not from earth, what turns peoples' heads aren't the orcs, the dwarfs, the goblins, dryads, or even the unicorn. No. It's when LaTeiqua walks with a literal god.

(Also he is still male. For a god who could turn into four leagues, a dragon, smoke—is it that really that hard to become a different gender?)

But the god is giving her the benefit of the doubt, which is why he accompanies her to where his subjects—or rather, ex-subjects— are living out their best lives. They recognize right away who he is, of course.

The troll shows the god the internet. Turns out the troll is really, *really* good in navigating the internet. The goblins squeak and go into a profusion of bowing. The ghost haunting the alleyway goes transparent, and LaTeiqua has to coax her into becoming opaque at least.

The dwarf and the willow nymph (who are now living together in a nice studio by the river) don't say anything, don't bow. But they tangle their fingers together and stand unblinking before their creator, ready for his judgement or punishment, but unwilling to be split apart.

The god takes all this in with his fiery eyes. When he speaks to his former subjects, his voice is a quiet rumble. He offers no opinion or judgement. He asks questions and listens.

It unnerves LaTeiqua a bit. She was expecting more fire, chastisement, anger. Bowing and scraping and whatnot.

Only one creature doesn't tremble or avert her eyes. The orc who had been weeping at the battlefield. LaTeiqua had brought her back to her world, set her up with a grief support group with other refugees in a similar situation. The orc, to LaTeiqua's surprise, requests to speak with the god alone in the laundry room. LaTeiqua heads upstairs. She washes dishes for the next hour while her floorboards rattle with the occasional scream, sob, curse. The god's replies are too low to hear.

When LaTeiqua is called back, the orc's face is puffy and red, but for the first time, she looks satisfied when she goes back into the portal. The god's face is its normal inscrutable mien.

"What did you say to her?"

Those eyes of flame shift to her as the air grows heavy. "None of your concern."

And finally there's Grok. Grok, who is wearing a "Kiss me" apron and is cooking a quiche. Grok, who loves cooking shows. Grok, who has learned to speak better English—and who had been teaching LaTeiqua the orc language, which was startling easy for her to learn. He cooks dinner for all of them.

Just as Grok pulls the quiche out of the oven, Lionel burst into the kitchen as if he has been in his room all this time playing video games. "Mama, have you seen my—" His eyes land on Grok and his mouth flops open. His left hand leaps to his right hip, reaching for a weapon that is not there.

"Lionel." The name spoken in warning does not come from LaTeiqua. Her son jerks his gaze over to the god sitting opposite her at the kitchen table. (It's a bear, this time, knife and fork clutched in dexterous paws.) On any other day, LaTeiqua would be tickled at her son's swiveling between Grok and the god, stunned to see two aspects of his magical world calmly sitting in his mother's kitchen having dinner. But although the god's fiery eyes are fixed on Lionel, for some reason, she feels herself the focus of the scrutinizing gaze.

"Yes," she says in her best "grownups are talking" voice. "What you need?"

"Uh... You seen my DMX Hoodie?"

"It's on your bed, along with the rest of the clothes you've yet to fold."

"Oh. Uh. Okay." He casts a final look at Grok, finally taking in the "Kiss Me" apron, the quiche's he's holding, and the fluffy pink slippers on his green feet. Grok stares back, expressionless, until Lionel shrugs and turns to go.

"Wait."

Still self-conscious of the god watching her, LaTeiqua gets up and goes to her son. She licks her thumb and wipes a streak of dirt from his cheek. It's stubbly, which is new. She should start adding razors to the shopping list. "You eating okay? Not just meat, but veggies too?"

He shifts, falling easily back into the embarrassed teenager she knows so well." Yes, Mama."

"Treating people right?" She takes his chin and tugs it down so he's looking right at her. She doesn't know if she'll get this chance again. Time is so immutable in the other world, and already she can see the hardened shell of age forming around him, burying the child within, encasing it in a form that's older, that has seen things she will never see or know. She can't stop it, and as far as she knows, the god whose scrutiny is searing her backside won't stop it either, so she speaks the only magic charm she knows. "You do good, you hear me? Always do the right thing; never forget what I taught you."

Lionel's eyes flick to the god, but then is drawn back to her, as if he finally recognizes the moment for what it is. "Okay, Mama."

She lets him go.

———⸦●⸧———

The sun is setting pink and orange through the buildings that surrounds LaTeiqua and the god when they sit in her backyard, drinking tea. Grok, still grinning from when the god declared his quiche "delicious," has left to go to the troll's new apartment studio to play some video game called *Legends*. Thus, it's just LaTeiqua and the god (and the unicorn, digging a hole at the far end of the backyard). Those flaming eyes rest on her, and LaTeiqua suppresses the urge to squirm.

He sips from the teacup, sets it down with a soft click. "You are not a god," he rumbles.

"I never said I was." The clink of teacups could be their own separate conversation. "I'm a social worker. I bring help where I can. Those creatures needed help, so I helped them the best I could."

"And you think I don't do this?"

"Why aren't you protecting my son?"

"Did you not teach him how to be good?"

This conversation isn't going the way she thought. The god watches her as she thinks of all the nights she worried about Lionel, how she realized that she was going to be one of "those" single mothers and told herself "no, not me" and gathered a network around her: friends, family, community resources. A bunch of men on speed dial, not for hook-ups (well, yes, okay, the occasional hookup), but who would also be able to take her son out for ice cream, to cheer for him at the baseball game, to be there during the times when she couldn't.

The nights she sat up when he slept, her worrying about how to pay his bills for school.

The girlfriends she called when she needed to rant on how he was playing video games all day. The way his grades rose and fell like a pendulum.

The moment when he dove into a magic portal to fight a war he had no stake in at all.

"Your son will be fine," the god replies, as if all of these quicksilver thoughts have streaked openly across her face. "You taught him well. Every decision he makes is birthed from the wisdom you instilled in him."

LaTeiqua scowls. Finishes her tea. "Why are you here? Are you going to stop me?"

"You are doing what needs to be done. In fact, I encourage you to continue." The twin flames shift slightly. "Besides, I think the portal likes you."

"You wanna help? Give me money so I can quit my day job."

Now the god smiles into his teacup. "I can't do that."

"Why not? What use is being a god if you don't use power? Don't you know people are dying? Your people! Bad enough that you have to pull people like my son to your realm to bail them out!" Once she starts, she can't stop. What's infuriating is that the god doesn't even blink. He sits there, in her deck chair, the eyes of flame still and steady as the dainty teacup balanced on his knee. She yells all sorts of things to get try to get a rise from him. She swears, she stomps, she accuses.

He says nothing.

And that's the worst part because at some point she realizes he's *allowing* her to rant. As if he's doing it to make *her* feel better.

So she stops and leans back in the chair, thinking. *Hell, I'm too old for this.*

"I know what you mean," the god responds, proving that, yes, he knows what she's thinking.

They talk far into the night. At some point, she asks why he's a male.

He says, "You only see what you want to see."

He says this in a very tired voice. And she is surprised to see him tired. So she takes a good hard look at him.

She thinks about the stories and how the stories are told. She thinks about how gods are supposed to be. Seeing a brand-new world being born, seeing children grow and make choices and doing your best to raise them, and seeing them fight and having the power to wipe out nations but never doing it. Because there are always those who are trying to make things right.

She thinks of her son, out there doing heroic things, doing what he thinks is right, and how some day, years in the future, when he is old and ready to return home, he will stumble back into the portal, blinking and disoriented. And she will welcome him back with open arms, no matter what he has done.

She thinks of the way Grok makes her shiver when he growls her name in orcish against her neck. How when he laughs, he screws his eyes shut, and it makes him look adorable. How he has forsaken his own world to live in hers, and how now she can't imagine her life without him. She thinks of Grok's world, and how she loves it and its people. How creatures are starting to call her a witch, and when she tries to say no, she's not, they just laugh and say "Don't worry. You're a *good* witch."

She thinks about stories and the people who tell the stories. How in those stories all queens who wield power are cast as evil, but kings are working for good—though thousands die under their hand. How there are never good witches, but there are good and evil wizards. And witches who did show wisdom don't appear much in the stories. Perhaps in another universe there is an evil wizard luring children to fight his battles for him, and there is a witch who goes by "The Shining Mother" who walks around encouraging, healing, caring for the wounded, telling those to not fall for bad stories but to rise, fight, and think for themselves.

And as LaTeiqua thinks, the unicorn approaches. The god, who is now an old woman, dark-skinned, like her grandma, reaches out to pet its mane. She's calm. Ancient. Still recognizable with her flames for eyes.

"All right," LaTeiqua tells the god as the sun rises in the opposite direction. "I'll do it."

The god smiles.

It's beautiful.

There are stories of a god who walks an enchanted land.

She has been seen at the side of weeping mothers. She cares for those cast out and abandoned. She walks with those who are deemed ugly, worthless, sex-crazed, stupid. She sees them for who they are.

Over time, the stories change. Her name fades because who can believe a god is named LaTeiqua? Instead, she is called the Shining Mother.

And even that fades. For everyone knows that there is only one god and he only has one form.

At least, that's how the stories go.

— ALL THE WORLD'S TREASURES —
by Kimberly Pauley

The antique brass shop bell tinkled—*ting-a-ling-a-ling*—as
Kristin pushed open the door.

"Hai ah, let me get a look at you!" Por Por grabbed her
by the shoulders before she could even step foot inside. Her
grandmother's round, wrinkled face broke into a big smile, eyes
crinkling. "You got fat!"

"Por Por, I'm seven months pregnant," said Kristin patiently.
She was sure her grandmother knew that already. Certainly, her
mother must have told her. She'd told *everyone*. Strangers she had
never met had congratulated her while walking down the streets
of Chinatown, as if it were a miracle that a woman over thirty-five
could possibly conceive.

"I know *that*! You look good. Healthy! Come in, don't just stand
there in the door letting in all the dirt of the world!"

Por Por's shop looked the same as it had always looked, probably
the same as it had looked when her mother, Kristin's great-grandmother, had run it. It had been in the family since the Gees had
immigrated to San Francisco in the 1880s. Possibly, thought
Kristin, some of the merchandise had been there just as long. A

little fresh dirt from the outside certainly wouldn't be noticeable in the dust of ages.

Not that the shop was grimy; Por Por cleaned it every day, picking up items with care, dusting them off, and setting them back down again. Every item had a home, every piece had a story, and Por Por knew them all. "Treasures of the World" said the ancient, hand-lettered sign outside—red letters, trimmed in gold, faded.

When she was little, Kristin had been sure the old curiosity shop did indeed have all the treasures of the world contained within it. Stepping through the door had felt like going from one world to another. Outside, a boring, mundane back alley in Chinatown, always full of the off-color bantering of shift workers, the clatter of the unloading of crates full of tourist tat, and the sweet smell of almond flavoring from the fortune cookie factory a little farther down that always kept its windows open because the heat of the industrial-sized oven was unbearable even in the foggy cool of a San Francisco summer. Inside the imperturbable darkness, dust motes caught in shafts of sunlight like tiny little pixies, the sounds of the city muffled by the packed shelves and cabinets creaking under the strain of holding Por Por's treasures. And, over it all, the faint scent of jasmine and cassia.

Some of the "treasures" were standard tourist trap fare: snow globes containing the Golden Gate bridge, even though it had last snowed in the Bay Area in the 1970s, and an entire metal cupboard covered in refrigerator magnets of landmarks like Coit Tower, Lombard Street, Pier 39, and Alcatraz—but, oddly enough, not even one of Chinatown.

Por Por led Kristin through the familiar maze. First, a quick trip past the table of hand carved Indonesian gods and goddesses that Por Por never let get dusty. Then, a squeeze around the rickety shelf of brightly painted Russian Matryoshka dolls, un-nested and lined up in a row, which always shook as she went by like they were laughing at her. Past the colorful rolls of Kente cloth upended in plump bolga baskets, and, finally, they were behind the glass topped counter at the back of the shop where the rarest of treasures were stored. Beyond that was the door that led to a little kitchenette, a storeroom just as packed as the shop, and the stairs up to Por Por's apartment.

"You, sit," said Por Por, pointing to an old wooden stool with an embroidered cushion so flat that it looked like it had become one with the wood. "I get you some water."

"Ice water, please?" asked Kristin, but Por Por merely clucked her tongue and swept past her to put a kettle on.

Kristin had expected as much but had thought it worth a try. She hadn't seen a glass of cold water from any of her relatives since she'd announced her condition, not even the cousins that were around her own age and younger. At least, not when any of the parents were around. Cold was considered bad for the baby, as were lots of things, including watching horror films and house renovations.

But the worst thing was that she couldn't stop craving all the foods she wasn't supposed to eat. Every night, she dreamed about juicy watermelon and ripe mangos and even the tartness of lychee, though it wasn't her favorite. Tom, her husband, couldn't understand the restrictions and thought them silly superstitions, though he certainly held her to all the ones that Western medicine advocated for, especially since this was officially a "geriatric pregnancy." No fish, in case the mercury content was too high. No soft cheeses or anything unpasteurized. No cleaning the litterbox. That one, to be fair, she didn't mind at all. But between her two worlds, it sometimes felt like nothing was allowed.

She watched through the door as Por Por bustled around the small kitchen in a well-practiced dance, no step out of place. She could probably make a cup of tea with her eyes closed. Por Por had been born above the shop, had grown up there and been caught, many times, sneaking down the fire escape. She had celebrated her marriage at the venerable Empress of China in its heyday, outlived a husband, and here she still was, stoop-shouldered and seemingly frail, but still sharp as a whip. A whip with many, many opinions.

"Why you come today? It's good to see you, but you should be home."

"I'll be stuck home long enough once the baby's here," said Kristin, "and this might be my last chance to see you in a while." She didn't mention that her auntie had told her about seeing tremors in Por Por's hands on her last visit or how the family was discussing amongst themselves how to get her to move in with someone and close down the shop. No one wanted to take it over; who would? It was amazing it had survived as long as it had. It was a relic of another time. A time before the Internet, before Amazon, before you could get anything delivered straight to your door on the back of a scooter within hours.

Kristin had been sent on a mission by the family. She was the first grandchild, which gave her a special place in Por Por's heart, at least according to Auntie Lian, her mother's younger sister. Of course, Auntie Lian had a small mahjong problem—she couldn't resist a game and Por Por *always* won. Any conversation between the two of them turned into epic, though outwardly unlikely, trash talking. Her younger cousins, much like their mom, were no one's favorite, not even their mother's. There were even rumors that Cousin Eric ran with a gang, but Kristin suspected he just dressed that way.

Her own mother, Mei, had bowed out of the difficult conversation as well. She was a sensitive, very traditional, but also easily swayed woman and she knew that if she broached the subject, she would somehow wind up agreeing to take over the shop herself. And no one wanted that. It would be bankrupt in a week.

So, here Kristin was. Kristin, the practical one. Kristin, who had graduated at the top of her class. Kristin, who wasn't a doctor but had married one, which was just as good even if he wasn't Chinese and could barely manage chopsticks. Kristin, who was heavily pregnant with aches and pains that she wasn't sure were baby related or just from being too close to forty. Kristin, who had no idea of how to bring up any of this to her por por, who only shut the shop on major holidays.

"Drink this," said Por Por, handing her a steaming mug of water. "You want some ginger? Your tummy okay? I remember when I was pregnant with your Auntie Lian, I threw up three times a day." She shook her head. "Your mother, though, she was easy. I ate like a horse! Of course, I was barely twenty then, not like you."

Yes, trust Por Por to know *exactly* the thing to say.

Kristin sighed and took the mug, wrapping her hands around it. It was a strange, misshapen thing with two handles, one low and one high, the low one barely big enough to fit a pinkie finger through. Had she made it when she was young and given it to Por Por? Surely she wouldn't have made anything that shade of chartreuse green. The mug practically gleamed in the dim light of the shop.

She blew across the top as she considered how to attack the topic. Tendrils of steam curled away and disappeared. Por Por watched her, a small smile on her face, all-knowing and as inscrutable as the statues in a temple.

"Go ahead, you say it," said Por Por. "You feel better after you do."

Kristin choked a little in surprise, even though she hadn't taken a sip yet. "What do you mean, Por Por?" She widened her eyes, trying to look innocent, knowing that she would be seen through in a minute. Por Por's dark brown eyes missed nothing.

But before her grandmother could answer, the bell above the door tinkled again and they both turned to look at it. But the door hadn't opened. It hadn't even moved.

"Ah, never you mind, we talk about it later," said Por Por, getting briskly to her feet and patting down a stray hair from her bun. "Customer coming! You just stay right there and drink your water." She hurried around the counter toward the door. The bell pinged one more time and then stilled mid-jingle.

"How—" Kristin started to ask, but the words fell away from her lips as an unearthly light sparked into being near the door and rapidly grew into a swirling mass, like a small galaxy full of stars, suddenly thrust into existence. It shimmered for a moment, dense and heavy, then expanded with a small *POP*, a miniature New Year's fireworks explosion, elongating as it sparkled into a blinding mini vertical event horizon. Then it stopped and settled into a vaguely human-like form, impossibly tall and thin, a barren winter tree come to life. The crisp smell of ozone cut through the small shop.

Kristin dropped the mug.

An arc of still steaming water spilled out. She might have screamed, or maybe it was just a mewl of surprise and shock, as she backpedalled, heavy-bellied, trying not to fall off the stool and to avoid the scalding water at the same time.

Apology! came a feeling, a word, a notion in the middle of her mind, and the thing at the door reached out an impossibly long, thin branch-like arm and waved. The mug stopped and obligingly hovered in the air, the water reversing course and settling back in with a *sploosh*. Ripples spread across the surface, a mini lake in an ugly mug.

Por Por rushed over and plucked the mug from where it hung in the air, clucking her tongue, acting for all the world like nothing unusual had happened. She handed the mug to Kristin, who took it back automatically. It wasn't Por Por's hands that were shaking.

Por Por turned back to the figure, still faintly glowing. "What can I get you today? You need some more incense? Tea? Some

Reshetylivka embroidery? I just got some in. Very nice, and I know you like the designs. All handmade!"

There was a question in the air, Kristin wasn't sure if it was hers or from the thing in the door. It wasn't a word; it was many—*okay?, who, safe, new, curious*. All of those things and more. The little hairs on her arm were all standing at attention. She felt like she'd been caught in a lightning storm.

Por Por patted her on the head like she had done when she was little. "Wài sūn nø. My daughter's daughter. Kristin, say hello to *Shneth*. That's not exactly her name, but it's the closest I can get to it outside of my head."

"Hello," Kristin said, still on automatic, bobbing her head. "Nice to meet you."

Greeting. Warmth, happy, family.

"I get you tea," said Por Por. "Lapsang souchong, yes?" She bustled off to the kitchen, not waiting for an answer.

Nervous, Kristin carefully set the mug down on a crocheted doily on the countertop. Even distracted as she was, she knew not to set it directly on the glass.

"You're, ah, not from around here, I guess," she said.

Far. She had a momentary, breath-taking sensation of floating through an unfamiliar, starlit sky.

The alien creature took a stuttering step forward, its body balancing gracefully on twig-like extensions descending from the long central stem. Now that the glow was nearly completely faded away, Kristin could see that its skin was a pale shade of green, speckled with darker flecks the colors of emerald and obsidian. Since Por Por was making tea, she guessed it must have a mouth, but she wasn't sure where it might be. Its upper half was only moderately thicker than its lower half, with more of the branch-like appendages. None of it held still; it looked like it was in constant motion.

It was almost all the way to her, already past the Matryoshka dolls, who were remarkably still on their rickety shelf, when it occurred to her that she was alone in a room with an alien tree thing. An alien that her grandmother seemed well acquainted with.

"Ah!" she said, struggling to stand up and then stopped there, hovering above the seat, jittering between wanting to run and wanting to sit down again.

"You, *sit,*" said Por Por, coming back out with another of the ugly mugs, this one smelling of smoke and pine and fire. Kristin sat, watching as the alien gently took the mug from the old woman's hands, wrapping around it and through the strange little handle until the mug was wound all around in the twig-like fingers of the thing. It brought the mug in to a point near its center, seeming to absorb in the smell. Did it have a nose? A mouth? Why was it here?

That, at least, seemed to be a question that Por Por shared with her. "So, what are you here for, if not more tea?" she asked.

Kristin had that sudden sense of falling through the stars again—no, *shooting* through them, like she was a comet, bypassing planets, traveling through meteor trails, out, out, *OUT*—and then, hanging motionless, looking over a mountainous planet of dark reds and deep blues. Not a planet she had ever seen before, but something reminiscent of both Mars and Earth. It looked forbidding, somehow. She took a deep, shuddering breath, glad that Por Por had made her sit and equally glad she hadn't had lunch yet, because she surely would have lost it.

Time again. Bargain.

Por Por clucked her tongue once more, clearly displeased. "Hai ah, again?"

"What again?" asked Kristin, her head still spinning.

"Oh, that'll mean the Ton LaToa will be here soon. They're not like Shneth. I'd best get ready, la. Come help me, Kristin. My old fingers have trouble these days." Por Por blinked innocently at her. "But you knew that already, lor?"

Kristin flushed red, not even sure why, but she obediently followed her grandmother up the steep stairs behind the shop, leaving the vine-like Shneth behind, delicately sniffing the tea.

Up the stairs they went, passing from the almost-reverent domain of the shop into the traditional comfort of Por Por's private rooms. The shop was a place no child had *ever* dared run in, but Por Por's apartment was freedom. The rooms had stopped accruing time decades ago and were permanently stuck in the 1940s. The ever-present smell of jasmine was there, mingled with sandalwood. The sturdy furniture was all dark and heavily polished, with more paper-thin cushions flattened by age.

"What...*who*...are the Ton LaToa?" asked Kristin, following Por Por into her bedroom.

"Aliens, obviously," said Por Por, opening her wardrobe and pointing to some folded red brocade on the top shelf. Kristin stood on her toes and got it down for her. "Now, help me put this on. They drive a hard bargain, and they're not impressed if you don't look the part."

"But *why* are they here?"

"They're customers, of course," said Por Por impatiently as she took off the simple dress she had been wearing, revealing a slip underneath.

Kristin helped unfold the old-fashioned cheongsam, mostly recognising it from pictures. She had seen Por Por wear it only once. The silk was thick and heavy, built to last for years, to be handed down generation after generation. The neck, high and stiff, was held closed by an elaborate golden pankou knot. That was the part that Por Por needed the help with.

Once it was on, she wasn't sure how they would get back down the stairs—an old woman swimming in a heavy silk dress and her pregnant granddaughter. Not to mention, Por Por had sunk into herself over the years, and the dress puddled around her, inches too long.

"*Tch*," said her grandmother, twitching the dress up and staring down at her feet. She was wearing simple slip-on black Tai Chi shoes. "I'll just have to wear these. I'm not putting on heels for anyone, not even the LaToa."

Somehow, they managed the stairs to find that a strange new figure had joined Shneth. This one was stocky and blue-skinned, with four arms. It had a bulbous face and a flower-like growth on its head. Kristin had to stifle a slightly hysterical giggle, suddenly reminded of her days collecting Pokémon. It reminded her of Bulbosaur.

"Is that a LaToa?" she whispered.

"La, no," said Por Por with a snort. "That's a harcraux. They're harmless. They love Swedish Fish, jellybeans, and ukiyo-e. You'll find some in the cupboard over there."

"Ukiyo-e?"

"No, no, the jellybeans and Swedish Fish. Put them in a flat dish. They have stubby fingers."

Kristin did as she was told, arranging the candy on a blue and white china platter that she remembered eating from at family dinners. It was a crowning course kind of dish, often fish, so the little red Swedish fish almost looked at home.

Meanwhile, Por Por was chatting with the newcomer and pulling out some woodblock prints for it to look at. It chortled excitedly, barely taking its frog-like eyes from them when Kristin set the platter down in front of it.

She was debating whether to interrupt and say hello or introduce herself when the bell on the door suddenly rang out madly, shaking as if an earthquake had hit the city. Unlike the brightness that had shone when the Shneth had arrived, this time there was a swallowing of light, the opening of a miniature black hole, an absence. Into that spot appeared something immovable. That was the first word that came to Kristin's mind.

Where Shneth was graceful and willowy and the harcraux stubby and blunt, this creature was solid. If obstinate had a physical presence, it would be this. Kristin's eyes slid over it, not quite wanting to stop, especially when its flat, pupil-less black eyes met hers. There were no hard angles on the thing's body, but somehow it still seemed sharp. At first, she thought it had no separate arms or legs, but then it moved and it had too many. Its hairless skin, if you could call it skin, was glossy purple and smooth with a tracing of red—veins?—just underneath. It clicked when it moved. The other creatures had felt alien. This one *was* alien.

Por Por elbowed her. This, then, was the LaToa. She wasn't sure what to do, so she awkwardly bowed, suddenly reminded of the first time she had gone to temple. It opened its mouth, which was full of three rows of blocky teeth, and snapped them at her three times. *Clack, clack, clack.*

Begin? came a whisper like a cooling breeze in everyone's mind from the Shneth. Even the LaToa seemed to relax a bit, or maybe it just seemed that way as it unclenched its jaw.

"So," said Por Por, suddenly all business. She inclined her head regally to the LaToa. "What are you asking for, Grix?"

Kristin held back a cheer. Por Por only came up to the creature's chin, but she stood as straight as she could, even with her age-stooped shoulders, and somehow managed to look it right in the eye. She had a pleasant smile on her face, but it was a smile Kristin knew well. They had once taken a family trip to China, where they still had relatives outside Shanghai. Even though Por Por had been born in San Francisco, she had somehow known exactly how to bargain in the markets. That was the smile she wore when she was about to get a trader to offer her a third of what they'd started at or maybe less. The negotiation had begun, though Kristin wasn't even sure what the negotiation was over.

"Want oceans," ground out Grix, his back row of teeth almost seeming to fold over his front. "All the water."

As if to assist, the Shneth moved its arms gracefully and they were all filled with an image of the sea. For a moment, Kristin was hung suspended in water, like when she had swum out past the breakers, bobbing gently in the waves; all was at peace, sun in her face, salt on her skin. She came out of that feeling with a gasp, the shock of cold water in her face. Had the LaToa just demanded all the water on the *planet*? On *Earth*? She looked at her grandmother.

But Por Por still had the slight smile on her face. She didn't look concerned or uneasy. *Never,* she had once told Kristin, *let them see you sweat. If you want something, don't show it. Always be ready to walk away. It's not a deal if you don't want it.*

But how did one walk away from a demand like this? What even was the alien bargaining with?

"La, that's a big demand," said Por Por, not even blinking. "What are you offering in exchange?"

"No destroy planet," said Grix.

Kristin took an involuntary step back, nearly stepping on the harcraux's stubby feet. It didn't even seem distracted by the conversation, or maybe it wasn't aware that the fate of the planet was being negotiated. It had set aside the Japanese woodblocks and had moved on to eating the candy one piece at a time. First a Swedish Fish, a brief chew, then a jellybean, another few chomps, and then back to the little red fish.

Por Por clucked her tongue. "That's not a very good deal at all," she said. "There's nothing in it for you or me if you do that. What good does a destroyed planet do you? It's a waste. And me, I'd have nothing, and you'd still have no water."

"I take water after," said the creature after a moment. He'd paused to look at the harcraux chewing.

"Oh, la, no," said Por Por, "that wouldn't work. Why, we'd just pollute the waters first before you got a chance to siphon them off. We're very good at that even when we don't mean to be. But imagine how fast we'd go about it if we *wanted* to and there was nothing to lose? Why, it'd be done in days. And, you do realise that there are things *living* in the water here, right? Creatures of all sizes, including things so small that you can't even see them without a microscope. We're fine drinking it and swimming in it because we're used to them, but what would they do to *you*? Might kill you. And how would you even transport all that liquid to your planet? Don't be silly."

The LaToa had been ponderously nodding its head along with Por Por's words, perhaps trying to follow them or keep track of her points. It ground its teeth at her and *clacked* them again. Kristin sidled farther away, a hand on her belly. Por Por didn't flinch, but she did nod at Shneth. The alien waved its twiggy arms about.

A vision of toxic green sewage-like water full of germs and microbes and algae and bacteria swept over them all. Slime. Tiny legs twitching in thick water. Bubbles of gases. The smell of methane and sulfur. Kristin gagged and closed her eyes, certain she was about to be violently, spectacularly ill. Even the baby kicked, a small footprint against the hand that still cradled her rounded tummy.

Then it was gone. Kristin opened her eyes to see that she wasn't the only one that had flinched. The LaToa's color seemed off; the shiny, slick purple had darkened. She didn't blame it. Maybe there was a point to only drinking heated water and killing anything bad that lurked inside.

"Need water," said Grix, but its tone was more unsure now.

"I think I can still help you, if you want to bargain nicely, lor," said Por Por. "Threats won't get you anywhere on this planet, not with me." She rubbed her hands together, a papery whisper. "So, what are you offering?"

Kristin's eyebrows rose and she stared at Por Por. *What* was she doing? Why was *she* doing it? Why were the aliens *here*, in this little shop in the middle of Chinatown, and not off threatening world leaders in the White House or Downing Street or the Hague?

There was the distinct sound of the grinding of many teeth. Grudgingly, Grix spoke again, each word harder than the last. "Many minerals," he said. "Trade. Okay?"

"Hmm," said Por Por as if she was considering it very carefully. "And you put them where I want them? And take only the water I tell you to take?"

There was nowhere else for Kristin's eyebrows to go. Any higher and they would disappear into her hairline. What was Por Por up to?

Grix *clacked* and did something so that all three rows of his teeth were visible at once. A wall of teeth. Por Por bared her teeth at him in response. "Done," she said. "Let me give you directions to the water you're allowed to touch. Even better, it's in solid form, so it will be easier to transport." She held out a hand to Shneth, who responded by twirling a vine-y appendage around her wrist.

Again, Kristin felt like she was moving impossibly fast, flying up through the roof of the shop, a split-second view of Chinatown, then they were over San Francisco, California receding away behind, past the moon, hurtling past Mars and picking up speed, then Jupiter swam into view and was gone in a flash, then bursting through Saturn's ring, slowing, slowing and then an all-too-sudden stop. They were floating above Uranus. Large, blue, serene. Cold.

"You see?" came Por Por's voice, as if through a dream. "Lots of water. All ice, easy to move. And not just water, magnesium too. I throw that in for free. You can take what you want from here, or from the next one. Neptune." A sudden dizzying shift, and they were above the other ice giant. "Same thing here too. And lucky you, both closer to your home planet, yes?"

A blink and they were back in the shop. The harcraux was down to the last jellybean and the last Swedish Fish; he stared down at the two remaining candy regretfully, as if he couldn't decide which one to end his feast on.

The LaToa nodded to Por Por, once, like boulders shifting. "Bring minerals after," it said.

"Drop them off *carefully*," said Por Por. "No big craters or massive splash downs, yes? We don't want a repeat of Chelyabinsk, do we?"

Grix clacked its teeth again, three times. On the last *clack*, light began to drain from the corners of the room, crawling toward the alien like he was some kind of vacuum. The room was nearly midnight dark when Kristin blinked and he was gone, the alien whisked away, a sudden absence.

The harcraux ate the jellybean and pushed the last Swedish Fish toward Por Por. She popped it in her mouth and chewed it thoughtfully. "I don't know why you like this so much," she said, "but I have a case of them for you in the back just like you asked. Usual agreement?"

The harcraux nodded and trundled off toward the storeroom, as if it knew exactly where to go.

"The usual agreement?" asked Kristin.

"Re-foresting," said Por Por and then laughed at the look on her granddaughter's face. "What, you think your Por Por doesn't know big words like that? The harcraux are talented gardeners. I have them sneak in and plant trees. Seems like a good exchange for plastic food." She grimaced. "Give me li hing mui any day. At least they started out as real food."

The Shneth waved its top half about. *For me?*

Por Por smiled fondly at the creature. "There's tea and incense for you, of course. You come any time."

Kristin felt a lightness, a thankfulness, a warmth. Then a brilliant glow that faded and that alien too was gone.

"Por Por," she said, "*how* did this happen? Who are they?"

"They're customers," said Por Por, as if that explained everything. "They show up one day for your tai por, oh, maybe seventy years ago? I was young then." She sighed, lost for a moment in dreams of youth. "My maa maa taught me always keep the customer happy."

"Ah. The customer is always right?" said Kristin. She'd heard that about a million times in her life. It was the American Mantra.

"Hai ah, no! I didn't say that at all," said Por por. "You give the customer what they want, you may get nothing, and they walk all over you. The LaToa are like that. But, you help them figure out what you want them to want, and then, you give them that. *That's* the key to a long and successful career. Everybody happy."

"Right," said Kristin.

"Now, you, sit," said Por por. "You on your feet too long."

Kristin sat.

"And now, we talk about the shop. Your maa maa is no good at negotiating and I'm getting old. I think it's about time you learned how to bargain, leh? You old enough now, have enough years not to act too silly when some alien pop in on a surprise visit." She gave a fond look at Kristin's rounded belly. "And, someday, who know? Maybe your baby take after me. Who knows what kind of deals she'll make someday?"

— STRANGE WINGS —
By Kathryn Ivey

Something massive was moving in Angelina Crawford's yard. The realization hit her through the early morning gloom as swift and true as an arrow, the awareness of something large and dangerous and wrong just beyond her sight. She went still, her back to the window, feeling the vibrations of heavy footsteps through the floor of the old house. Nothing that lived here was that big. It sounded like an elephant, moving in her yard at the edge of the forest in the heart of Appalachia. Her breath caught and she turned slowly, hot mug of coffee still in her hands, both terrified to face that doorway and terrified to keep her back to it.

A knock pierced the morning quiet. A quick rap on the glass, *one-two*, intentional and eerie and completely at odds with the sound of rumbling movement out in the pre-dawn dark. Angie froze again, heart hammering in her chest, going cold with the rush of adrenaline that flooded her body. Everything slowed and she willed herself just to look, to see—

Then, again.

Tap tap.

Angie's body flew from the window before her mind could catch up. Instinct told her several things, all at once: the knock was too solid and rhythmic to be trees against the glass or the cat scratching at the screen, and whatever knocked reached the ten-foot-high window to do it. She scrambled back, trying to get away from the window that felt like a black hole in her living room, like something evil and unknown had ripped itself out of old stories and come to call her.

She finally, finally looked toward the window with her back against the opposite wall, clutching the mug like it was a weapon and a lifeline, and she bit back a scream as a single golden eye, slitted and enormous, stared back at her. She thought again of legends, of basilisks and dragons and things that lurked around the edges of a map as she held that golden gaze. The fear loosened in her chest, just a little, just enough. Another emotion began to take hold, something deeper and older than even fear: wonder.

A scream ripped through the quiet and Angie's budding wonder. The pupil of that great eye flashed away, faster than Angie could comprehend, then disappeared into the dark. Angie scrambled to her feet as something rustled outside like the sound of a very large bird shaking itself—then a thud she felt more than heard, low and deep, then another. The creature was moving back to the woods, toward the direction of the scream—

Toward her children's bedrooms. Toward Ellie, who always slept with her window open this time of year. Time slowed and stretched and Angie ran, faster than she'd ever run in her life, the hallways stretching on forever and ever like she was running through a dream. The heavy thudding of the creature's footsteps moved faster and she heard something else as she ran, a weird scraping and scratching above her head.

She wrenched open her daughter's door to see Ellie awake and pale, pressed against the wall with her blankets clutched to her chest, her eyes wide and terrified. The window gaped above her, open to the night and all its horror. Those petrified eyes flew to Angie and the scraping and scrabbling sounds like long claws against a hard surface came from just above them.

Angie closed the distance in a leap and covered her daughter's mouth with one hand, throwing the other arm over the girl's skinny shoulders. She braced her thighs against the side of the bed and wrenched her body backward, pulling her daughter out of the bed and onto the floor just as the sounds came from right outside the window—

"*Mom*," Ellie tried to shout but Angie clamped her hand tighter over her daughter's mouth, shaking her head and meeting her daughter's terrified eyes. "Be quiet," she hissed through her teeth, and something shifted in the teenager's eyes. Angie forced herself to breathe slowly, silently, as something above them began to scrape and scratch along the glass of the window. Angie realized that there were two creatures out in the night, the large golden-eyed beast whose gaze she'd held and something else, something on the verge of crawling in through the window, something that reeked of malevolence.

The giant's footsteps were right outside the window. The scraping stopped and something *hissed*, an awful, guttural sound that was so close Angie wanted to scream for her husband, for help, for anything.

A low, rumbling growl, as if in response to the hissing creature above them. Angie had the feeling—bizarre, unfounded, but certain—that the creatures were communicating, that the large one was warning the small one. The world felt upside down, uncertain, and under the terror Angie wondered how the hell she'd never heard of anything like these creatures before.

Through the haze of years and memories came her grand-mother's voice, the old woman's often-cryptic warnings; and the way she knew things she shouldn't, the way she seemed more alive in the woods than anywhere else—

A great rustling from the window, like the unfurling of great wings. A low growl, almost a rumble, and a deep guttural clicking that triggered some very old fear deep at the base of Angie's spine. The skittering thing moved again, the last hiss as if from a great distance.

A gust of air blew through the window, hard and unnatural and carrying some familiar smell Angie couldn't place, of smoke and metal and strange musk.

The great wings flapped again and sent another gust through the window, then again, and Angie fought the sudden urge to rise and see the creature before it vanished into the night—she felt that pull of wonder deep in her chest, the desire to follow some ancient call to dark places. But her daughter still trembled in her arms and the wild desire vanished, along with the creature that rose into the air and away from her home.

"We're okay," she whispered into her daughter's hair. "It's gone, we're okay."

Ellie was shaking so hard that for a wild moment Angie thought she was actually having a seizure. Then the girl gasped and Angie saw the tears on her face, the anguish in her eyes.

"I told you," she sobbed, still shaking with terror. "I *told* you something was coming for me."

And she had.

Earlier that week, Ellie—fifteen years old, awkward and hopeful and brimming with belief that magic still lurked in the unknown places of the world—came home from school with stars in her eyes about a new substitute teacher. He was a little older, she said, which coming from her could have meant twenty or fifty-five, and he taught their English class about Arthurian legends.

"He said that everyone got Morgana wrong, that she only became a villain later on when the church wanted to demonize powerful women. He said she was the most powerful out of all of them, that she had these connections with the land and animals and that even dragons listened to her—"

"I didn't know there were dragons in Arthurian England," said Joel from the table, dryly. Ellie shot him a withering look and continued. Angie tuned it all out, the chatter of her children and the clanking of the dishes under her hands. Her mind drifted more and more lately to the great expanse of green just beyond their door, as if being pulled by an old tether to something she couldn't name. She stared out the window over the sink, taking in the trees and mountains beyond their little cabin.

"—He told me something else, too." The tone in Ellie's voice jerked Angie back to reality. It was the tone of a child divulging information that was requested to remain secret, filled to the brim with the air of knowing something she shouldn't. Trepidation, too. Angie's eyes flashed to her teen daughter and saw the same concerns etched in her husband's face. She said nothing, waiting for Ellie to continue. The girl looked between her parents, face nervous.

"He asked to talk to me after class and he said he—he had to warn me about something?" Her voice lilted up as if asking a question. Angie's heart beat faster. Ellie swallowed hard. "Apparently—well, he said something weird about the doors under the mountain and that there has to be a guardian. To save everyone from what's behind the doors. He said that—that he thinks I'm the guardian, that's why he came to the school today, to tell me—" She was speaking very quickly now, twisting her hands together but looking unflinchingly between both of her parents, who were decidedly not meeting each other's gaze. "—and he said that there's proof, that it's all real, there's a place I can go to see that he's not lying—"

"Did he ask you to meet him there?" Joel's voice was very calm, and Angie watched his hands shaking in fists under the kitchen table. Ellie nodded and Angie thought her heart might break as she looked at her child, who still believed magic could be found at the backs of wardrobes, who would have walked into Mordor in a heartbeat, who was being lied to by an older man who wanted to manipulate her.

"Ellie," she said, softly. "Do you believe him?"

Confusion crossed Ellie's features. "Of course I do. It's *proof,* mom, proof that magic is real—"

Joel was shaking his head, pinching the bridge of his nose. Angie tried but couldn't keep the concern and sadness off of her face and Ellie looked between them again, eyebrows tightening in anger.

"Why don't you believe me? This is important, it could be life or death. He said that something would be coming for the guardian, the person that was chosen, and that I need to be ready. I *have* to see if it's real." There was desperation in her voice, the desperation of a girl clinging to childhood beliefs with tight fists. Angie wished that the world was different, that it was better, that girls could go on believing in magic and mystery and wonderful things instead of seeing the monsters that lurked at every turn.

"He was telling you a story, Eleanor," Angie said, more sharply than she meant to. "He was telling you what you wanted to hear so that he could get you alone."

"No, he wouldn't do that, he was really nice—"

"He wouldn't be a troll to you if the point was to get you alone, would he?" she snapped, her hand tightening on the wooden spatula. The spaghetti sauce burned on the stove, forgotten. Ellie looked as though she'd been slapped and Angie wanted so badly to tell her it was okay, that maybe the story was true, but she knew, in the way that all older women know, what dangers awaited her daughter if she followed this older man into the woods.

Something scratched deep at her memory, something about men and woods and danger. Something her grandmother had said, long ago, in this very cabin. The memory bobbed just beyond her reach and Angie felt, suddenly, that she was missing something vital about all of this.

"I'm sorry," she said quietly. "I'm sorry that you have to think about these things, but you do."

Ellie's eyes brimmed with tears. "Just because you don't believe in *anything* doesn't mean there's nothing to believe in."

"Ellie—"

She was already up from the table, stalking to her bedroom. She stopped with her hand on the door, turning halfway back to her parents. "I hope that nothing comes for me when you won't even let me prepare for it," she said with all the drama of an indignant teen. And then she slammed the door behind her.

Now, still crouching beside Ellie's bed and shaking with adrenaline, Angie tried desperately to make sense of it all. She knew there were odd things that called the Appalachian hills home, everyone who lived here knew that, but the local haints were a far cry from whatever the fuck had just been in her yard. Angie twisted back and up, peering at the window and the early dawn beyond. Deep claw marks gouged deep into the bottom of the window, like something had dug the window open by force. Angie wanted to throw up.

"I told you," Ellie sobbed again. "I *told* you."

"I know," said Angie, climbing to her feet. "I know. Where did he tell you to go, in the woods? Did he tell you how to get there?"

Ellie froze and the realization hit Angie like a train. "Ellie. Did you go out there?"

"Yes, and he wasn't there like you and dad were so afraid of. Nothing was there. It was just a freaking clearing in the woods—"

"When did you go?" Angie interrupted her. Ellie didn't meet her eye. "Eleanor."

"Yesterday afternoon."

Angie drew in a deep breath, mind spinning. She wanted to think that none of this was real, that it had just been a bear and a cougar out in the yard—but cougars didn't have claws like that and neither did bears. And something had *knocked*.

She wished her grandmother was still alive.

She pushed all of it away—the wishing and the swirling doubt and the lingering terror—and fixed her eyes on her daughter.

"I need you to tell me how to get there."

"Joel. Joel, wake up," Angie hissed, shaking her husband's shoulder. Joel grunted blearily and squinted at her, his face lined and hair mussed from sleep.

"What's on?" He mumbled and her lips twitched up in a smile.

"I need you to get up. We have to go into the woods."

His squint intensified. "For why?"

"You remember Ellie telling us about the teacher that we thought was just a creep, which could still very well be the case, but there is now new information—"

He put a hand on her mouth. "Too many words. Less words, please."

Part of her wanted to laugh and the other part wanted to shake him. She sighed and moved his hand.

"There were monsters in our front yard, Joel. Big ones. I think it has something to do with Ellie. We need to go into the woods."

It spoke to the type of man Joel was and the respect he had for his wife that he did not question her assertion that monsters were real and in their front yard. He dressed quickly, took the family gun from the safe at the back of the closet, and followed Angie out of the cabin. She froze at the edge of the porch, breathing heavily. That pull in her chest was stronger than ever, stronger than it had been since she was a child, and she knew that even if Ellie hadn't told them how to get to the place in the woods where magic was real, she would have found it. She was being led to it.

"Holy shit," murmured Joel at her side and she started out of her trance, following his gaze to the forest.

"Oh my god."

Massive tracks covered the yard. Three-pronged toes, like some sort of lizard, but enormous, far bigger than any lizard she'd ever heard of—and with a six year old son obsessed with everything dinosaurs and reptiles, she'd have heard of it. She followed the tracks with her eyes, moving off the porch and into the yard as if in a dream. There, right outside the kitchen window. That golden eye flashed again into her mind, ancient and almost warm, like it knew her.

"There were two," she heard herself saying as if from a great distance. She pointed at the larger tracks. "I think—I *think* this one may have been protecting us. Protecting us from—" She whirled, eyes scanning the ground for the tracks of another creature, long-clawed and soaked with evil. At the base of the house, just beyond the kitchen, she saw them. Almost human but wrong, the feet too long and too narrow, and the claw marks on the side of the house.

The scratching above her as she'd sprinted for Ellie's room. The evil she'd felt at the window, malevolent and cold.

"—protecting us from that." Her voice was low as she stared at those claw marks. Joel took her hand and held it, tightly. She forced herself to turn away from the house, away from her children, and toward the woods.

"Did Ellie want to come?"

"Of course she did." She didn't need to say that she would sooner die than lead her child into danger.

"Do...do you think it's possible? That she's some sort of...like, a chosen one?"

"Our nerdy-ass child is not Harry Potter, no matter what she'd like to think," said Angie firmly. "Could you imagine trying to live with her if she was the chosen one?"

"Good luck trying to get her to clean the bathroom."

"Like she needs another excuse to ignore me. She already thinks I'm lame, we cannot allow her to gain superpowers on top of the precision teenage sass."

Joel grinned and nudged her with an elbow. "She learned that sass from the best. And I think you're great. Warrior mom."

Angie rolled her eyes. Together they faced the wood, the daunting wall of green and birdsong that was apparently home to monsters.

They began to walk. Angie followed Ellie's directions as well as the pull under her collarbones, the relentless urge to follow *some-thing*, to find *something*. The woods were quiet and still in the early morning. The birds singing from their perches comforted Angie, who feared the sudden onset of silence and heavy air. The forest floor crunched under her feet, solid and familiar. Joel's breathing beside her was rhythmic, steady, and a swell of love rose within her for this man and his steadfast presence.

"Thank you," she said quietly, glancing at him. His blue eyes met her green and she took in that face, as familiar to her as her own, the lines around his eyes and mouth, the stubble over his chin. "For believing me."

He nodded, just once. "You always said weird things happened in the woods."

"Yeah, but there's *weird* and then there's—"

"Fairy tale shit."

"Is that what this is? With our kid as some sort of chosen one? It feels more like a nightmare."

For a moment he was silent, and the sounds of the wild filled the gap where his voice had been.

"What do you think it means?" He asked, finally. "'The guardian'. That's what she said, right? Something about the doors in the mountain or under the mountain and a guardian?"

Angie nodded.

"Do you think—whatever was in our yard?"

"I don't know. Maybe. Maybe one of them, the smaller one with the claws. The other one felt...I don't know how to describe it. Evil leaves a mark, you know? It has this unmistakable feeling about it that can't be masked or ignored once you know what it is. The golden eyed one didn't feel that way. It just felt old. And curious."

They fell back into tense silence. The sky above the trees glowed with the pink light of sunrise and the fear in Angie loosened a little more as the darkness of night faded.

There was something familiar about all of this. Like it was a story she'd heard long ago.

"I told you about some of the weird stuff that happened to me as a kid, right?" She hadn't realized she was going to say it until the words were out of her mouth, the goosebumps crawling up her skin as they always did when she talked about certain events of her adolescence. She felt Joel tense next to her.

"Not really. You hinted at it, but never really explained anything."

"It's hard to explain. I'd have dreams about things, really weird, specific stuff, and then it would happen. I dreamt about my best friend's mom getting cancer the night before she got the diagnosis. And another time I dreamed that the same friend was—that she got raped by a teacher at our school. Because the other dreams had come true, I went by where I saw them in the dream, and I was able to stop it." She shivered. "There was other stuff, too. Things I heard and—and saw, in the woods. No monsters, not like today, but things that felt wrong. A doorway to nowhere, these stone circles with runes or some kind of markings in the middle."

"Did May ever tell you anything?"

"She told me a lot of things. Most of it cryptic and confusing, like she couldn't just give me a straight answer. It was all riddles and warnings."

"About..?"

She gestured around them and the gnarled old trees and the steadily sloping ground. "The forest, mostly. She loved nature but it was like she never really trusted it and she didn't want me to trust it either. She really wanted me to understand that the woods were dangerous."

The woods and danger and a man. Angie shook her head, trying to clear away the fog around the memory, wondering why she kept coming back to those three things—

She remembered. She remembered her grandmother, May, looking at her with the same green eyes in her own face, warning her. About the woods and danger and a man.

"There was one thing, when I was about Ellie's age," Angie formed the words slowly, as if she was afraid speaking about the memory would chase it away. "She told me that one day a man in the woods would call my name and that I must not ever, ever answer."

"*Any* man? That's not terrible advice if weirdos hang out in the trees and try to talk to teenagers—"

"No, you dingus, I think she meant a specific man."

"That's weird."

"She was a weird lady. She definitely never talked about anything like this."

"Did she say what would happen if you *did* answer?"

"No. At least, not that I can remember."

As her words trailed off, Angie realized that the woods had gone quiet. Goosebumps rose over her arms and the back of her neck prickled—she felt eyes on her, eyes as old as the trees themselves.

"Your grandmother gave you every answer you needed. You chose not to listen."

The voice came from between the trees, deep but decidedly human, and out of the corner of her eye Angie saw Joel's hand go to the gun at his hip. Angie whirled around, looking for the voice, and a man stepped out of the air as if from behind a curtain. Power flowed from him like a flood, and Angie knew at once that this was the man from her grandmother's warnings. Her skin tingled and she tasted metal as that power washed over her; she wondered how it was she recognized it as power when she had never encountered it before, hadn't even believed in magic yesterday.

"Who are you?" she demanded, hands balling into fists at her sides. "How do you know my grandmother?"

His head tilted, a strange, almost animal gesture. "Your grandmother was the finest guardian these mountains have had in a very, very long time. She protected you well. Too well."

"What the fuck are you talking about?" she snapped, just as Joel said: "Are you the one who told our teen daughter to meet you in the woods?"

The man's brows furrowed as he looked between the husband and wife, and he stepped closer.

"Your daughter would have answered the call," he said, softly, moving silently toward them. "She wants to. She has the makings of greatness in her."

"Stay away from our daughter," Joel said hoarsely, voice low and full of the threat of violence. But the man's eyes—green eyes—fixed on Angie's.

"I want nothing to do with your daughter," said the man calmly, still looking at Angie. "She is young and untested, and the burden that must be borne is as great as it is terrible. This gift, this curse is passed among the women of your bloodline when the mountain has had need of it. The doors have opened and the old magic is free. The call is not for your daughter. It is for you."

Those eyes flashed, beautiful and terrible. The tingle of magic was around her, inside her, so strong that she didn't know if she could speak; some long-forgotten dam had burst within her and set the magic free. The man stepped closer again, and Angie grabbed Joel's arm with a surprisingly steady hand as her husband tried to put himself between her and the man. She knew she was not in danger. Not yet.

"You ran, girl." The man's voice was soft, as soft as the rustle of leaves in the breeze. "You ran from this place and the magic it promised, ran from your gifts and into the city so you could convince yourself that you were normal, that you weren't made of something different, something older—"

The world swayed under her feet. She felt power everywhere, not just his or hers, but power and magic deep within the forest itself, calling her. It was as though the veil itself was vanishing. She could almost see it, she thought, could almost see the veil stretched over everything, shimmering as finely as gossamer in the light. What mysteries lay just beyond; what magic lurked just out of her reach? The feeling in her chest was on the verge of exploding as she realized how she yearned to see the world beyond the world, yearned for the mystery of that great golden eye meeting hers, yearned for the wonder of legends and stories.

She grabbed her husband's hand tightly and met the green gaze that was so much like her grandmother's, like her own.

"Angeline Crawford," said the man, green eyes glowing. "Are you ready to see the naked truth of the world?"

— THE MOUNTAIN WITCH —
By Lucy A. Snyder

Swordmistress Ruby's heart swelled with bittersweet pride as her apprentice Finch scrambled up onto the granite cliff where the Witch of Fangsdun dwelled. Ruby carefully folded her legs into a more comfortable position in the blind she'd made from brush, dry tall grass, and scrubby deadfall branches the night before on the western slope. She refocused her brass spyglass on his lanky figure and watched, breath bated, as he drew his falchion and pointed it at the dark fissure that led to the Witch's cavern lair. The monks had forbidden any to follow the champions onto the mountain to offer aid, but Ruby was desperate to see him succeed with her own eyes. Surely hanging back a few hundred yards couldn't hurt? He was still facing the Witch alone.

Finch's voice was as bright and strong as his sword: "Foul Enchantress! Come forth and face..."

The rest of his ritual challenge was snatched from her ears by a sudden gust of frigid mountain wind.

Ruby prayed he'd remember the rest of the incantation that was supposed to render the witch vulnerable and careless. She'd drilled him for hours on the warspell, and his memory was good.

But she knew from awful experience that a bad case of nerves could drive a youth's mind as blank as a salt flat. He was the last of her prospects, the final seventh son of a seventh son who the monks declared could fulfill the prophecy God-Emperor Bornath carved into the Obelisk of Xanos ten thousand years before.

Young Finch *had* to fulfill it.

For if he did not, it was foretold that during the next full eclipse, the Witch would use her dread sorceries to awaken the Ur-Dragon who slept beneath the mountains. The vast black beast would rise from the earth, shattering their lands like an eggshell. The entire continent would erupt in hellfire from deep in the world's core, and after everything burned, impossibly tall waves from the oceans would rise from the depths to drown any souls who had managed to survive the conflagration.

Ruby had sworn that she would never let that happen. She'd sworn it first as a twelve-year-old apprentice and sworn it again before each of the five duels that she herself had fought with the Witch upon that wind-wracked cliff. There, Finch now stood proud in his tall, polished leather boots and shining chainmail, his mop of blond hair hidden beneath a steel sallet that bore the monks' hieroglyphic blessings in gold paint.

Despite her lifelong resolve, Ruby had never fully believed in the orthodox monks' interpretation of the prophecy. The dragon? Yes, she accepted its existence and threat without question or qualm. But surely, she'd thought, any skilled, resolute warrior could defeat the Witch by cutting her heart from her chest. Many of the passages on the Obelisk has been blurred by wind and time; no one alive could point to any lines that specified either a son or a specific birth order. She'd been certain to the core of her soul that the monks' declaration of the ancient magic was a chauvinistic fiction.

But when she awoke battered, bleeding, and mud-caked in the starveling heather at the foot of Mount Fangsdun for the fifth time, she was forced to admit to herself that perhaps the patriarchs were right: only a male descendant of Bornath's holy loins could sunder their ancient nemesis. Only a seventh son of a seventh son.

Fortunately, the God-Emperor had sired at least forty children on his wives and concubines. Male descendants were plentiful as grapes on twisting vines. For two long decades, Ruby set her own dreams of heroism aside and dedicated herself to teaching the art of the sword to all the promising lads of the land. Poured all her hard-won wisdom into their coltish skulls. All to save their world.

"Witch!" Finch shouted. "Come forth! I adjure thee, by the power of Bornath, thou must face me!"

Ruby sucked in her breath and ducked lower behind a twisting bit of cedar as the Witch stepped from the shadows, tall and powerfully built, her face hidden in shadow beneath her black leather cowl. Only once, when Ruby and the Witch had wrestled, sweating and straining on the flat slate stones beneath the twisted white tree near the cavern entrance, had the cowl fallen back, revealing the Witch's true visage.

The swordmistress still wasn't sure what she had quite expected to see—a bald, scarred head, perhaps. Dry, yellowed skin stretched tight over a pit-eyed, grinning skull. Or toadstool-green flesh hanging loose from a bloated face. Maybe a hooked, warty nose. She'd heard the old weapons masters describing all manner of grotesque features late at night around crackling bonfires or grog-damp tavern tables.

But Ruby had most certainly not expected smooth, dewy skin burnished like bronze, nor full, rose-red lips. Fierce eyes, yes, those she would have laid odds on at the tavern...but she'd never have wagered they'd be half-obscured by locks of thick, raven-black hair. And she never reckoned those eyes would be as deeply green as a rose's leaves. Nor sharp as its thorns.

And she would never have imagined that for nearly every night after that battle, she'd see those green eyes in her dreams. Feel herself embraced by those lean, strong, leather-clad arms. Taste those red lips upon her own.

For ten thousand nights she'd awakened with a start, her linen nightclothes drenched in sweat, her body burning with desire and shame. How could she have let herself become so bewitched? But, she reasoned, endless private torture was a fit punishment for having failed at the task she'd sworn to do.

When the Witch was dead at the hands of a champion she had trained and taught herself, surely the cursed dreams would end?

"Save me, lad," she whispered as Finch shouted the ritual third challenge into the wind.

Her heart leapt as she saw the black, cowled figure who haunted her dreams step from the dark chasm. Yes. The Witch was answering the call of his spell. Decades of hard work had come down to this. At long last, was victory finally at hand?

Finch, bless the boy, sprinted straight at the Witch, clearly intending to run her through with his blade. Cut her heart from her chest. The gory image that rose unbidden in Ruby's mind made her feel intensely sick to her soul. Tears welled in her eyes.

What is the matter with you? she angrily scolded herself. No woman was a stranger to blood. She'd cleaved enemies in half in battle. Gouged out a man's eyes with her bare thumbs to defend her own life in her bedchamber once. Why should the scene playing out before her shake her so?

The sorceress made a casual stirring motion with the index finger of her left hand. Ruby watched in horror as a whirlwind rose around Finch, stopping him in his tracks, lifting him off his feet. The lad flailed and slashed at the wind, trying to free himself from his airy bonds to no avail. To the lad's credit, he did not drop his sword in his struggle.

The Witch made a flicking motion and the whirlwind whisked Finch off the mountain and carried him away toward the sea.

"Finch! No!" Ruby shouted. The sickness in the pit of her stomach curdled into a dizzying panic.

Before she had quite realized what she was doing, Ruby dropped her spyglass, stood, and kicked herself free of the branches of her blind. She sprinted up the narrow trail to the granite cliff, knowing she was not remotely prepared to face the Witch in battle. Her leather jerkin and canvas breeches might as well have been a diaphanous chemise as far as any protection in a serious duel was concerned. Even worse, she had no sword, just a hunting knife strapped to her thigh for trimming twigs, and a sling in case she encountered a poisonous snake or hungry arachnid. She'd deliberately left her weapons behind in case her stealth failed and someone caught her out on the mountainside. She couldn't very well claim to simply be watching if she was armed and ready to take Finch's place, could she?

And by now, at least one of the spectators below had certainly spotted her. Probably so had the Witch from above. Prison and dishonor waited for her at the foot of the mountain. Death waited for her within it.

But she could not stop herself from running, not even when her knees and ankles began to hurt with every pounding step and her breath ached bloody in her throat. The patriarchs would declare Finch's defeat to be her own final failure, and she had to do *something* in the face of it. Had to do something to fix it. Her life's work couldn't end with her meekly sneaking back down the mountain to receive half-hearted condolences. There would be nothing for her after that but to fade into obscurity, live out her years as any other forgotten old woman with no husband and no children would. If she outlived her modest savings, she'd be reduced to begging on the city square. Toothless in every way.

Better that the Witch burn her alive than to suffer such a graceless, powerless existence.

Ruby was shocked to find the Witch still standing on the cliff when she hauled herself to the top. She got to her feet as fast as she could, lest the Witch attack, but for a mortifying moment, all the swordmistress could do was lean on her knees and gasp for air. Meanwhile, the Witch remained motionless, hands clasped behind her back as she gazed out at the horizon.

Is she toying with me? Ruby wondered as she wiped the perspiration from her eyes.

But that seemed unlikely. The Witch could have mocked her for being so out of breath before their battle had even begun. Or given her a withering stare and sidelong smirk. She could have done something to try to bait the swordmistress into making a rageful misstep. But instead, her adversary seemed to be politely ignoring her weakness and giving her time to recover. Professional courtesy? Pity? A ruse? Ruby just wasn't certain.

The wind against Ruby's sweat-soaked chemise drew all the heat from her body despite her exertion. With a shaking, exhausted hand, she slid her hunting knife from its leather thigh sheath, straightened her complaining spine, and pointed the well-worn blade at the sorceress. Her entire arm trembled with cold and fatigue. Would the day's humiliations ever end?

"H-how could you kill Finch like that?" Her voice wasn't any steadier than the rest of her. And the question seemed stupid the moment she uttered it. Clearly, the Witch could *easily* kill Finch. What else did she expect from the immortal embodiment of evil?

The Witch sighed, still gazing out at the land. "The fool is alive. Stuck in a tree in the valley, I expect. I'm not in the habit of murdering children."

A lie, surely. Trickery designed to convince her to drop her guard. Ruby began to utter the old challenge despite her shaky voice: "F-foul ench-chantress, c-come forth—"

"Oh, stop this nonsense." The Witch turned toward Ruby and pushed back the leather cowl, revealing her face. She was just as beautiful and youthful as she'd been before, and despite her bone-deep cold, Ruby felt her cheeks flush with envy and embarrassment.

The Witch gazed at her with a mixture of irritation and concern. "I have *already* come forth, and *you* are in no condition to fight off so much as an angry wasp. Come inside and get yourself warm before you give yourself pneumonia."

Ruby blinked. These were not words she'd ever expected to hear. "W-what trickery is this?"

The Witch pinched the bridge of her nose and sighed as if the weight of the entire world had settled on her shoulders. "I offer no trickery. Can't we just talk? Like civilized people? Sit and talk, instead of repeating this pointless dance of blood? I've grown so *weary* of the ridiculousness that Bornath and his apostles inflicted on us all."

Ruby's cheeks flushed hot again. "Do not utter such heresy before me, Witch."

The Witch threw up her hands. "Oh, for the love of all the dead. I *know* you know better, Ruby. You're a very smart woman. I know you've doubted the fairy tales the monks teach the common folk in this land. Haven't you ever once been curious to hear my side of the old story?"

Ruby bit her lip. She'd lain awake at night wondering if the stories she'd been told were true. But she'd sworn an oath to be faithful to her kingdom, and that meant she had to accept the monks' gospels as unerring truth. She could never give a voice to her own doubts.

So, she simply stood, silent and shivering, as the Witch stared at her with expectantly raised eyebrows.

"For pity's sake," the Witch finally sighed. "Are you *really* so eager to die today? Why not come inside, get warm, hear my tale, and *then* we can come back out here and fight if you're so dead set upon it. What have you got to lose?"

This *had* to be a ruse. On the other hand, if the Witch knifed her in the kidneys when her back was turned? That would still be one of the better outcomes Ruby faced. "I...um..."

The sorceress clicked her tongue impatiently and spread her hands. "Die now or die later. What difference will it make? But *please* make a decision. I'm cold, too, and my toes are going numb."

"All right." Ruby uncertainly sheathed her knife. "Let's go inside and talk."

Rough granite gave way to slick cavern walls, which in turn gave way to plaster and brick. Finally the passageway ended at a stout oaken door reinforced with thick riveted iron straps. It swung open noiselessly when the Witch approached, revealing a huge domed room with thousands of tomes shelved on the polished wood walls. The floors were gleaming white granite. Enchanted torches floated in the dome above, which was painted to look like the night's sky.

"Please, sit down." The Witch gestured toward the rightmost of a pair of well-upholstered red leather reading chairs facing each other a few feet away from a broad fireplace at the other end of the room.

Ruby crossed the room and cautiously settled in the chair, stifling a groan as the stiff muscles in her lower back and hips painfully stretched and reluctantly released.

A pewter plate bearing a blue crockery mug of steaming liquid floated through the air to Ruby.

"Hot tea?" the Witch asked. A seemingly identical plate floated to her as she seated herself.

Ruby eyed the hovering mug suspiciously. "What's in it?"

"Red leaf from the southern archipelago, dried rose hips, cinnamon, and a spoonful of honey." The Witch took her own mug and sipped it gingerly. "Nothing poisonous, nothing that would impair your mind or cloud your judgement. It's just a bit warmer than I intended, so mind your tongue."

Ruby grunted neutrally and took the mug. The hot ceramic soothed her aching knuckles through her goat leather gloves. The wafting fragrance awakened a long-forgotten memory of her aunt making her tea when she was a child. "I haven't had red tea in years."

"Few in this kingdom have." The Witch blew across her mug and took another sip. "The monks' hatred of foreigners has closed countless trade routes. But I needn't tell you that."

"'A good solider needs neither tea nor grog as long as he has water blessed by Bornath.'" Ruby mostly kept the sarcasm out of her voice as she quoted the city's Knight Primus, who seemed to relish new deprivations amongst the troops.

"If this keeps up," the Witch said, "in another thirty years, I expect the monks will claim that tea is but a myth designed to lead the faithful astray. And no one who knows better will dare say a word to counter the lie."

Ruby pursed her lips, frowning. The Witch's prediction was heresy, but nonetheless she knew in her heart it was likely to come to pass. The monks were the arbiters of truth, and so anything they said was true. Facts and reality were irrelevant.

"Would you like anything else?" the Witch asked. "A biscuit, perhaps?"

"No, thank you." Ruby eyed the Witch and sipped her tea, trying to gauge her true intent. "To what do I owe this exceptional hospitality?"

The Witch's gaze dropped to her mug. Was she turning a little red? Blushing? "It's...good to see you again, after so many years.

I've missed our encounters, and I had started to lose hope that you might come here again."

Ruby nearly spat out her drink in surprise and indignation. "'Encounters'? I was trying to kill you, sorceress."

The Witch met her gaze. Mischief gleamed in her eye. "Were you, though?"

Heat rose in Ruby's cheeks, and her heart pounded, whether from anger or something else she wasn't certain. "H-how dare you suggest—" she began to stammer.

The Witch raised her hands palms up in an appeasing gesture. Her mug hung in the air where she'd released it. "I meant no offense! I cast no aspersions upon your skills or loyalties! Of course you were trying to kill me. Of *course*."

Ruby took a deep breath, trying to calm down. "And you were trying to kill me."

The Witch smiled crookedly and retrieved her tea. "At first."

"What in the six hells do you mean?"

"At first, I thought you were yet another earnest, tediously violent lad who fancied himself a chosen champion of his god and country. But then, I realized that neither were you a lad, nor were you tedious. You were...unusually skilled at countering my spells. I had to work hard to win that day. It was honestly more fun than I'd had in hundreds of years."

"Fun." Ruby stared at her, not sure whether to be flattered or mortally offended. "If I'd been a bit luckier that day, you would be dead."

"That's true. But knowing there was a real risk—that's *exactly* what made it fun. Our battles made me feel alive in a way that I hadn't in a very long time. And so, yes, I've missed them a great deal."

"So you went easy on me? Is that what you're saying?"

"Oh, not at all," the Witch laughed. "Every time, I had to use all my skills and wits to get the better of you. I just abstained from killing spells and fatal blows, avoided breaking your bones, that kind of thing."

"You certainly didn't extend that courtesy to any of my students," Ruby grumbled. Most of them had to spend weeks in the infirmary after facing the Witch.

"Well, I had to dissuade them from returning, didn't I?"

"Dissuade them? You tore Tauron limb from limb and incinerated his corpse!"

"Tauron..." The Witch squinted, apparently trying to remember. "The tall redhead with the bull tattoo on his neck?"

"Yes."

"He called me a whore and bragged that he would violate me before he killed me. I don't tolerate that kind of disrespect in my own house. And I couldn't tell if he was profanely bluffing or nakedly expressing his intent. So, I erred on the side of caution and made very, very sure that he could never rape anyone again."

"Oh." Ruby felt sick. "He seemed so polite..."

"Of course he did. He knew you could utterly destroy him. When your body is healthy, you are the finest, deadliest sword fighter I have seen in ten thousand years. Even a thickheaded, arrogant, woman-hating lout like Tauron had to recognize the danger you present."

Ruby's cheeks warmed at the seemingly earnest flattery and she gave a nervous, surprised laugh. "Surely I am not the finest. Surely Bornath—"

"Ugh." The Witch rolled her eyes. "I do so tire of hearing about the Fraud-Emperor. I knew him. Better than I ever wanted to, I promise you. He was barely a man, and certainly no god. You are a thousand times the warrior he ever was."

Hearing such heresy spoken out loud made a reflexive panic churn Ruby's guts. She glanced at the domed ceiling, half afraid that holy lightning would strike them both down. "You must not say such things."

The Witch spread her arms wide. "If I cannot speak the truth in my own home, where can I speak it?"

Ruby shook her head anxiously. "What you say cannot be true."

"Why not? I could put you directly inside my memories so you could experience them for yourself...but of course your monks have probably told you that such magic is always an unholy deception, and you can never trust it."

"They told us that, yes."

"Then I have no way to prove that I speak the truth. And so, my story must stand on its own merits. I believe it does. But if your mind is closed and your beliefs carved in temple stone, I wouldn't want to waste my breath. Or your time, which is more precious than mine."

Ruby swallowed, still dreading a bolt from above. "Tell me. I want to know."

The Witch raised her eyebrows skeptically. "Truly? You'll listen with open ears?"

"Yes."

"All right." The Witch took a long drink of her tea and settled back in her chair. "I was born in the Atrian province and spent my youth in the mountains there. My mother led the local coven of witches, and she started teaching me the old magics when I was barely out of diapers. I was twelve when Bornath inherited the throne from his father. When I was fifteen, he sent his emissaries to our mountain enclave, and they told me and the other young witches that they were recruiting magic adepts from across the land for special training at the capital. We would be provided with room and board and tuition, and we would learn mysteries that had previously only been accessible to royal wizard apprentices. My mother didn't want me to leave the mountains, but I was eager to experience the glamour of life in the city."

"I've never heard of such a magical training program," Ruby said.

"You never heard of it because it was all a lie." The Witch paused, looking grimly furious. "We were drugged and interrogated. Afterward, the strongest boys were marched off to the docks to be pressed into the navy. The young boys and girls were sorted according to our handlers' estimations of our beauty. Those they deemed plain or ugly were sent to the slave auction houses. The rest of us were lined up in the courtyard, and Bornath chose twelve of us for his harem. The others he gave as gifts to his political and military allies, and those he hoped to recruit as allies. Hundreds of promising youths fed into a meat grinder to satisfy old wealthy perverts."

Ruby felt dizzy and ill. "I... I never heard about this, either."

"Of course you haven't. Why should the first monks tell anyone that their exalted God-Emperor was a liar, a slave-monger, a pedophile, and a pimp? 'Holy' is not a word I'd use to describe a man who does such vile things."

"If you know so much about that time, then what was written on the Obelisk of Xanos?" Ruby demanded. "What was the full prophecy?"

The Witch arched an eyebrow. "I myself have wondered what fictions Bornath's monks carved upon that ostentatious rock. But alas, I never saw if for myself. By the time he commissioned the Obelisk, his wizards had cast powerful warding enchantments upon the foot of this mountain to keep me from entering the kingdom. I have not been able to walk or fly from this mountain, and I cannot break the magic from here."

Ruby shook her head, not wanting to believe it all. It was one thing to have doubts about some of the stories the monks preached, to have heard whispered rumors about corrupt clerics. She knew how badly men behaved when they had more power than they deserved. And the monks never claimed to be anything but men.

But the God-Emperor was supposed to be the son of the Maker himself, the noblest, most perfect human to have ever been born to a woman. And for him to be an utter deceit? For Ruby to have spent her entire life and the lives of her students in service to nothing but a lie?

She shook her head again. "No. It's not possible."

"It is."

Her mind strained for a rational explanation, something to shore up the fast-crumbling foundation of her faith. "But...but ten thousand years is such a long time. Memories fade, they change, perhaps you mistook some other noble—"

"*I am not mistaken.*" The Witch's voice had turned as cold and strong as the wind outside. "Bornath was a villain and a fraud. As I said before, I can put you inside my memories of what he did to us, but I promise you that you'll sleep much better if you just take my word."

Ruby looked the Witch in the eye, and she could see profound pain and fury in the ancient woman's gaze. If she'd ever lied, she was certainly not lying now.

"How...how did you escape him?"

Her eyes went unfocused. "In some ways, I never did. The shortest version is that I bided my time, swallowed my disgust. Made him believe I was in his thrall. I waited for my moment, and when it arrived, I fled."

A single tear dripped down her cheek, but she didn't move to wipe it away. "He was furious. Obsessed. He had hundreds of women at his fingertips, but he mobilized all his forces to find me. And when he could not, he took revenge and destroyed my village."

A shock of surprise washed through Ruby as she realized she'd grown up hearing a version of this story in the Temple.

"The Purge of the Witches," she gasped.

The Witch's lip curled. "Ah, yes. They did find a way to twist that brutal atrocity into a tale of noble heroism, didn't they? Turned the slaughter of parents, children, herbalists, and midwives into a rousing tale of brave knights hunting wicked child thieves."

This was all too much. Ruby's head spun. Panic gripped her heart. "No. No, no, no, this can't be. You're...you're lying. This is a trick to keep me from stopping you from awakening the Dragon—"

"Ruby, there's no dragon—"

"Liar! You're going to destroy us all!"

"Why in the name of the blessed dead would I do that?"

"Because...because you're evil!"

"In the name of the Mother, I thought you were smarter than this, Ruby. Evil is a behavior, not a state of existence. People don't just do evil for the sake of it. Not even Bornath. He sought pleasure, and wealth, and power, and he didn't care if he hurt other people in the process. Even those weird island cultists who sacrifice children to that octopus god, well, they're doing it to please their god, aren't they? They're doing it to secure power in the afterlife. People have a *reason* for doing evil, even if it's simple spite or boredom."

The Witch gestured broadly at the room around them. "This is my home. I have spent centuries making this exactly how I like it. Why would I want this destroyed? Why would I want to burn the tea I love? The hills and forests I love looking at every morning? What would I possibly have to gain? How does that damned fairy tale about me make a single grain of sense?"

Ruby felt stunned, and she was silent for a long time as her mind reluctantly digested the Witch's words. "It doesn't, does it."

"It's all just a lie to keep people afraid. A lie to convince people that their one true enemy lives here in this mountain. A lie to keep them distracted from the evil inside their own Temple and government."

Evil, and more evil. Ruby's mind drifted back to the story of the Purge.

"Bornath killed your mother?" she asked numbly.

"He tried. But she and the other coven leaders found a way to open an ancient, hidden door to other worlds. Many died, but she and the other mothers led many more to safety."

Ruby wasn't sure she'd heard correctly. "Other worlds?"

The Witch nodded. "They are as numerous as the stars in the sky. I have only been to fourteen myself. Fortunately, Bornath's wards do not block me from opening portals to other planets and universes. Seeing them has made me so much more frustrated with our own realm."

"Why?"

"Other human civilizations have accomplished *so much* in ten thousand years. Even in places with not a single bit of magic, they've created advancements and inventions that I could scarcely believe myself. But because of the monks and their hidebound beliefs, our world has stagnated. People wear the same clothes, fight the same wars, die of the same pointless injuries and preventable diseases. There is so much more our people could be!"

"Why don't you live in one of those better worlds?"

"Because *this* is my home. *This* is the place I want to be better!"

Better. Not once had the nobles or monks spoken of making anyone's lives better. Ruby's own missions and vows had never been about changing anything for the better; her work had been entirely focused on keeping disasters at bay. On keeping things the same. Her mind finally turned a corner, and she saw her past with fresh eyes. Saw all the evils and injustices she'd been blind to, all the lies she'd trusted as truth. All the opportunities she'd been denied, or simply missed.

She gave an anguished, frustrated growl and buried her face in her gloved hands, wishing the mountain would open beneath her and swallow her in darkness. "I have been such a fool. I have wasted my damned life."

She heard the Witch rise and cross the marble floor to stand beside her. The Witch rested her tea-warmed hand on the back of Ruby's neck, sending a thrill through her whole body.

"Your life is not over," the Witch said. "It's not too late to make this a world worth saving. And if you and I work together, I think that in time we can make this land and its people blossom."

Ruby rose, embraced the Witch, and kissed her deeply.

Even better, the Witch kissed her back.

The next morning, Ruby awoke on satin sheets fit for a queen, warm in the Witch's embrace. Her entire body ached, and she didn't care in the slightest.

"You've enchanted me," she accused sleepily.

"No more than you have enchanted me." The Witch sighed. "I think I fell in love with you the first time you tried to kill me."

Ruby laughed. "To think we spent all that time fighting when we could have been doing this instead."

"Clearly, we have a lot of catching up to do." The Witch paused. "Are you ever going to ask the question?"

"Oh. Uh. Will you marry me?"

"First: that seems sudden, don't you think? Second: yes, I will. But third: that's not the question I was referring to."

"...I'm lost."

The Witch made an exasperated noise. "Are you ever going to ask me my name, you silly goose?"

"Oh. Yes. What's your name?"

"It's Loralai."

"I could get used to saying that."

"You'd better, because if you address me as 'foul enchantress' again, you're going to get *such* a spanking, young lady."

Ruby grinned. "Promise?"

"Absolutely."

— ABOUT THE EDITORS —

ALANA JOLI ABBOTT is Editor in Chief of Outland Entertainment, where she co-edits fantasy and science fiction anthologies, such as *Where the Veil Is Thin, APEX: World of Dinosaurs,* and *Bridge to Elsewhere.* As a writer, her multiple choice novels, including *Choice of the Pirate* and *Blackstone Academy for Magical Beginners,* are published by Choice of Games. She is the author of three novels, several short stories (including one for this anthology), and many role playing game supplements. You can find her online at VirgilandBeatrice.com.

ADDIE J. KING is an attorney by day and author by nights, evenings, weekends, and whenever else she can find a spare moment. Her novels, *The Grimm Legacy, The Andersen Ancestry, The Wonderland Woes, The Bunyon Barter,* and *The Perrault Vow* are now available from Loconeal Publishing, now an imprint of Hydra Publications. Her novel, *Shades of Gray,* is the first book in The Hochenwalt Files series and is also available. A collection of her short stories has been published, entitled *Demons, Heroes, and Robots, Oh My!* She has also contributed a story to this anthology. Her website is http://www.addiejking.com

— ABOUT THE AUTHORS —

JOHN F. ALLEN is an American author born in Indianapolis, IN, where he currently resides. He is a founding member of the Speculative Fiction Guild and is a faculty member of the Indiana Writers Center. John has penned several published short stories, a novel and two novellas. His short stories have appeared in such works as *Black Pulp II, Spyfunk, Thunder on the Battlefield Vol. I: Sword, Trajectories,* and he has a short story collection titled *The Best is Yet to Come.* His novel is titled *The God Killers* and his novellas include *Codename: Knight Ranger* and its follow-up, *The God Particle Conspiracy.* John is also a poet, visual artist, and podcaster. He is married to an amazing woman named Mia, and between them have seven adult children and nine grandchildren. You can find him online at www.johnfallenauthor.com.

JD BLACKROSE loves all things storytelling and celebrates great writing by posting about it on her website, www.slipperywords. com. She's fearful that so-called normal people will discover exactly how often she thinks about wicked fairies, nasty wizards, homicidal elevators, treacherous forests, and the odd murder, even when she is supposed to be having coffee with a friend or paying something called "bills." As a survival tactic, she has mastered the art of looking interested. She would like to thank her parents for teaching her to ask questions, and in lieu of facts, how to make things up.

MAURICE BROADDUS is an accidental teacher (at the Oaks Academy Middle School), an accidental librarian (the School Library Manager, which is part of the IndyPL Shared System), and a purposeful community organizer (resident Afrofuturist at the Kheprw Institute), his work has appeared in such places as *Magazine of Fantasy & Science Fiction, Lightspeed Magazine, Black*

Panther: Tales from Wakanda, Asimov's, and *Uncanny Magazine,* with some of his stories having been collected in *The Voices of Martyrs.* His novels include the urban fantasy trilogy, *The Knights of Breton Court,* the steampunk novel, *Pimp My Airship,* and the middle grade detective novel series, *The Usual Suspects.* As an editor, he's worked on *Dark Faith, Fireside Magazine,* and *Apex Magazine.* His gaming work includes writing for the *Marvel Super-Heroes, Leverage,* and *Firefly* role-playing games as well as working as a consultant on *Watch Dogs 2.* Learn more about him at MauriceBroaddus.com.

SARAH HANS is an award-winning writer, editor, and teacher whose stories have appeared in more than 40 publications, including *Love Letters to Poe* and *Pseudopod.* She is the author of the horror novel *Entomophobia* as well as the short story collection *Dead Girls Don't Love.* You can also find her on Twitter, Instagram, and TikTok under the handle @witchwithabook, where she loves to talk about living the spooky life. She lives in Ohio with her partner, stepdaughter, and an entirely reasonable number of pets.

JIM C. HINES is the author of the *Magic ex Libris* series, the Princess series of fairy tale retellings, the humorous Goblin Quest trilogy, and the Fable Legends tie-in *Blood of Heroes.* He also won the 2012 Hugo Award for Best Fan Writer. His latest novel is *Terminal Peace,* book three in the humorous science fiction Janitors of the Post-Apocalypse trilogy. He lives in mid-Michigan with his family.

KATHRYN IVEY is a full-time intensive care nurse, part-time artist, and part-time writer who enjoys escaping into worlds of color and wonder. She has written constantly since she was a child, with the subject matter ranging from rich fantasy worlds to the grim reality of the COVID-19 pandemic. A firm believer in the ability of stories to teach us how to live, her stories often feature ordinary people who find themselves at the heart of extraordinary and impossible things. She is still not fully convinced that magic doesn't lurk in some old corner of the world, waiting patiently to be remembered. She is often found in the company of her dachshund, Badger, who was a dragon in a previous life and won't let anyone forget it.

ERICKA KAHLER has lived in eight states, all of them progressively further north. At this rate her nursing home will be above the Arctic Circle, even though she really HATES snow. She graduated from the University of West Florida with a BA in History. She has worked in fields ranging from radio to construction to law to finance, finally landing at eLearning design. Once she escaped the cult she began writing and editing. Her short fiction has been published in genre magazines as well as the anthologies *Under a Dark Sign* and *Dark Light 3*. Her creative non-fiction has appeared in *Chicken Soup for the Soul: Time to Thrive* and *Zest Literary Journal*.

VASEEM KHAN is the author of two award-winning crime series set in India, the Baby Ganesh Agency series set in modern Mumbai, and the Malabar House historical crime novels set in 1950s Bombay. His first book, *The Unexpected Inheritance of Inspector Chopra*, was selected by the Sunday Times as one of the 40 best crime novels published 2015-2020, and is translated into 16 languages. The second in the series won the Shamus Award in the US. In 2018, he was awarded the Eastern Eye Arts, Culture and Theatre Award for Literature. Vaseem was born in England, but spent a decade working in India. In 2021, *Midnight at Malabar House* won the Crime Writers Association Historical Dagger, the world's premier award for historical crime fiction. When he isn't writing, he works at the Jill Dando Institute of Security and Crime Science at University College London. Vaseem also co-hosts the popular crime fiction podcast, The Red Hot Chilli Writers.

Born and raised in Eagle Pass, Texas, **GUADALUPE GARCIA MCCALL** is the award-winning author of several young adult novels, some short stories for adults, and many children's poems. Guadalupe has received the Prestigious Pura Belpre Award, a Westchester Young Adult Fiction Award, the Tomás Rivera Mexican-American Children's Book Award, and was a finalist for the William C. Morris Award and the Andre Norton Award for Young Adult Science Fiction and Fantasy, among many other accolades. She is an advocate for literacy, diverse books, and Own Voices. In her travels, she is always looking for a good taco place and, she never met a chocolate mole sauce she didn't love! She loves to garden, cook, read, write, go for walks and take pictures of nature.

KIMBERLY PAULEY wanted to grow up to be Douglas Adams, Robert Heinlein, or Edgar Allen Poe when she was little, but has since settled for being herself and writing her own brand of funny quirky fantasy. Born in California, she has lived everywhere from Florida to Chicago and has now gone international to live in the UK with her husband (a numbers man) and son (her geeky partner in crime). She is the award-winning author of four young adult novels and 2020 marks her debut as a middle grade novelist, with *The Accidental Wizard*.

ALEXANDRA PITCHFORD is an author and freelance game designer who has worked on game settings such as *Shadowrun* and *Vampire: the Masquerade*. She has also written third-party material for *Pathfinder* 1st edition. Originally from the United States, she now lives in Victoria, Australia with her partner.

LINDA ROBERTSON is an internationally published novelist and her short stories have appeared in several anthologies. In addition to writing fantasy and urban fantasy, she is also a musician and award-winning composer. She has written and produced full orchestral scores to accompany her novels as well as a few short, independent films. Her music is available on most streaming channels. She's also a graphic artist. A mother of four boys, Linda is married and lives in Ohio.

LUCY A. SNYDER is the Shirley Jackson Award-nominated and five-time Bram Stoker Award-winning author of 15 books and over 100 published short stories. Her most recent books are the collection *Halloween Season* and the forthcoming novel *Sister, Maiden, Monster*. She also wrote the novels *Spellbent, Shotgun Sorceress,* and *Switchblade Goddess,* the nonfiction book *Shooting Yourself in the Head for Fun and Profit: A Writer's Survival Guide,* and the collections *Garden of Eldritch Delights, While the Black Stars Burn, Soft Apocalypses, Orchid Carousals, Sparks and Shadows, Chimeric Machines,* and *Installing Linux on a Dead Badger.* Her writing has been translated into French, Russian, Italian, Spanish, Czech, and Japanese editions and has appeared in publications such as *Asimov's Science Fiction, Apex Magazine, Nightmare Magazine, Pseudopod, Strange Horizons,* and *Best Horror of the Year.* She lives in Columbus, Ohio. You can learn more about her at www.lucysnyder.com and you can follow her on Twitter at @LucyASnyder.

R.J. SULLIVAN'S short fantastic fiction has appeared in the Stoker-nominated anthology *Dark Faith: Invocations, Vampires Don't Sparkle, Short and Twisted Western Tales,* and the magazine retrospectives *A Big Book of Strange, Weird and Wonderful, Books I and II.* His short story collection is titled *Darkness with a Chance of Whimsy.* R.J. publishes paranormal thriller series books through DarkWhimsy Books and his science fiction spaceship adventure series through Hydra Publications. Learn more at https://rjsullivanfiction.com/

JAYMIE WAGNER is a queer, trans, divorced, and polyamorous writer who lives near Minneapolis, Minnesota. She has been a semi-professional NHL writer, a blogger, and a BBQ chef at different parts of her life, and lives with her cat and an increasingly alarming number of tiny giant robots. Her work is available in several short story collections and anthologies, and her werewolf romance series Sing For Me is available from JMS Books.

LASHAWN M. WANAK lives in Wisconsin with her husband, son, and numerous knitting projects. She writes short fiction, essays, and poetry, and has been published in venues including *Fireside Magazine, FIYAH, Uncanny Magazine,* and *2019 Best American Science Fiction and Fantasy Anthology.* She is the editor of the online speculative magazine *GigaNotoSaurus* and previously wrote book reviews for *Lightspeed Magazine.* She enjoys knitting, anime, and wrestling with theological truths from a Womanist's perspective. Writing stories keeps her sane. Also, pie.

URSULA VERNON, aka T. Kingfisher, is an author and illustrator. She has written over fifteen books for children, at least a dozen novels for adults, an epic webcomic called "Digger" and various short stories and other odds and ends. Her work has been nominated for the Eisner, World Fantasy, and longlisted for the British Science Fiction Awards. It has garnered a number of Webcomics Choice Awards, the Hugo Award for Best Graphic Story, the Mythopoeic Award for Children's Literature, the Nebula for Best Short Story, the Sequoyah Award, and many others.